Tomorrow is here. Are you ready?

Year's
Best
SF
15

Praise for previous volumes

"An impressive roster of authors."
Locus

"The finest modern science fiction writing."
Pittsburgh Tribune

Edited by David G. Hartwell

Edited by David G. Hartwell
& Kathryn Cramer

YEAR'S BEST SF 15

EDITED BY

DAVID G. HARTWELL
and KATHRYN CRAMER

An Imprint of HarperCollinsPublishers

Additional copyright information appears on pages 493–494.

EOS
An Imprint of HarperCollins*Publishers*
10 East 53rd Street
New York, New York 10022-5299

Copyright © 2010 by David G. Hartwell and Kathryn Cramer
ISBN 978-0-06-172175-5
www.eosbooks.com

First Eos paperback printing: June 2010

HarperCollins® and Eos® are registered trademarks of HarperCollins Publishers.

Printed in the U.S.A.

10 9 8 7 6 5 4 3 2 1

To Canadian Fandom, especially to those we know and those we do not, who made our time in Montreal at the World SF convention a special treat. Thanks Eugene, thanks Rene, thanks Elisabeth, and special thanks to the people who created the necktie exhibit. And to the city of Montreal, for being itself.

And to Charles N. Brown, a Giant of SF, who would have enjoyed this dedication, and who had to miss Montreal. Death will do that to you.

And to *Tor.com*, for making our year harder, but better.

Acknowledgments

Ellen Datlow, Gardner R. Dozois, Jonathan Strahan, Nick Gevers, Pete Crowther, especially among the anthologists, gave us some real help as well as publishing some good stories, and Alice Krasnostein, Jed Hartman, Trevor Quachri, Brian Bienowski, and Gordon Van Gelder answered a lot of last-minute queries and send a lot of files quickly.

Contents

x CONTENTS

Introduction

The year 2009 began with some layoffs and firings in publishing, but not many affecting SF. Still, some SF people lost their jobs. The really good news is that SF and fantasy sales held up throughout the year for most publishing lines in spite of comparative disasters in other areas of publishing. But it was for the most part not a year of expansion and commercial ambition.

The year 2010 is announced as one of economic recovery, and we certainly hope that is the case. In publishing, that means mostly holding the line, not growth. Several online venues for fantasy and SF, including the ambitious Baen's Universe, have announced closings in early 2010. At least one of them, Internet Review of SF, has said they can no longer afford to lose money and that they see no way to break even, never mind profit.

Marketing genres associated with fantasy, paranormal romance, vampire and zombie books for teenagers, and "urban fantasy" were notably successful in 2009. One might even claim that F&SF expanded in 2009, but that would require ignoring that fact that the associated genres are not notable for much variation from the commercial formulas of the horror or romance genres; they are about feelings more than thought or knowledge.

The general quality of SF short fiction was no less in 2009, but from our vantage point there was a lot of SF with thinly-painted settings as backdrops for their characters, and in which not much happened. Sometimes, at least, this was done with style and sophistication, but not actually often enough for us to praise this trend.

The electronic book was hysterically discussed and promoted all year, but the sales of electronic text did not increase to as high as 4 percent of any major publisher's income. Ian Randal Strock of SF Scope reported double-digit sales on his electronic "bestseller." So print is still the principal venue for SF and fantasy in terms of economics for writers and for publishers. Bless my soul, someone even mentioned publically that Amazon.com might be inflating its sales claims for electronic books or Kindle readers. Its figures are of course secret.

And there was a scandal when it was discovered that one could lose an electronic book that one had bought if the seller decided it must take it back—and how easily it could be done with, in this case, a book by George Orwell. Welcome to the cloud where you don't actually own, but just lease or license.

We are reminded of the feudal system, where we serfs don't actually own the property. The lords own it. It is the stuff of paranoid SF novels. They can come into your computer or reader or phone and delete. That information is no longer, as President Nixon once said of his previous statement of fact, operative. *1984*, anyone?

The magazines and original anthologies published a lot of good fiction but appeared to be commercially hard-pressed (with the occasional anthologies of vampire, zombie, and fantasy romance fiction the exception). Delivery and distribution bankruptcies hurt magazines and mass market books most of all. Trade paperbacks have been forced into prominence but costs, and therefore prices, are rising. This was also the year of the oversized ten-dollar ($9.99) mass market paperback. And of the highly discounted bestseller—at least four major retailers were selling select bestsellers at less than they paid for them. There was a good analysis of this in *The New Yorker*, showing who it would hurt (bookstores) and how.

And perhaps most important, this was the year that Google attempted to establish that it could violate copyright with impunity; 2010 will be the year that that happens, or doesn't. It is still in court.

Yet we still offer cautious optimism for the SF field. A lot of what has grown up on the internet in the last decade depends on the free time of employed people, or the free time generated by a person with a job in the household, and maybe even some of the household discretionary spending or borrowing. Some of that free time and money (and optimism) has evaporated, along with trillions of dollars from the national economies of the developed countries. So we look forward to creativity on a shoestring and less sleep.

There are still three professional magazines that publish SF, and several online venues that pay more than a token for fiction. However, much of the new fiction of high quality is showcased in original anthologies these days, and they are the source for just about half the wordage in this book (nine of the stories). Only mentioning the SF anthologies, among the best are: *X6*, an Australian small press collection of novellas; *Other Earths*, edited by Nick Gevers; *We Think Therefore We Are*, edited by Pete Crowther; *When It Changed*, edited by Geoff Ryman; and the *Solaris Book of New Science Fiction #3*, edited by George Mann.

Our Year's Best SF is an anthology series about what's going on now in SF. We try in each volume of this series to represent the varieties of tones and voices and attitudes that keep the genre vigorous and responsive to the changing realities out of which it emerges, in science and daily life. It is supposed to be fun to read, a special kind of fun you cannot find elsewhere. The stories that follow show, and the story notes point out, the strengths of the evolving genre in the year 2009.

This book is full of science fiction—every story in the book is fairly clearly that and not something else. It is our opinion that it is a good thing to have genre boundaries. If we didn't, young writers would probably feel compelled to find something else, perhaps less interesting, to transgress or attack to draw attention to themselves. We have a high regard for horror, fantasy, speculative fiction, and slipstream, and postmodern literature. We (Kathryn Cramer and David G. Hartwell) edit the *Year's Best Fantasy* as well, a companion volume to this one—look for it if you enjoy short fantasy fiction too. But here, we choose science fiction.

We make a lot of additional comments about the writers and the stories, and what's happening in SF, in the individual introductions accompanying the stories in this book. Welcome to the *Year's Best SF* in 2009.

David G. Hartwell & Kathryn Cramer
Pleasantville, NY

Infinities

VANDANA SINGH

Vandana Singh (users.rcn.com/singhvan/) is from India and lives in Framingham, Massachusetts, where she is an assistant professor of physics. Her stories are collected in The Woman Who Thought She Was a Planet *(2008). Her novella "Distances" was published in 2008 by Aqueduct Press. She has also published two YA novels,* Younguncle Comes to Town *and* Younguncle in the Himalayas. *And she is the editor of* To Each Her Own: Anthology of Contemporary Hindi Stories. *In an interview she says, "The city of Delhi is thousands of years old and I grew up surrounded by history, almost literally in the shadows of crumbling fort walls and nameless medieval monuments (among the modern highrises). The very air was—and still is—thick with stories. But I had to go away, to take the view from a far shore, to see all this."*

"Infinities" was published in The Woman Who Thought She Was a Planet, *which came out at the end of 2008 in India. She says, "Physics is a way of viewing the world, and it is one of my most important lenses. One of the most exciting things about science is that it reveals the sub-text of the physical world. In other words, surface reality isn't all there is, the world is full of hidden stories, connections, patterns, and the scientific as well as the literary and psychological aspects of this multi-textured reality are, to me, fascinating." This is a story about a man in India who loves mathematics.*

*An equation means nothing to me unless it expresses
a thought of God.*

—Srinivasa Ramanujan,
Indian mathematician (1887–1920)

Abdul Karim is his name. He is a small, thin man, precise to the point of affectation in his appearance and manner. He walks very straight; there is gray in his hair and in his short, pointed beard. When he goes out of the house to buy vegetables, people on the street greet him respectfully. "Salaam, Master sahib," they say, or "Namaste, Master Sahib," according to the religion of the speaker. They know him as the mathematics master at the municipal school. He has been there so long that he sees the faces of his former students everywhere: the autorickshaw driver Ramdas who refuses to charge him, the man who sells paan from a shack at the street corner, with whom he has an account, who never reminds him when his payment is late—his name is Imran and he goes to the mosque far more regularly than Abdul Karim.

They all know him, the kindly mathematics master, but he has his secrets. They know he lives in the old yellow house, where the plaster is flaking off in chunks to reveal the underlying brick. The windows of the house are hung with faded curtains that flutter tremulously in the breeze, giving passersby an occasional glimpse of his genteel poverty—the threadbare covers on the sofa, the wooden furniture as gaunt and lean and resigned as the rest of the house,

2

waiting to fall into dust. The house is built in the old-fashioned way about a courtyard, which is paved with brick except for a circular omission where a great litchi tree grows. There is a high wall around the courtyard, and one door in it that leads to the patch of wilderness that was once a vegetable garden. But the hands that tended it—his mother's hands—are no longer able to do more than hold a mouthful of rice between the tips of the fingers, tremblingly conveyed to the mouth. The mother sits nodding in the sun in the courtyard while the son goes about the house, dusting and cleaning as fastidiously as a woman. The master has two sons—one is in distant America, married to a gori bibi, a white woman—how unimaginable! He never comes home and writes only a few times a year. The wife writes cheery letters in English that the master reads carefully with finger under each word. She talks about his grandsons, about baseball (a form of cricket, apparently), about their plans to visit, which never materialize. Her letters are as incomprehensible to him as the thought that there might be aliens on Mars, but he senses a kindness, a reaching out, among the foreign words. His mother has refused to have anything to do with that woman.

The other son has gone into business in Mumbai. He comes home rarely, but when he does he brings with him expensive things—a television set, an air-conditioner. The TV is draped reverently with an embroidered white cloth and dusted every day but the master can't bring himself to turn it on. There is too much trouble in the world. The air-conditioner gives him asthma so he never turns it on, even in the searing heat of summer. His son is a mystery to him—his mother dotes on the boy but the master can't help fearing that this young man has become a stranger, that he is involved in some shady business. The son always has a cell phone with him and is always calling nameless friends in Mumbai, bursting into cheery laughter, dropping his voice to a whisper, walking up and down the pathetically clean drawing-room as he speaks. Although he would never admit it to anybody other than Allah, Abdul Karim has the distinct impression that his son is waiting for him to die. He is always relieved when his son leaves.

Still, these are domestic worries. What father does not worry about his children? Nobody would be particularly surprised to know that the quiet, kindly master of mathematics shares them also. What they don't know is that he has a secret, an obsession, a passion that makes him different from them all. It is because of this, perhaps, that he seems always to be looking at something just beyond their field of vision, that he seems a little lost in the cruel, mundane world in which they live.

He wants to see infinity.

It is not strange for a mathematics master to be obsessed with numbers. But for Abdul Karim, numbers are the stepping stones, rungs in the ladder that will take him (Inshallah!) from the prosaic ugliness of the world to infinity.

When he was a child he used to see things from the corners of his eyes. Shapes moving at the very edge of his field of vision. Haven't we all felt that there was someone to our left or right, darting away when we turned our heads? In his childhood he had thought they were farishte, angelic beings keeping a watch over him. And he had felt secure, loved, nurtured by a great, benign, invisible presence.

One day he asked his mother:

"Why don't the farishte stay and talk to me? Why do they run away when I turn my head?"

Inexplicably to the child he had been, this innocent question led to visits to the Hakim. Abdul Karim had always been frightened of the Hakim's shop, the walls of which were lined from top to bottom with old clocks. The clocks ticked and hummed and whirred while tea came in chipped glasses and there were questions about spirits and possessions, and bitter herbs were dispensed in antique bottles that looked as though they contained djinns. An amulet was given to the boy to wear around his neck; there were verses from the Qur'an he was to recite every day. The boy he had been sat at the edge of the worn velvet seat and trembled; after two weeks of treatment, when his mother asked him about the farishte, he had said:

"They're gone."

That was a lie.

*　*　*

My theory stands as firm as a rock; every arrow directed against it will quickly return to the archer. How do I know this? Because I have studied it from all sides for many years; because I have examined all objections which have ever been made against the infinite numbers; and above all because I have followed its roots, so to speak, to the first infallible cause of all created things.

—Georg Cantor, German mathematician (1845–1918)

In a finite world, Abdul Karim ponders infinity. He has met infinities of various kinds in mathematics. If mathematics is the language of Nature, then it follows that there are infinities in the physical world around us as well. They confound us because we are such limited things. Our lives, our science, our religions are all smaller than the cosmos. Is the cosmos infinite? Perhaps. As far as we are concerned, it might as well be.

In mathematics there is the sequence of natural numbers, walking like small, determined soldiers into infinity. But there are less obvious infinities as well, as Abdul Karim knows. Draw a straight line, mark zero on one end and the number one at the other. How many numbers between zero and one? If you start counting now, you'll still be counting when the universe ends, and you'll be nowhere near one. In your journey from one end to the other you'll encounter the rational numbers and the irrational numbers, most notably the transcendentals. The transcendental numbers are the most intriguing—you can't generate them from integers by division, or by solving simple equations. Yet in the simple number line there are nearly impenetrable thickets of them; they are the densest, most numerous of all numbers. It is only when you take certain ratios like the circumference of a circle to its diameter, or add an infinite number of terms in a series, or negotiate the countless steps of infinite continued fractions, do these transcendental numbers emerge. The most famous of these is, of course, pi, 3.14159 . . . , where there is an infinity of non-repeating numbers after the decimal point. The transcendentals! Theirs is a universe richer in infinities than we can imagine.

In finiteness—in that little stick of a number line—there is infinity. What a deep and beautiful concept, thinks Abdul Karim! Perhaps there are infinities in us too, universes of them.

The prime numbers are another category that capture his imagination. The atoms of integer arithmetic, the select few that generate all other integers, as the letters of an alphabet generate all words. There are an infinite number of primes, as befits what he thinks of as God's alphabet . . .

How ineffably mysterious the primes are! They seem to occur at random in the sequence of numbers: 2, 3, 5, 7, 11 . . . There is no way to predict the next number in the sequence without actually testing it. No formula that generates all the primes. And yet, there is a mysterious regularity in these numbers that has eluded the greatest mathematicians of the world. Glimpsed by Riemann, but as yet unproven, there are hints of order so deep, so profound, that it is as yet beyond us.

To look for infinity in an apparently finite world—what nobler occupation for a human being, and one like Abdul Karim, in particular?

As a child he questioned the elders at the mosque: What does it mean to say that Allah is simultaneously one, and infinite? When he was older he read the philosophies of Al Kindi and Al Ghazali, Ibn Sina and Iqbal, but his restless mind found no answers. For much of his life he has been convinced that mathematics, not the quarrels of philosophers, is the key to the deepest mysteries.

He wonders whether the farishte that have kept him company all his life know the answer to what he seeks. Sometimes, when he sees one at the edge of his vision, he asks a question into the silence. Without turning around.

Is the Riemann Hypothesis true?

Silence.

Are prime numbers the key to understanding infinity?

Silence.

Is there a connection between transcendental numbers and the primes?

There has never been an answer.

But sometimes, a hint, a whisper of a voice that speaks in his mind. Abdul Karim does not know whether his mind is playing tricks upon him or not, because he cannot make out what the voice is saying. He sighs and buries himself in his studies.

He reads about prime numbers in Nature. He learns that the distribution of energy level spacings of excited uranium nuclei seem to match the distribution of spacings between prime numbers. Feverishly he turns the pages of the article, studies the graphs, tries to understand. How strange that Allah has left a hint in the depths of atomic nuclei! He is barely familiar with modern physics—he raids the library to learn about the structure of atoms.

His imagination ranges far. Meditating on his readings, he grows suspicious now that perhaps matter is infinitely divisible. He is beset by the notion that maybe there is no such thing as an elementary particle. Take a quark and it's full of preons. Perhaps preons themselves are full of smaller and smaller things. There is no limit to this increasingly fine graininess of matter.

How much more palatable this is than the thought that the process stops somewhere, that at some point there is a pre-preon, for example, that is composed of nothing else but itself. How fractally sound, how beautiful if matter is a matter of infinitely nested boxes.

There is a symmetry in it that pleases him. After all, there is infinity in the very large too. Our universe, ever expanding, apparently without limit.

He turns to the work of Georg Cantor, who had the audacity to formalize the mathematical study of infinity. Abdul Karim painstakingly goes over the mathematics, drawing his finger under every line, every equation in the yellowing textbook, scribbling frantically with his pencil. Cantor is the one who discovered that certain infinite sets are more infinite than others—that there are tiers and strata of infinity. Look at the integers, 1, 2, 3, 4 . . . Infinite, but of a lower order of infinity than the real numbers like 1.67, 2.93, etc. Let us say the set of integers is of order Aleph-null, the set of real numbers of order Aleph-One, like the hierarchical ranks of a king's courtiers. The question that plagued Cantor and eventually cost him his life and sanity was the Continuum Hypothesis, which states that there is no infinite set of numbers with order *between* Aleph-Null and Aleph-One. In other words, Aleph-One succeeds Aleph-Null; there is no intermediate rank. But Cantor could not prove this.

He developed the mathematics of infinite sets. Infinity plus infinity equals infinity. Infinity minus infinity equals infinity. But the Continuum Hypothesis remained beyond his reach.

Abdul Karim thinks of Cantor as a cartographer in a bizarre new world. Here the cliffs of infinity reach endlessly toward the sky, and Cantor is a tiny figure lost in the grandeur, a fly on a precipice. And yet, what boldness! What spirit! To have the gall to actually *classify* infinity . . .

His explorations take him to an article on the mathematicians of ancient India. They had specific words for large numbers. One purvi, a unit of time, is seven hundred and fifty-six thousand billion years. One sirsaprahelika is eight point four million Purvis raised to the twenty-eighth power. What did they see that caused them to play with such large numbers? What vistas were revealed before them? What wonderful arrogance possessed them that they, puny things, could dream so large?

He mentions this once to his friend, a Hindu called Gangadhar, who lives not far away. Gangadhar's hands pause over the chessboard (their weekly game is in progress) and he intones a verse from the Vedas:

From the Infinite, take the Infinite, and lo! Infinity remains . . .

Abdul Karim is astounded. That his ancestors could anticipate Georg Cantor by four millennia!

That fondness for science . . . that affability and condescension which God shows to the learned, that promptitude with which he protects and supports them in the elucidation of obscurities and in the removal of difficulties, has encouraged me to compose a short work on calculating by al-jabr *and* al-muqabala, *confining it to what is easiest and most useful in arithmetic.*

—Al Khwarizmi, eighth century Arab mathematician

Mathematics came to the boy almost as naturally as breathing. He made a clean sweep of the exams in the little municipal school. The neighborhood was provincial, dominated by small tradesmen, minor government officials and the like, and their children seemed to have inherited or acquired their plodding practicality. Nobody understood that strangely clever Muslim boy, except for a Hindu classmate, Gangadhar, who was a well-liked, outgoing fellow. Although Gangadhar played gulli-danda on the streets and could run faster than anybody, he had a passion for literature, especially poetry— a pursuit perhaps as impractical as pure mathematics. The two were drawn together and spent many hours sitting on the compound wall at the back of the school, eating stolen jamuns from the trees overhead and talking about subjects ranging from Urdu poetry and Sanskrit verse to whether mathematics pervaded everything, including human emotions. They felt very grown-up and mature for their stations. Gangadhar was the one who, shyly, and with many giggles, first introduced Kalidasa's erotic poetry to Abdul Karim. At that time girls were a mystery to them both: although they shared classrooms it seemed to them that girls (a completely different species from their sisters, of course) were strange, graceful, alien creatures from another world. Kalidasa's lyrical descriptions of breasts and hips evoked in them unarticulated longings.

They had the occasional fight, as friends do. The first serious one happened when there were some Hindu-Muslim tensions in the city just before the elections. Gangadhar came to Abdul in the school playground and knocked him flat.

"You're a bloodthirsty Muslim!" he said, almost as though he had just realized it.

"You're a hell-bound kafir!"

They punched each other, wrestled the other to the ground. Finally, with cut lips and bruises, they stared fiercely at each other and staggered away. The next day they played gulli-danda in the street on opposite sides for the first time.

Then they ran into each other in the school library. Abdul Karim tensed, ready to hit back if Gangadhar hit him. Gangadhar looked as if he was thinking about it for a moment, but then, somewhat embarrassedly, he held out a book.

"New book . . . on mathematics. Thought you'd want to see it . . ."

After that they were sitting on the wall again, as usual.

Their friendship had even survived the great riots four years later, when the city became a charnel house—buildings and bodies burned, and unspeakable atrocities were committed by both Hindus and Muslims. Some political leader of one side or another had made a provocative proclamation that he could not even remember, and tempers had been inflamed. There was an incident—a fight at a bus-stop, accusations of police brutality against the Muslim side, and things had spiraled out of control. Abdul's elder sister Ayesha had been at the market with a cousin when the worst of the violence broke out. They had been separated in the stampede; the cousin had come back, bloodied but alive, and nobody had ever seen Ayesha again.

The family never recovered. Abdul's mother went through the motions of living but her heart wasn't in it. His father lost weight, became a shrunken mockery of his old, vigorous self—he would die only a few years later. As for Abdul— the news reports about atrocities fed his nightmares and in his dreams he saw his sister bludgeoned, raped, torn to pieces again and again and again. When the city calmed down, he spent his days roaming the streets of the market, hoping for a sign of Ayesha—a body even—torn between hope and feverish rage.

Their father stopped seeing his Hindu friends. The only reason Abdul did not follow suit was because Gangadhar's people had sheltered a Muslim family during the carnage, and had turned off a mob of enraged Hindus.

Over time the wound—if it did not quite heal—became bearable enough that he could start living again. He threw himself into his beloved mathematics, isolating himself from everyone but his family and Gangadhar. The world had wronged him. He did not owe it anything.

Aryabhata is the master who, after reaching the furthest shores and plumbing the inmost depths of the sea of ultimate knowledge of mathematics, kinematics and spherics, handed over the three sciences to the learned world.
> —The Mathematician Bhaskara, commenting on the 6th century Indian mathematician Aryabhata, a hundred years later

Abdul Karim was the first in his family to go to college. By a stroke of great luck, Gangadhar went to the same regional institution, majoring in Hindi literature while Abdul Karim buried himself in mathematical arcana. Abdul's father had become reconciled to his son's obsession and obvious talent. Abdul Karim himself, glowing with praise from his teachers, wanted to follow in the footsteps of Ramanujan. Just as the goddess Namakkal had appeared to that untutored genius in his dreams, writing mathematical formulas on his tongue (or so Ramanujan had said), Abdul Karim wondered if the farishte had been sent by Allah so that he, too, might be blessed with mathematical insight.

During that time an event occurred that convinced him of this.

Abdul was in the college library, working on a problem in differential geometry, when he sensed a farishta at the edge of his field of vision. As he had done countless times before, he turned his head slowly, expecting the vision to vanish.

Instead he saw a dark shadow standing in front of the long bookcase. It was vaguely human-shaped. It turned slowly, revealing itself to be thin as paper—but as it turned it seemed to acquire thickness, hints of features over its dark, slender form. And then it seemed to Abdul that a door opened in the air, just a crack, and he had a vision of an unutterably strange world beyond. The shadow stood at the door, beckoning with one arm, but Abdul Karim sat still, frozen with wonder. Before he could rouse himself and get up, the door and the shadow both rotated swiftly and vanished, and he was left staring at the stack of books on the shelf.

After this he was convinced of his destiny. He dreamed obsessively of the strange world he had glimpsed; every time he sensed a farishta he turned his head slowly toward it—and every time it vanished. He told himself it was just a matter of time before one of them came, remained, and perhaps—wonder of wonders—took him to that other world.

Then his father died unexpectedly. That was the end of Abdul Karim's career as a mathematician. He had to return home to take care of his mother, his two remaining sisters and a brother. The only thing he was qualified for was teaching. Ultimately he would find a job at the same municipal school from which he had graduated.

On the train home, he saw a woman. The train was stopped on a bridge. Below him was the sleepy curve of a small river, gold in the early morning light, mists rising faintly off it, and on the shore a woman with a clay water pot. She had taken a dip in the river—her pale, ragged sari clung wetly to her as she picked up the pot and set it on her hip and began to climb the bank. In the light of dawn she was luminous, an apparition in the mist, the curve of the pot against the curve of her hip. Their eyes met from a distance—he imagined what he thought she saw, the silent train, a young man with a sparse beard looking at her as though she was the first woman in the world. Her own eyes gazed at him fearlessly as though she were a goddess looking into his soul. For a moment there were no barriers between them, no boundaries of gender, religion, caste or class. Then she turned and vanished behind a stand of shisham trees.

He wasn't sure if she had really been there in the half-light or whether he had conjured her up, but for a long time she represented something elemental to him. Sometimes he thought of her as Woman, sometimes as a river.

He got home in time for the funeral. His job kept him busy, and kept the moneylender from their door. With the stubborn optimism of the young, he kept hoping that one day his fortunes would change, that he would go back to college and complete his degree. In the meantime, he knew his mother wanted to find him a bride . . .

Abdul Karim got married, had children. Slowly, over the years of managing rowdy classrooms, tutoring students in the afternoons and saving, paisa by paisa, from his meager salary for his sisters' weddings and other expenses, Abdul Karim lost touch with that youthful, fiery talent he had once had, and with it the ambition to scale the heights to which Ramanujan, Cantor and Riemann had climbed. Things came more slowly to him now. An intellect burdened by years of worry wears out. When his wife died and his children grew up and went away, his steadily decreasing needs finally caught up with his meager income, and he found for the first time that he could think about mathematics again. He no longer hoped to dazzle the world of mathematics with some new insight, such as a proof of Riemann's hypothesis. Those dreams were gone. All he could hope for was to be illumined by the efforts of those who had gone before him, and to re-live, vicariously, the joys of insight. It was a cruel trick of Time, that when he had the leisure he had lost the ability, but that is no bar to true obsession. Now, in the autumn of his life it was as though Spring had come again, bringing with it his old love.

In this world, brought to its knees by hunger and thirst
Love is not the only reality, there are other Truths . . .
—Sahir Ludhianvi, Indian poet (1921–1980)

There are times when Abdul Karim tires of his mathematical obsessions. After all, he is old. Sitting in the courtyard with his notebook, pencil and books of mathematics for so many hours at a stretch can take its toll. He gets up, aching all over, sees to his mother's needs and goes out to the graveyard where his wife is buried.

His wife Zainab had been a plump, fair-skinned woman, hardly able to read or write, who moved about the house with indolent grace, her good-natured laugh ringing out in the courtyard as she chattered with the washerwoman. She had loved to eat—he still remembered the delicate tips of her plump fingers, how they would curl around a piece of lamb, scooping up with it a few grains of saffron rice, the morsel conveyed reverently to her mouth. Her girth gave an impression of strength, but ultimately she had not been able to hold out against her mother-in-law. The laughter in her eyes faded gradually as her two boys grew out of babyhood, coddled and put to bed by the grandmother in her own corner of the women's quarters. Abdul Karim himself had been unaware of the silent war between his wife and mother—he had been young and obsessed with teaching mathematics to his recalcitrant students. He had noticed how the grandmother always seemed to be holding the younger son, crooning to him, and how the elder boy followed his mother around, but he did not see in this any connection to his wife's growing pallor. One night he had requested her to come to him and massage his feet—their euphemism for sex—and he had waited for her to come to him from the women's quarters, impatient for the comfort of her plump nakedness, her soft, silken breasts. When she came at last she had knelt at the foot of the bed, her chest heaving with muffled sobs, her hands covering her face. As he took her in his arms, wondering what could have ruffled her calm good nature, she had collapsed completely against him. No comfort he could offer would make her tell what it was that was breaking her heart. At last she begged him, between great, shuddering breaths, that all she wanted in the world was another baby.

Abdul Karim had been influenced by modern ideas—he considered two children, boys at that, to be quite sufficient for a family. As one of five children, he had known poverty and the pain of giving up his dream of a university career to help support his family. He wasn't going to have his children go through the same thing. But when his wife whispered to him that she wanted one more, he relented.

Now, when he looked back, he wished he had tried to understand the real reason for her distress. The pregnancy had been a troublesome one. His mother had taken charge of both boys almost entirely while Zainab lay in bed in the women's quarters, too sick to do anything but weep silently and call upon Allah to rescue her. "It's a girl," Abdul Karim's mother had said grimly. "Only a girl would cause so much trouble." She had looked away out of the window into the courtyard, where her own daughter, Abdul Karim's dead sister, Ayesha, had once played and helped hang the wash.

And finally it had been a girl, stillborn, who had taken her mother with her. They were buried together in the small, unkempt graveyard where Abdul Karim went whenever he was depressed. By now the gravestone was awry and grass had grown over the mound. His father was buried here also, and three of his siblings who had died before he was six. Only Ayesha, lost Ayesha, the one he remembered as a source of comfort to a small boy—strong, generous arms, hands delicate and fragrant with henna, a smooth cheek—she was not here.

In the graveyard Abdul Karim pays his respects to his wife's memory while his heart quails at the way the graveyard itself is disintegrating. He is afraid that if it goes to rack and ruin, overcome by vegetation and time, he will forget Zainab and the child and his guilt. Sometimes he tries to clear the weeds and tall grasses with his hands, but his delicate scholar's hands become bruised and sore quite quickly, and he sighs and thinks about the Sufi poetess Jahanara, who had written, centuries earlier: "Let the green grass grow above my grave!"

I have often pondered over the roles of knowledge or experience, on the one hand, and imagination or intuition, on the other, in the process of discovery. I believe that there is a certain fundamental conflict between the two, and knowledge, by advocating caution, tends to inhibit the flight of imagination. Therefore, a certain naivete, unburdened by conventional wisdom, can sometimes be a positive asset.
—Harish-Chandra, Indian mathematician (1923–1983)

Gangadhar, his friend from school, was briefly a master of Hindi literature at the municipal school and is now an academician at the Amravati Heritage Library, and a poet in his spare time. He is the only person to whom Abdul Karim can confide his secret passion.

In time, he too becomes intrigued with the idea of infinity. While Abdul Karim pores over Cantor and Riemann, and tries to make meaning from the Prime Number theorem, Gangadhar raids the library and brings forth treasures. Every week, when Abdul Karim walks the two miles to Gangadhar's house, where he is led by the servant to the comfortable drawing room with its gracious, if aging mahogany furniture, the two men share what they've learned over cups of cardamom tea and a chess game. Gangadhar cannot understand higher mathematics but he can sympathize with the frustrations of the knowledge-seeker, and he has known what it is like to chip away at the wall of ignorance and burst into the light of understanding. He digs out quotes from Aryabhata and Al-Khwarizmi, and tells his friend such things as:

"Did you know, Abdul, that the Greeks and Romans did not like the idea of infinity? Aristotle argued against it, and proposed a finite universe. Of the yunaanis, only Archimedes dared to attempt to scale that peak. He came up with the notion that different infinite quantities could be compared, that one infinite could be greater or smaller than another infinite . . ."

And on another occasion:

"The French mathematician, Jacques Hadamard . . . He was the one who proved the Prime Number theorem that has you in such ecstasies . . . he says there are four stages to mathematical discovery. Not very different from the experience of the artist or poet, if you think about it. The first is to study and be familiar with what is known. The next is to let these ideas turn in your mind, as the earth regenerates by lying fallow between plantings. Then—with luck—there is the flash of insight, the illuminating moment when you discover something new and feel in your bones that it must be true. The final stage is to verify—to subject that epiphany to the rigors of mathematical proof . . ."

Abdul Karim feels that if he can simply go through Hadamard's first two stages, perhaps Allah will reward him with a flash of insight. And perhaps not. If he had hopes of being another Ramanujan, those hopes are gone now. But no true Lover has ever turned from the threshold of the Beloved's house, even knowing he will not be admitted through the doors.

"What worries me," he confides to Gangadhar during one of these discussions, "what has always worried me, is Gödel's Incompleteness Theorem. According to Gödel, there can be statements in mathematics that are not provable. He showed that the Continuum Hypothesis of Cantor was one of these statements. Poor Cantor, he lost his sanity trying to prove something that cannot be proved or disproved! What if all our unproven ideas on prime numbers, on infinity, are statements like that? If they can't be tested against the constraints of mathematical logic, how will we ever know if they are true?"

This bothers him very much. He pores over the proof of Gödel's theorem, seeking to understand it, to get around it. Gangadhar encourages him:

"You know, in the old tales, every great treasure is guarded by a proportionally great monster. Perhaps Gödel's theorem is the djinn that guards the truth you seek. Maybe instead of slaying it, you have to, you know, befriend it . . ."

Through his own studies, through discussions with Gangadhar, Abdul Karim begins to feel again that his true companions are Archimedes, Al-Khwarizmi. Khayyam, Aryabhata, Bhaskar. Riemann, Cantor, Gauss, Ramanujan, Hardy.

They are the masters, before whom he is as a humble student, an apprentice following their footprints up the mountainside. The going is rough. He is getting old, after all. He gives himself up to dreams of mathematics, rousing himself only to look after the needs of his mother, who is growing more and more frail.

After a while, even Gangadhar admonishes him.

"A man cannot live like this, so obsessed. Will you let yourself go the way of Cantor and Gödel? Guard your sanity, my friend. You have a duty to your mother, to society."

Abdul Karim cannot make Gangadhar understand. His mind sings with mathematics.

The limit of a function f(N) as N goes to infinity. . . .

So many questions he asks himself begin like this. The function f(N) may be the prime counting function, or the number of nested dolls of matter, or the extent of the universe. It may be abstract, like a parameter in a mathematical space, or earthy, like the branching of wrinkles in the face of his mother, growing older and older in the paved courtyard of his house, under the litchi trees. Older and older, without quite dying, as though she were determined to live Zeno's paradox.

He loves his mother the way he loves the litchi tree; for being there, for making him what he is, for giving him shelter and succor.

The limit . . . as N goes to infinity . . .

So begin many theorems of calculus. Abdul Karim wonders what kind of calculus governs his mother's slow arc into dying. What if life did not require a minimum threshold of conditions—what if death were merely a limit of some function f(N) as N goes to infinity?

> *A world in which human life is but a pawn*
> *A world filled with death-worshipers,*
> *Where death is cheaper than life . . .*
> *That world is not my world . . .*
> —Sahir Ludhianvi, Indian poet (1921–1980)

While Abdul Karim dabbles in the mathematics of the infinite, as so many deluded fools and geniuses have done, the world changes.

He is vaguely aware that there are things going on in the world—that people live and die, that there are political upheavals, that this is the hottest summer yet and already a thousand people have died of the heat wave in Northern India. He knows that Death also stands at his mother's shoulder, waiting, and he does what he can for her. Although he has not always observed the five daily prayers, he does the namaz now, with her. She has already started becoming the citizen of another country—she lives in little leaps and bends of time long gone, calling for Ayesha one moment, and for her long-dead husband the next. Conversations from her lost girlhood emerge from her trembling mouth. In her few moments of clarity she calls upon Allah to take her away.

Dutiful as he is to his mother, Abdul Karim is relieved to be able to get away once a week for a chess game and conversation with Gangadhar. He has a neighbor's aunt look in on his mother during that time. Heaving a sigh or two, he makes his way through the familiar lanes of his childhood, his shoes scuffing up dust under the ancient jamun trees that he once climbed as a child. He greets his neighbors: old Ameen Khan Sahib sitting on his charpai, wheezing over his hookah, the Ali twins, madcap boys chasing a bicycle tire with a stick, Imran at the paan shop. He crosses, with some trepidation, the increasingly congested market road, past the faded awnings of Munshilal and Sons, past a rickshaw stand into another quiet lane, this one shaded with jacaranda trees. Gangadhar's house is a modest white bungalow, stained an indeterminate gray from many monsoons. The creak of the wooden gate in the compound wall is as familiar a greeting as Gangadhar's welcome.

But the day comes when there is no chess game at Gangadhar's house.

The servant boy—not Gangadhar—ushers him into the familiar room. Sitting down in his usual chair, Abdul Karim notices that the chess board has not been laid out. Sounds come from the inner rooms of the house: women's voices, heavy objects being dragged across the floor.

An elderly man comes into the room and stops short as though surprised to see Abdul Karim. He looks vaguely familiar—then Abdul remembers that he is some relative of Gangadhar's wife—an uncle, perhaps—and he lives on the other side of the city. They have met once or twice at some family celebration.

"What are you doing here?" the man says, without any of the usual courtesies. He is white-haired but of vigorous build.

Puzzled and a little affronted, Abdul Karim says:

"I am here for my chess game with Gangadhar. Is he not at home?"

"There will be no chess game today. Haven't you people done enough harm? Are you here to mock us in our sorrow? Well, let me tell you . . ."

"What happened?" Abdul Karim's indignation is dissolving in a wave of apprehension. "What are you talking about? Is Gangadhar all right?"

"Perhaps you don't know," says the man, his tone mocking. "Some of your people burned a bus on Paharia road yesterday evening. There were ten people on it, all Hindus, coming back from a family ceremony at a temple. They all perished horribly. Word has it that you people did it. Didn't even let the children get off the bus. Now the whole town is in turmoil. Who knows what might happen? Gangadhar and I are taking his family to a safer part of town."

Abdul Karim's eyes are wide with shock. He can find no words.

"All these hundreds of years we Hindus have tolerated you people. Even though you Muslims raided and pillaged us over the centuries, we let you build your mosques, worship your God. And this is how you pay us!"

In one instant Abdul Karim has become "you people." He wants to say that he did not lift an arm to hurt those who perished on the bus. His were not the hands that set the fire. But no words come out.

"Can you imagine it, Master Sahib? Can you see the flames? Hear their screams? Those people will never go home . . ."

"I can imagine it," Abdul Karim says, grimly now. He rises to his feet, but just then Gangadhar enters the room. He has surely heard part of the conversation because he puts his hands on Abdul Karim's shoulders, gently, recognizing him as the other man has not done. This is Abdul Karim, his friend, whose sister, all those years ago, never came home.

Gangadhar turns to his wife's uncle.

"Uncle, please. Abdul Karim is not like those miscreants. A kinder man I have never known! And as yet it is not known who the ruffians are, although the whole town is filled with rumors. Abdul, please sit down! This is a measure of the times we live in, that we can say such things to each other. Alas! Kalyug is indeed upon us."

Abdul Karim sits down, but he is shaking. All thoughts of mathematics have vanished from his mind. He is filled with disgust and revulsion for the barbarians who committed this atrocity, for human beings in general. What a degraded species we are! To take the name of Ram or Allah, or Jesus, and to burn and destroy under one aegis or another—that is what our history has been.

The uncle, shaking his head, has left the room. Gangadhar is talking history to Abdul, apologizing for his uncle.

". . . a matter of political manipulation," he says. "The British colonialists looked for our weakness, exploited it, set us against each other. Opening the door to hell is easy enough—but closing it is hard. All those years, before British rule, we lived in relative peace. Why is it that we cannot close that door they opened? After all, what religion tells us to slay our neighbor?"

"Does it matter?" Abdul Karim says bitterly. "We humans are a depraved species, my friend. My fellow Muslims address every prayer to Allah, the Merciful and Compassionate. You Hindus, with your "Isha Vasyam Idam Sarvam"—the divine pervades all. The Christians talk on about turning the other cheek. And yet each of them has hands that are stained in blood. We pervert everything—we take the words of peace spoken by prophets and holy men and turn them into weapons with which to kill each other!"

He is shaking so hard that he can barely speak.

"It is in mathematics . . . only in mathematics that I see Allah . . ."

"Quiet now," Gangadhar says. He calls for the servant to bring some water for the master sahib. Abdul Karim drinks and wipes his mouth. The suitcases are being brought out from inside the house. There is a taxi in front.

"Listen, my friend," Gangadhar says, "you must look to your safety. Go home now and lock your doors, and look after your mother. I am sending my family away and I will join them in a day or so. When this madness has passed I will come and look for you!"

Abdul Karim goes home. So far everything looks normal—the wind is blowing litter along in the streets, the paan shop is open, people throng the bus-stop. Then he notices that there aren't any children, even though the summer holidays are going on. The vegetable market is very busy. People are buying up everything like crazy. He buys a few potatoes, onions and a large gourd, and goes home. He locks the door. His mother, no longer up to cooking meals, watches as he cooks. After they eat and he has her tucked into bed, he goes to his study and opens a book on mathematics.

One day passes, perhaps two—he does not keep track. He remembers to take care of his mother but often forgets to eat. His mother lives, more and more, in that other world. His sisters and brother call from other towns, anxious about the reports of escalating violence; he tells them not to worry. When things are back to normal they will come and see him and their mother.

> How marvelous, the Universal Mystery
> That only a true Lover can comprehend!
> —Bulleh Shah, eighteenth century Punjabi Sufi poet

> Logic merely sanctions the conquests of the intuition.
> —Jacques Hadamard, French mathematician (1865–1963)

One morning he emerges from the darkness of his study into the sunny courtyard. Around him the old city writhes and burns, but Abdul Karim sees and hears nothing but mathematics. He sits in his old cane chair, picks up a stick lying on the ground and begins to draw mathematical symbols in the dust.

There is a farishta standing at the edge of his vision.

He turns slowly. The dark shadow stays there, waits. This time Abdul Karim is quick on his feet, despite a sudden twinge of pain in one knee. He walks toward the door, the beckoning arm, and steps through.

For a moment he is violently disoriented—it occurs to

him that he has spun through a different dimension into this hidden world. Then the darkness before his eyes dissipates, and he beholds wonders.

All is hushed. He is looking at a vast sweep of land and sky unlike anything he has ever seen. Dark, pyramidal shapes stud the landscape, great monuments to something beyond his understanding. There is a vast, polyhedral object suspended in a pale orange sky that has no sun. Only a diffuse luminescence pervades this sky. He looks at his feet, still in his familiar, worn sandals, and sees all around, in the sand, little fish-like creatures wriggling and spawning. Some of the sand has worked its way between his toes, and it feels warm and rubbery, not like sand at all. He takes a deep breath and smells something strange, like burnt rubber mixed with his own sweat. The shadow stands by his side, looking solid at last, almost human but for the absence of neck and the profusion of limbs—their number seems to vary with time—at the moment Abdul Karim counts five.

The dark orifice in the head opens and closes, but no sound comes out. Instead Abdul feels as though a thought has been placed in his mind, a package that he will open later.

He walks with the shadow across the sands to the edge of a quiet sea. The water, if that is what it is, is foaming and bubbling gently, and within its depths he sees ghostly shapes moving, and the hints of complex structure far below. Arabesques form in the depths, break up, and form again. He licks his dry lips, tastes metal and salt.

He looks at his companion, who bids him pause. A door opens. They step through into another universe.

It is different, this one. It is all air and light, the whole space hung with great, translucent webbing. Each strand in the web is a hollow tube within which liquid creatures flow. Smaller, solid beings float in the emptiness between the web strands.

Speechless, he stretches out his hand toward a web-strand. Its delicacy reminds him of the filigreed silver anklets his wife used to wear. To his complete surprise a tiny being floating within the strand stops. It is like a plump, watery comma, translucent and without any features he can recognize, and yet he has the notion that he is being looked at, examined, and that at the other end is also wonder.

The web-strand touches him, and he feels its cool, alien smoothness on a fingertip.

A door opens. They step through.

It is dizzying, this wild ride. Sometimes he gets flashes of his own world, scenes of trees and streets, and distant blue hills. There are indications that these flashes are at different points in time—at one point he sees a vast army of soldiers, their plumed helmets catching the sunlight, and thinks he must be in the time of the Roman Empire. Another time he thinks he is back home, because he sees before him his own courtyard. But there is an old man sitting in his cane chair, drawing patterns in the dust with a stick. A shadow falls across the ground. Someone he cannot see is stealing up behind the old man. Is that a knife agleam in the stranger's hand? What is this he is seeing? He tries to call out, but no sound emerges. The scene blurs—a door opens, and they step through.

Abdul Karim is trembling. Has he just witnessed his own death?

He remembers that Archimedes died that way—he had been drawing circles, engrossed with a problem in geometry, when a barbarian of a soldier came up behind him and killed him.

But there is no time to ponder. He is lost in a merry-go-round of universes, each different and strange. The shadow gives him a glimpse of so many, Abdul Karim has long lost count. He puts thoughts of Death away from him and loses himself in wonder.

His companion opens door after door. The face, featureless except for the orifice that opens and shuts, gives no hint of what the shadow is thinking. Abdul Karim wants to ask: who are you? Why are you doing this? He knows, of course, the old story of how the angel Gabriel came to the Prophet Mohammad one night and took him on a celestial journey, a grand tour of the heavens. But the shadow does not look like an angel; it has no face, no wings, its gender is indeterminate. And in any case, why should the angel Gabriel concern himself with a humble mathematics master in a provincial town, a person of no consequence in the world?

And yet, he is here. Perhaps Allah has a message for him; His ways are ineffable, after all. Exultation fills Abdul Karim as he beholds marvel after marvel.

At last they pause in a place where they are suspended in a yellow sky. As Abdul Karim experiences the giddy absence of gravity, accompanied by a sudden jolt of nausea that slowly recedes—as he turns in mid-air, he notices that the sky is not featureless but covered with delicate tessellations: geometric shapes intertwine, merge and new ones emerge. The colors change too, from yellow to green, lilac, mauve. All at once it seems as though numberless eyes are opening in the sky, one after the other, and as he turns he sees all the other universes flashing past him. A kaleidoscope, vast beyond his imaginings. He is at the center of it all, in a space between all spaces, and he can feel in his bones a low, irregular throbbing, like the beating of a drum. Boom, boom, goes the drum. Boom boom boom. Slowly he realizes that what he is seeing and feeling is part of a vast pattern.

In that moment Abdul Karim has the flash of understanding he has been waiting for all his life.

For so long he has been playing with the transcendental numbers, trying to fathom Cantor's ideas; at the same time Riemann's notions of the prime numbers have fascinated him. In idle moments he has wondered if they are connected at a deeper level. Despite their apparent randomness the primes have their own regularity, as hinted by the unproven Riemann Hypothesis; he sees at last that if you think of prime numbers as the terrain of a vast country, and if your view of reality is a two-dimensional plane that intersects this terrain at some height above the surface, perhaps at an angle, then of course what you see will appear to be random. Tops of hills. Bits of valleys. Only the parts of the terrain that cross your plane of reality will be apparent. Unless you can see the entire landscape in its multi-dimensional splendor, the topography will make no sense.

He sees it: the bare bones of creation, here, in this place where all the universes branch off, the thudding heart of the metacosmos. In the scaffolding, the skeletal structure of the multiverse is beautifully apparent. This is what Cantor had a glimpse of, then, this vast topography. Understanding opens in his mind as though the metacosmos has itself spoken to him. He sees that of all the transcendental numbers, only a few—infinite still, but not the whole set—are marked as doorways to other universes, and each is labeled by a prime number. Yes. Yes. Why this is so, what deeper symmetry it reflects, what law or regularity of Nature undreamed of by the physicists of his world, he does not know.

The space where primes live—the topology of the infinite universes—he sees it in that moment. No puny function as yet dreamed of by humans can encompass the vastness—the inexhaustible beauty of this place. He knows that he can never describe this in the familiar symbols of the mathematics that he knows, that while he experiences the truth of the Riemann Hypothesis, as a corollary to this greater, more luminous reality, he cannot sit down and verify it through a conventional proof. No human language as yet exists, mathematical or otherwise, that can describe what he knows in his bones to be true. Perhaps he, Abdul Karim, will invent the beginnings of such a language. Hadn't the great poet Iqbal interpreted the Prophet's celestial journey to mean that the heavens are within our grasp?

A twist, and a door opens. He steps into the courtyard of his house. He turns around, but the courtyard is empty. The farishta is gone.

Abdul Karim raises his eyes to the heavens. Rain clouds, dark as the proverbial beloved's hair, sweep across the sky; the litchi tree over his head is dancing in the swift breeze. The wind has drowned out the sounds of a ravaged city. A red flower comes blowing over the courtyard wall and is deposited at his feet.

Abdul Karim's hair is blown back, a nameless ecstasy fills him; he feels Allah's breath on his face.

He says into the wind:

Dear Merciful and Compassionate God, I stand before

your wondrous universe, filled with awe; help me, weak mortal that I am, to raise my gaze above the sordid pettiness of everyday life, the struggles and quarrels of mean humanity . . . Help me to see the beauty of your Works, from the full flower of the red silk cotton tree to the exquisite mathematical grace by which you have created numberless universes in the space of a man's step. I know now that my true purpose in this sad world is to stand in humble awe before your magnificence, and to sing a paean of praise to you with every breath I take . . .

He feels weak with joy. Leaves whirl in the courtyard like mad dervishes; a drop or two of rain falls, obliterating the equation he had scratched in the dust with his stick. He has lost his chance at mathematical genius a long time ago; he is nobody, only a teacher of mathematics at a school, humbler than a clerk in a government office—yet Allah has favored him with this great insight. Perhaps he is now worthy of speech with Ramanujan and Archimedes and all the ones in between. But all he wants to do is to run out into the lane and go shouting through the city: see, my friends, open your eyes and see what I see! But he knows they would think him mad; only Gangadhar would understand . . . if not the mathematics then the impulse, the importance of the whole discovery.

He leaps out of the house, into the lane.

> *This blemished radiance . . . this night-stung dawn*
> *Is not the dawn we waited for . . .*
> —Faiz Ahmed Faiz, Pakistani poet (1911–1984)

> *Where all is broken*
> *Where each soul's athirst, each glance*
> *Filled with confusion, each heart*
> *Weighed with sorrow . . .*
> *Is this a world, or chaos?*
> —Sahir Ludhianvi, Indian poet (1921–1980)

But what is this?

The lane is empty. There are broken bottles everywhere.

The windows and doors of his neighbors' houses are shuttered and barred, like closed eyes. Above the sound of the rain he hears shouting in the distance. Why is there a smell of burning?

He remembers then, what he had learned at Gangadhar's house. Securing the door behind him, he begins to run as fast as his old-man legs will carry him.

The market is burning.

Smoke pours out of smashed store fronts, even as the rain falls. There is broken glass on the pavement; a child's wooden doll in the middle of the road, decapitated. Soggy pages filled with neat columns of figures lie scattered everywhere, the remains of a ledger. Quickly he crosses the road.

Gangadhar's house is in ruins. Abdul Karim wanders through the open doors, stares blindly at the blackened walls. The furniture is mostly gone. Only the chess table stands untouched in the middle of the front room.

Frantically he searches through the house, entering the inner rooms for the first time. Even the curtains have been ripped from the windows.

There is no body.

He runs out of the house. Gangadhar's wife's family—he does not know where they live. How to find out if Gangadhar is safe?

The neighboring house belongs to a Muslim family that Abdul Karim knows only from visits to the mosque. He pounds on the door. He thinks he hears movement behind the door, sees the upstairs curtains twitch—but nobody answers his frantic entreaties. At last, defeated, his hands bleeding, he walks slowly home, looking about him in horror. Is this truly his city, his world?

Allah, Allah, why have you abandoned me?

He has beheld the glory of Allah's workmanship. Then why this? Were all those other universes, other realities a dream?

The rain pours down.

There is someone lying on his face in a ditch. The rain has wet the shirt on his back, made the blood run. As Abdul Karim starts toward him, wondering who it is, whether he is dead or alive—young, from the back it could be Ramdas or Imran—he sees behind him, at the entrance to the lane, a horde of young men. Some of them may be his students—they can help.

They are moving with a predatory sureness that frightens him. He sees that they have sticks and stones.

They are coming like a tsunami, a thunderclap, leaving death and ruin in their wake. He hears their shouts through the rain.

Abdul Karim's courage fails him. He runs to his house, enters, locks and bars the door and closes all the windows. He checks on his mother, who is sleeping. The telephone is dead. The dal for their meal has boiled away. He turns off the gas and goes back to the door, putting his ear against it. He does not want to risk looking out of the window.

Over the rain he hears the young men go past at a run. In the distance there is a fusillade of shots. More sounds of running feet, then, just the rain.

Are the police here? The army?

Something or someone is scratching at the door. Abdul Karim is transfixed with terror. He stands there, straining to hear over the pitter patter of the rain. On the other side, somebody moans.

Abdul Karim opens the door. The lane is empty, roaring with rain. At his feet there is the body of a young woman.

She opens her eyes. She's dressed in a salwaar kameez that has been half-torn off her body—her long hair is wet with rain and blood, plastered over her neck and shoulders. There is blood on her salwaar, blood oozing from a hundred little cuts and welts on her skin.

Her gaze focuses.

"Master Sahib."

He is taken aback. Is she someone he knows? Perhaps an old student, grown up?

Quickly he half-carries, half-pulls her into the house and secures the door. With some difficulty he lifts her carefully on to the divan in the drawing room, which is already staining with her blood. She coughs.

"My child, who did this to you? Let me find a doctor . . ."

"No," she says. "It's too late." Her breath rasps and she coughs again. Tears well up in the dark eyes.

"Master Sahib, please, let me die! My husband . . . my son . . . They must not see me take my last breath. Not like this. They will suffer. They will want revenge . . . Please . . . cut my wrists . . ."

She's raising her wrists to his horrified face, but all he can do is to take them in his shaking hands.

"My daughter," he says, and doesn't know what to say. Where will he find a doctor in the mayhem? Can he bind her cuts? Even as he thinks these thoughts he knows that life is ebbing from her. Blood is pooling on his divan, dripping down to the floor. She does not need him to cut her wrists.

"Tell me, who are the ruffians who did this?"

She whispers:

"I don't know who they were. I had just stepped out of the house for a moment. My family . . . don't tell them, Master Sahib! When I'm gone just tell them . . . tell them I died in a safe place . . ."

"Daughter, what is your husband's name?"

Her eyes are enormous. She is gazing at him without comprehension, as though she is already in another world.

He can't tell if she is Muslim or Hindu. If she wore a vermilion dot on her forehead, it has long since been washed off by the rain.

His mother is standing at the door of the drawing room. She wails suddenly and loudly, flings herself by the side of the dying woman.

"Ayesha! Ayesha, my life!"

Tears fall down Abdul Karim's face. He tries to disengage his mother. Tries to tell her: this is not Ayesha, just another woman whose body has become a battleground over which men make war. At last he has to lift his mother in his arms, her body so frail that he fears it might break—he takes her to her bed, where she crumples, sobbing and calling Ayesha's name.

Back in the drawing room, the young woman's eyes flicker to him. Her voice is barely above a whisper.

"Master Sahib, cut my wrists . . . I beseech you, in the

Almighty's name! Take me somewhere safe . . . Let me die . . ."

Then the veil falls over her eyes again and her body goes limp.

Time stands still for Abdul Karim.

Then he senses something familiar, and turns slowly. The farishta is waiting.

Abdul Karim picks up the woman in his arms, awkwardly arranging the bloody divan cover over her half-naked body. In the air, a door opens.

Staggering a little, his knees protesting, he steps through the door.

After three universes he finds the place.

It is peaceful. There is a rock rising from a great turquoise sea of sand. The blue sand laps against the rock, making lulling, sibilant sounds. In the high, clear air, winged creatures call to each other between endless rays of light. He squints in the sudden brightness.

He closes her eyes, buries her deep at the base of the rock, under the blue, flowing sand.

He stands there, breathing hard from the exertion, his hands bruised, thinking he should say something. But what? He does not even know if she's Muslim or Hindu. When she spoke to him earlier, what word had she used for God? Was it Allah or Ishwar, or something neutral?

He can't remember.

At last he says the Al-Fatihah, and, stumbling a little, recites whatever little he knows of the Hindu scriptures. He ends with the phrase *Isha Vasyamidam Sarvam*.

Tears run off his cheeks into the blue sand, and disappear without leaving a trace.

The farishta waits.

"Why didn't you do something!" Abdul Karim rails at the shadow. He falls to his knees in the blue sand, weeping. "Why, if you are truly a farishta, didn't you save my sister?"

He sees now that he has been a fool—this shadow creature is no angel, and he, Abdul Karim, no Prophet.

He weeps for Ayesha, for this nameless young woman, for the body he saw in the ditch, for his lost friend Gangadhar.

The shadow leans toward him. Abdul Karim gets up, looks around once, and steps through the door.

He steps out into his drawing room. The first thing he discovers is that his mother is dead. She looks quite peaceful, lying in her bed, her white hair flowing over the pillow.

She might be asleep, her face is so calm.

He stands there for a long time, unable to weep. He picks up the phone—there is still no dial tone. After that he goes about methodically cleaning up the drawing room, washing the floor, taking the bedding off the divan. Later, after the rain has stopped, he will burn it in the courtyard. Who will notice another fire in the burning city?

When everything is cleaned up, he lies down next to his mother's body like a small boy and goes to sleep.

When you left me, my brother, you took away the book
In which is writ the story of my life . . .
    —Faiz Ahmed Faiz, Pakistani poet (1911–1984)

The sun is out. An uneasy peace lies over the city. His mother's funeral is over. Relatives have come and gone— his younger son came, but did not stay. The older son sent a sympathy card from America.

Gangadhar's house is still empty, a blackened ruin. Whenever he has ventured out, Abdul Karim has asked about his friend's whereabouts. The last he heard was that Gangadhar was alone in the house when the mob came, and his Muslim neighbors sheltered him until he could join his wife and children at her parents' house. But it has been so long that he does not believe it any more. He has also heard that Gangadhar was dragged out, hacked to pieces and his body set on fire. The city has calmed down—the army had to be called in—but it is still rife with rumors. Hundreds of people are missing. Civil rights groups comb the town, interviewing people, revealing, in clipped, angry press statements, the negligence of the state government, the collusion of the police in some of the violence. Some of them came to his house, too, very clean, very young people, burning with an idealism that, however misplaced, is comforting to see.

He has said nothing about the young woman who died in his arms, but he prays for that bereft family every day.

For days he has ignored the shadow at his shoulder. But now he knows that the sense of betrayal will fade. Whose fault is it, after all, that he ascribed to the creatures he once called farishte the attributes of angels? Could angels, even, save human beings from themselves?

The creatures watch us with a child's curiosity, he thinks, but they do not understand. Just as their own worlds are incomprehensible to me, so are our ways to them. They are not Allah's minions.

The space where the universes branch off—the heart of the metacosmos—now appears remote to him, like a dream. He is ashamed of his earlier arrogance. How can he possibly fathom Allah's creation in one glance? No finite mind can, in one meager lifetime, truly comprehend the vastness, the grandeur of Allah's scheme. All we can do is to discover a bit of the truth here, a bit there, and thus to sing His praises.

But there is so much pain in Abdul Karim's soul that he cannot imagine writing down one syllable of the new language of the infinite. His dreams are haunted by the horrors he has seen, the images of his mother and the young woman who died in his arms. He cannot even say his prayers. It is as though Allah has abandoned him, after all.

The daily task of living—waking up, performing his ablutions, setting the little pot on the gas stove to boil water for one cup of tea, to drink that tea alone—unbearable thought! To go on, after so many have died—to go on without his mother, his children, without Gangadhar . . . Everything appears strangely remote: his aging face in the mirror, the old house, even the litchi tree in his courtyard. The familiar lanes of his childhood hold memories that no longer seem to belong to him. Outside, the neighbors are in mourning; old Ameen Khan Sahib weeps for his grandson; Ramdas is gone, Imran is gone. The wind still carries the soot of the burnings. He finds little piles of ashes everywhere, in the cracks in the cement of his courtyard, between the roots of the trees in the lane. He breathes the dead. How can he regain his heart, living in a world so wracked with pain? In this world there is no place for the likes of him. No place for henna-scented hands rocking a child to sleep, for old-woman hands tending a garden. And no place at all for the austere beauty of mathematics.

He's thinking this when a shadow falls across the ground in front of him. He has been sitting in his courtyard, idly writing mathematical expressions with his stick on the dusty ground. He does not know whether the knife bearer is his son, or an enraged Hindu, but he finds himself ready for his death. The creatures who have watched him for so long will witness it, and wonder. Their uncomprehending presence comforts him.

He turns and rises. It is Gangadhar, his friend, who holds out his empty arms in an embrace.

Abdul Karim lets his tears run over Gangadhar's shirt. As waves of relief wash over him he knows that he has held Death at bay this time, but it will come. It will come, he has seen it. Archimedes and Ramanujan, Khayyam and Cantor died with epiphanies on their lips before an indifferent world. But this moment is eternal.

"Allah be praised!" says Abdul Karim.

This Peaceable Land; or, The Unbearable Vision of Harriet Beecher Stowe

ROBERT CHARLES WILSON

Robert Charles Wilson (www.robertcharleswilson.com) *lives in Toronto, Ontario, in Canada. Wilson's first novel,* A Hidden Place, *was published in 1986. Since then he has written more than a dozen novels, including* Spin, *which received the Hugo Award, Germany's Kurd Lasswitz Prize, and the French Grand Prix de l'Imaginaire. Among his other works are* Darwinia, Blind Lake, *and* The Chronoliths. *His most recent novel is* Julian Comstock: A Story of 22nd-Century America *(2009). He published two especially distinguished SF stories in 2009, of which this is one.*

"This Peaceable Land; or, the Unbearable Vision of Harriet Beacher Stowe" appeared in Other Earths, *edited by Nick Gevers, a paperback anthology of original stories that is in our opinion one of the best anthologies of the year. Set in the southern U.S., in an alternate late nineteenth century, it takes place in a universe in which the U.S. Civil War was avoided. It is the first of several alternate universe stories in this volume.*

It's worth your life to go up there," the tavernkeeper's wife said. "What do you want to go up there for, anyway?"

"The property is for sale," I said.

"Property!" The landlady of the roadside tavern nearly spat out the word. "There's nothing up there but sand hills and saggy old sheds. That, and a family of crazy colored people. Someone claims they sold you that? You ought to check with the bank, Mister, see about getting your money back."

She smiled at her own joke, showing tobacco-stained teeth. In this part of the country there were spittoons in every taproom and Bull Durham advertisements on every wall. It was 1895. It was August. It was hot, and we were in the South.

I was only posing as an investor. I had no money in all the baggage I was carrying—very little, anyhow. I had photographic equipment instead.

"You go up those hills," the tavernkeeper's wife said more soberly, "you carry a gun, and you keep it handy. I mean that."

I had no gun.

I wasn't worried about what I might find up in the pine barrens.

I was worried about what I would tell my daughter.

I paid the lady for the meal she had served me and for a second meal she had put up in a neat small box. I asked her whether a room was available for the night. There was. We discussed the arrangements and came to an agreement. Then I went out to where Percy was waiting in the carriage.

"You'll have to sleep outside," I said. "But I got this for you." I gave him the wrapped dinner. "And the landlady says she'll bring you a box breakfast in the morning, as long as there's nobody around to see her."

Percy nodded. None of this came as a surprise to him. He knew where he was, and who he was, and what was expected of him. "And then," he said, "we'll drive up to the place, weather permitting."

To Percy it was always "the place"—each place we found.

Storm clouds had dallied along this river valley all the hot day, but no rain had come. If it came tonight, and if it was torrential, the dirt roads would quickly become useless creeks of mud. We would be stuck here for days.

And Percy would get wet, sleeping in the carriage as he did. But he preferred the carriage to the stable where our horses were put up. The carriage was covered with rubberized cloth, and there was a big sheet of mosquito netting he stretched over the open places during the night. But a truly stiff rain was bound to get in the cracks and make him miserable.

Percy Camber was an educated black man. He wrote columns and articles for the *Tocsin*, a Negro paper published out of Windsor, Canada. Three years ago a Boston press had put out a book he'd written, though he admitted the sales had been slight.

I wondered what the landlady would say if I told her Percy was a book writer. Most likely she would have denied the possibility of an educated black man. Except perhaps as a circus act, like that Barnum horse that counts to ten with its hoof.

"Make sure your gear is ready first thing," Percy said, keeping his voice low although there was nobody else about—this was a poor tavern on a poor road in an undeveloped county. "And don't drink too much tonight, Tom, if you can help it."

"That's sound advice," I agreed, by way of not pledging

an answer. "Oh, and the keeper's wife tells me we ought to carry a gun. Wild men up there, she says."

"I don't go armed."

"Nor do I."

"Then I guess we'll be prey for the wild men," said Percy, smiling.

The room where I spent the night was not fancy, which made me feel better about leaving my employer to sleep out-of-doors. It was debatable which of us was better off. The carriage seat where Percy curled up was not infested with fleas, as was the mattress on which I lay. Percy customarily slept on a folded jacket, while my pillow was a sugar sack stuffed with corn huskings, which rattled beneath my ear as if the beetles inside were putting on a musical show.

I slept a little, woke up, scratched myself, lit the lamp, took a drink.

I will not drink, I told myself as I poured the liquor. I will not drink "to excess." I will not become drunk. I will only calm the noise in my head.

My companion in this campaign was a bottle of rye whisky. Mister Whiskey Bottle, unfortunately, was only half full and not up to the task assigned him. I drank but kept on thinking unwelcome thoughts, while the night simmered and creaked with insect noises.

"Why do you have to go away for so long?" Elsebeth asked me.

In this incarnation she wore a white dress. It looked like her christening dress. She was thirteen years old.

"Taking pictures," I told her. "Same as always."

"Why can't you take pictures at the portrait studio?"

"These are different pictures, Elsie. The kind you have to travel for."

Her flawless young face took on an accusatory cast. "Mama says you're stirring up old trouble. She says you're poking into things nobody wants to hear about any more, much less see photographs of."

"She may be right. But I'm being paid money, and money buys pretty dresses, among other good things."

"Why make such trouble, though? Why do you want to make people feel bad?"

Elsie was a phantom. I blinked her away. These were questions she had not yet actually posed, though our last conversation, before I left Detroit, had come uncomfortably close. But they were questions I would sooner or later have to answer.

I slept very little, despite the drink. I woke up before dawn.

I inventoried my photographic equipment by lamplight, just to make sure everything was ready.

It had not rained during the night. I settled up with the landlady and removed my baggage from the room. Percy had already hitched the horses to the carriage. The sky was drab under high cloud, the sun a spot of light like a candle flame burning through a linen handkerchief.

The landlady's husband was nowhere to be seen. He had gone down to Crib Lake for supplies, she said, as she packed up two box lunches, cold cuts of beef with pickles and bread, which I had requested of her. She had two adult sons living with her, one of whom I had met in the stables, and she felt safe enough, she told me, even with her husband absent. "But we're a long way from anywhere," she added, "and the traffic along this road has been light ever since— well, ever since the Lodge closed down. I wasn't kidding about those sand hills, Mister. Be careful up there."

"We mean to be back by nightfall," I said.

My daughter Elsebeth had met Percy Camber just once, when he came to the house in Detroit to discuss his plans with me. Elsie had been meticulously polite to him. Percy had offered her his hand, and she, wide-eyed, had taken it. "You're very neatly dressed," she had said.

She was not used to well-dressed black men. The only blacks Elsebeth had seen were the day laborers who gathered on the wharves. Detroit housed a small community of Negroes who had come north with the decline of slavery, before Congress passed the Labor Protection Act. They did "the jobs white men won't do," for wages to which white men would not submit.

"You're very prettily dressed yourself," Percy Camber said, ignoring the unintended insult.

Maggie, my wife, had simply refused to see him.

"I'm not some radical old Congregationalist," she told me, "eager to socialize with every tawny Moor who comes down the pike. That's your side of the family, Tom, not mine."

True enough. Maggie's people were Episcopalians who had prospered in Michigan since before it was a State— sturdy, reliable folks. They ran a string of warehouses that catered to the lake trade. My father was a disappointed Whig who had spent a single term in the Massachusetts legislature pursuing the chimera of Free Education before he died at an early age, and my mother's bookshelves still groaned under the weight of faded tomes on the subjects of Enlightened Marriage and Women's Suffrage. I came from a genteel family of radical tendencies and modest means. I was never sure Maggie's people understood that poverty and gentility could truly coexist.

"Maggie's indisposed today," I had told Percy, who may or may not have believed me, and then we had settled down to the business of planning our three-month tour of the South, according to the map he had made.

"There ought to be photographs," Percy said, "before it's all gone."

We traveled several miles from the tavern, sweating in the airless heat of the morning, following directions Percy had deduced from bills-of-transfer, railway records, and old advertisements placed in the Richmond and Atlanta papers.

The locality to which we were headed had been called Pilgassi Acres. It had been chartered as a business by two brothers, Marcus and Benjamin Pilgassi of South Carolina, in 1879, and it had operated for five years before the Ritter Inquiry shut it down.

There were no existing photographs of Pilgassi Acres, or any of the institutions like it, unless the Ritter Inquiry had commissioned them. And the Final Report of the Ritter Inquiry had been sealed from the public by consent of Congress, not to be reopened until some time in the twentieth century.

Percy Camber intended to shed some light into that officially ordained darkness.

He sat with me on the driver's board of the carriage as I coaxed the team over the rutted and runneled trail. This had once been a wider road, much used, but it had been bypassed by a Federal turnpike in 1887. Since then nature and the seasons had mauled it, so the ride was tedious and slow. We subdued the boredom by swapping stories: Percy of his home in Canada, me of my time in the army.

Percy "talked white." That was the verdict Elsebeth had passed after meeting him. It was a condescending thing to say, excusable only from the lips of a child, but I knew what she meant. Percy was two generations out of slavery. If I closed my eyes and listened to his voice, I could imagine that I had been hired by some soft-spoken Harvard graduate. He was articulate, even for a newspaper man. And we had learned, over the course of this lengthy expedition, to make allowances for our differences. We had some common ground. We were both the offspring of radical parents, for example. The "madness of the fifties" had touched us both, in different ways.

"You suppose we'll find anything substantial at the end of this road?" Percy asked.

"The landlady mentioned some old sheds."

"Sheds would be acceptable," Percy said, his weariness showing. "It's been a long haul for you, Tom. And not much substantial work. Maybe this time?"

"Maybe."

"Documents, oral accounts, that's all useful, but a photograph—just one, just to show that something remains—well, that would be important."

"I'll photograph any old shed you like, Percy, if it pleases you." Though on this trip I had seen more open fields—long since burned over and regrown—than anything worthy of being immortalized. Places edited from history. Absences constructed as carefully as architecture. I had no reason to think Pilgassi Acres would be different.

Percy seldom spoke out loud about the deeper purpose of his quest or the book he was currently writing. Fair enough, I thought; it was a sensitive subject. Like the way I don't talk much about Cuba, though I had served a year and a half there under Lee. The spot is too tender to touch.

These hills were low and covered with stunted pines and other rude vegetation. The road soon grew even more rough, but we began to encounter evidence of a prior human presence. A few fenceposts. Scraps of rusted barbwire. The traces of an old narrow-gauge railbed. Then we passed under a wooden sign suspended between two lodgepoles, on which the words *PILGASSI ACRES* in an ornate script were still legible, though the seasons had bleached the letters to ghosts.

There was also the remains of a wire fence, tangled over with brambles.

"Stop here," Percy said.

"Might be more ahead," I suggested.

"This is already more than we've seen elsewhere. I want a picture of that sign."

"I can't guarantee it'll be legible," I said, given the way the sun was striking it, and the faint color of the letters, pale as chalk on the white wood.

"Well, try," Percy said shortly.

So I set up my equipment and did that. For the first time in a long while, I felt as though I was earning my keep.

The first book Percy had written was called *Every Measure Short of War*, and it was a history of Abolitionism from the Negro point of view.

The one he was writing now was to be called *Where Are the Three Million?*

I made a dozen or so exposures and put my gear back in the carriage. Percy took the reins this time and urged the horses farther up the trail. Scrub grass and runt pines closed in on both sides of us, and I found myself watching the undergrowth for motion. The landlady's warning had come back to haunt me.

But the woods were empty. An old stray dog paced us for a few minutes, then fell behind.

My mother had once corresponded with Mrs. Harriet Beecher Stowe, who was a well-known abolitionist at one time, though the name is now mostly forgotten. Percy had contacted my parents in order to obtain copies of that correspondence, which he had quoted in an article for the *Tocsin*.

My mother, of course, was flattered, and she continued her correspondence with Percy on an occasional basis. In one of his replies Percy happened to remark that he was looking for a reliable photographer to hire for the new project he had in mind. My mother, of course, sent him to me. Perhaps she thought she was doing me a favor.

Thus it was not money but conscience that had propelled me on this journey. Conscience, that crabbed and ecclesiastical nag, which inevitably spoke, whether I heeded it or not, in a voice much like my mother's.

The remains of Pilgassi Acres became visible as we rounded a final bend, and I was frankly astonished that so much of it remained intact. Percy Camber drew in his breath.

Here were the administrators' quarters (a small building with pretensions to the Colonial style), as well as five huge barnlike buildings and fragments of paving stones and mortared brick where more substantial structures had been demolished.

All silent, all empty. No glass in the small windows. A breeze like the breath from a hard-coal stove seeped around the buildings and tousled the meadow weeds that lapped at them. There was the smell of old wood that had stood in the sunlight for a long time. There was, beneath that, the smell of something less pleasant, like an abandoned latrine doused with lime and left to simmer in the heat.

Percy was working to conceal his excitement. He pretended to be casual, but I could see that every muscle in him had gone tense.

"Your camera, Tom," he said, as if the scene were in some danger of evaporating before our eyes.

"You don't want to explore the place a little first?"

"Not yet. I want to capture it as we see it now—from a distance, all the buildings all together."

And I did that. The sun, though masked by light high clouds, was a feverish nuisance over my right shoulder.

I thought of my daughter Elsebeth. She would see these pictures some day. "What place is this?" she would ask.

But what would I say in return?

Any answer I could think of amounted to drilling a hole in her innocence and pouring poison in.

Every Measure Short of War, the title of Percy's first book, implied that there might have been one—a war over Abolition, that is, a war between the States. My mother agreed. "Though it was not the North that would have brought it on," she insisted. (A conversation we had had on the eve of my marriage to Maggie.) "People forget how sullen the South was in the years before the Douglas Compromise. How fierce in the defense of slavery. Their 'Peculiar Institution'! Strange, isn't it, how people cling most desperately to a thing when it becomes least useful to them?"

My mother's dream, and Mrs. Stowe's, for that matter, had never been achieved. No Abolition by federal statute had ever been legislated. Slavery had simply become unprofitable, as its milder opponents and apologists used to insist it inevitably would. Scientific farming killed it. Crop rotation killed it. Deep plowing killed it, mechanized harvesters killed it, soil fertilization killed it.

Embarrassment killed it, once Southern farmers began to take seriously the condescension and disapproval of the European powers whose textile and tobacco markets they craved. Organized labor killed it.

Ultimately, the expense and absurdity of maintaining human beings as farm chattel killed it.

A few slaves were still held under permissive state laws (in Virginia and South Carolina for example), but they tended to be the pets of the old Planter aristocracy—kept, as pets might be kept, because the children of the household had grown fond of them and objected to their eviction.

I walked with Percy Camber through the abandoned administration building at Pilgassi Acres. It had been stripped of everything—all furniture, every document, any scrap that might have testified to its human utility. Even the wallpaper had peeled or rotted away. One well-placed lightning strike would have burned the whole thing to the ground.

Its decomposing stairs were too hazardous to attempt. Animals had covered the floorboards with dung, and birds lofted out of every room we opened. Our progress could have been charted by the uprisings of the swallows and the indignation of the owls.

"It's just an empty building," I said to Percy, who had been silent throughout the visit, his features knotted and tense.

"Empty of what, though?" he asked.

I took a few more exposures on the outside. The crumbling pillars. The worm-tunneled verandah casting a sinister shade. A chimney leaning sideways like a drunken man.

I did not believe, could not bring myself to believe, that a war within the boundaries of the Union could ever have been fought, though historians still worry about that question like a loose tooth. If the years after '55 had been less prosperous, if Douglas had not been elected President, if the terrorist John Brown had not been tried in a Northern court and hanged on a Northern gallows . . . *if, if,* and *if, ad infinitum.*

All nonsense, it seemed to me. Whatever Harriet Beecher Stowe might have dreamed, whatever Percy Camber might have uncovered, this was fundamentally a peaceable land.

This is a peaceable land, I imagined myself telling my daughter Elsebeth; but my imagination would extend itself no farther.

* * *

"Now the barracks," Percy said.

It had been even hotter in the administration building than it was outside, and Percy's clothes were drenched through. So were mine. "You mean those barns?"

"Barracks," Percy repeated.

Barracks or barns—they were a little of both, as it turned out. The one we inspected was a cavernous wooden box, held up by mildew and inertia. Percy wanted photographs of the rusted iron brackets that had supported rows of wooden platforms—a few of these remained—on which men and women had once slept. There were a great many of these brackets, and I estimated that a single barracks-barn might have housed as many as two hundred persons in its day. An even larger number if mattresses had been laid on the floors.

I took the pictures he wanted by the light that came through fallen boards. The air in the barn was stale, despite all the holes in the walls, and it was a relief to finish my work and step out into the relentless, dull sunshine.

The presence of so many people must have necessitated a dining hall, a communal kitchen, sanitary facilities at Pilgassi Acres. Those structures had not survived except as barren patches among the weeds. Dig down a little—Percy had learned this technique in his research—and you would find a layer of charcoal for each burned building or outhouse. Not every structure in Pilgassi Acres had survived the years, but each had left its subtle mark.

One of the five barns was not like the others, and I made this observation to Percy Camber as soon as I noticed it. "The rest of these barracks, the doors and windows are open to the breeze. The far one in the north quarter has been boarded up—d'you see?"

"That's the one we should inspect next, then," Percy said.

We were on our way there when the first bullet struck.

My mother had always been an embarrassment to me, with her faded enthusiasms, her Bible verses and Congregationalist poetry, her missionary zeal on behalf of people whose lives were so tangential to mine that I could barely imagine them.

She didn't like it when I volunteered for Cuba in 1880. It wasn't a proper war, she said. She said it was yet another concession to the South, to the aristocracy's greed for expansion toward the equator. "A war engineered at the Virginia Military Institute," she called it, "fought for no good reason."

But it blended Northerners and Southerners on a neutral field of battle, where we were all just American soldiers. It was the glue that repaired many ancient sectional rifts. Out of it emerged great leaders, like old Robert E. Lee, who transcended regional loyalties (though when he spoke of "America," I often suspected he used the word as a synonym for "Virginia"), and his son, also a talented commander. In Cuba we all wore a common uniform, and we all learned, rich and poor, North and South, to duck the Spaniards' bullets.

The bullet hit a shed wall just above Percy Camber's skull. Splinters flew through the air like a cloud of mosquitoes. The sound of the gunshot arrived a split second later, damped by the humid afternoon to a harmless-sounding *pop*. The rifleman was some distance away. But he was accurate.

I dropped to the ground—or, rather, discovered that I had already dropped to the ground, obeying an instinct swifter than reason.

Percy, who had never been to war, lacked that ingrained impulse. I'm not sure he understood what had happened. He stood there in the rising heat, bewildered.

"Get down," I said.

"What is it, Tom?"

"Your doom, if you don't get down. *Get down!*"

He understood then. But it was as if the excitement had loosened all the strings of his body. He couldn't decide which way to fold. He was the picture of confusion.

Then a second bullet struck him in the shoulder.

"Liberty Lodges," they had been called at first.

I mean the places like Pilgassi Acres, back when they were allowed to flourish.

They were a response to a difficult time. Slavery had died, but the slaves had not. That was the dilemma of the South. Black men without skills, along with their families and countless unaccompanied children, crowded the roads— more of them every day, as "free-labor cotton" became a rallying cry for progressive French and English buyers.

Who were Marcus and Benjamin Pilgassi? Probably nothing more than a pair of Richmond investors jumping on a bandwagon. The Liberty Lodges bore no onus then. The appeal of the business was explicit: Don't put your slaves on the road and risk prosecution or fines for "abandonment of property." We will take your aging and unprofitable chattel and house them. The men will be kept separate from the women to prevent any reckless reproduction. They will live out their lives with their basic needs attended to for an annual fee only a fraction of what it would cost to keep them privately.

What the Pilgassi brothers (and businessmen like them) did not say directly—but implied in every line of their advertisements—was that the Liberty Lodge movement aimed to achieve an absolute and irreversible decline in the Negro population in the South.

In time, Percy had told me, the clients of these businesses came to include entire state governments, which had tired of the expense and notoriety incurred by the existence of temporary camps in which tens of thousands of "intramural refugees" could neither be fed economically nor be allowed to starve. It had been less onerous for them to subsidize the Lodges, which tended to be built in isolated places, away from casual observation.

Percy's grandfather had escaped slavery in the 1830s and settled in Boston, where he picked up enough education to make himself prominent in the Abolition movement. Percy's father, an ordained minister, had spoken at Lyman Beecher's famous church, in the days before he founded the journal that became the *Tocsin*.

Percy had taken up the moral burden of his forebears in a way I had not, but there was still a similarity between us. We were the children of crusaders. We had inherited their disappointments and drunk the lees of their bitterness.

I was not a medical man, but I had witnessed bullet wounds in Cuba. Percy had been shot in the shoulder. He lay on the ground with his eyes open, blinking, his left hand pressed against the wound. I pried his hand away so that I could examine his injury.

The wound was bleeding badly, but the blood did not spurt out, a good sign. I took a handkerchief from my pocket, folded it and pressed it against the hole.

"Am I dying?" Percy asked. "I don't feel like I'm dying."

"You're not all that badly hurt or you wouldn't be talking. You need attention, though."

A third shot rang out. I couldn't tell where the bullet went.

"And we need to get under cover," I added.

The nearest building was the boarded-up barracks. I told Percy to hold the handkerchief in place. His right arm didn't seem to work correctly, perhaps because the bullet had damaged some bundle of muscles or nerves. But I got him crouching, and we hurried toward shelter.

We came into the shadow of the building and stumbled to the side of it away from the direction from which the shots had come. Grasshoppers buzzed out of the weeds in fierce brown flurries, some of them lighting on our clothes. There was the sound of dry thunder down the valley. This barracks had a door—a wooden door on a rail, large enough to admit dozens of people at once. But it was closed, and there was a brass latch and a padlock on it.

So we had no real shelter—just some shade and a moment's peace.

I used the time to put a fresh handkerchief on Percy's wound and to bind it with a strip of cloth torn from my own shirt.

"Thank you," Percy said breathlessly.

"Welcome. The problem now is how to get back to the carriage." We had no weapons, and we could hardly withstand a siege, no matter where we hid. Our only hope was escape, and I could not see any likely way of achieving it.

Then the question became moot, for the man who had tried to kill us came around the corner of the barracks.

* * *

"Why do you want to make these pictures?" Elsie asked yet again, from a dim cavern at the back of my mind.

In an adjoining chamber of my skull a different voice reminded me that I wanted a drink, a strong one, immediately.

The ancient Greeks (I imagined myself telling Elsebeth) believed that vision is a force that flies out from the eyes when directed by the human will. They were wrong. There is no force or will in vision. There is only light. Light direct or light reflected. Light, which behaves in predictable ways. Put a prism in front of it, and it breaks into colors. Open a shuttered lens, and some fraction of it can be trapped in nitrocellulose or collodion as neatly as a bug in a killing jar.

A man with a camera is like a naturalist, I told Elsebeth. Where one man might catch butterflies, another catches wasps.

I did not make these pictures.

I only caught them.

The man with the rifle stood five or six yards away at the corner of the barracks. He was a black man in threadbare coveralls. He was sweating in the heat. For a while there was silence, the three of us blinking at each other.

Then, "I didn't mean to shoot him," the black man said.

"Then you shouldn't have aimed a rifle at him and pulled the trigger," I said back, recklessly.

Our assailant made no immediate response. He seemed to be thinking this over. Grasshoppers lit on the cuffs of his ragged pants. His head was large, his hair cut crudely close to the skull. His eyes were narrow and suspicious. He was barefoot.

"It was not my intention to hurt anyone," he said again. "I was shooting from a distance, sir."

By this time Percy had managed to sit up. He seemed less afraid of the rifleman than he ought to have been. Less afraid, at any rate, than I was. "What *did* you intend?"

He gave his attention to Percy. "To warn you away, is all."

"Away from what?"

"This building."

"Why? What's in this building?"

"My son."

* * *

The "three million" in Percy's title were the men, women and children of African descent held in bondage in the South in the year 1860. For obvious reasons, the number is approximate. Percy always tried to be conservative in his estimates, for he did not want to be vulnerable to accusations of sensationalizing history.

Given that number to begin with, what Percy had done was to tally up census polls, where they existed, alongside the archived reports of various state and local governments, tax and business statements, Federal surveys, rail records, etc., over the years between then and now.

What befell the three million?

A great many—as many as one third—emigrated North, before changes in the law made that difficult. Some of those who migrated continued on up to Canada. Others made lives for themselves in the big cities, insofar as they were allowed to. A smaller number were taken up against their will and shipped to certain inhospitable "colonies" in Africa, until the excesses and horrors of repatriation became notorious and the whole enterprise was outlawed.

Some found a place among the freemen of New Orleans or worked boats, largely unmolested, along the Gulf Coast. A great many went West, where they were received with varying degrees of hostility. Five thousand "irredeemably criminal" black prisoners were taken from Southern jails and deposited in a Utah desert, where they died not long after.

Certain jobs remained open to black men and women— as servants, rail porters, and so forth—and many did well enough in these professions.

But add the numbers, Percy said, even with a generous allowance for error, and it still comes up shy of the requisite three million.

How many were delivered into the Liberty Lodges? No one can answer that question with any certainty, at least not until the evidence sealed by the Ritter Inquiry is opened to the public. Percy's estimate was somewhere in the neighborhood of 50,000. But as I said, he tended to be conservative in his figures.

"We were warned there was a family of wild men up here," I said.

"I'm no wilder than I have to be," the gunman said. "I didn't ask you to come visit."

"You hurt Percy bad enough, whether you're wild or not. Look at him. He needs a medic."

"I see him all right, sir."

"Then, unless you mean to shoot us both to death, will you help me get him back to our carriage?"

There was another lengthy pause.

"I don't like to do that," the black man said finally. "There won't be any end to the trouble. But I don't suppose I have a choice, except, as you say, sir, to kill you. And that I cannot bring myself to do."

He said these words calmly enough, but he had a way of forming his vowels, and pronouncing them deep in his throat, that defies transcription. It was like listening to a volcano rumble.

"Take his right arm, then," I said. "I'll get on his left. The carriage is beyond that ridge."

"I know where your carriage is. But, sir, I won't put down this rifle. I don't think that would be wise. You can help him yourself."

I went to where Percy sat and began to lift him up. Percy startled me by saying, "No, Tom, I don't want to go to the carriage."

"What do you mean?" the assailant asked, before I could pose the same question.

"Do you have a name?" Percy asked him.

"Ephraim," the man said, reluctantly.

"Ephraim, my name is Percy Camber. What did you mean when you said your son was inside this barracks?"

"I don't like to tell you that," Ephraim said, shifting his gaze between Percy and me.

"Percy," I said, "you need a doctor. We're wasting time."

He looked at me sharply. "I'll live a while longer. Let me talk to Ephraim, please, Tom."

"Stand off there where I can see you, sir," Ephraim directed. "I know this man needs a doctor. I'm not stupid. This won't take long."

I concluded from all this that the family of wild Negroes the landlady had warned me about was real and that they were living in the sealed barn.

Why they should want to inhabit such a place I could not say.

I stood apart while Percy, wounded as he was, held a hushed conversation with Ephraim, who had shot him.

I understood that they could talk more freely without me as an auditor. I was a white man. It was true that I worked for Percy, but that fact would not have been obvious to Ephraim any more than it had been obvious to the dozens of hotelkeepers who had assumed without asking that I was the master, and Percy was the servant. My closeness to Percy was unique and all but invisible.

After a while Ephraim allowed me to gather up my photographic gear, which had been scattered in the crisis.

I had been fascinated by photography even as a child. It had seemed like such patent magic! The magic of stopped time, places and persons rescued from their ephemeral natures. My parents had given me books containing photographs of Indian elephants, of the pyramids of Egypt, of the natural wonders of Florida.

I put my gear together and waited for Percy to finish his talk with the armed lunatic who had shot him.

The high cloud that had polluted the sky all morning had dissipated during the afternoon. The air was still scaldingly hot, but it was a touch less humid. A certain brittle clarity had set in. The light was hard, crystalline. A fine light for photography, though it was beginning to grow long.

"Percy," I called out.

"What is it, Tom?"

"We have to leave now, before the sun gets any lower. It's a long journey to Crib Lake." There was a doctor at Crib Lake. I remembered seeing his shingle when we passed through that town. Some rural bonesetter, probably, a doughty relic of the mustard-plaster era. But better than no doctor at all.

Percy's voice sounded weak; but what he said was, "We're not finished here yet."

"What do you mean, not finished?"

"We've been invited inside," he said. "To see Ephraim's son."

Some bird, perhaps a mourning dove, called out from the gathering shadows among the trees where the meadow ended.

I did not want to meet Ephraim's son. There was a dreadful aspect to the whole affair. If Ephraim's son was in the barn, why had he not come out at the sound of gunshots and voices? (Ephraim, as far as I could tell, was an old man, and his son wasn't likely to be an infant.) Why, for that matter, was the barracks closed and locked? To keep the world away from Ephraim's son? Or to keep Ephraim's son away from the world?

"What is his name?" I asked. "This son of yours."

"Jordan," he said.

I had married Maggie not long after I got back from Cuba. I had been trying to set up my photography business at the time. I was far from wealthy, and what resources I had I had put into my business. But there was a vogue among young women of the better type for manly veterans. I was manly enough, I suppose, or at least presentable, and I was authentically a veteran. I met Maggie when she came to my shop to sit for a portrait. I escorted her to dinner. Maggie was fond of me; and I was fond of Maggie, in part because she had no political convictions or fierce unorthodox ideals. She took the world as she found it.

Elsebeth came along a year or so after the wedding. It was a difficult birth. I remember the sound of Maggie's screams. I remember Elsebeth as a newborn, bloody in a towel, handed to me by the doctor. I wiped the remnant blood and fluid from her tiny body. She had been unspeakably beautiful.

Ephraim wore the key to the barn on a string around his

neck. He applied it to the massive lock, still giving me suspicious glances. He kept his rifle in the crook of his arm as he did this. He slid the huge door open. Inside, the barn was dark. The air that wafted out was a degree or two cooler than outside, and it carried a sour tang, as of long-rotten hay or clover.

Ephraim did not call out to his son, and there was no sound inside the abandoned barracks.

Had Ephraim once held his newborn son in his arms, as I had held Elsebeth?

The last of the Liberty Lodges were closed down in 1888. Scandal had swirled around them for years, but no sweeping legal action had been taken. In part this was because the Lodges were not a monolithic enterprise; a hundred independent companies held title to them. In part it was because various state legislatures were afraid of disclosing their own involvement. The Lodges had not proved as profitable as their founders expected; the plans had not anticipated, for instance, all the ancillary costs of keeping human beings confined in what amounted to a jail (guards, walls, fences, discipline, etc.) for life. But the *utility* of the Lodges was undisputed, and several states had quietly subsidized them. A "full accounting," as Percy called it, would have tainted every government south of the Mason Dixon Line and not a few above it. Old wounds might have been reopened.

The Ritter Inquiry was called by Congress when the abuses inherent in the Lodge system began to come to light, inch by inch. By that time, though, there had been many other scandals, many other inquests, and the public had grown weary of all such issues. Newspapers, apart from papers like the *Tocsin*, hardly touched the story. The Inquiry sealed its own evidence, the surviving Lodges were hastily dismantled, and the general population (apart from a handful of aged reformers) paid no significant attention.

"Why dredge up all that ugliness?" Maggie had asked me. *Nobody wants to see those pictures*, Elsebeth whispered. Nobody but a few old scolds.

* * *

It was too dark in the immense barracks to be certain, but it seemed to me there was nobody inside but the three of us.

"I came here with Jordan in '78," Ephraim said. "Jordan was twelve years old at the time. I don't know what happened to his mama. We got separated at the Federal camp on the Kansas border. Jordan and I were housed in different buildings."

He looked around, his eyes abstracted, and seemed to see more than an old and ruined barracks. Perhaps he could see in the dark—it was dark in here, the only light coming through the fractionally open door. All I could see was a board floor, immaculately swept, picked out in that wedge of sun. All else was shadow.

He found an old crate for Percy to sit on. The crate was the only thing like furniture I could see. There was nothing to suggest a family resided here apart from the neatness, the sealed entrances and windows, the absence of bird dung. I began to feel impatient.

"You said your son was here," I prompted him.

"Oh, yes, sir. Jordan's here."

"Where? I don't see him."

Percy shot me an angry look.

"He's everywhere in here," the madman said.

Oh, I thought, it's not Jordan, then, it's the spirit of Jordan, or some conceit like that. This barn is a shrine the man has been keeping. I had the unpleasant idea that Jordan's body might be tucked away in one of its shadowed corners, dry and lifeless as an old Egyptian king.

"Or at least," Ephraim said, "from about eight foot down."

He found and lit a lantern.

One evening in the midst of our journey through the South I had got drunk and shared with Percy, too ebulliently, my idea that we were really very much alike.

This was in Atlanta, in one of the hotels that provides separate quarters for colored servants traveling with their employers. That was good because it meant Percy could sleep in relative comfort. I had snuck down to his room, which was little more than a cubicle, and I had brought a bottle with me, although Percy refused to share it. He was an abstinent man.

I talked freely about my mother's fervent abolitionism and how it had hovered over my childhood like a storm cloud stitched with lightning. I told Percy how we were both the children of idealists, and so forth.

He listened patiently, but at the end, when I had finally run down, or my jaw was too weary to continue, he rummaged through the papers he carried with him and drew out a letter that had been written to him by Mrs. Harriet Beecher Stowe.

Mrs. Stowe is best remembered for her work on behalf of the China Inland Mission, but she came from an abolitionist family. Her father was the first president of the famous Lane Theological Seminary. At one point in her life she had attempted a novel meant to expose the evils of slavery, but she could not find a publisher.

Percy handed me the woman's letter.

I have received your book "Every Measure Short of War," the letter began, *and it brings back terrible memories and forebodings. I remember all too distinctly what it meant to love my country in those troubled years and to tremble at the coming day of wrath.*

"You want me to read this?" I asked drunkenly.

"Just that next part," Percy said.

Perhaps because of your book, Mr. Camber, Mrs. Stowe wrote, *or because of the memories it aroused, I suffered an unbearable dream last night. It was about that war. I mean the war that was so much discussed but that never took place, the war from which both North and South stepped back as from the brink of a terrible abyss.*

In my dream that precipice loomed again, and this time there was no Stephen Douglas to call us away with concessions and compromises and his disgusting deference to the Slave Aristocracy. In my dream, the war took place. And it was an awful war, Mr. Camber. It seemed to flow before my eyes in a series of bloody tableaux. A half a million dead. Battlefields too awful to contemplate, North and South. Industries crippled, both the print and the cotton presses silenced, thriving cities reduced to smoldering ruins—all this I saw, or knew, as one sees or knows in dreams.

But that was not the unbearable part of it.

Let me say that I have known death altogether too intimately. I have suffered the loss of children. I love peace just as fervently as I despise injustice. I would not wish grief or heartbreak on any mother of any section of this country, or any other country. And yet—!

And yet, in light of what I have inferred from recent numbers of your newspaper, and from the letters you have written me, and from what old friends and acquaintances have said or written about the camps, the deportations, the Lodges, etc.,—because of all that, a part of me wishes that that war had indeed been fought if only because it might have ended slavery. Ended it cleanly, I mean, with a sane and straightforward liberation, or even a liberation partial and incomplete—a declaration, at least, of the immorality and unacceptability of human bondage—anything but this sickening decline by extinction, this surreptitious (as you so bitterly describe it) "cleansing."

I suppose this makes me sound like a monster, a sort of female John Brown, confusing righteousness with violence and murder with redemption.

I am not such a monster. I confess a certain admiration for those who, like President Douglas, worked so very hard to prevent the apocalypse of which I dreamed last night, even if I distrust their motives and condemn their means. The instinct for peace is the most honorable of all Christian impulses. My conscience rebels at a single death, much less one million.

But if a War could have ended Slavery . . . would I have wished it? Welcomed it?

What is unbearable, Mr. Camber, is that I don't know that I can answer my own horrifying question either honestly or decently. And so I have to ask: Can you?

I puzzled it out. Then I gave Percy a blank stare. "Why are you showing me this?"

"We're alike in many ways, as you say, Tom. But not all ways. Not all ways. Mrs. Stowe asks an interesting question.

Answering it isn't easy. I don't know your mind, but fundamentally, Tom, despite all the sympathies between us, the fact
is, I suspect that in the end you might give the *wrong* answer
to that question—and I expect you think the same of me."

There was another difference, which I did not mention to
Percy, and that was that every time I remarked on our simi-
larities, I could hear my wife's scornful voice saying (as she
had said when I first shared the idea of this project with her),
"Oh, Tom, don't be ridiculous. You're nothing like that
Percy Camber. That's your mother talking—all that abolitionist guilt she burdened you with. As if you need to prove
you haven't betrayed the *cause*, whatever the *cause* is, exactly."

Maggie failed to change my mind, though what she said
was true.

"From about eight feet down," Ephraim said cryptically,
lifting the lantern.

Eight feet is as high an average man can reach without
standing on something. Between eight feet and the floor is
the span of a man's reach.

"You see, sir," Ephraim said, "my son and I were held in
separate barracks. The idea behind that was that a man
might be less eager to escape if it meant leaving behind a
son or father or uncle. The overseers said, if you run, your
people will suffer for it. But when my chance come I took it.
I don't know if that's a sin. I think about it often." He walked
toward the nearest wall, the lantern breaking up the darkness as it swayed in his grip. "This barracks here was my
son's barracks."

"Were there many escapes?" Percy asked.

I began to see that something might have been written on
the wall, though at first it looked more like an *idea* of writing: a text as crabbed and indecipherable as the scratchings
of the Persians or the Medes.

"Yes, many," Ephraim said, "though not many successful.
At first there was fewer guards on the gates. They built the
walls up, too, over time. Problem is, you get away, where is

there to go? Even if you get past these sandy hills, the country's not welcoming. And the guards had rifles, sir, the guards had dogs."

"But you got away, Ephraim."

"Not far away. When I escaped it was very near the last days of Pilgassi Acres." (He pronounced it *Pigassi*, with a reflexive curl of contempt on his lips.) "Company men coming in from Richmond to the overseer's house, you could hear the shouting some nights. Rations went from meat twice a week to a handful of cornmeal a day and green bacon on Sundays. They fired the little Dutch doctor who used to tend to us. Sickness come to us. They let the old ones die in place, took the bodies away to bury or burn. Pretty soon we knew what was meant to happen next. They could not keep us, sir, nor could they set us free."

"That was when you escaped?"

"Very near the end, sir, yes, that's when. I did not want to go without Jordan. But if I waited, I knew I'd be too weak to run. I told myself I could live in the woods and get stronger, that I would come back for Jordan when I was more myself."

He held the lantern close to the board wall of this abandoned barracks.

Percy was suffering more from his wound now than he had seemed to when he received it, and he grimaced as I helped him follow Ephraim. We stood close to the wild man and his circle of light, though not too close—I was still conscious of his rifle and of his willingness to use it, even if he was not in a killing mood right now.

The writing on the wall consisted of names. Hundreds of names. They chased each other around the whole of the barn in tight horizontal bands.

"I expect the overseers would have let us starve if they had the time. But they were afraid federal men would come digging around. There ought to be nothing of us left to find, I think was the reasoning. By that time the cholera had taken many of us anyhow, weak and hungry as we were, and the rest . . . well, death is a house, Mr. Camber, with many doorways. This is my son's name right here."

Jordan Nash was picked out by the yellow lantern light.

"Dear God," said Percy Camber, softly.

"I don't think God come into it, sir."

"Did he write his own name?"

"Oh, yes, sir. A northern lady taught us both to read, back in the Missouri camp. I had a Bible and a copybook from her. I still read that Bible to this day. Jordan was proud of his letters." Ephraim turned to me as if I, not Percy, had asked the question: "Most of these men couldn't write nor read. Jordan didn't just write his own name. He wrote *all* these names. Each and every one. A new man came in, he would ask the name and put it down as best he could. The list grew as we came and went. Many years' worth, sir. All the prisoners talked about it, how he did that. He had no pencil or chalk, you know. He made a kind of pen or brush by chewing down sapling twigs to soften their ends. Ink he made all kind of ways. He was very clever about that. Riverbottom clay, soot, blood even. In the autumns the work crews drawing water from the river might find mushrooms which turn black when you picked them, and they brought them back to Jordan—those made fine ink, he said."

The pride in Ephraim's voice was unmistakable. He marched along the wall with his lantern held high so we could see his son's work in all its complexity. All those names, written in the space between a man's reach and the floor. The letters were meticulously formed, the lines as level as the sea. Some of the names were whole names, some were single names, some were the kind of whimsical names given to house servants. They all ran together, to conserve space, so that in places you had to guess whether the names represented one person or two.

. . . *John Kincaid Tom Abel Fortune Bob Swift Pompey Atticus Joseph Wilson Elijah Elijah Jim Jim's Son Rufus Moses Deerborn Moses Raffity* . . .

"I don't know altogether why he did it," Ephraim said. "I think it made him feel better to see the men's names written down. Just so somebody might know we passed this way, he said."

Jordan lived in this barracks from eight foot down. And so did shockingly many others.

"This is why you shot at us," Percy whispered, a kind of awe or dread constricting his throat.

"I make it seem dangerous up here, yes, sir, so that nobody won't come back and take it down or burn it. And yet I suppose they will sooner or later whether I scare anybody or not. Or if not that, then the weather will wear it down. I keep it best I can against the rain, sir. I don't let birds or animals inside. Or even the daylight, sir, because the daylight fades things, that ink of Jordan's is sensitive to it. All be gone one day, I suppose, but I will too, bye and bye, and yourselves as well, of course."

"Perhaps we can make it last a little longer," Percy said.

Of course I knew what he meant.

"I'll need light," I said.

The fierce, hot light of the fading day.

Ephraim was anxious to help, once Percy explained the notion to him. He threw open the barracks door. He took down the wood he had tacked over the south-facing windows. There were still iron bars in the window frames.

In the corners the light was not adequate despite our best efforts. Ephraim said he had a sheet of polished tin he used for a mirror, which might help reflect the sunlight in. He went to his encampment to get it. By that time he trusted us enough to leave us alone for a short time.

Once again I suggested escape, but Percy refused to leave. So I kept about my work.

There were only so many exposures I could make, and I wanted the names to be legible. In the end I could not capture everything. But I did my best.

Ephraim told us about the end of Pilgassi Acres. He had been nearby, hidden half starving in a grove of dwarf pines, when he heard the initial volley of gunshots. It was the first of many over the several hours that followed. Gunfire in waves, and then the cries of the dying. By that sound he knew he would never see his son Jordan again.

Trenches were dug in the ground. Smoke from the chimneys lay over the low country for days. But the owners had been hasty to finish their work, Ephraim said. They had not bothered to burn the empty barracks before they rode off in their trucks and carriages.

Ever since that time Ephraim had sheltered in the barn of a poor white farmer who was sympathetic to him. Ephraim trapped game in exchange for this modest shelter. Eventually the farmer lent him his rifle so that Ephraim could bring back an occasional deer as well as rabbits and birds. The farmer didn't talk much, Ephraim said, but there were age-browned copies of Garrison's *Liberator* stored in the barn; and Ephraim read these with interest, and improved his vocabulary and his understanding of the world.

Hardly anyone came up to Pilgassi Acres nowadays except hunters following game trails. He scared them off with his rifle if they got too close to Jordan's barracks.

There was no point leaving the barracks after dark, since we could not travel in the carriage until sunrise. Percy's condition worsened during the night. He came down with a fever, and as he shivered, his wound began to seep. I made him as comfortable as possible with blankets from the carriage, and Ephraim brought him water in a cracked clay jug.

Percy was lucid, but his ideas began to run in whimsical directions as midnight passed. He insisted that I take Mrs. Stowe's letter from where he kept it in his satchel and read it aloud by lamplight. It was this letter, he said, that had been the genesis of the book he was writing now, about the three million. He wanted to know what Ephraim would make of it.

I kept my voice neutral as I read, so that Mrs. Stowe's stark words might speak for themselves.

"That is a decent white woman," Ephraim said when he had heard the letter and given it some thought. "A Christian woman. She reminds me of the woman that taught me and Jordan to read. But I don't know what she's so troubled about, Mr. Camber. This idea there was no war. I suppose there wasn't, if by war you mean the children of white men fighting the children of white men. But, sir, I have seen the guns, sir, and I have seen them used, sir, all my life—*all* my life. And in my father's time and before him. Isn't that war? And if it *is* war, how can she say war was avoided? There were many casualties, sir, though their names are not generally recorded; many graves, though not marked; and many battlefields, though not admitted to the history books."

"I will pass that thought on to Mrs. Stowe," Percy whispered, smiling in his discomfort, "although she's very old now and might not live to receive it."

And I decided I would pass it on to Elsebeth, my daughter.

I packed up my gear very carefully, come morning.

This is Jordan's name, I imagined myself telling Elsie, pointing to a picture in a book, the book Percy Camber would write.

This photograph, I would tell her, represents light cast in a dark place. Like an old cellar gone musty for lack of sun. Sunlight has a cleansing property, I would tell her. See: I caught a little of it here.

I supposed there was enough of her grandmother in her that Elsebeth might understand.

I began to feel hopeful about the prospect.

Ephraim was less talkative in the morning light. I helped poor shivering Percy into the carriage. I told Ephraim my mother had once published a poem in the *Liberator*, years ago. I couldn't remember which issue.

"I may not have seen that number," Ephraim said. "But I'm sure it was a fine poem."

I drove Percy to the doctor in Crib Lake. The doctor was an old man with pinch-nose glasses and dirty fingernails. I told him I had shot my servant accidentally, while hunting. The doctor said he did not usually work on colored men, but an extra ten dollars on top of his fee changed his mind.

He told me there was a good chance Percy would pull through, if the fever didn't worsen.

I thanked him, and went off to buy myself a drink.

The Unstrung Zither

YOON HA LEE

Yoon Ha Lee (pegasus.cityofveils.com) lives in Pasadena, California. She has a degree in mathematics and writes about mathematics in her website. She has been publishing her carefully crafted stories in the genre for about ten years. Her fiction has appeared in Fantasy & Science Fiction, Lady Churchill's Rosebud Wristlet, Ideomancer, *and* Shadows of Saturn, *among others. When we first included her fiction in a Year's Best volume, she lived in Massachusetts with "a motley assortment of musical instruments, and a glass Klein bottle." We hope she still has them.*

"The Unstrung Zither" was published in F & SF, *a leading magazine that went bi-monthly in 2009, but nevertheless continued to publish a lot of excellent fiction (including two more stories found in this volume). This is the second "math" story in this volume. Kathryn, who has a degree in math, says, "I appreciate the story for its mathematical/musical aesthetic logic. Getting to the ending is like reading a good proof." David, whose doctorate is in literature, says, "the emotional logic is convincing, and the characterization deep and suggestive."*

"**T**hey don't look very dangerous," Xiao Ling Yun said to the aide. Ling Yun wished she understood what Phoenix Command wanted from her. Not that she minded the excuse to take a break from the composition for two flutes and hammered dulcimer that had been stymieing her for the past two weeks.

Through a one-way window in the observation chamber, Xiao Ling Yun saw five adolescents sitting cross-legged on the floor in a semicircle. Before them was a tablet and two brushes. No ink; these were not calligraphy brushes. One of the adolescents, a girl with short, dark hair, leaned over and drew two characters with quick strokes. All five studied the map that appeared on the tablet.

"Nevertheless," the aide said. "They attempted to assassinate the Phoenix General. We are fortunate to have captured them."

The aide wrote something on her own tablet, and a map appeared. She circled a region of the map. The tablet enlarged it until it filled the screen. "Circles represent gliders," the aide said. "Triangles represent dragons."

Ling Yun peered at the formations. "Who's winning?"

At the aide's instigation, the tablet replayed the last move. A squadron of dragons engaged a squadron of gliders. One dragon turned white—white for death—and vanished from the map. The aide smiled. "The assassins are starting to slip."

Ling Yun had thought that the Phoenix General desired

the services of a musician to restore order to the fractious ashworlds. She was not the best person for such a purpose, nor the worst: a master musician, yes, but without a sage's philosophical bent of mind. Perhaps they had chosen her on account of her uncle's position as a logistician. She was pragmatic enough not to be offended by the possibility.

"I had not expected prisoners to be offered entertainment," Ling Yun said, a little dubious. She was surprised that they hadn't been executed, in fact.

"It is not entertainment," the aide said reprovingly. "Every citizen has a right to education."

Of course. The government's stance was that the ashworlds already belonged to the empire, whatever the physical reality might be. "Including the classical arts, I presume," she said. "But I am a musician, not a painter." Did they want her to tutor the assassins? And if so, why?

"Music is the queen of the arts, is it not?" the aide said.

She had not expected to be discussing the philosophy of music with a soldier. "According to tradition, yes," Ling Yun said carefully. Her career had been spent writing music that never strayed too much from the boundaries of tradition.

The most important music lesson she had had came not from her tutor, but from a servant in her parents' house. The servant, whose name Ling Yun had deliberately forgotten, liked to sing as he stirred the soup or pounded the day's bread. He didn't have a particularly notable voice. It wavered in the upper register and his vowels drifted when he wasn't paying attention. (She didn't tell him any of this. She didn't talk to him at all. Her parents would have disapproved.) But the servant had two small children who helped him with his tasks, and they chanted the songs, boisterously out of tune.

From watching that servant and his children, Ling Yun learned that the importance of music came not from its ability to move the five elements, but from its ability to affect the heart. She wanted to write music that anyone could hum, music that anyone could enjoy. It was the opposite of the haughty ideal that her tutor taught her to strive toward. Naturally, Ling Yun kept this thought to herself.

The aide scribbled some more on the tablet. In response, an image of a mechanical dragon drew itself across the tablet. It had been painted white, with jagged red markings on its jointed wings.

"Is this a captured dragon?" Ling Yun asked.

"Unfortunately, no," the aide said. "We caught glimpses of two of the assassins as they came down on dragons, but the dragons disappeared as though they'd been erased. We want to know where they're hiding, and how they're being hidden."

Ling Yun stared at the dragon. Whoever had drawn it did not have an artist's fluency of line. But everything was precise and carefully proportioned. She could see where the wings connected to the body and the articulations that made motion possible, even, if she squinted, some of the controls by the pilot's seat.

"Who produced this?"

The aide turned her head toward the window. "The dark-haired girl did. Her name is Wu Wen Zhi."

It was a masculine name, but they probably did things differently in the ashworlds. Ling Yun felt a rebellious twinge of approval.

Ling Yun said, "Wen Zhi draws you a picture, and you expect it to yield the ashworlders' secrets. Surely she's not as incompetent an assassin as all that. Or did you torture this out of her?"

"No, it's part of the game they're playing with the general," the aide said.

"I don't see the connection," she said. And why was the general playing a game with them in the first place? *Wei qi* involved no such thing, nor had the tablet games she had played as a student.

The aide smiled as though she had heard the thought. "It personalizes the experience. When the game calculates the results of combat, it refers to the pilot's emblem to determine her strengths and weaknesses. Take Wen Zhi's dragon, for instance. First of all, the dragon's design indicates that it specializes in close combat, as opposed to Mesketalioth's—" she switched briefly to another dragon painting "—which has repeating crossbows mounted on its shoulders." She returned to Wen Zhi's white dragon. "However, notice the stiffness of the lines. The pilot is always alert, but in a way that makes her tense. This can be exploited."

"The general has an emblem in the game, too, I presume," Ling Yun said.

"Of course," the aide said, but she didn't volunteer to show it to Ling Yun. "Let me tell you about our five assassins.

"Wu Wen Zhi comes from Colony One." The empire's two original colonies had been given numbers rather than names. "Wen Zhi has tried to kill herself three times already. She doesn't sleep well at night, but she refuses to meditate, and she won't take medications."

I wouldn't either, Ling Yun thought.

"The young man with the long braid is Ko. He's lived on several of the ashworlds and speaks multiple languages, but his accent suggests that he comes from Arani. Interestingly enough, Ko alerted us to the third of Wen Zhi's suicide attempts. Wen Zhi didn't take this well.

"The scarred one sitting next to Ko is Mesketalioth. He's from Straken Okh. We suspect that he worked for Straken's intelligence division before he was recruited by the Dragon Corps.

"The girl with the light hair is Periet, although the others call her Perias. We haven't figured out why, and they look at us as though we're crazy when we ask them about it, although she'll answer to either name. Our linguists tell us that Perias is the masculine form of her name; our doctors confirm that she is indeed a girl. She comes from Kiris. Don't be fooled by her sweet manners. She's the one who destroyed Shang Yuan."

Ling Yun opened her mouth, then found her voice. "*Her*?" Shang Yuan had been a city of several million people. It had been obliterated during the Festival of Lanterns, for which it had been famous. "I thought that the concussive storm was a natural disaster."

The aide gave Ling Yun a singularly cynical look. "Natural disasters don't flatten every building in the city and cause all the lanterns to explode. It was an elemental attack."

"I suppose this is classified information."

"It is, technically, not that many people haven't guessed."

"How much help did she have?"

The aide's mouth twisted. "Ashworld Kiris didn't authorize the attack. As near as we can determine, Periet did it all by herself."

"All right," Ling Yun said. She paced to the one-way window and watched Periet-Perias, trying to map the massacre onto the girl's open, cheerful expression. "Who's the fifth one now skulking in a corner?"

"That's Li Cheng Guo, from Colony Two," the aide said. "He killed two of our guards on the first day. Actually, they all did their share of killing on the way in, although Periet takes the prize."

"That's terrible," Ling Yun said. But what she was thinking was, *The ashworlds must be terribly desperate, to send children.* The Phoenix General had had the ashworlds' leader assassinated two years ago; this must be their counterstroke. "So," she said, "one assassin from each ashworld." Colony One and Colony Two; Arani, Straken Okh, and Kiris. The latter three had been founded by nations that had since been conquered by the empire.

"Correct." The aide rolled the brush around in her hand. "The Phoenix General wants you to discover the assassins' secret."

Oh no, Ling Yun thought. For all the honors that the empress had lavished on the Phoenix General, he was still known as the Mad General. He had started out as a glider pilot, and everyone knew that glider pilots were crazy. Their extreme affinity for fire and wood unbalanced their minds.

On the other hand, Ling Yun had a lifetime's practice of bowing before those of greater standing, however much it chafed, and the man had produced undeniable results. She could respect that.

"I'm no soldier," Ling Yun said, "and no interrogator. What would you like me to do?"

The aide smiled. "Each assassin has an emblem in the game."

Ling Yun had a sudden memory of a self-portrait she had

drawn when she was a child. It was still in the hallway of her parents' house, to her embarrassment: lopsided face with tiny eyes and a dot for a nose, scribbly hair, arms spread wide. "Why did they agree to this game?" she asked.

"They are playing because it was that or die. But they have some hidden purpose of their own, and time may be running out. You must study the game—we'll provide analyses for you, as we hardly expect you to become a tactician—and study the dragons. Compose a suite of five pieces, one for each dragon—for each pilot."

"Pilot?"

"They're pilots in their minds, although we're only certain that Periet and Mesketalioth have the training. Maybe the secret is just that they found blockade runners to drop them off." The aide didn't sound convinced.

"One piece for each dragon. You think that by translating their self-representations into music, the supreme art, you will learn their secret, and how to defeat them."

"Precisely."

"I will do what I can," Xiao Ling Yun said.

"I'm sure you will," the aide said.

Xiao Ling Yun's ancestors had worshipped dragons. At the harvest festival, they poured libations of rice wine to the twin dragons of the greatmoon and the smallmoon. When the empire's skies were afire with the summer's meteor showers, people would burn incense for the souls of the falling stars.

You could still see fire in the sky, most nights, festive and beautiful, but no one brought out incense. The light came from battles high in the atmosphere, battles between the ashworlders' metal dragons and the empire's Phoenix Corps.

When she was a child, Ling Yun's uncle had made her a toy glider, a flimsy-looking thing of bamboo and paper, with tiny slivers to represent the wing-mounted flame-throwers. He had painted the red-and-gold emblem of the Phoenix Corps on each wing. "Uncle," she asked, "why do we fight with fire when the gliders are made of wood? Isn't it dangerous?"

Her uncle patted her hand and smiled. "Remember the cycle of elements, little one."

She thought about it: metal cut wood, wood split earth, earth drank water, water doused fire, and—"Fire melts metal," she said.

"Indeed," he said. "The ashworlds abound in metal, mined from the asteroid belts. Therefore their dragons are built of metal. We must use fire to defeat metal."

"But wood *burns*," Ling Yun said, wondering, despite all her lessons and the habits of obedience, if her uncle were right in the head. She turned the glider around in her hands, testing the paper wings. They flexed under her touch.

"So does the phoenix," her uncle said.

Ling Yun squinted, trying to reconcile fire-defeats-metal with fire-burns-wood and fire-goes-down-in-flames.

Taking pity on her, her uncle added, "The phoenix is a symbol that came to us by conquest, from the southern spicelands." He laughed at her wide eyes. "Oh, yes—do you think that for thousands and thousands of years, the empire has never been conquered? You'll find all the old, ugly stories in the history books, of the Boar Banner and the Tiger Banner, the woman who brought down the wall, the Outsider Dynasty with its great fleets. . . ."

Ling Yun took note of the things that he had mentioned so she could look them up later.

"Come, Ling Yun," her uncle said. "Why don't we go outside and test the glider?"

She sensed that he was preventing her from asking further questions. But if he didn't want her to know, why had he told her about the phoenix in the first place?

Still, she loved the way the glider felt in her hand, and her uncle didn't visit very often. "All right," she said.

They went into the courtyard with its broad flagstones and pond, and spoke no more of the elements.

Ling Yun started composing the suite on the *wuxian qin*, the five-stringed zither. She had brought her favorite one with her. The military was accustomed to transporting fragile instruments, thanks to the Phoenix Corps, whose gliders had to be attuned to the elements.

For suicidal, dark-haired Wu Wen Zhi, Ling Yun wrote a disjunct melody with tense articulations, reflecting the mixed power and turmoil she saw in the girl's white dragon. White and red, bone and blood, death and fortune. The aide said Wen Zhi had killed six people since landing in the empire. The dragon had nine markings. Ling Yun trusted the dragon. Wen Zhi did not strike her as the subtle type. The aide's response to this observation was a pained laugh.

Ko's drawing was more of a sketch, in a relaxed, spontaneous style that Ling Yun's calligraphy tutor would have approved of. The colors worried her, however: black and gray, no sign of color, a sense of aching incompleteness. Yet the reports that came every morning noted Ko's unshakable good cheer and cooperativeness. Ling Yun felt a strange affinity to what she knew of the boy. She had no illusions that she understood what it was like to be a killer, but she knew something about hiding part of yourself from the outside world. She gave Ko's piece a roving melody with ever-shifting rhythms and playful sliding tones.

Mesketalioth's blue dragon was the most militant-looking of the five, at least to Ling Yun's untrained eye. Ko's dragon, if you looked at it from a distance, might pass as a picture of a god out of legend, not a war automaton. Meskctalioth's diagram included not only the dragon, but cross-sections and insets showing the mechanisms of the repeating crossbows and the way the joints were put together. The aide assured her that it was a known type of ashworlder dragon, and provided Ling Yun with explanations from the engineers. Ling Yun thought that the aide was trying to be reassuring for her benefit, and failing. For Mesketalioth, she wrote a military air in theme and variations, shadows falling in upon themselves, the last note an infinitely subtle vibrato informed by the pulse in the finger holding down the string.

Periet was the best painter of the five. She had drawn her dragon out of scale so it looked no larger than a large cat, its head tilted to watch two butterflies, one sky-blue and the other star-spotted black. It was surrounded by flowers and gears and neatly organized mechanics' tools. Ling Yun thought of Shang Yuan, with its shattered lanterns and ashes, wind blowing through streets inhabited only by grasshoppers and mice. No one had attempted to rebuild the City of Lanterns. The song she wrote for Periet had an utterly conventional pentatonic melody. The countermelody, on the other hand, was sweet, logical, and in a foreign mode.

As for the last of them, Li Cheng Guo had drawn a flamboyant red dragon with golden eyes. Ling Yun wondered if he meant some mockery of the Phoenix General by this. On the other hand, red did indicate good fortune. The gliders were always painted in fire-colors, while the dragons came in every color imaginable. Obligingly, Ling Yun wrote a rapid, skirling piece for Cheng Guo, martial in its motifs, but hostile where Mesketalioth's was subtle.

Ling Yun slept surrounded by the five assassins' pictures. She was disturbed to realize that, no matter where she rearranged them on the walls, she always woke up facing Periet's butterfly dragon.

Careful inquiry revealed the assassins' sleeping arrangements: in separate cells, although they were permitted in a room together for the purposes of lessons—probably a euphemism for interrogation sessions—and the general's game. Ling Yun asked how they kept the assassins from killing their guards or tutors.

"After the first few incidents, they swore to the Phoenix General that they would abide by the terms of the game," the aide said.

"And you trust them?" Ling Yun said.

"They've sworn," the aide said emphatically. "And if they break oath, he'll have them executed."

Sooner or later, she was going to have to speak with the Phoenix General, if he didn't demand a report from her first. She presumed that Phoenix Command had other precautions in place.

Two weeks into the assignment, Ling Yun said to the aide, "I'd like to speak with the assassins."

"If you draw up a list of questions," she said, "our interrogators can obtain the answers you want."

"In person," Ling Yun said.

"That's unwise for a whole list of reasons I'm sure you've already thought of."

"Surely one musician more or less is expendable in the general's game," Ling Yun said, keeping all traces of irony from her voice. She doubted the aide was fooled.

Sure enough, the aide said, with exasperation, "Do you know why we requested you, Musician Xiao? When we could have asked for the empress's personal troupe and had them do the general's bidding?"

"I had wondered, yes."

"Most musicians at your level of mastery have, shall we say, a philosophical bent of mind."

Ling Yun could think of a number of less flattering expressions. "I've heard that criticism," she said noncommittally.

The aide snorted. "Of course you have. We wanted you because you have a reputation for pragmatism. Or did you think it would go unnoticed? The psychological profiles for the empire's musicians aren't completely worthless."

"Will you trust that I have a pragmatic reason for wanting to talk to the assassins, then?" Ling Yun said. "Tell them it's part of the game. Surely that isn't far from the truth. It's one thing for me to study your game transcripts, but I want to know what the assassins are like as people. I'm no interrogator, but I am accustomed to listening to the hidden timbres of the human voice. I might hear something useful."

"We will consider it," the aide said.

"Thank you," Ling Yun said, certain she had won.

The first time Ling Yun tuned a glider to the elements with her music, she was shaking so badly that her fingers jerked on her zither's peg and she broke a string.

Ling Yun's tutor looked down at her with imperturbable eyes. "Perhaps the flute—" he suggested. Many of the Phoenix Corps' musicians preferred the bamboo flute for its association with birdsong, and therefore the heavens.

Ling Yun had come prepared with an extra set of strings. "I will try again," she said. Instead of trying to block the presence of the pilot and engineers from her mind, she raised her head and studied them. The pilot was a woman scarcely older than Ling Yun herself, who met Ling Yun's gaze with a quirk to her mouth, as if in challenge. The engineers had an expression of studied politeness; they had been through this before.

Carefully, mindful of the others' time but also mindful of the necessity of precision, Ling Yun replaced the broken string. The new one was going to be temperamental. She would have to play to compensate.

After tuning the zither to her satisfaction, she breathed in and breathed out several times. Then she began "The Crane Flies Home," the traditional blessing-piece. At first, the simple task of getting her fingers through the piece occupied her.

Then, Ling Yun became aware of the glider responding. It was a small, scarred creature, with gouges in the wood from past battles, and it thrummed almost imperceptibly whenever she played the strings that corresponded to wood and fire. Remembering her tutor's advice not to neglect the other strings, she coaxed the glider with delicate harmonics, reminding it that it would have to face water, fight metal, return to earth.

Only when she had finished did she realize that her fingers were bleeding, despite her calluses. That hadn't happened in years. She blotted the blood against the hem of her jacket. *Water feeds wood*, she thought.

The engineers, who had their own training in music, checked the glider over. They consulted with her tutor, using terminology she didn't understand. The tutor turned to her and nodded once, smiling.

"You haven't even flown it," Ling Yun said, bewildered. The winch was all the way down the airfield. "How do you know I tuned it properly?"

"I listened," he said simply. "It must fly in spirit before it can fly in truth. You have achieved this."

All her dreams that night were of gliders arcing into the air, launched by winch and changing into birds at the moment of release: herons and cranes and sparrows, hawks and geese and swallows, but not a single red-and-gold phoenix.

The five pilots— Ling Yun wasn't sure when she had started thinking of them as dragon pilots rather than assassins, a shift she hoped to keep from Phoenix Command—wore clothes that fit them indifferently. Dark-haired Wu Wen Zhi stood stiffly, her arms crossed. Ko, the boy with the braid, was smiling. Mesketalioth, whose face was calmly expressionless, had his hands clasped behind his back. The scars at his temple were startlingly white. Periet's blue eyes were downcast, although Ling Yun knew better than to mistake the girl's demeanor for submissiveness. Li Cheng Guo, the tallest, stood farthest from the others and scowled openly.

"I'm—"

"Another interrogator," Wen Zhi said. The girl's voice was high, precise, and rapid. It put Ling Yun in mind of stone chimes.

"Yes and no," Ling Yun said. "I have questions, but I'm not a soldier; do you see me wearing a uniform?" She had worn a respectable gray dress, the kind she would have worn to speak with a client.

Wen Zhi grabbed Ling Yun's wrist and twisted. Ling Yun bit back a cry. "It's all right!" she said quickly, knowing that the guards were monitoring the situation.

The girl ran her hand over Ling Yun's fingertips, lingering over the calluses. "You're an engineer."

"Also yes and no," Ling Yun said. "I'm a musician." Wen Zhi must not play the zither, or she would have noticed immediately that Ling Yun's fingernails were slightly long to facilitate plucking the strings. Ling Yun could practically hear the aide's reproof, but what was she supposed to do? Deny the obvious?

Ko tossed his head. "The correct response, Wen Zhi," he said, "is to say, 'Hello, I am honored to meet you.' Then to give your name, although I'm sure you already know ours, madam." His Imperial was startlingly good, despite the broadened vowels. "I'm Ko."

"I'm Xiao Ling Yun," she said gravely. Did they not use surnames on Arani? Or Straken Okh or Kiris, for that matter?

The others gave their names. Mesketalioth had a quiet, clipped voice, distantly polite. Periet called herself by that name. She had a pleasant alto and spoke with a heavier accent than the others. Li Cheng Guo's Imperial was completely idiomatic; he addressed Ling Yun with a directness that was just short of insulting.

Ling Yun wondered if any of them had vocal training, then felt silly. Of course they did. Not in the populist styles of their homes, surely, but in the way that all glider pilots did, the ability to hold a tune and the more important ability to listen for a glider's minute reverberations. What would it be like to write for their voices?

The question was moot, as she doubted the aide would stand for any such endeavor.

On a whim, Ling Yun had brought her uncle's toy glider with her. Keeping her motions slow, she drew it from her jacket.

"Pretty," Periet said. "Does it fly?" She was smiling.

Mesketalioth opened his hands toward Ling Yun. She gave the toy glider to him. He studied its proportions, and she was suddenly chilled. Could he draw diagrams of gliders, too?

"Yes, it flies," Mesketalioth said. "It's never been tuned, has it?"

"No," Ling Yun said. "It's just a toy." Surely the adolescents had had toys in childhood. What kinds of lives had they led in the ashworlds, constantly under assault from glider bombing runs?

"Even a toy can be a weapon," Cheng Guo said with a sneer. "I would have had it tuned. Especially if you're already a musician."

"Oh, for pity's sake, Cheng Guo," Ko said, "what's it going to do? Drop little origami bombs?" He made flicking motions with his fingers. Cheng Guo glowered at him, and Ko only grinned back.

They sounded like the students she had attended classes with as an adolescent herself, fractious and earnest. However, unlike those fellow students, they carried themselves alertly. She noticed that, despite standing around her, they deliberately left her path to the exit unblocked.

"I have permission to ask you some questions," Ling Yun said. She wanted them to be clear on her place in the hierarchy, which was to say, low.

"Are you part of the game?" Wen Zhi asked.

Ling Yun wondered if the girl ever smiled, and was struck by a sudden urge to ruffle that short hair. The thought of the nine red marks on Wen Zhi's dragon made the urge entirely resistible. "No," she said, afraid that they would refuse to talk to her further.

"Good," Cheng Guo said shortly. "You're not prepared." He trained his glower on Ling Yun, as though it would cause her to go away. It seemed to her that ignoring her would be much more effective.

"What does it feel like to kill?" Ling Yun said.

Ko had sauntered over to the wall across from Cheng Guo and was leaning against it, worrying at the fraying end of his braid. They hadn't given him a clip for his hair, and the aide had said that he refused to get it cut. Ko gave Ling Yun a shrewd look and said, "You could ask that of your own soldiers, couldn't you?"

"I'd know how they felt, but I'm interested in you," she said.

"Ask what you mean," Periet said. Her tone had shifted, just below the surface. Ling Yun wondered if the others could hear that undercurrent of ferocity. "You're interested in how we're different."

"All right," Ling Yun said. "Yes." It cost her nothing to be agreeable, a lesson she had applied all her life.

"Don't listen to her," Wen Zhi said to the others. "She's trying to get inside our heads."

"Well, yes," Ling Yun said mildly. "But the longer you talk to me, the longer you draw out the game, the longer you live."

Mesketalioth raised his chin. His scars went livid. "Living isn't the point."

"Then what is?" she asked.

With no warning—at least, not to Ling Yun's slow senses—Mesketalioth snapped the glider between his hands.

Ling Yun stared at him, fists pressed to her sides. Her eyes stung. She had known, theoretically, that she might lose the glider. What had she been thinking, bringing it into a room full of assassins? Assassins who knew the importance of symbols and would think of a glider as a hostile one, at that. She just hadn't expected them to break this reminder of her childhood.

It's a toy, she reminded herself. She could make another herself if she had to.

How much had these children lost, before coming here?

Periet's blue eyes met Ling Yun's gaze. The girl made a tiny nod.

" 'Even a toy can be a weapon,' " Mesketalioth said, without inflection. "There are many kinds of weapons."

"Hey," Ko said to Ling Yun. He sounded genuinely concerned. "We can fix it. They'll let us have some glue, won't they? Besides, your general likes you. He'd have our heads if we didn't."

I've never even met the Phoenix General, Ling Yun thought, chewing her lip before she caught herself. "How many people did *you* take down?" she asked, trying to remind herself that these children were assassins and killers.

Ko rebraided the ends of his hair. "I keep a tally in my head," he said.

"He's killed sixteen gliders in the game," Wen Zhi said contemptuously. "That's information that you should have gotten from studying the game."

"You're still losing territory," Ling Yun said, remembering the latest report. "How do you expect to win?"

Cheng Guo laughed from his corner. "As if we'd tell you? Please."

General, Ling Yun thought, *how in the empress's name is this a good idea*? She hoped she wasn't the only musician they had working on the problem. The whole conversation was giving her a jittery sense of urgency.

"Indeed," she said. "Thank you."

"Leave the glider," Ko said. "We'll fix it. You'll see."

"If you like," Ling Yun said, wondering what her uncle would say if he knew. Well, she didn't have to tell him. "Perhaps I'll see you another time, if they permit it."

Periet touched Ling Yun's hand lightly. Ling Yun half-turned. "Yes?"

Periet said, "There should be six, not five. But you've always known that, haven't you?"

The hairs on the back of Ling Yun's neck prickled.

Periet smiled again.

Ling Yun thought of the two butterflies in Periet's dragon-portrait, and wondered if dragons ate butterflies. Or musicians, for that matter. "It was pleasant meeting you all," she said, because her parents had raised her to be polite.

Wu Wen Zhi and Li Cheng Guo ignored her, but the others murmured their good-byes.

Shaking her head, Ling Yun made the signal that the guards had taught her, and the door opened. None of the assassins made an attempt to escape. It scared her.

Ling Yun was in the midst of revising Mesketalioth's piece in tablature when the summons came. She knew it had to be the Phoenix General because the soldiers would not disrupt her concentration for anything else. But Ling Yun used to practice composing in adverse circumstances: sitting in a clattering train; at a street puppet theater while children shouted out their favorite characters' names; during tedious parties when she had had too much rice wine. She didn't compose courtly lays or ballads, but cheerful ditties that she could hum in the bath where no one else had to know. But the aides had certain ideas about how musicians worked, and it was hardly for her to overturn those ideas.

The aide asked, "Will you need your zither?"

"That depends," Ling Yun said. "Will he want me to play what I have so far?"

"No," the aide said, a little hesitantly. "He'll make arrangements when he wants to hear a performance, I'm sure."

Surreptitiously, Ling Yun curled and uncurled her fingers to limber them up, just in case.

The aide escorted her to a briefing room painted with

Phoenix Command's flame-and-spear on the door. She slid the door open with a surprising lack of ceremony. "General," she called out, "Musician Xiao is here." She patted Ling Yun's shoulder. "Go on. You'll be fine."

Ling Yun stepped through the minimum distance possible and knelt in full obeisance, catching a glimpse of the Phoenix General on the way down. He had gray-streaked hair and a strong-jawed profile.

"Enough," the general said. "Let's not waste time on ceremony."

Slowly, she rose, trying to interpret his expression. *He hasn't heard your work yet*, she reminded herself, *so he can't hate it already*.

"Sir," she said, dipping in a bow despite herself.

"You've been too well trained, I see," the general said wryly. "I swear, it's true of every musician I meet. Sit down."

Ling Yun had no idea what to say to this, so she sat cross-legged at the table and settled for looking helpful.

"What dreams do you dream?" the general asked. His fingers tapped the wall. Indeed, he seemed unable to stop them.

"My last dream was about the fish I had for dinner," Ling Yun said, taken aback. "It swam up out of my mouth and chastised me for using too much salt. When I woke up, I was facing the butterfly dragon."

"Ah, yes," the general said. "Periet, destroyer of Shang Yuan. I lost an entire glider squadron when she flew in. Dragon pilots are unstable too, as you might guess, so we thought she was a rogue. We'd seen her take down a couple of her own comrades on the way in. Then her dragon roared, and the concussive storm shattered everything in its path, and the City of Lanterns exploded in fire."

"You were there, General?"

He didn't answer her. "How is the dragon suite progressing?"

"I have revisions to make based on this morning's results in the game, sir," Ling Yun said.

"Do you play *wei qi*, Musician?" he asked.

"Only poorly," Ling Yun said. "My mother taught me the rules, but it's been years. It concerns territory and influence and patterns, doesn't it? It's strange—musical patterns are so easy for me to perceive, but the visual ones are more difficult."

The general sat across from her. "If musicians were automatically as skilled at *wei qi* as they were at music," he said, "they would be unbeatable."

A tablet rested on the table. He picked up the larger of two brushes and wrote *game*, then several other characters. There were no triangles—no dragons—to be seen anywhere. "I didn't know they could do that," the general mused. "This is what happens when you allow the game to modify its own rules." He met Ling Yun's inquisitive gaze. "Somehow I don't think they've conceded."

"So the dragons haven't been captured," she said, slipping back into the terminology of *wei qi*. "What else mediates this game, General?"

"It's tuned the way a glider might be tuned by a musician, the way a tablet is calibrated by a calligrapher. It's tuned by developments in the living war."

"I had understood," Ling Yun said, "that the suite was to reflect the pilots, not to influence them. I must confess that so far I haven't seen anything that would explain the vanishing dragons."

The general said, "In music, the ideal is a silent song upon an unstrung zither. Is this not so?"

Ling Yun drew the characters in her mind: *wuxian* meant "five," *qin* meant "zither." But the *wu* of "five," in the third tone, brought to mind the *wu* of "nothing" or "emptiness," which was in the first tone. The unstrung zither, favored instrument of the sages. The ancients had preferred subtlety and restraint in all things; the unstrung zither took this to the natural conclusion. Ling Yun had applied herself to her lessons with the same patient dedication that she did all things musical, but the unstrung zither had vexed her. "That was the view of the traditional theorists," she said neutrally, "although modern musicians don't necessarily agree."

The Phoenix General's smile only widened, as though he saw right through her temporizing. "Music is the highest expression of the world's patterns. The sages have told us so, time and again. The music in the empress's court provides order to her subjects. We must apply the same principles in war."

She already knew what he was going to say.

"Thus, in war, the ideal must be a bloodless engagement upon an empty battlefield."

"Are you sure it is wise to keep the ashworlder children alive, then?" Ling Yun said. It made her uneasy to ask, for she didn't want to change the general's mind. Perhaps the thought was traitorous.

"They'll die when they're no longer useful," the general said frankly.

Traitorous or not, there was something wrong with a war that involved killing children. Even deadly children. Even Periet, with her eyes that hid such lethality.

Wei qi was a game of territory, of colonialism. Ling Yun thought of all the things she owed to her parents, who had made sure she had the best tutors; to her uncle, who had brought her the glider and other treats over the years. But she no longer lived in her parents' house. And three of the colonies, Arani and Straken Okh and Kiris, had not been founded by the empire at all. What did they owe the Phoenix Banner?

In her history lessons, she had learned that the phoenix and dragon were wedding symbols, and that this was a sign that the ashworlds, with their dragons, needed to be joined to the empire. But surely there were ways to cooperate—in trade, say—without conquering the ashworlds outright.

The general closed his eyes for a second and sighed. "If we could win the war without expending lives, it would be a marvel indeed. Imagine gliders that fly themselves, set against the ashworlds' dragons."

"The ashworlders are hardly stupid, sir," Ling Yun said. "They'll send pilotless dragons of their own." *Or*, she thought suddenly, *dragonless pilots*.

Maybe the ashworlds were ahead of the Phoenix General. From Ling Yun's vantage point, it was impossible to tell.

"Then there's no point sending army against army, is there?" the general said, amused. "But people are people. I doubt anyone would be so foolish as to disarm entirely, and commit a war solely on paper, as a game."

Ling Yun bowed, even knowing it would annoy him, to give herself time to think.

"Enough," the general said. "It is through music we will win the game, and through the game we will win the war. I commend your work, Musician. Take the time you need, but no longer."

"As you will, sir," Ling Yun said.

The population of the empire on the planet proper, at the last census, was 110 million people.

The population of the five ashworlds was estimated at 70 million people, although this number was much less certain, due to the transients who lived in the asteroid belts.

The number of gliders in the Phoenix Corps was classified. The number of dragons in the Dragon Corps was likewise classified.

Ling Yun stayed up late into the night reviewing the game's statistics. Visual patterns were not her forte, but she remembered the general's words. She had heard the eagerness in his voice, the way she heard echoes of the massacre of Shang Yuan in Periet's. Even now, there had to be pilotless gliders speeding toward the colonies.

Many of the reports compared the pilots' strategy in the game to actual engagements. Ling Yun had skimmed these earlier, because of all the unfamiliar names and places—the Serpent's Corridor, the Siege of Uln Okh, the Greater Vortex—but now she added up the ashworlders' estimated casualties and felt ill. They had lost their own Shang Yuans. She doubted that the general would stop until they lost many more.

Ling Yun had been right. The ashworlders were desperate, to send children.

Something else that interested her was the rate of replenishment. In the game, you could build new units to replace the ones you had lost. The five pilots kept losing dragons. Over the course of the game, the rate at which the game permitted them to build new dragons dropped slowly but significantly. Based on the general's remarks, Ling Yun was willing to bet that this was based on actual intelligence about the Dragon Corps' attrition rate.

It was too bad she couldn't ask her uncle, who had probably helped plan the general's grand attack. Her uncle once told her that, so far, the ashworlds had held their own because they had a relatively large number of dragon pilots. Metal was not nearly as unstable an element as fire; people who worked almost exclusively with metal did not self-destruct quite as regularly.

It was no coincidence that each colony sent an assassin, and also no coincidence that the Phoenix General had kept all of them captive. Five was an important number, one that Ling Yun had taken for granted until Periet told her that the key was *six*.

The empire, with its emphasis on tradition, had accepted the sages' cycle of five elements since antiquity, even after it founded Colony One and Colony Two in the vast reaches of space. But what of space itself?

Numbers were Ling Yun's domain as much as they were any musician's. Now she knew what to do.

Ling Yun's head hurt, and even the tea wasn't going to keep her awake much longer. Still, she felt a quiet glow of triumph. She had finished the suite, including the sixth piece. The sixth piece wasn't for the *wuxian qin* at all. It was meant to be hummed, or whistled, like a folk melody or a child's song, like the music she had wanted to write all her life.

There was no place in the empire for such music, but she didn't have to accept that anymore.

If the toy glider had a song, it would be this one, even if the glider was broken. It was whole in her mind. That was what mattered.

Five strings braided together were coiled in her jacket sleeve, an uncomfortable reminder of what she was about to do.

Ling Yun wrote a letter on the tablet and marked it urgent, for the general's eyes only: *I must speak to you concerning the five assassins.* Her hand shook and her calligraphy looked unsteady. Let the general interpret that however he pleased.

A handful of moments passed. The character for *message* drew itself in the upper right corner. Ling Yun touched the tip of her brush to it.

The general's response was, simply: *Come.*

Shaking slightly, Ling Yun waited until her escort arrived. Under her breath, she hummed one of the variations from Mesketalioth's piece. In composing the suite, she had attuned herself to the pilots and their cause, but she did this by choice.

Be awake, she urged him, urged all the young pilots. *Be prepared.* Would the music pluck at the inner movements of their souls, the way it happened in the stories of old?

The escort arrived. "You are dedicated to work so long into the night," the taller of the two soldiers said, with every appearance of sincerity.

"We do what we can," Ling Yun said, thinking, *You have no idea.* People thought musicians were crazy, too. Perhaps everybody looked crazy to someone.

After tonight, she was going to look crazy to everyone, assuming Phoenix Command allowed the story to escape.

The Phoenix General met her in a different room this time. It had silk scrolls on the walls. "They're pretty, aren't they?" he said. Ling Yun was eerily reminded of Periet looking at her glider. "Some of them are generations old."

One of the scrolls had crisp, dark lines. Ling Yun's eyes were drawn to it: a phoenix hatching from a *wei qi* stone. "You painted that," she said.

"I was younger," the general said, "and never subtle. Please, there's tea. Your profile said you preferred citron, so I had them brew some for us."

The citron smelled sweet and sharp. Ling Yun knew that if she tasted it, she would lose her nerve. But courtesy was courtesy. "Thank you, sir," she said.

She held the first five movements of the dragon suite in her head, to give her Wu Wen Zhi's fixity of purpose and

Ko's relaxed mien, Mesketalioth's reflexes and Periet's hidden ferocity, and Li Cheng Guo's quick wits.

The braided silk strings slipped down into Ling Yun's palm. She whipped them around the Phoenix General's neck. He was a large man, but she was fighting with the strength of six, not one. And she was fighting for five ashworlds rather than one empire.

As the Phoenix General struggled, Ling Yun tightened the strings. She fixed her gaze upon the painting of the hatching stone.

Ling Yun had been the Phoenix General's creature. The phoenix destroyed itself; it was only fitting that she destroy him.

It would not occur to her until later that it had begun with the general assassinating the ashworlders' leader, that justice was circular.

Now I know what it is like to kill.

There was—not happiness, precisely, but a peculiar singing relief that the other was dead, and not she. She let go of the strings and listened to the thump as the general's body hit the floor.

The door crashed open. Wen Zhi and Periet held pistols. Wen Zhi's was pointed straight at Ling Yun.

Ling Yun looked up, heart thudding in her chest. She pulled her shoulders back and straightened. It turned out that she cared to die with some dignity, after all. "Make it quick," she said. "You have to get out of here."

Ko showed up behind the other two; he had apparently found a cord to tie his braid. "Come *on*, madam," he said. "We haven't any time to waste."

"So you were right," Wen Zhi said to him, sounding irritable. "The musician took care of the general, but that doesn't guarantee that she's an ally."

"Is this really the best time to be arguing?" Periet asked, with an air of, *Have you ever known me to be wrong?*

The other girl lowered her pistol. "All right, Perias. Are you coming with us, Musician?"

It was unlikely that Ling Yun's family would ever forgive her, even if she evaded capture by the imperial magistrates. She hurried after the pilots, who seemed to know exactly where they were going. "Perias?" she asked Periet, hoping that she might get an answer where Phoenix Command had not.

"Was the sixth one," Mesketalioth said without slowing down.

"What exactly is your plan for getting out of here?" Ling Yun said diffidently, between breaths. "We'll be hunted—"

"You of all people have no excuse to be so slow-witted," Cheng Guo called back. He was at the head of the group. "How do you think we got here?"

"All we need is a piece of sky," Periet said yearningly. She struck the wall with the heel of her hand.

I was right, Ling Yun thought. The edges of her vision went black; the reverberations sounded like a great gong.

Mesketalioth caught her. His arm was steady and warm. "Next time, a warning would be appreciated," he said, deadpan as ever.

The wall split outwards. *Metal cuts wood.*

"Let's fly," Periet said. A great wind was blowing through the hallway. They stepped through the hole in the wall, avoiding the jagged, broken planks. Above them, stars glittered in the dark sky.

"The void is the sixth element," Ling Yun said, looking up.

Five dragons manifested in a half circle, summoned through the void, white black blue yellow red. In the center, tethered to the red dragon by shimmering cables, was an unpainted glider. The sleek curves of its fuselage reminded Ling Yun of her zither.

"See?" Ko said. "I told you we'd fix it."

"Thank you," Ling Yun said, overwhelmed. They had written her into the game after all.

"It only works if there's six of us," Cheng Guo said. "You're the sixth pilot."

Mesketalioth helped Ling Yun into the glider's cockpit. "When we release the cables," he said, "follow Cheng Guo. He understands glider theory best, and he'll safely keep you on the void's thermal paths." Despite the scars, his expression was almost kind.

"It's time!" Wen Zhi shouted from her white dragon. There were now ten red marks on it. "We have to warn the seedworlds."

Soldiers shouted from the courtyard. A bolt glanced from one dragon in a shower of sparks. Mesketalioth's dragon reared up and laid down covering fire while Wen Zhi's dragon raked the ground with its claws. The soldiers, overmatched, scattered.

Then they were aloft, all six of them, dragons returning to the sky where they had been born.

Ling Yun spared not a glance backwards, but sang a quiet little melody to herself as they headed for the stars.

Black Swan

BRUCE STERLING

Bruce Sterling (www.wired.com/beyond_the_beyond/) *lives usually in exotic places in Europe, from which he continues his lifelong habit of cultural commentary. He reports that he "is dividing his atemporal time-zones among Austin, Turin, and Belgrade, and his alternate global identities as Bruce Sterling, Bruno Argento, and Boris Srebro." "Black Swan" is one of those "Bruno Argento" efforts, written in Torino and originally published in Italy. His most recent novel is SF,* The Caryatids *(2009). His short fiction is collected in* Ascendancies: The Best of Bruce Sterling *(2007). Throughout Sterling's career, his project has been to put us in touch with the larger world in which we live, giving us glimpses of not only speculative and fantastic realities but also the bedrock of politics in human behavior. He is an American and citizen of the world, drawn to events and especially people tipping the present over into the future. His short fiction, now as likely to be fantasy as SF, is one of the finest bodies of work in the genre over the last three decades.*

"Black Swan" originally appeared in Italian as "Cigno Nero" in the Spring 2009 issue of ROBOT *magazine. It was subsequently published in* Interzone, *which in spite of its small circulation continues to be a major venue for SF and fantasy. The title refers to the concept behind Nassim Nicholas Taleb's book* The Black Swan: The Impact of the Highly Improbable.

The ethical journalist protects a confidential source. So I protected 'Massimo Montaldo,' although I knew that wasn't his name.

Massimo shambled through the tall glass doors, dropped his valise with a thump, and sat across the table. We were meeting where we always met: inside the Caffe Elena, a dark and cozy spot that fronts on the biggest plaza in Europe.

The Elena has two rooms as narrow and dignified as mahogany coffins, with lofty red ceilings. The little place has seen its share of stricken wanderers. Massimo never confided his personal troubles to me, but they were obvious, as if he'd smuggled monkeys into the cafe and hidden them under his clothes.

Like every other hacker in the world, Massimo Montaldo was bright. Being Italian, he struggled to look suave. Massimo wore stain-proof, wrinkle-proof travel gear: a black merino wool jacket, an American black denim shirt, and black cargo pants. Massimo also sported black athletic trainers, not any brand I could recognize, with eerie bubble-filled soles.

These skeletal shoes of his were half-ruined. They were strapped together with rawhide boot-laces.

To judge by his Swiss-Italian accent, Massimo had spent a lot of time in Geneva. Four times he'd leaked chip secrets to me—crisp engineering graphics, apparently snipped right out of Swiss patent applications. However, the various bureaus in Geneva had no records of these patents. They had no records of any 'Massimo Montaldo,' either.

Each time I'd made use of Massimo's indiscretions, the traffic to my weblog had doubled.

I knew that Massimo's commercial sponsor, or more likely his spymaster, was using me to manipulate the industry I covered. Big bets were going down in the markets somewhere. Somebody was cashing in like a bandit.

That profiteer wasn't me, and I had to doubt that it was him. I never financially speculate in the companies I cover as a journalist, because that is the road to hell. As for young Massimo, his road to hell was already well-trampled.

Massimo twirled the frail stem of his glass of Barolo. His shoes were wrecked, his hair was unwashed, and he looked like he'd shaved in an airplane toilet. He handled the best wine in Europe like a scorpion poised to sting his liver. Then he gulped it down.

Unasked, the waiter poured him another. They know me at the Elena.

Massimo and I had a certain understanding. As we chatted about Italian tech companies—he knew them from Alessi to Zanotti—I discreetly passed him useful favors. A cellphone chip—bought in another man's name. A plastic hotel pass key for a local hotel room, rented by a third party. Massimo could use these without ever showing a passport or any identification.

There were eight 'Massimo Montaldos' on Google and none of them were him. Massimo flew in from places unknown, he laid his eggs of golden information, then he paddled off into dark waters. I was protecting him by giving him those favors. Surely there were other people very curious about him, besides myself.

The second glass of Barolo eased that ugly crease in his brow. He rubbed his beak of a nose, and smoothed his unruly black hair, and leaned onto the thick stone table with both of his black woolen elbows.

"Luca, I brought something special for you this time. Are you ready for that? Something you can't even imagine."

"I suppose," I said.

Massimo reached into his battered leather valise and brought out a no-name PC laptop. This much-worn machine, its corners bumped with use and its keyboard dingy, had one of those thick super-batteries clamped onto its base. All that extra power must have tripled the computer's weight. Small wonder that Massimo never carried spare shoes.

He busied himself with his grimy screen, fixated by his private world there.

The Elena is not a celebrity bar, which is why celebrities like it. A blonde television presenter swayed into the place. Massimo, who was now deep into his third glass, whipped his intense gaze from his laptop screen. He closely studied her curves, which were upholstered in Gucci.

An Italian television presenter bears the relationship to news that American fast food bears to food. So I couldn't feel sorry for her—yet I didn't like the way he sized her up. Genius gears were turning visibly in Massimo's brilliant geek head. That woman had all the raw, compelling appeal to him of some difficult math problem.

Left alone with her, he would chew on that problem until something clicked loose and fell into his hands, and, to do her credit, she could feel that. She opened her dainty crocodile purse and slipped on a big pair of sunglasses.

"Signor Montaldo," I said.

He was rapt.

"Massimo?"

This woke him from his lustful reverie. He twisted the computer and exhibited his screen to me.

I don't design chips, but I've seen the programs used for that purpose. Back in the 1980s, there were thirty different chip-design programs. Nowadays there are only three survivors. None of them are nativized in the Italian language, because every chip geek in the world speaks English.

This program was in Italian. It looked elegant. It looked like a very stylish way to design computer chips. Computer chip engineers are not stylish people. Not in this world, anyway.

Massimo tapped at his weird screen with a gnawed fingernail. "This is just a cheap, 24-K embed. But do you see these?"

"Yes I do. What are they?"

"These are memristors."

In heartfelt alarm, I stared around the cafe, but nobody in the Elena knew or cared in the least about Massimo's stunning revelation. He could have thrown memristors onto their tables in heaps. They'd never realize that he was tossing them the keys to riches.

I could explain now, in gruelling detail, exactly what memristors are, and how different they are from any standard electronic component. Suffice to understand that, in electronic engineering, memristors did not exist. Not at all. They were technically possible—we'd known that for thirty years, since the 1980s—but nobody had ever manufactured one.

A chip with memristors was like a racetrack where the jockeys rode unicorns.

I sipped the Barolo so I could find my voice again. "You brought me schematics for memristors? What happened, did your UFO crash?"

"That's very witty, Luca."

"You can't hand me something like that! What on Earth do you expect me to do with that?"

"I am not giving these memristor plans to you. I have decided to give them to Olivetti. I will tell you what to do: you make one confidential call to your good friend, the Olivetti Chief Technical Officer. You tell him to look hard in his junk folder where he keeps the spam with no return address. Interesting things will happen, then. He'll be grateful to you."

"Olivetti is a fine company," I said. "But they're not the outfit to handle a monster like that. A memristor is strictly for the big boys—Intel, Samsung, Fujitsu."

Massimo laced his hands together on the table—he might have been at prayer—and stared at me with weary sarcasm. "Luca," he said, "don't you ever get tired of seeing Italian genius repressed?"

The Italian chip business is rather modest. It can't always make its ends meet. I spent fifteen years covering chip tech in Route 128 in Boston. When the almighty dollar ruled the tech world, I was glad that I'd made those connections.

But times do change. Nations change, industries change. Industries change the times.

Massimo had just shown me something that changes industries. A disruptive innovation. A breaker of the rules.

"This matter is serious," I said. "Yes, Olivetti's people do read my weblog—they even comment there. But that doesn't mean that I can leak some breakthrough that deserves a Nobel Prize. Olivetti would want to know, they would *have* to know, the source of that."

He shook his head. "They don't want to know, and neither do you."

"Oh yes, I most definitely do want to know."

"No, you don't. Trust me."

"Massimo, I'm a journalist. That means that I always want to know, and I never trust anybody."

He slapped the table. "Maybe you were a 'journalist' when they still printed paper 'journals.' But your dot-com journals are all dead. Nowadays you're a blogger. You're an influence peddler and you spread rumors for a living." Massimo shrugged, because he didn't think he was insulting me. "So: shut up! Just do what you always do! That's all I'm asking."

That might be all that he was asking, but my whole business was in asking. "Who created that chip?" I asked him. "I know it wasn't you. You know a lot about tech investment, but you're not Leonardo da Vinci."

"No, I'm not Leonardo." He emptied his glass.

"Look, I know that you're not even 'Massimo Montaldo'— whoever that is. I'll do a lot to get news out on my blog. But I'm not going to act as your cut-out in a scheme like this! That's totally unethical! Where did you steal that chip? Who made it? What are they, Chinese super-engineers in some bunker under Beijing?"

Massimo was struggling not to laugh at me. "I can't reveal that. Could we have another round? Maybe a sandwich? I need a nice toasty pancetta."

I got the waiter's attention. I noted that the TV star's boyfriend had shown up. Her boyfriend was not her husband. Unfortunately, I was not in the celebrity tabloid business. It wasn't the first time I'd missed a good bet by consorting with computer geeks.

"So you're an industrial spy," I told him. "And you must be Italian to boot, because you're always such a patriot about it. Okay: so you stole those plans somewhere. I won't ask you how or why. But let me give you some good advice: no sane man would leak that to Olivetti. Olivetti's a consumer outfit. They make pretty toys for cute secretaries. A memristor chip is dynamite."

Massimo was staring raptly at the TV blonde as he awaited his sandwich.

"Massimo, pay attention. If you leak something that advanced, that radical . . . a chip like that could change the world's military balance of power. Never mind Olivetti. Big American spy agencies with three letters in their names will come calling."

Massimo scratched his dirty scalp and rolled his eyes in derision. "Are you so terrorized by the CIA? They don't read your sorry little one-man tech blog."

This crass remark irritated me keenly. "Listen to me, boy genius: do you know what the CIA does here in Italy? We're their 'rendition' playground. People vanish off the streets."

"Anybody can 'vanish off the streets.' I do that all the time."

I took out my Moleskin notebook and my shiny Rotring technical pen. I placed them both on the Elena's neat little marble table. Then I slipped them both back inside my jacket. "Massimo, I'm trying hard to be sensible about this. Your snotty attitude is not helping your case with me."

With an effort, my source composed himself. "It's all very simple," he lied. "I've been here a while, and now I'm tired of this place. So I'm leaving. I want to hand the future of electronics to an Italian company. With no questions asked and no strings attached. You won't help me do that simple thing?"

"No, of course I won't! Not under conditions like these. I don't know where you got that data, what, how, when, whom, or why . . . I don't even know who you are! Do I look like that kind of idiot? Unless you tell me your story, I can't trust you."

He made that evil gesture: I had no balls. Twenty years ago—well, twenty-five—and we would have stepped outside the bar. Of course I was angry with him—but I also knew he was about to crack. My source was drunk and he was clearly in trouble. He didn't need a fist-fight with a journalist. He needed confession.

Massimo put a bold sneer on his face, watching himself in one of the Elena's tall spotted mirrors. "If this tiny gadget is too big for your closed mind, then I've got to find another blogger! A blogger with some guts!"

"Great. Sure. Go do that. You might try Beppe Grillo."

Massimo tore his gaze from his own reflection. "That washed-up TV comedian? What does he know about technology?"

"Try Berlusconi, then. He owns all the television stations and half the Italian Internet. Prime Minister Berlusconi is just the kind of hustler you need. He'll free you from all your troubles. He'll make you Minister of something."

Massimo lost all patience. "I don't need that! I've been to a lot of versions of Italy. Yours is a complete disgrace! I don't know how you people get along with yourselves!"

Now the story was tearing loose. I offered an encouraging nod. "How many 'versions of Italy' do you need, Massimo?"

"I have sixty-four versions of Italy." He patted his thick laptop. "Got them all right here."

I humored him. "Only sixty-four?"

His tipsy face turned red. "I had to borrow CERN's supercomputers to calculate all those coordinates! Thirty-two Italies were too few! A hundred twenty-eight . . . I'd never have the time to visit all those! And as for *your* Italy . . . well . . . I wouldn't be here at all, if it wasn't for that Turinese girl."

"Cherchez la femme," I told him. "That's the oldest trouble-story in the world."

"I did her some favors," he admitted, mournfully twisting his wineglass. "Like with you. But much more so."

I felt lost, but I knew that his story was coming. Once I'd coaxed it out of him, I could put it into better order later.

"So, tell me: what did she do to you?"

"She dumped me," he said. He was telling me the truth,

but with a lost, forlorn, bewildered air, like he couldn't believe it himself. "She dumped me and she married the President of France." Massimo glanced up, his eyelashes wet with grief. "I don't blame her. I know why she did that. I'm a very handy guy for a woman like her, but Mother of God, I'm not the President of France!"

"No, no, you're not the President of France," I agreed. The President of France was a hyperactive Hungarian Jewish guy who liked to sing karaoke songs. President Nicolas Sarkozy was an exceedingly unlikely character, but he was odd in a very different way from Massimo Montaldo.

Massimo's voice was cracking with passion. "She says that he'll make her the First Lady of Europe! All I've got to offer her is insider-trading hints and a few extra millions for her millions."

The waiter brought Massimo a toasted sandwich.

Despite his broken heart, Massimo was starving. He tore into his food like a chained dog, then glanced up from his mayonnaise dip. "Do I sound jealous? I'm not jealous."

Massimo was bitterly jealous, but I shook my head so as to encourage him.

"I can't be jealous of a woman like her!" Massimo lied. "Eric Clapton can be jealous, Mick Jagger can be jealous! She's a rock star's groupie who's become the Premiere Dame of France! She married Sarkozy! Your world is full of journalists—spies, cops, creeps, whatever—and not for one minute did they ever stop and consider: 'Oh! This must be the work of a computer geek from another world!' "

"No," I agreed.

"Nobody ever imagines that!"

I called the waiter back and ordered myself a double espresso. The waiter seemed quite pleased at the way things were going for me. They were a kindly bunch at the Elena. Friedrich Nietzsche had been one of their favorite patrons. Their dark old mahogany walls had absorbed all kinds of lunacy.

Massimo jabbed his sandwich in the dip and licked his fingers. "So, if I leak a memristor chip to you, nobody will ever stop and say: 'some unknown geek eating a sandwich

in Torino is the most important man in world technology.'
Because that truth is inconceivable."

Massimo stabbed a roaming olive with a toothpick. His
hands were shaking: with rage, romantic heartbreak, and
frustrated fury. He was also drunk.

He glared at me. "You're not following what I tell you.
Are you really that stupid?"

"I do understand," I assured him. "Of course I understand.
I'm a computer geek myself."

"You know who designed that memristor chip, Luca? You
did it. You. But not here, not in this version of Italy. Here,
you're just some small-time tech journalist. You created that
device in *my* Italy. In my Italy, you are the guru of computational aesthetics. You're a famous author, you're a culture
critic, you're a multi-talented genius. Here, you've got no
guts and no imagination. You're so entirely useless here that
you can't even change your own world."

It was hard to say why I believed him, but I did. I believed
him instantly.

Massimo devoured his food to the last scrap. He thrust his
bare plate aside and pulled a huge nylon wallet from his
cargo pants. This overstuffed wallet had color-coded plastic
pop-up tags, like the monster files of some Orwellian bu-
reaucracy. Twenty different kinds of paper currency jammed
in there. A huge riffling file of varicolored plastic ID cards.

He selected a large bill and tossed it contemptuously onto
the Elena's cold marble table. It looked very much like
money—it looked much more like money than the money
that I handled every day. It had a splendid portrait of Galileo
and it was denominated in 'Euro-Lira.'

Then he rose and stumbled out of the cafe. I hastily
slipped the weird bill in my pocket. I threw some euros onto
the table. Then I pursued him.

With his head down, muttering and sour, Massimo was
weaving across the millions of square stone cobbles of the
huge Piazza Vittorio Veneto. As if through long experience,
he found the emptiest spot in the plaza, a stony desert between a handsome line of ornate lamp-posts and the sleek
steel railings of an underground parking garage.

He dug into a trouser pocket and plucked out tethered foam earplugs, the kind you get from Alitalia for long overseas flights. Then he flipped his laptop open.

I caught up with him. "What are you doing over here? Looking for wifi signals?"

"I'm leaving." He tucked the foam plugs in his ears.

"Mind if I come along?"

"When I count to three," he told me, too loudly, "you have to jump high into the air. Also, stay within range of my laptop."

"All right. Sure."

"Oh, and put your hands over your ears."

I objected. "How can I hear you count to three if I have my hands over my ears?"

"Uno." He pressed the F1 function key, and his laptop screen blazed with sudden light. "Due." The F2 emitted a humming, cracking buzz. "Tre." He hopped in the air.

Thunder blasted. My lungs were crushed in a violent billow of wind. My feet stung as if they'd been burned.

Massimo staggered for a moment, then turned by instinct back toward the Elena. "Let's go!" he shouted. He plucked one yellow earplug from his head. Then he tripped.

I caught his computer as he stumbled. Its monster battery was sizzling hot.

Massimo grabbed his overheated machine. He stuffed it awkwardly into his valise.

Massimo had tripped on a loose cobblestone. We were standing in a steaming pile of loose cobblestones. Somehow, these cobblestones had been plucked from the pavement beneath our shoes and scattered around us like dice.

Of course we were not alone. Some witnesses sat in the vast plaza, the everyday Italians of Turin, sipping their drinks at little tables under distant, elegant umbrellas. They were sensibly minding their own business. A few were gazing puzzled at the rich blue evening sky, as if they suspected some passing sonic boom. Certainly none of them cared about us.

We limped back toward the cafe. My shoes squeaked like the shoes of a bad TV comedian. The cobbles under our feet had broken and tumbled, and the seams of my shoes had gone loose. My shining patent-leather shoes were foul and grimy.

We stepped through the arched double-doors of the Elena, and, somehow, despite all sense and reason, I found some immediate comfort. Because the Elena was the Elena: it had those round marble tables with their curvilinear legs, those maroon leather chairs with their shiny brass studs, those colossal time-stained mirrors . . . and a smell I hadn't noticed there in years.

Cigarettes. Everyone in the cafe was smoking. The air in the bar was cooler—it felt chilly, even. People wore sweaters.

Massimo had friends there. A woman and her man. This woman beckoned us over, and the man, although he knew Massimo, was clearly unhappy to see him.

This man was Swiss, but he wasn't the jolly kind of Swiss I was used to seeing in Turin, some harmless Swiss banker on holiday who pops over the Alps to pick up some ham and cheese. This Swiss guy was young, yet as tough as old nails, with aviator shades and a long narrow scar in his hairline. He wore black nylon gloves and a raw canvas jacket with holster room in its armpits.

The woman had tucked her impressive bust into a hand-knitted peasant sweater. Her sweater was gaudy, complex and aggressively gorgeous, and so was she. She had smoldering eyes thick with mascara, and talon-like red painted nails, and a thick gold watch that could have doubled as brass knuckles.

"So Massimo is back," said the woman. She had a cordial yet guarded tone, like a woman who has escaped a man's bed and needs compelling reasons to return.

"I brought a friend for you tonight," said Massimo, helping himself to a chair.

"So I see. And what does your friend have in mind for us? Does he play backgammon?"

The pair had a backgammon set on their table. The Swiss mercenary rattled dice in a cup. "We're very good at backgammon," he told me mildly. He had the extremely menacing tone of a practiced killer who can't even bother to be scary.

"My friend here is from the American CIA," said Massimo. "We're here to do some serious drinking."

"How nice! I can speak American to you, Mr. CIA," the woman volunteered. She aimed a dazzling smile at me. "What is your favorite American baseball team?"

"I root for the Boston Red Sox."

"I love the Seattle Green Sox," she told us, just to be coy.

The waiter brought us a bottle of Croatian fruit brandy. The peoples of the Balkans take their drinking seriously, so their bottles tend toward a rather florid design. This bottle was frankly fantastic: it was squat, acid-etched, curvilinear, and flute-necked, and with a triple portrait of Tito, Nasser and Nehru, all toasting one another. There were thick flakes of gold floating in its paralyzing murk.

Massimo yanked the gilded cork, stole the woman's cigarettes, and tucked an unfiltered cig in the corner of his mouth. With his slopping shot-glass in his fingers he was a different man.

"Zhivali!" the woman pronounced, and we all tossed back a hearty shot of venom.

The temptress chose to call herself 'Svetlana,' while her Swiss bodyguard was calling himself 'Simon.'

I had naturally thought that it was insane for Massimo to announce me as a CIA spy, yet this gambit was clearly helping the situation. As an American spy, I wasn't required to say much. No one expected me to know anything useful, or to do anything worthwhile.

However, I was hungry, so I ordered the snack plate. The attentive waiter was not my favorite Elena waiter. He might have been a cousin. He brought us raw onions, pickles, black bread, a hefty link of sausage, and a wooden tub of creamed butter. We also got a notched pig-iron knife and a battered chopping board.

Simon put the backgammon set away.

All these crude and ugly things on the table—the knife, the chopping board, even the bad sausage—had all been made in Italy. I could see little Italian maker's marks hand-etched into all of them.

"So you're hunting here in Torino, like us?" probed Svet-lana.

I smiled back at her. "Yes, certainly!"

"So, what do you plan to do with him when you catch him? Will you put him on trial?"

"A fair trial is the American way!" I told them. Simon thought this remark was quite funny. Simon was not an evil man by nature. Simon probably suffered long nights of existential regret whenever he cut a man's throat.

"So," Simon offered, caressing the rim of his dirty shot glass with one nylon-gloved finger, "So even the Americans expect 'the Rat' to show his whiskers in here!"

"The Elena does pull a crowd," I agreed. "So it all makes good sense. Don't you think?"

Everyone loves to be told that their thinking makes good sense. They were happy to hear me allege this. Maybe I didn't look or talk much like an American agent, but when you're a spy, and guzzling fruit brandy, and gnawing sausage, these minor inconsistencies don't upset anybody.

We were all being sensible.

Leaning his black elbows on our little table, Massimo weighed in. "The Rat is clever. He plans to sneak over the Alps again. He'll go back to Nice and Marseilles. He'll rally his militias."

Simon stopped with a knife-stabbed chunk of blood sausage on the way to his gullet. "You really believe that?"

"Of course I do! What did Napoleon say? 'The death of a million men means nothing to a man like me!' It's impossible to corner Nicolas the Rat. The Rat has a star of destiny."

The woman watched Massimo's eyes. Massimo was one of her informants. Being a woman, she had heard his lies before and was used to them. She also knew that no informant lies all the time.

"Then he's here in Torino tonight," she concluded.

Massimo offered her nothing.

She immediately looked to me. I silently stroked my chin in a sagely fashion.

"Listen, American spy," she told me politely, "you Americans are a simple, honest people, so good at tapping phone calls . . . It won't hurt your feelings any if Nicolas Sarkozy is found floating face-down in the River Po. Instead of teasing me here, as Massimo is so fond of doing, why don't you just tell me where Sarkozy is? I do want to know."

I knew very well where President Nicolas Sarkozy was supposed to be. He was supposed to be in the Elysee Palace carrying out extensive economic reforms.

Simon was more urgent. "You do want us to know where the Rat is, don't you?" He showed me a set of teeth edged in Swiss gold. "Let us know! That would save the International Courts of Justice a lot of trouble."

I didn't know Nicolas Sarkozy. I had met him twice when he was French Minister of Communication, when he proved that he knew a lot about the Internet. Still, if Nicolas Sarkozy was not the President of France, and if he was not in the Elysee Palace, then, being a journalist, I had a pretty good guess of his whereabouts.

"Cherchez la femme," I said.

Simon and Svetlana exchanged thoughtful glances. Knowing one another well, and knowing their situation, they didn't have to debate their next course of action. Simon signalled the waiter. Svetlana threw a gleaming coin onto the table. They bundled their backgammon set and kicked their leather chairs back. They left the cafe without another word.

Massimo rose. He sat in Svetlana's abandoned chair, so that he could keep a wary eye on the café's double-door to the street. Then he helped himself to her abandoned pack of Turkish cigarettes.

I examined Svetlana's abandoned coin. It was large, round, and minted from pure silver, with a gaudy engraving of the Taj Mahal. 'Fifty Dinars,' it read, in Latin script, Hindi, Arabic, and Cyrillic.

"The booze around here really gets on top of me," Massimo complained. Unsteadily, he stuffed the ornate cork back into the brandy bottle. He set a slashed pickle on a buttered slice of black bread.

"Is he coming here?"

"Who?"

"Nicolas Sarkozy. 'Nicolas the Rat.'"

"Oh, him," said Massimo, chewing his bread. "In this version of Italy, I think Sarkozy's already dead. God knows there's enough people trying to kill him. The Arabs, Chinese, Africans . . . he turned the south of France upside down! There's a bounty on him big enough to buy Olivetti—not that there's much left of Olivetti."

I had my summer jacket on, and I was freezing. "Why is it so damn cold in here?"

"That's climate change," said Massimo. "Not in *this* Italy—in *your* Italy. In your Italy, you've got a messed-up climate. In this Italy, it's the *human race* that's messed-up. Here, as soon as Chernobyl collapsed, a big French reactor blew up on the German border . . . and they all went for each other's throats! Here NATO and the European Union are even deader than the Warsaw Pact."

Massimo was proud to be telling me this. I drummed my fingers on the chilly tabletop. "It took you a while to find that out, did it?"

"The big transition always hinges in the 1980s," said Massimo, "because that's when we made the big breakthroughs."

"In your Italy, you mean."

"That's right. Before the 1980s, nobody understood the physics of parallel worlds . . . but after that transition, we could pack a zero-point energy generator into a laptop. Just boil the whole problem down into one single micro-electronic mechanical system."

"So you've got zero-point energy MEMS chips," I said.

He chewed more bread and pickle. Then he nodded.

"You've got MEMS chips and you were offering me some fucking lousy memristor? You must think I'm a real chump!"

"You're not a chump." Massimo sawed a fresh slice of bad bread. "But you're from the wrong Italy. It was your own stupid world that made you this stupid, Luca. In my Italy, you were one of the few men who could talk sense to my Dad. My Dad used to confide in you. He trusted you, he thought you were a great writer. You wrote his biography."

" 'Massimo Montaldo, Senior,' " I said.

Massimo was startled. "Yeah. That's him." He narrowed his eyes. "You're not supposed to know that."

I had guessed it. A lot of news is made from good guesses.

"Tell me how you feel about that," I said, because this is always a useful question for an interviewer who has lost his way.

"I feel desperate," he told me, grinning. "Desperate! But I feel much *less* desperate here than I was when I was the spoilt-brat dope-addict son of the world's most famous scientist. Before you met me—Massimo Montaldo—had you ever heard of any 'Massimo Montaldo'?"

"No. I never did."

"That's right. I'm never in any of the other Italies. There's never any other Massimo Montaldo. I never meet another version of myself—and I never meet another version of my father, either. That's got to mean something crucial. I know it means something important."

"Yes," I told him, "that surely does mean something."

"I think," he said, "that I know what it means. It means that space and time are not just about physics and computation. It means that human beings really matter in the course of world events. It means that human beings can truly change the world. It means that our actions have consequence."

"The human angle," I said, "always makes a good story."

"It's true. But try telling that story," he said, and he looked on the point of tears. "Tell that story to any human being. Go on, do it! Tell anybody in here! Help yourself."

I looked around the Elena. There were some people in there, the local customers, normal people, decent people, maybe a dozen of them. Not remarkable people, not freakish, not weird or strange, but normal. Being normal people, they were quite at ease with their lot and accepting their daily existences.

Once upon a time, the Elena used to carry daily newspapers. Newspapers were supplied for customers on those special long wooden bars.

In my world, the Elena didn't do that any more. Too few newspapers, and too much Internet.

Here the Elena still had those newspapers on those handy wooden bars. I rose from my chair and I had a good look at them. There were stylish imported newspapers, written in Hindi, Arabic and Serbo-Croatian. I had to look hard to find a local paper in Italian. There were two, both printed on a foul gray paper full of flecks of badly-pulped wood.

I took the larger Italian paper to the cafe table. I flicked through the headlines and I read all the lead paragraphs. I knew immediately I was reading lies.

It wasn't that the news was so terrible, or so deceitful. But it was clear that the people reading this newspaper were not expected to make any practical use of news. The Italians were a modest, colonial people. The news that they were offered was a set of feeble fantasies. All the serious news was going on elsewhere.

There was something very strong and lively in the world called the 'Non-Aligned Movement.' It stretched from the Baltics all the way to the Balkans, throughout the Arab world, and all the way through India. Japan and China were places that the giant Non-Aligned superpower treated with guarded respect. America was some kind of humbled farm where the Yankees spent their time in church.

Those other places, the places that used to matter— France, Germany, Britain, 'Brussels'—these were obscure and poor and miserable places. Their names and locales were badly spelled.

Cheap black ink was coming off on my fingers. I no longer had questions for Massimo, except for one. "When do we get out of here?"

Massimo buttered his tattered slice of black bread. "I was never searching for the best of all possible worlds," he told me. "I was looking for the best of all possible me's. In an Italy like this Italy, I really matter. Your version of Italy is pretty backward—but *this* world had a nuclear exchange. Europe had a civil war, and most cities in the Soviet Union are big puddles of black glass."

I took my Moleskin notebook from my jacket pocket. How pretty and sleek that fancy notebook looked, next to that gray pulp newspaper. "You don't mind if I jot this down, I hope?"

"I know that this sounds bad to you—but trust me, that's not how history works. History doesn't have any 'badness' or 'goodness.' This world has a future. The food's cheap, the climate is stable, the women are gorgeous . . . and since there's only three billion people left alive on Earth, there's a lot of room."

Massimo pointed his crude sausage-knife at the cafe's glass double door. "Nobody here ever asks for ID, nobody cares about passports . . . They never even heard of electronic banking! A smart guy like you, you could walk out of here and start a hundred tech companies."

"If I didn't get my throat cut."

"Oh, people always overstate that little problem! The big problem is—you know—who wants to *work* that hard? I got to know this place, because I knew that I could be a hero here. Bigger than my father. I'd be smarter than him, richer than him, more famous, more powerful. I would be better! But that is a *burden*. 'Improving the world,' that doesn't make me happy at all. That's a *curse,* it's like slavery."

"What *does* make you happy, Massimo?"

Clearly Massimo had given this matter some thought. "Waking up in a fine hotel with a gorgeous stranger in my bed. That's the truth! And that would be true of every man in every world, if he was honest."

Massimo tapped the neck of the garish brandy bottle with the back of the carving knife. "My girlfriend Svetlana, she understands all that pretty well, but—there's one other thing. I drink here. I like to drink, I admit that—but they *really* drink around here. This version of Italy is in the almighty Yugoslav sphere of influence."

I had been doing fine so far, given my circumstances. Suddenly the nightmare sprang upon me, unfiltered, total, and wholesale. Chills of terror climbed my spine like icy scorpions. I felt a strong, irrational, animal urge to abandon my comfortable chair and run for my life.

I could run out of the handsome cafe and into the twilight streets of Turin. I knew Turin, and I knew that Massimo would never find me there. Likely he wouldn't bother to look. I also knew that I would run straight into the world so badly described by that grimy newspaper. That terrifying world would be where, henceforth, I existed. That world would not be strange to me, or strange to anybody. Because that world was reality. It was not a strange world, it was a normal world. It was I, me, who was strange here. I was desperately strange here, and that was normal.

This conclusion made me reach for my shot glass. I drank. It was not what I would call a 'good' brandy. It did have strong character. It was powerful and it was ruthless. It was a brandy beyond good and evil.

My feet ached and itched in my ruined shoes. Blisters were rising and stinging. Maybe I should consider myself lucky that my aching alien feet were still attached to my body. My feet were not simply slashed off and abandoned in some black limbo between the worlds.

I put my shot-glass down. "Can we leave now? Is that possible?"

"Absolutely," said Massimo, sinking deeper into his cozy red leather chair. "Let's sober up first with a coffee, eh? It's always Arabic coffee here at the Elena. They boil it in big brass pots."

I showed him the silver coin. "No, she settled our bill for us, eh? So let's just leave."

Massimo stared at the coin, flipped it from head to tails, then slipped it in a pants pocket. "Fine. I'll describe our options. We can call this place the 'Yugoslav Italy,' and, like I said, this place has a lot of potential. But there are other versions." He started ticking off his fingers.

"There's an Italy where the 'No Nukes' movement won big in the 1980s. You remember them? Gorbachev and Reagan made world peace. Everybody disarmed and was happy. There were no more wars, the economy boomed everywhere . . . Peace and justice and prosperity, everywhere on Earth. So the climate exploded. The last Italian survivors are living high in the Alps."

I stared at him. "No."

"Oh yes. Yes, and those are very nice people. They really treasure and support each other. There are hardly any of them left alive. They're very sweet and civilized. They're wonderful people. You'd be amazed what nice Italians they are."

"Can't we just go straight back to my own version of Italy?"

"Not directly, no. But there's a version of Italy quite close to yours. After John Paul the First died, they quickly elected another Pope. He was not that Polish anticommunist—instead, that Pope was a pedophile. There was a colossal scandal and the Church collapsed. In that version of Italy, even the Moslems are secular. The churches are brothels and discotheques. They never use the words 'faith' or 'morality.' "

Massimo sighed, then rubbed his nose. "You might think the death of religion would make a lot of difference to people. Well, it doesn't. Because they think it's normal. They don't miss believing in God any more than you miss believing in Marx."

"So first we can go to that Italy, and then nearby into my own Italy—is that the idea?"

"That Italy is boring! The girls there are boring! They're so matter-of-fact about sex there that they're like girls from Holland." Massimo shook his head ruefully. "Now I'm going to tell you about a version of Italy that's truly different and interesting."

I was staring at a round of the sausage. The bright piece of gristle in it seemed to be the severed foot of some small animal. "All right, Massimo, tell me."

"Whenever I move from world to world, I always materialize in the Piazza Vittorio Veneto," he said, "because that plaza is so huge and usually pretty empty, and I don't want to hurt anyone with the explosion. Plus, I know Torino—I know all the tech companies here, so I can make my way around. But once I saw a Torino with no electronics."

I wiped clammy sweat from my hands with the cafe's rough cloth napkin. "Tell me, Massimo, how did you feel about that?"

"It's incredible. There's no electricity there. There's no wires for the electrical trolleys. There are plenty of people there, very well-dressed, and bright colored lights, and some things are flying in the sky . . . big aircraft, big as oceanliners. So they've got some kind of power there—but it's not electricity. They stopped using electricity, somehow. Since the 1980s."

"A Turin with no electricity," I repeated, to convince him that I was listening.

"Yeah, that's fascinating, isn't it? How could Italy abandon electricity and replace it with another power source? I think that they use cold fusion! Because cold fusion was another world-changing event from the 1980s. I can't explore that Torino—because where would I plug in my laptop? But you could find out how they do all that! Because you're just a journalist, right? All you need is a pencil!"

"I'm not a big expert on physics," I said.

"My God, I keep forgetting I'm talking to somebody from the hopeless George Bush World," he said. "Listen, stupid: physics isn't complicated. Physics is very simple and elegant, because it's *structured*. I knew that from the age of three."

"I'm just a writer, I'm not a scientist."

"Well, surely you've heard of 'consilience.' "

"No. Never."

"Yes you have! Even people in your stupid world know about 'consilience.' Consilience means that all forms of human knowledge have an underlying unity!"

The gleam in his eyes was tiring me. "Why does that matter?"

"It's makes all the difference between your world and my world! In your world there was a great physicist once . . . Dr. Italo Calvino."

"Famous literary writer," I said, "he died in the 1980s."

"Calvino didn't die in my Italy," he said, "because in my Italy, Italo Calvino completed his 'Six Core Principles.' "

"Calvino wrote 'Six Memos,' " I said. "He wrote 'Six Memos for the Next Millennium.' And he only finished five of those before he had a stroke and died."

"In my world Calvino did not have a stroke. He had a stroke of genius, instead. When Calvino completed his work, those six lectures weren't just 'memos.' He delivered six major public addresses at Princeton. When Calvino gave that sixth, great, final speech, on 'Consistency,' the halls were crammed with physicists. Mathematicians, too. My father was there."

I took refuge in my notebook. 'Six Core Principles,' I scribbled hastily, 'Calvino, Princeton, consilience.'

"Calvino's parents were both scientists," Massimo insisted. "Calvino's brother was also a scientist. His Oulipo literary group was obsessed with mathematics. When Calvino delivered lectures worthy of a genius, nobody was surprised."

"I knew Calvino was a genius," I said. I'd been young, but you can't write in Italian and not know Calvino. I'd seen him trudging the porticoes in Turin, hunch-shouldered, slapping his feet, always looking sly and preoccupied. You only had to see the man to know that he had an agenda like no other writer in the world.

"When Calvino finished his six lectures," mused Massimo, "they carried him off to CERN in Geneva and they made him work on the 'Semantic Web.' The Semantic Web works beautifully, by the way. It's not like your foul little Internet—so full of spam and crime." He wiped the sausage knife on an oil-stained napkin. "I should qualify that remark. The Semantic Web works beautifully—*in the Italian language.* Because the Semantic Web was built by Italians. They had a little bit of help from a few French Oulipo writers."

"Can we leave this place now? And visit this Italy you boast so much about? And then drop by my Italy?"

"That situation is complicated," Massimo hedged, and stood up. "Watch my bag, will you?"

He then departed to the toilet, leaving me to wonder about all the ways in which our situation could be complicated.

Now I was sitting alone, staring at that corked brandy bottle. My brain was boiling. The strangeness of my situation had broken some important throttle inside my head.

I considered myself bright—because I could write in three languages, and I understood technical matters. I could speak to engineers, designers, programmers, venture capitalists and government officials on serious, adult issues that we all agreed were important. So, yes, surely I was bright.

But I'd spent my whole life being far more stupid than I was at this moment.

In this terrible extremity, here in the cigarette-choked Elena, where the half-ragged denizens pored over their grimy newspapers, I knew I possessed a true potential for genius. I was Italian, and, being Italian, I had the knack to shake the world to its roots. My genius had never embraced me, because genius had never been required of me. I had been stupid because I dwelled in a stupefied world.

I now lived in no world at all. I had no world. So my thoughts were rocketing through empty space.

Ideas changed the world. Thoughts changed the world— and thoughts could be written down. I had forgotten that writing could have such urgency, that writing could matter to history, that literature might have consequence. Strangely, tragically, I'd forgotten that such things were even possible.

Calvino had died of a stroke: I knew that. Some artery broke inside the man's skull as he gamely struggled with his manifesto to transform the next millennium. Surely that was a great loss, but how could anybody guess the extent of that loss? A stroke of genius is a black swan, beyond prediction, beyond expectation. If a black swan never arrives, how on Earth could its absence be guessed?

The chasm between Massimo's version of Italy and my Italy was invisible—yet all encompassing. It was exactly like the stark difference between the man I was now, and the man I'd been one short hour ago.

A black swan can never be predicted, expected, or categorized. A black swan, when it arrives, cannot even be recognized as a black swan. When the black swan assaults us, with the wingbeats of some rapist Jupiter, then we must rewrite history.

Maybe a newsman writes a news story, which is history's first draft.

Yet the news never shouts that history has black swans. The news never tells us that our universe is contingent, that our fate hinges on changes too huge for us to comprehend, or too small for us to see. We can never accept the black swan's arbitrary carelessness. So our news is never about how the news can make no sense to human beings. Our news is always about how well we understand.

Whenever our wits are shattered by the impossible, we swiftly knit the world back together again, so that our wits can return to us. We pretend that we've lost nothing, not one single illusion. Especially, certainly, we never lose our minds. No matter how strange the news is, we're always sane and sensible. That is what we tell each other.

Massimo returned to our table. He was very drunk, and he looked greenish. "You ever been in a squat-down Turkish toilet?" he said, pinching his nose. "Trust me: don't go in there."

"I think we should go to your Italy now," I said.

"I could do that," he allowed idly, "although I've made some trouble for myself there. . . my real problem is you."

"Why am I trouble?"

"There's another Luca in my Italy. He's not like you: because he's a great author, and a very dignified and very wealthy man. He wouldn't find you funny."

I considered this. He was inviting me to be bitterly jealous of myself. I couldn't manage that, yet I was angry anyway. "Am I funny, Massimo?"

He'd stopped drinking, but that killer brandy was still percolating through his gut.

"Yes, you're funny, Luca. You're weird. You're a terrible joke. Especially in this version of Italy. And especially now that you're finally catching on. You've got a look on your face now like a drowned fish." He belched into his fist. "Now, at last, you think that you understand, but no, you don't. Not yet. Listen: in order to arrive here—I *created* this world. When I press the Function-Three key, and the field transports me here—without me as the observer, this universe doesn't even exist."

I glanced around the thing that Massimo called a universe. It was an Italian cafe. The marble table in front of me was every bit as solid as a rock. Everything around me was very solid, normal, realistic, acceptable and predictable.

"Of course," I told him. "And you also created my universe, too. Because you're not just a black swan. You're God."

" 'Black swan,' is that what you call me?" He smirked, and preened in the mirror. "You journalists need a tag-line for everything."

"You always wear black," I said. "Does that keep our dirt from showing?"

Massimo buttoned his black woolen jacket. "It gets worse," he told me. "When I press that Function-Two key, before the field settles in . . . I generate millions of potential histories. Billions of histories. All with their souls, ethics, thoughts, histories, destinies—whatever. Worlds blink into existence for a few nanoseconds while the chip runs through the program—and then they all blink out. As if they never were."

"That's how you move? From world to world?"

"That's right, my friend. This ugly duckling can fly."

The Elena's waiter arrived to tidy up our table. "A little rice pudding?" he asked.

Massimo was cordial. "No, thank you, sir."

"Got some very nice chocolate in this week! All the way from South America."

"My, that's the very best kind of chocolate." Massimo jabbed his hand into a cargo pocket. "I believe I need some chocolate. What will you give me for this?"

The waiter examined it carefully. "This is a woman's engagement ring."

"Yes, it is."

"It can't be a real diamond, though. This stone's much too big to be a real diamond."

"You're an idiot," said Massimo, "but I don't care much. I've got a big appetite for sweets. Why don't you bring me an entire chocolate pie?"

The waiter shrugged and left us.

"So," Massimo resumed, "I wouldn't call myself a 'God'—because I'm much better described as several million billion Gods. Except, you know, that the zero-point transport field always settles down. Then, here I am. I'm standing outside some cafe, in a cloud of dirt, with my feet aching. With nothing to my name, except what I've got in my brain and my pockets. It's always like that."

The door of the Elena banged open, with the harsh jangle of brass Indian bells. A gang of five men stomped in. I might have taken them for cops, because they had jackets, belts, hats, batons and pistols, but Turinese cops do not arrive on duty drunk. Nor do they wear scarlet armbands with crossed lightning bolts.

The cafe fell silent as the new guests muscled up to the dented bar. Bellowing threats, they proceeded to shake-down the staff.

Massimo turned up his collar and gazed serenely at his knotted hands. Massimo was studiously minding his own business. He was in his corner, silent, black, inexplicable. He might have been at prayer.

I didn't turn to stare at the intruders. It wasn't a pleasant scene, but even for a stranger, it wasn't hard to understand.

The door of the men's room opened. A short man in a trenchcoat emerged. He had a dead cigar clenched in his teeth, and a snappy Alain Delon fedora.

He was surprisingly handsome. People always underesti-mated the good looks, the male charm of Nicolas Sarkozy. Sarkozy sometimes seemed a little odd when sunbathing half-naked in newsstand tabloids, but in person, his cha-risma was overwhelming. He was a man that any world had to reckon with.

Sarkozy glanced about the cafe, for a matter of seconds. Then he sidled, silent and decisive, along the dark mahog-any wall. He bent one elbow. There was a thunderclap. Mas-simo pitched face-forward onto the small marble table.

Sarkozy glanced with mild chagrin at the smoking hole blown through the pocket of his stylish trenchcoat. Then he stared at me.

"You're that journalist," he said.

"You've got a good memory for faces, Monsieur Sarkozy."

"That's right, asshole, I do." His Italian was bad, but it was better than my French. "Are you still eager to 'protect' your dead source here?" Sarkozy gave Massimo's heavy chair one quick, vindictive kick, and the dead man, and his chair, and his table, and his ruined, gushing head all fell to the hard cafe floor with one complicated clatter.

"There's your big scoop of a story, my friend," Sarkozy told me. "I just gave that to you. You should use that in your lying commie magazine."

Then he barked orders at the uniformed thugs. They grouped themselves around him in a helpful cluster, their faces pale with respect.

"You can come out now, baby," crowed Sarkozy, and she emerged from the men's room. She was wearing a cute little gangster-moll hat, and a tailored camouflage jacket. She lugged a big black guitar case. She also had a primitive radio-telephone bigger than a brick.

How he'd enticed that woman to lurk for half an hour in the reeking cafe toilet, that I'll never know. But it was her. It was definitely her, and she couldn't have been any more demure and serene if she were meeting the Queen of England.

They all left together in one heavily armed body.

The thunderclap inside the Elena had left a mess. I rescued Massimo's leather valise from the encroaching pool of blood.

My fellow patrons were bemused. They were deeply bemused, even confounded. Their options for action seemed to lack constructive possibilities.

So, one by one, they rose and left the bar. They left that fine old place, silently and without haste, and without meeting each other's eyes. They stepped out the jangling door and into Europe's biggest plaza.

Then they vanished, each hastening toward his own private world.

I strolled into the piazza, under a pleasant spring sky. It was cold, that spring night, but that infinite dark blue sky was so lucid and clear.

The laptop's screen flickered brightly as I touched the F1 key. Then I pressed 2, and then 3.

Exegesis

NANCY KRESS

Nancy Kress (www.sff.net/people/nankress/) *lives in Seattle, Washington. She recently moved to the west coast. Her novel* Steal Across the Sky, *a near-future SF novel about alien crime, punishment, and the strange paths that atonement can take, was published in 2009. Her short fiction, for which she won her second Hugo Award in 2009, is collected in* Nano Comes to Clifford Falls and Other Stories *(2008). She is one of today's leading SF writers, a popular guest at SF conventions, and an eminent teacher of writing. She published several distinguished SF stories in 2009. This is one of the shortest and most amusing, a new twist on an old idea.*

"Exegesis" was published in Asimov's, *still a leader in SF (the source of five stories in this volume), and the place where Kress published a majority of her best work in 2009. This is linguistic SF, on the evolution of language and erosion of meaning, in the tradition of such classics as Robert Nathan's "Digging the Weans."*

1950

from *Branson's Quotations for Book Lovers*
ed. Roger Branson, Random House

"Frankly, my dear, I don't give a damn." One of the
world's most famous quotations, this is the film version
of Rhett Butler's (Clark Gable) immortal farewell to
Scarlett O'Hara (Vivien Leigh) in Margaret Mitchell's
1936 novel *Gone With the Wind*, a crowning achievement of American literature. It occurs at the end of the
film when Scarlett asks Rhett, "Where shall I go? What
shall I do?" if he leaves her. The print version does not
include the word "frankly," which was added by director
David O. Selznik. The line was bitterly objected to by
the Hays Office, but remained in the 1939 film, due to a
last-minute amendment to the Production Code.

2050

from *Critical Interpretations of Twentieth Century
Literature*, Random House,
eds. Jared Morvais and Hannah Brown

TEXT: "Frankly, my dear, I don't give a damn."[1]

[1]Line from a twentieth-century American novel,
Gone With the Wind by Margaret Mitchell, now largely
dismissed as both racist and romanticized. The male
protagonist, Rhett Butler, speaks the line to the abra-
sive heroine, Scarlett O'Hara, as he leaves their marriage.

2150
Dictionary of Modern Sayings for the Faithful
Church of Renewed Enlightenment
ENTRY: "Frankly, my dear, I don't give a damn."
Line from a twentieth-century novel written by Margaret Mitchell in Southern Ezra (a section of the former United States of America), in which a man, Rhett Butler, abandons his legal wife, an adulteress ("scarlet woman"). The passage is a stark illustration of the sinfulness and irresponsibility of pre-Ezran so-called "Christianity." Praise!

2250
from *Studees in Lawst Litrucher*, Reformd Langwij
Co-ullishun, Han Goldman
SUBJECT: "Franklee, my der, I dont giv a dam."
Line frum Pre-Kolapse novul—awther unown—that twoday iz mostlee fowk sayeen in Suthern Ezra. The prahverb means—ruffly—that the speeker wil not giv even wun "dam"—wich may hav bin a tipe of lokul munee—to by a "der," an xtinkt meet animul. Implikashun is that watever iz beein diskused is over prised. This interpretashun is reinforced by the tradishunul usoceeashun of the line with peepul hoo served meels, known as "butlers."

2350
Harox College Download 6753-J-ENLIT
TEXT: "Frankly[1], my dear[2], I don't give a damn[3]."
New research sheds interesting light on this folk saying from Mubela (formerly Southern Ezra.) The Pre-Collapse Antiquarian Grove humbly makes this offering to the Forest of Enlightened Endolas:
 [1]"Frankly" means that the speaker is talking without subterfuge or lies. Since only liars emphasize their truthfulness—enlightened endolas, of course, represent truth with their very beings—the speaker is openly announcing that he is lying, signaling to the hearer that everything which follows is therefore

untrue. In fact, the speaker *does* give a damn. This sort of convoluted speech was often necessary in pre-Collapse societies, in which "governments" were so politically oppressive that truth could not be openly spoken.

[2]"My dear" is an honorific, similar in construction to the equally archaic, hierarchical "my lord" or "your excellency." This suggests that in the original, the speaker was addressing some sort of lord or commander.

[3]"Damn." Rigorous scholarship by Kral BlackG3 reveals that this was a curse. Its presence in a coded message to a high official is intriguing. For centuries the folk saying has been associated with an extinct "servant class" that included ditch diggers, butlers, and dentists. It may be that in ancient times, when humans compelled other humans rather than robots to provide services, a folk saying was the only acceptable way to "curse" or condemn the owner class, even as the speaker obediently transmits whatever coded information followed. Unfortunately, the sentences following "Frankly, my dear, I don't give a damn" in this political drama have been lost.

NOTE: The common variation, still occasionally seen even in scholarly forums, is scripted in the short-lived and silly "Reformed English": "Franklee, my der, I dont giv a dam."

2450
Fragment of a Download Recovered After the EMP Catastrophe of 2396, with Exegesis

"Frank Lee, my dear, I don't give a dam." "Frank Lee"[1] means that the speaker is talking without subterfuge or lies. Since only liars emphasize their truthfulness—enlightened endolas[2], of course, represent truth with their very beings—the speaker is openly announcing that he is lying, signaling to the hearer that everything which follows is therefore untrue. In fact, the speaker *does* give a damn.[3] This sort

of convoluted speech was often necessary in pre-Collapse[4] societies, in which "governments"[5] were so politically oppressive that truth could not be openly spoken.[6]

[1]Frank Lee—Unknown folk persona who seems to have represented "straight shooting," either verbal or (as is to be expected in violent historical periods) the use of personal arms. See *Frank and Jesse James.*

[2]endolas—religious scholars of the pre-Catastrophe EuroPolar Coalition. They conflated some solid learning with much mysticism. Organized into "groves," "forests," and "amazons," in the eco-heavy nomenclature of that era.

[3]This explanation is typical of the confused and ignorant thinking that prevailed in the Endola Age.

[4]Collapse—one name given to the economic and social upheavals, circa 2190-2210. Exact dates have, of course, disappeared with much other history in the EMP Catastrophe. Other names: Crash, Cave-in, the Big Oops (etymology unknown).

[5]governments—vernacular name for ruling bodies, some consensual and some not. All pre-date Electronic Fair Facilitation and Enforcement.

[6]"so politically oppressive that truth could not be openly spoken." Unable to say whether this analysis is or is not correct.

2850, i
Unified Link Information, Quantum-Entangled
Energy Center
DB 549867207 (Historical)

DATUM: "Franklee, my dear, I don't give a damn."

VARIATIONS: "Frankly, my dear, I don't give a damn."

"Frankly, my dear, I don't give a dam."

"Franklee, my der, I dont giv a dam."

CLASSIFICATION: Proverb, class 32

DATE: Pre-QUENTIAM, probably pre-twenty-second century, specifics unknown

ORIGIN: Human, Sol 3, specifics unknown

LANGUAGES: Many (recite list?). Original probably Late English

EXPLICATION: "Franklee" (or "Frankly") indicates origin in era pre-telepathic-implants, with choice of offering true or untrue information. "My dear" is an archaic term of endearment for members of a "family"; indicates pre-gene-donate society. "Don't give a damn" is antique idiom meaning the speaker/projector is not involved in a current project. Equivalents: "apathy," "independence," "non-functioning implant."

LAST REQUEST FOR THIS INFORMATION: No requests to date

2850, ii

Ser, don't screen your implant from me!

I go now.

Why? Why leave me? Why leave the pod? We desire you!

I go now.

But why?

I tell you, pod mate, I no longer care.

Erosion

IAN CREASEY

Ian Creasey (www.iancreasey.com) lives in Leeds in the UK. Since 1999, he has published over forty short stories. He began writing "when rock & roll stardom failed to return his calls." His spare-time interests include hiking, gardening, and environmental conservation work—anything to get him outdoors and away from the computer screen. He occasionally attends the Milford UK workshop held annually in Wales. "I'm a big believer in the workshopping process: I personally find it very helpful to both critique and be critiqued. I've written hundreds of critiques over the years, and I think that's the main source of my development as a writer." We think Creasey is a major talent to emerge in SF in the last four years, and this story is proof of it.

"Erosion" was published in Asimov's. *A man who has had himself physically altered so he can survive on other planets tells the story of his last week on Earth, when he had an accident. What this story does best is manage point of view in the service of plot, and this it does impressively and to powerful effect. The use of setting details to clarify a moment in the future is no less impressive.*

Let me tell you about my last week on Earth. . . .

Before those final days, I'd already said my farewells. My family gave me their blessing: my grandfather, who came to England from Jamaica as a young man, understood why I signed up for the colony program. He warned me that a new world, however enticing, would have its own frustrations. We both knew I didn't need the warning, but he wanted to pass on what he'd learned in life, and I wanted to hear it. I still remember the clasp of his fingers on my new skin; I can replay the exo-skin's sensory log whenever I wish.

My girlfriend was less forgiving. She accused me of cowardice, of running away. I replied that when your house is on fire, running away is the sensible thing to do. The Earth is burning up, and so we set forth to find a new home elsewhere. She said—she shouted—that when our house is on fire, we should stay and fight the flames. She wanted to help the firefighters. I respected her for that, and I didn't try to persuade her to come with me. That only made her all the more angry.

The sea will douse the land, in time, but it rises slowly. Most of the coastline still resembled the old maps. I'd decided that I would spend my last few days walking along the coast, partly to say goodbye to Earth, and partly to settle into my fresh skin and hone my augments. I'd tested it all in the post-op suite, of course, and in the colony simulator, but I wanted to practice in a natural setting. Reality throws up challenges that a simulator would never devise.

And so I traveled north. People stared at me on the train. I'm accustomed to that—when they see a freakishly tall black man, even the British overcome their famed (and largely mythical) reserve, and stare like scientists at a new specimen. The stares had become more hostile in recent years, as waves of African refugees fled their burning lands. I was born in Newcastle, like my parents, but that isn't written on my face. When I spoke, people smiled to hear a black guy with a Geordie accent, and their hostility melted.

Now I was no longer black, but people still stared. My grey exo-skin, formed of myriad tiny nodules, was iridescent as a butterfly's wings. I'd been told I could create patterns on it, like a cuttlefish, but I hadn't yet learned the fine control required. There'd be plenty of shipboard time after departure for such sedentary trifles. I wanted to be active, to run and jump and swim, and test all the augments in the wild outdoors, under the winter sky.

Scarborough is, or was, a town on two levels. The old North Bay and South Bay beaches had long since drowned, but up on the cliffs the shops and quaint houses and the ruined castle stood firm. I hurried out of town and soon reached the coastal path—or rather, the latest incarnation of the coastal path, each a little further inland than the last. The Yorkshire coast had always been nibbled by erosion, even in more tranquil times. Now the process was accelerating. The rising sea level gouged its own scars from higher tides, and the warmer globe stirred up fiercer storms that lashed the cliffs and tore them down. Unstable slopes of clay alternated with fresh rock, exposed for the first time in millennia. Piles of jagged rubble shifted restlessly, the new stones not yet worn down into rounded pebbles.

After leaving the last house behind, I stopped to take off my shirt, jeans and shoes. I'd only worn them until now as a concession to blending in with the naturals (as we called the unaugmented). I hid the clothes under some gorse, for collection on my return. When naked, I stretched my arms wide, embracing the world and its weather and everything the future could throw at me.

The air was calm yet oppressive, in a brooding sulk

between stormy tantrums. Grey clouds lay heavy on the sky, like celestial loft insulation. My augmented eyes detected polarized light from the sun behind the clouds, beyond the castle standing starkly on its promontory. I tried to remember why I could see polarized light, and failed. Perhaps there was no reason, and the designers had simply installed the ability because they could. Like software, I suffered feature bloat. But when we arrived at our new planet, who could guess what hazards lay in store? One day, seeing polarized light might save my life.

I smelled the mud of the path, the salt of the waves, and a slight whiff of raw sewage. Experimentally, I filtered out the sewage, leaving a smell more like my memories from childhood walks. Then I returned to defaults. I didn't want to make a habit of ignoring reality and receiving only the sense impressions I found aesthetic.

Picking up speed, I marched beside the barbed wire fences that enclosed the farmers' shrinking fields. At this season the fields contained only stubble and weeds, the wheat long since harvested. Crows pecked desultorily at the sodden ground. I barged through patches of gorse; the sharp spines tickled my exo-skin, but did not harm it. With my botanist's eye, I noted all the inhabitants of the little cliff-edge habitat. Bracken and clover and thistles and horsetail— the names rattled through my head, an incantation of farewell. The starship's seedbanks included many species, on the precautionary principle. But initially we'd concentrate on growing food crops, aiming to breed strains that would flourish on the colony world. The other plants . . . this might be the last time I'd ever see them.

It was once said that the prospect of being hanged in the morning concentrated a man's mind wonderfully. Leaving Earth might be almost as drastic, and it had the same effect of making me feel euphorically alive. I registered every detail of the environment: the glistening spiders' webs in the dead bracken, the harsh calls of squabbling crows, the distant roar of the ever-present sea below. When I reached a gully with a storm-fed river at the bottom, I didn't bother following the path inland to a bridge; I charged down the slope, sliding on mud but keeping my balance, then splashed through the water and up the other side.

I found myself on a headland, crunching along a graveled path. An ancient notice-board asked me to clean up after my dog. Ahead lay a row of benches, on the seaward side of the path, much closer to the cliff edge than perhaps they once had been. They all bore commemorative plaques, with lettering mostly faded or rubbed away. I came upon a legible one that read:

In memory of Katriona Grady
2021–2098
She Loved This Coast

Grass had grown up through the slats of the bench, and the wood had weathered to a mottled beige. I brushed aside the detritus of twigs and hawthorn berries, then smiled at myself for the outdated gesture. I wore no clothes to be dirtied, and my exo-skin could hardly be harmed by a few spiky twigs. In time I would abandon the foibles of a fragile human body, and stride confidently into any environment.

I sat, and looked out to sea. The wind whipped the waves into white froth, urging them to the coast. Gulls scudded on the breeze, their cries as jagged as the rocks they nested on. A childhood memory shot through me—eating chips on the seafront, a gull swooping to snatch a morsel. Within me swelled an emotion I couldn't name.

After a moment I became aware of someone sitting next to me. Yet the bench hadn't creaked under any additional weight. A hologram, then. When I turned to look, I saw the characteristic bright edges of a cheap hologram from the previous century.

"Hello, I'm Katriona. Would you like to talk?" The question had a rote quality, and I guessed that all visitors were greeted the same way; a negative answer would dismiss the hologram so that people could sit in peace. But I had several days of solitude ahead of me, and I didn't mind pausing for a while. It seemed appropriate that my last conversation on a dying world would be with a dead person.

"Pleased to meet you," I said. "I'm Winston."

The hologram showed a middle-aged white woman, her hair as grey as riverbed stones, her clothes a tasteful expanse of soft-toned lavender skirt and low-heeled expensive shoes. I wondered if she'd chosen this conventional self-effacing look, or if some memorial designer had imposed a template projecting the dead as aged and faded, not upstaging the living. Perhaps she'd have preferred to be depicted as young and wild and beautiful, as she'd no doubt once been—or would like to have been.

"It's a cold day to be wandering around starkers," she said, smiling.

I had forgotten I wore no clothes. I gave her a brief account of my augmentations. "I'm going to the stars!" I said, the excitement of it suddenly bursting out.

"What, all of them? Do they make copies of you, and send you all across the sky?"

"No, it's not like that." However, the suggestion caused me a moment of disorientation. I had walked into the hospital on my old human feet, been anaesthetized, then—quite some time later—had walked out in shiny new augmented form. Did only one of me leave, or had others emerged elsewhere, discarded for defects or optimized for different missions? *Don't be silly,* I told myself. *It's only an exo-skin. The same heart still beats underneath.* That heart, along with the rest of me, had yesterday passed the final pre-departure medical checks.

"We go to one planet first," I said, "which will be challenge enough. But later—who knows?" No one had any idea what the lifespan of an augmented human might prove to be; since all the mechanical components could be upgraded, the limit would be reached by any biological parts that couldn't be replaced. "It does depend on discovering other planets worth visiting. There are many worlds out there, but only a few even barely habitable."

I described our destination world, hugging a red dwarf sun, its elliptical orbit creating temperature swings, fierce weather and huge tides. "The colonists are a mixed bunch: naturals who'll mostly have to stay back at base; then the augmented, people like me who should be able to survive outside; and the gene-modders—they reckon they'll be best off in the long run, but it'll take them generations to get the gene-tweaks right." There'd already been tension between the groups, as we squabbled over the starship's finite cargo capacity, but I refrained from mentioning it. "I'm sorry— I've gone on long enough. Tell me about yourself. Did you live around here? Was this your favorite place?"

"Yorkshire lass born and bred, that's me," said Katriona's hologram. "Born in Whitby, spent a few years on a farm in Dentdale, but came back—*suck my flabby tits*—to the coast when I married my husband. He was a fisherman, God rest his soul. *Arsewipe!* When he was away, I used to walk along the coast and watch the North Sea, imagining him out there on the waves."

My face must have showed my surprise.

"Is it happening again?" asked Katriona. "I was hacked a long time ago, I think. I don't remember very much since I died—I'm more of a recording than a simulation. I only have a little memory, enough for short-term interaction." She spoke in a bitter tone, as though resenting her limitations. "What more does a memorial bench need? Ah, I loved this coast, but that doesn't mean I wanted to sit here forever. . . . *Nose-picking tournament, prize for the biggest booger!*"

"Would you like me to take you away?" I asked. It would be easy enough to pry loose the chip. The encoded personality could perhaps be installed on the starship's computer with the other uploaded colonists, yet I sensed that Katriona wouldn't pass the entrance tests. She was obsolete, and the dead were awfully snobbish about the company they kept. I'd worked with them in the simulator, and I could envisage what they'd say. "Why, Winston, I know you mean well, but she's not the right sort for a mission like this. She has no relevant expertise. Her encoding is coarse, her algorithms are outdated, and she's absolutely riddled with parasitic memes."

Just imagining this response made me all the more determined to fight it. But Katriona saved me the necessity. "That's all right, dear. I'm too old and set in my ways to go to the stars. I just want to rejoin my husband, and one day I will." She stared out to sea again, and I had a sudden intuition of what had happened to her husband.

"I'm sorry for your loss," I said. "I take it he was never"—I groped for an appropriate word—"memorialized."

"There's a marker in the *fuckflaps* graveyard," she said, "but he was never recorded like me. Drowning's a quick death, but it's not something you plan for. And we never recovered the body, so it couldn't be done afterward. He's still down there somewhere. . . ."

It struck me that if Katriona's husband had been augmented, he need not have drowned. My limbs could tirelessly swim, and my exo-skin could filter oxygen from the water. As it would be tactless to proclaim my hardiness, I cast about for a neutral reply. "The North Sea was all land, once. Your ancestors hunted mammoths there, before the sea rose."

"And now the sea is rising again." She spoke with such finality that I knew our conversation was over.

"God speed you to your rest," I said. When I stood up, the hologram vanished.

I walked onward, and the rain began.

I relished the storm. It blew down from the northeast, with ice in its teeth. They call it the lazy wind, because it doesn't bother to go around you—it just goes straight through you.

The afternoon darkened, with winter twilight soon expiring. The rain thickened into hail, bouncing off me with an audible rattle. Cracks of thunder rang out, an ominous rumbling as though the raging sea had washed away the pillars of the sky, pulling the heavens down. Lightning flashed somewhere behind me.

I turned and looked along the coastal path, back to the necropolis of benches I had passed earlier. The holograms were all lit up. I wondered who would sit on the benches in this weather, until I realized that the lightning must have short-circuited the activation protocols.

The holograms were the only bright colors in a washed-out world of slate-grey cloud and gun-dark sea. Images of men and women flickered on the benches, an audience for

Nature's show. I saw Katriona standing at the top of the cliff, raising her arms as if calling down the storm. Other figures sat frozen like reproachful ghosts, tethered to their wooden anchors, waiting for the storm to fade. Did they relish the brief moment of pseudo-life? Did they talk among themselves? Or did they resent their evanescent existence, at the mercy of any hikers and hackers wandering by?

I felt I should not intrude. I returned to my trek, slogging on as the day eroded into night. My augmented eyes harvested stray photons from lights in distant houses and the occasional car gliding along inland roads. To my right, the sea throbbed with the pale glitter of bioluminescent pollution. The waves sounded loud in the darkness, their crashes like a secret heartbeat of the world.

The pounding rain churned the path into mud. My mouth curved into a fierce grin. Of course, conditions were nowhere near as intense as the extremes of the simulator. But this was *real*. The sight of all the dead people behind me, chained to their memorials, made me feel sharply alive. Each raindrop on my face was another instant to be cherished. I wanted the night never to end. I wanted to be both here and gone, to stand on the colony world under its red, red sun.

I hurried, as if I could stride across the stars and get there sooner. I trod on an old tree branch that proved to be soggy and rotten. My foot slid off the path. I lurched violently, skidding a few yards sideways and down, until I arrested my fall by grabbing onto a nearby rock. The muscles in my left arm sent pangs of protest at the sharp wrench. Carefully I swung myself round, my feet groping for toeholds. Soon I steadied myself. Hanging fifty feet above the sea, I must have only imagined that I felt spray whipping up from the waves. It must have been the rain, caught by the wind and sheeting from all angles.

The slip exhilarated me. I know that makes little sense, but I can only tell you how I felt.

But I couldn't cling there all night. I scrambled my way across the exposed crags, at first shuffling sideways by inches, then gaining confidence and swinging along, trusting my augmented muscles to keep me aloft.

My muscles gripped. My exo-skin held. The rock did not.

In mid-swing, I heard a *crack*. My anchoring left hand felt the rock shudder. Instinctively I scrabbled for another hold with my right hand. I grasped one, but nevertheless found myself falling. For a moment I didn't understand what was happening. Then, as the cliff-face crumbled with a noise like the tearing of a sky-sized newspaper, I realized that when the bottom gives way, the top must follow.

As I fell, still clinging to the falling rock, I was drenched by the splashback from the lower boulders hitting the sea below me. Time passed slowly, frame by frame, the scene changing gradually like an exhibition of cels from an animated movie. The hefty rock that I grasped was rotating as it fell. Soon I'd be underneath it. If I still clung on, I would be crushed when it landed.

I leapt free, aiming out to sea. If the cliff had been higher, I'd have had enough time to get clear. But very soon I hit the water, and so did the boulder behind me, and so too—it seemed—did half of the Yorkshire coast.

It sounded like a duel between a volcano and an earthquake. I flailed frantically, trying to swim away, not understanding why I made no progress. Only when I stopped thrashing around did I realize the problem.

My right foot was trapped underwater, somewhere within the pile of rocks that came down from the cliff. At the time, I'd felt nothing. Now, belatedly, a dull pounding pain crept up my leg. I breathed deeply, gulping air between the waves crashing around my head. Then I began attempting to wriggle free, with no success.

I tried to lift up the heavy boulders, but it was impossible. My imprisoned foot kept me in place, constricting my position and preventing me from finding any leverage. After many useless heaves, and much splashing and cursing, I had to give up.

All this time, panic had been building within me. As soon as I stopped struggling, terror flooded my brain with the fear of drowning, the fear of freezing in the cold sea, the fear of more rocks falling on top of me. My thoughts were overwhelmed by the prospect of imminent death.

It took long minutes to regain any coherence. Gradually I asserted some self-command, telling myself that the panic was a relic of my old body, which wouldn't have survived long floating in the North Sea in winter. My new form was far more robust. I wouldn't drown, or freeze to death. If I could compose myself, I'd get through this.

I concentrated on my exo-skin. Normally its texture approximated natural skin's slight roughness and imperfections. Now my leg became utterly smooth, in the hope that a friction-free surface might allow me to slip free. I felt a tiny amount of give, which sent a surge of hope through me, but then I could pull my foot no further. The bulge of my ankle prevented any further progress. Even friction-free, you can't tug a knot through a needle's eye.

Impatient and frustrated, I let the exo-skin revert to default. I needed to get free, and I couldn't simply wait for the next storm to rattle the rocks around. My starship would soon leave Earth. If I missed it, I would have no other chance.

At this point I began to wonder whether I'd subconsciously wanted to miss the boat. Had I courted disaster, just to prevent myself from going?

I couldn't deny that I'd in some sense brought this on myself. I'd been deliberately reckless, pushing myself until the inevitable accident occurred. Why?

Thinking about it, as the cold waves frothed around me, I realized that I'd wanted to push beyond the bounds of my old body, in order to prove to myself that I was worthy of going. We'd heard so much of the harsh rigors of the destination world, and so much had been said about the naturals' inability to survive there unaided, that I'd felt compelled to test the augments to their limit.

Unconsciously, I'd wanted to put myself in a situation that a natural body couldn't survive. Then if I did survive, that would prove I'd been truly transformed, and I'd be confident of thriving on the colony world, among the tides and hurricanes.

Well, I'd accomplished the first stage of this plan. I'd got myself into trouble. Now I just had to get out of it.

But how?

I had an emergency radio-beacon in my skull. I could activate it and no doubt someone would come along to scoop me out of the water. Yet that would be embarrassing. It would show that I couldn't handle my new body, even in the benign conditions of Earth. If I asked for rescue, then some excuse would be found to remove me from the starship roster. Colonists needed to be self-reliant and solve their own problems. There were plenty of reserves on the waiting list—plenty of people who hadn't fallen off a cliff and got themselves stuck under a pile of rocks.

The same applied if I waited until dawn and shouted up to the next person to walk along the coastal path. No, I couldn't ask for rescue. I had to save myself.

Yet asserting the need for a solution did not reveal its nature. At least, not at first. As the wind died down, and the rain softened into drizzle, I found myself thinking coldly and logically, squashing trepidation with the hard facts of the situation.

I needed to extract my leg from the rock. I couldn't move the rock. Therefore I had to move my leg.

I needed to move my leg, but the foot was stuck. Therefore I had to leave my foot behind.

Once I realized this, a calmness descended upon me. It was very simple. That was the price I must pay, if I wanted to free myself. I thought back to the option of calling for help. I could keep my foot, and stay on Earth. Or I could lose my foot, and go to the stars.

Did I long to go so badly?

I'd already decided to leave my family behind and leave my girlfriend. If I jibbed at leaving a mere foot, a minor bodily extremity, then what did that say about my values? Surely there wasn't even a choice to make; I merely had to accept the consequences of the decision I'd already made.

And yet I delayed and delayed, hoping that some other option would present itself, hoping that I could evade the results of my choices.

I'm almost ashamed to admit what finally prompted me to action. It wasn't logic or strong-willed decisiveness. It was the pain from my squashed foot, a throbbing that had steadily intensified while I mulled the possibilities. And it was no fun floating in the cold sea, either. The sooner I acted, the sooner I could get away.

I concentrated upon my exo-skin, that marvel of programmable integument, and commanded it to flow up from my foot. Then I pinched it into my leg, just above my right ankle.

Ouch! Ouch, ouch, ouch, owwww!

Trying to ignore the pain, I steered the exo-skin further in. I wished I could perform the whole operation in an instant, slicing off my foot as if chopping a cucumber. But the exo-skin had limits, and it wasn't designed to do this. I was stretching the spec already.

Soon—sooner than I would have hoped—I had to halt. I needed to access my pain overrides. It had been constantly drilled into us that this was a last resort, that pain existed for a reason and we shouldn't casually shut it off. But if amputating one's own foot wasn't an emergency, I didn't ever want to encounter a true last resort. I turned off the pain signals.

The numbness intoxicated me. What a blessing, to be free from the hurts of the flesh! In the absence of pain, the remaining tasks seemed to elapse much more swiftly. Soon the exo-skin had completely cut through the bone, severing my lower leg and sealing off the wound. Freed from the rockfall, I swam away and dragged myself ashore. There I collapsed into sleep.

When I woke, the tide had receded, leaving behind a beach clogged with fallen clumps of grass, soggy dead bracken, and the ever-present plastic trash that was humanity's legacy to the world. The pain signals had returned—they could only be temporarily suspended, not permanently switched off. For about a minute I tried to live with my lower calf's agonized protestations; then I succumbed to temptation and suppressed them again. As I tried to stand up, I discovered that I was now lopsided. At the bottom of my right leg I had some spare exo-skin, since it no longer covered a foot. I instructed the surplus material to extend a few inches into a peg-leg, so that I could balance. I shaped the peg to avoid pressing on my stump, with the force of my steps being borne by the exo-skin higher up my leg.

I tottered across the trash-strewn pebbles. I could walk! I shouted in triumph, and disturbed a magpie busy pecking at the freshly revealed soil on the new shoreline. It chittered reprovingly as it flew away.

Then I must have blacked out for a while. Later, I woke with a weak sun shining in my face. My first thought was to return to the landslip and move the rocks to retrieve my missing foot.

My second thought was—*where is it?*

The whole coast was a jumble of fallen boulders. The cliff had been eroding for years, and last night's storm was only the most recent attrition. I couldn't tell where I'd fallen, or where I'd been trapped. Somewhere in there lay a chunk of flesh, of great sentimental value. But I had no idea where it might be.

I'd lost my foot.

Only at that moment did the loss hit home. I raged at myself for getting into such a stupid situation, and for going through with the amputation rather than summoning help, like a young boy too proud to call for his mother when he hurts himself.

And I felt a deep regret that I'd lost a piece of myself I'd never get back. Sure, the exo-skin could replace it. Sure, I could augment myself beyond what I ever was before.

But the line between man and machine seemed like the coastline around me: constantly being nibbled away. I'd lost a foot, just like the coast had lost a few more rocks. Yet no matter what it swallowed, the sea kept rising.

What would I lose next?

I turned south, back toward town, and walked along the shoreline, looking for a spot where I could easily climb from the beach to the path above the cliff. Perhaps I could have employed my augments and simply clawed my way up the sheer cliff-face, but I had become less keen on using them.

The irony did not escape me. I'd embarked on this expedition with the intent of pushing the augments to the full. Now

I found myself shunning them. Yet the augments themselves hadn't failed.

Only I had failed. I'd exercised bad judgment, and ended up trapped and truncated. That was my entirely human brain, thinking stupidly.

Perhaps if my brain had been augmented, I would have acted more rationally.

My steps crunched on banks of pebbles, the peg-leg making a different sound than my remaining foot, so that my gait created an alternating rhythm like the bass-snare drumbeat of old-fashioned pop music. The beach smelled of sea-salt, and of the decaying vegetation that had fallen with the landslip. Chunks of driftwood lay everywhere.

The day was quiet; the wind had dropped and the tide was out, so the only sounds came from my own steps and the occasional cry of the gulls far out to sea. Otherwise I would never have heard the voice, barely more than a scratchy whisper.

"Soon, my darling. Soon we'll be together. Ah, how long has it been?"

I looked around and saw no one. Then I realized that the voice came from low down, from somewhere among the pebbles and the ever-present trash. I sifted through the debris and found a small square of plastic. When I lifted it to my ear, it swore at me.

"Arsewipe! Fuckflaps!"

The voice was so tinny and distorted that I couldn't be sure I recognized it. "Katriona?" I asked.

"How long, how long? Oh, the sea, the dear blessed sea. Speed the waves. . . ."

I asked again, but the voice wouldn't respond to me. Maybe the broken chip, which no longer projected a hologram, had also lost its aural input. Or maybe it had stopped bothering to speak to passersby.

Now I saw that some of the driftwood planks were slats of benches. The memorial benches, which over the years had inched closer to the eroding cliff-edge, had finally succumbed to the waves.

Yet perhaps they hadn't succumbed, but rather had finally

attained their goal—or would do soon enough when the next high tide carried the detritus away. I remembered the holograms lighting up last night, how they'd seemed to summon the storm. I remembered Katriona telling me about her husband who'd drowned. For all the years of her death, she must have longed to join him in the watery deeps.

I strode out toward the distant waves. My steps squelched as I neared the waterline, and I had to pick my way between clumps of seaweed. As I walked, I crunched the plastic chip to shreds in my palm, my exo-skin easily strong enough to break it. When I reached the spume, I flung the fragments into the sea.

"Goodbye," I said, "and God rest you."

I shivered as I returned to the upper beach. I felt an irrational need to clamber up the rocks to the cliff-top path, further from the hungry sea.

I'd seen my own future. The exo-skin and the other augments would become more and more of me, and the flesh less and less. One day only the augments would be left, an electronic ghost of the person I used to be.

As I retrieved my clothes from where I'd cached them, I experienced a surge of relief at donning them to rejoin society. Putting on my shoes proved difficult, since I lacked a right foot. I had to reshape my exo-skin into a hollow shell, in order to fill the shoes of a human being.

Tomorrow I would return to the launch base. I'd seek medical attention after we lifted off, when they couldn't remove me from the colony roster for my foolishness. I smiled as I wondered what similar indiscretions my comrades might reveal, when it was too late for meaningful punishment. What would we all have left behind?

What flaws would we take with us? And what would remain of us, at the last?

Now we approach the end of my story, and there is little left. As I once helped a shadow fade, long ago and far away, I hope that someday you will do the same for me.

Collision

GWYNETH JONES

Gwyneth Jones (homepage.ntlworld.com/gwynethann/) is a speculative fiction writer and Young Adult author who lives in Brighton in the UK. Her YA books are written under the name Anne Halam, and her SF and fantasy is written under her real name, Gwyneth Jones. Gwyneth Jones writes ambitious, feminist science fiction and fantasy, and criticism. She has won a number of awards for fiction, and the Pilgrim Award of the Science Fiction Research Association for her achievements in SF and fantasy criticism. She writes in the tradition of Ursula K. Le Guin and Joanna Russ. Her major SF includes Divine Endurance *(1984), the Bold as Love sequence of novels, and the White Queen trilogy and its associated stories, of which this is one.*

"Collision" was published in Geoff Ryman's anthology When It Changed, *a book of stories based on real science and including commentary on the science involved in each of them (see Ryman story note, later in this book). This story fills in a crucial moment in the White Queen future history, and elucidates a unique mode of interstellar transportation, as well as questions of gender.*

Does size matter? You can build a particle accelerator on a desktop, but the Buonarotti Torus was huge, its internal dimensions dwarfing the two avatars who strolled, gazing about them like tourists in a virtual museum. Malin had heard that the scale was unnecessary, it was just meant to flatter the human passion for Big Dumb Objects: a startling thought, but maybe it was true. The Aleutians, the only aliens humanity had yet encountered, had never been very good at explaining themselves.

Nobody would have been allowed to keep the Buonarotti on a desktop on Earth, anyway. The voters were afraid an Instantaneous Transit Collider might rend the fabric of reality and wanted it as far away as possible. So the aliens had created the Torus, and set it afloat out here in the Kuiper Belt as a kind of goodbye present—when they'd tired of plundering planet Earth, and gone back from whence they came.

Wherever that was.

But the Aleutians had departed before Malin was born. The problem right now was the new, Traditionalist government of the World State. A fact-finding mission was soon to arrive at the Panhandle station, and the Torus scientists were scared. They were mostly Reformers, notionally, but politics wasn't the issue. Nobody cared if Flat-Earthers were in charge at home, as long as they *stayed* at home. The issue was survival.

Malin and Lou Tiresias, the Director of Torus Research,

were checking rad levels after a recent gamma burst, using high-rez medical avatars. There was a gruesome fascination in watching the awesome tissue damage rack up on their eyeball screens . . . Luckily the beast needed little in-person, hands-on maintenance. Especially these days, when it was so rarely fired-up.

No transiters would ever take any harm, either. They weren't flesh and blood when they passed through this convoluted way-station.

'At least they're scientists,' said Lou. 'My replacement, the Interim Director, is a high-flying gold-medal neurophysicist, *and* a media star.'

'Huh. I bet she's a Flat-Earther of the worst kind,' growled Malin. 'What d'you think's going to happen, Lou?'

The World Government was supposed to leave the Panhandle scientists alone. *That was the deal*. In return, it must be admitted, for past services the researchers would rather forget—

'I'm afraid they're going to shut us down, my child.'

Lou gave a twirl, and a crooked grin. Hir avatar wore a draped white gown, a blue-rinsed perm, rhinestone wingtip glasses and a pantomime beard: an ensemble actually quite close to the Director's real world appearance. With some members of the Torus station community, you had to ask them if they preferred 'he,' 'she' or the unisex pronoun. Lou, the funky, reassuringly daft, all-purpose parent figure was obviously a 'hir.'

'It's a question of style,' he explained, ruefully.

There were few of Malin's colleagues who hadn't fooled around most *un*-traditionally with their meat-bodies, and few who respected the boring notion of mere male or female sex.

Malin digested the thought that Lou was to be replaced by some brutal, totalitarian, politicised stranger.

'Will we be black-listed?'

'Not at all! They'll send us home, that's all.'

Malin had glimpsed movement, on the edge of her screen: sensed a prick-eared scampering, a glint of bright eyes. Who was that, and in what playful form? People often came to the

Torus: just to hang out in the gleaming, giant's cavern, just to delight in the sheer improbablity of it . . . They say deep space is cold and bare, but Malin lived in a wild wood, a rich coral reef, blossoming with endless, insouciant variety. It thrilled her. She loved to feel herself embedded in the ecology of information, set free from drab constraint: a droplet in the teeming ocean, a pebble on the endless shore—

'I don't want to go home,' she said. '*This* is home.'

To the Deep Spacers, mainly asteroid miners, who used their sector of the Panhandle as an R&R station, the Torus was a dangerous slot machine that occasionally spat out big money. They didn't care. The scientists were convinced their project was doomed, and terrified they'd never work again once the IT Collider had been declared a staggering waste of money. The night before the Slingshot was due to dock they held a wake, in the big canteen full of greenery and living flowers, under the rippling banners that proclaimed the ideals of Reform, *Liberté Egalité Amitié* . . . They toasted each other in the Semillion they'd produced that season, and talked about the good times. It all became very emotional. Dr. Fortune, of the DARPA detector lab, inveterate gamer and curator of all their virtualities, had arrived already drunk, attired in full Three Kingdoms warrior regalia. He had to be carried out in the end, still wildly insisting that the Torus staff should make a last stand like the Spartans at Thermopylae and sobbing—

'An army of lovers cannot lose!'

Nobody blamed him. The DARPA bums (the lab teams were all nicknamed after ancient search engines) had switched off their circadians and worked flat out for the last 240 hours, gobbling glucose and creatine, trying to nail one of those elusive *turnaround* results that might save this small, beloved world; and they had failed.

The 'fact-finders' arrived, and immediately retired to the visitors' quarters, where they could enjoy stronger gravity and conduct their assessment without bothersome personal contact. The Interim Director herself, alas, was less tactful.

The science sector was a 4-spaced environment, permeated by the digital: Dr. Caterina Marie Skodlodowska didn't have to signal her approach by moving around in the flesh. You never knew when or where she would pop up—and her questions were casual, but merciless.

She asked Lou could 'he' envisage building *another* Torus. (Dr. Skodlodowska didn't buy unisex pronouns.)

'Of course! Eventually we'll need a whole network.'

Lou was wise, but 'he' lacked cunning.

'Eventually. Mm. But you've analysed all those esoteric Aleutian materials, and you can synthesise? Strange that we haven't been told.'

'We don't have to synthesise, we can *clone* the stuff. Like growing a cell culture, er, on a very large scale.'

'So you don't yet know what the T is made of?'

'But we know it *works*! Hey, you use Aleutian gadgets you don't understand all the time on Earth!'

She asked Lemuel Reason, the fox-tailed, clever-pawed technical manager of the Yahoo lab, exactly how many lives had been lost.

'Very few!' said Lemuel, glad to be on safe ground. 'Er, relatively. We don't fire-up unless we're pretty sure the destination is safe.'

The Deep Spacers were volunteer guinea pigs, in a lottery sanctioned and encouraged by the World Government. They could apply for rights to a sector of Local-Space, and transit out there to see what they could find. Some went missing, or returned in rather poor shape, but a respectable minority hit paydirt: an asteroid rich in gold or exotics; an exploitable brown dwarf. These sites couldn't yet be exploited, but they were already worth big bucks on the Space Development futures market.

'I was thinking of the so-called Damned, the political and Death Row prisoners shipped out here for so-called Transportation. I believe you'll find the losses were 100%, and the numbers run into many hundreds.'

Skodlodowska was referring to a sorry episode in the Panhandle's history. The 'Damned' had been dispatched to supposedly Earth-type habitable planets, the nearest of them thousands of light years 'away' by conventional measure. They'd been told that their safe arrival would be monitored, but that had been a soothing lie, for only consciousness, the *information* that holds mind and body together, can 'travel' by the Buonarotti method. Did Lemuel have to explain the laws of neurophysics?

'The mass transits were recorded as successful!' cried the Yahoo.

Dr. Skodlodowska smiled sadly.

'The operation was successful, but the patient died, eh?'

They did their best to look busy, to disguise the fact that the great Collider had been more or less in mothballs for years. It was useless, Skodlodowska knew everything, but they had to try. Malin was a JANET, a wake-field analyst. She worked on her core task, sifting archived bit-streams for proof that non-Local transiters had actually arrived somewhere: but she couldn't concentrate. She was poking around in an out-of-bounds area, when her screen flagged a warning and switched to the Buonarotti video, digitised from analogue, that she was using as a safety net . . . One of the few records of the real Buonarotti to have survived, and quite possibly her only media interview.

'You're going to break the speed of light this way?' asks the journalist.

'Break the what?' says the direly dressed, slightly obese young woman, in faux 4D: twisting her hands, knitting her scanty brows, speaking English with a pronounced, hesitant European accent. 'I don't understand you. Speed, or light, neither is relevant at all. Where there is no duration there is no *speed*.'

Coming over as both arrogant and bewildered—

'Terrible combination,' muttered Malin, shaking her head.

'The shiny blue suit and the hair? Or the genius and the journalist?'

The new boss was at Malin's shoulder. Dr. Caterina Marie in the flesh, slender yet voluptuous in her snow-white labsuit and bootees, and (you betcha) absolutely darling lingerie underneath. The female lead for a C20 sci-fi movie: brave, maverick, beautiful lady scientist. *But there's a Y chromosome in there somewhere*, thought Malin, malignly. She didn't have the genemod for detecting precise shades of sexual identity, but she had friends who did, and something must have rubbed off—

'The format.' Shame at her secret rudeness made Malin more open. 'Imagine how it sounded. Kirlian photography. Auras. Breaking the mind-matter barrier. All those ideas, totally bizarre to the general public of the time. But TV interviews aren't everything. Give her a smartboard, let her turn her back on the audience, she'd dazzle you.'

'I think you like her,' remarked Caterina, in a voice like dark honey.

'What I know of her, I think I like. But Buonarotti is ancient history and we don't have her notes. The important thing is that our Torus *works*.'

'I keep hearing that. The Torus does *something*,' corrected the Director, 'It makes people disappear, *very* expensively. I grant you that.'

Malin forced a smile: it hurt her face. The Transportation episode had been before her time, but she still felt that guilt. So now it was Malin's turn to get fried, or to win the boss over. Ten seconds to save the world—

They didn't have Buonarotti's notes. Everything had been lost in the chaos of the Gender Wars: all they had were fragments and the prototype 'device' that had been rescued by the Aleutians from the wreckage of battle. To Malin the truth was still self-evident: but Skodlodowska and her bosses might well feel differently. They were Flat-Earthers, after all—

'Peenemunde Buonarotti invented a means of sending human beings, translated into code by her scanner-couches, around a big collider buried under the rocks of Europe. She split those transcendental packets of code into two, and ramped up the energies so that when they collided, they broke the mind-matter barrier. Nobody understood her, but the Aleutians *did*, and that's how we got the Torus. For an instant, transiters are where speed, time, duration, distance don't exist.

If they've been programmed with a 4-space destination, then *instantly* that's where they'll be. No matter how far—'

She took a deep breath.

The Torus was a black box that seemed, fairly definitely, to take people instantaneously across light years. But proof was elusive.

'You can't shut us down!' Malin began to babble, unnerved by Dr. Skodlodowska's silence. 'This is the gateway to the stars! We have gas giant moons, asteroid areas, planetoids, where the prospects for mining are *fabulous*. We have the habitable planets, where you could move in next week. Okay, okay, it's all in need of development, but what we do isn't magical, it's *proven*. There's absolutely no doubt that instantaneous transit happens. We see the event. The only thing we don't have—'

She was out of breath, out of time.

'Is a repeatable experiment,' said Caterina, dryly. 'Isn't that what divides science from pseudoscience? Oh, don't look like that—' She laid a hand on Malin's arm, and the touch was a shock, warm and steady. Her dark eyes glowed. 'Your enemies are back on Earth. *I'm on your side.*'

Yeah, right, thought Malin. That's why you're asking all the awkward questions, and sending our stupid babbling straight back to Earth. But when Caterina had gone she thought it over, staring at the movie of Buonarotti: and then, with sudden decision, opened the file she'd been working on before the boss appeared. Not exactly *secret*, but a little hard to explain.

The DARPA team, as their nickname suggested, were all about destination coordinates: how the linkage between consciousness and specific 4-space location happened. The Yahoos and the Googles studied the human element, the transiters themselves. The possible JANETs (named for a long ago academic and science network) looked for news from nowhere, postcards from Botany Bay . . . Somewhere in the wake of the monstrous energies of collision, there should be buried fragments of sense-perceptions from the other side. The S-factor, the physical organism, had arrived in another place. Eyes had opened on alien scenes, skin had felt the touch of another planet's air. There must be some irefutable trace of that landfall, leaking back from the future. The JANETs hadn't found it yet but they lived in hope.

Malin had been figuring out ways of reducing the P-factor interference (essentially, stray thoughts) that disturbed the wake of a collision. It had been observed that certain transiters, paradoxically, seemed to *dream* in non-duration. There were brainstates, neuronal maps that cognitive analysis translated as weird images, emotional storms, flashes of narrative. It was rich stuff, but all useless crap, since everything had the signature of internally generated perception. But *why* were some transiters having these dense and complex dreams? What did it mean?

What if you flip the gestalt, see the noise as signal?

Malin searched in forbidden territory, the personal files of the Damned. Alone in a virtual archive room, in the middle of the night, she felt herself watched. She looked over her virtual shoulder and, inevitably, there was Caterina—leaning against a filing cabinet, dark hair a shining tumble: hands in the pockets of a white silk dressing-gown.

Malin's avatar wore nubbly old Rocketkid pyjamas.

'Of course, you can explain yourself,' said the vision. 'You wouldn't be doing something so illegal and unprofessional if you didn't have very good reason. Do you know how much trouble you're in?'

Malin nodded. 'Yes, but these files are banned because of data protection, nothing scientific, and I'm not looking at personal information. I think I'm onto something. See here—' She shared her view. 'See this? Hyper-development in the *anterior insula*, and the *frontal operculum*? That's not uncommon, it indicates a natural-born, life-experience augmented talent for handling virtual worlds: a gamer, a fantasist, a creative scientist. I have a group of these people, all showing the same very unusual P-stream activity in the event-wake. The backwash of the collision, that is. Like layers of new neuronal architecture—'

'What's that extraordinary *spike*?'

'That's what I'm talking about.'

'But these are induction scans, decades old. Are you telling me that what happened in the Collider retroactively *appeared* in their files?'

'Yep, it's entanglement effect. We get them, spooky effects. In terms of intentionality, we're *very* close to the Torus.'

Ouch. Traditionalists, Malin reminded herself, were *repelled* by the strangeness of the new science.

The boss did not flinch. 'What d'you think's going on?'

Desperation generates blinding insight. Back in the JANET lab, Malin had seen, grasped, *guessed*, that Caterina Marie Skodlodowska really was on their side. Her questions were tough, but that was because she had hardliners to convince at home. She wanted the Torus to live!

Malin drew a breath. 'I've been trying to eliminate "stray thoughts" from the information-volume where we'd hope to find S-traces from the remote site. Probability-tunnelling back to us. In certain cases I'm seeing P-fragments of extraordinary complexity. I think they're mapping the equation of the transit. When you have a problem that's too big to handle, subsitituting imagery for the values is a useful technique.'

Caterina paid attention. 'You mean, like a memory palace?'

'Yes! I think I'm seeing prepared minds, impelled by the collision with the mind/matter barrier to *know* what's happening: where they're going and how. They're experiencing, processing this knowledge as a virtual world!'

'That sounds dangerously like meddling with the supernatural.'

It's a bit late to worry about that, thought Malin, exasperated, and forgetting that Cat was not the enemy. Down all the millennia, people like you have said science is 'challenging the Throne of God.' The funny thing is, your 'God' doesn't seem to mind. Your 'God' keeps saying to us, *Hey, wonderful! You noticed! Follow me, I have some other great stuff to show you—*

'Not supernatural, purely neurology. Brain-training. We could do the work here on the Panhandle. We need to be able to handle complex virtual worlds, so we have the equipment. We're just not allowed to ramp it up, because of that "destroying the fabric of reality" thing, you know, creating exotic brainstates close to the Torus.'

'I see you've given this some thought,' said Caterina, without a sign of alarm. 'There would certainly be some risk.'

'I think it's worth it. What's happening here, in these files, is involuntary and uncontrolled. If we could get people to do the trick voluntarily, we'd have your repeatable experiment! I could be a candidate myself, I've spent enough time in virtuality—'

'You could turn yourself into a quantum computer?'

'I *am* a quantum computer,' said Malin (and heard herself, arrogant and bewildered as Buonarotti). 'That's what consciousness is, like the universe: a staggering mass of simultaneous, superimposed calculations—'

Caterina's avatar was ripping through the data. 'You're saying that some of the Damned made successful transits. Why didn't they come back?'

'Would you?'

'Good point.'

'Theoretically there's no problem about "coming back." Imagine a stretched elastic. It *wants* to rebound. The difficulty should be *staying*, at the remote site, I mean. That is, until we have a presence there, to anchor people in the new reality. Another station.'

'What about the Lost? Why didn't they "rebound"?'

They died, thought Malin. They were annihilated, unless they had this fortuitous ability; or at least someone in the party did.

'I don't know.'

That strange glow rose in Caterina's eyes (her virtual eyes); which Malin had seen before and could not quite interpret.

'Well . . . I think you've set us a challenge, Malin.'

So they were off, Malin the possible JANET and her polar opposite. Skodlodowska chose the destination. She decided they might as well go for the big prize: one of the Transportation planets, where they should find Earth-type conditions. Maybe they'd meet some of the Damned! The science teams, in a fever of hope, prepared to fire-up the Torus. The fact-finders stayed in their quarters, and communications with Earth (as far as Lou could discover) continued undisturbed. It looked as if Caterina wasn't telling her Flat-Earth bosses that she planned to take this crazy leap into the void.

Malin spent hours in the neuro-labs, getting her brain trained under the supervision of Dr. Fortune, gamer-lord of the Panhandle's virtualities.

'You're fraternising with the enemy,' he warned her.

'Fraternising's a dirty word. I'm offering the hand of friendship.'

'You'll be sorry. You don't know what she really wants.'

'She wants to make a transit, obviously. It's her secret dream.'

'Yes, but *why*?'

'I'm hoping it's the everlasting fame and glory,' said Malin. The mystery bothered her, too.

All transiters, even the humble 'prospectors' had to do some brain-training. They were schooled in handling, visualising, internalising their survival kit: so that the pressure suit, rations, air supply would transit with them, imprinted on the somatosensory cortex; and they wouldn't turn up naked in hard vacuum. Malin had to do a lot more. She was building her memory palace, a map for the equation of the transit. They had decided, playing safe, that it should be a starship. Visualise this, Malin. Choose the details and imprint them. Internalise this skin, this complex exo-skeleton. The ship is the journey. You are the ship, and you are with your crew, inside the ship—

'Conditions for supporting *human* life?' wondered Caterina. 'Is that necessary? Why not a completely new body and chemistry?'

'Maybe it could be done,' said Malin. 'Not easily. We unravel S from P by mathematical tricks in the lab, but consciousness and embodiment evolved together. They're inextricable, far as we can tell.'

'So on the other side, it's the real me, who I always was?'

'Yeah, I suppose.'

They had lain down like prospectors, in the Buonarotti couches in the transit chamber: and they had 'woken up' on board. Malin remembered the transition, vaguely as a dream, but she'd forgotten it was real. Reality was the ship, the saloon, their cabins; the subliminal hum of the great engines. Malin's desk of instruments, the headset that fastened on her cranium, sending ethereal filaments deep into her brain. She was the Navigator.

Caterina, of course, was the captain.

They lived together, playing games, preparing food, talking away the long idle hours, as they crossed the boundless ocean of information—

'My name isn't really Skodlodowska,' Cat confessed.

'I didn't think it was!'

'I liked you straight away, Mal, because you're so *normal*, except kind of unisex. I'm sorry, but I find bodymods unnatural and repulsive—'

Oh yeah?, thought Malin: but she understood. Caterina hadn't chosen her genemods. She had been compelled, by pressures no Reformer could understand, to make herself into a beautiful, risk-loving woman.

'My *thoughts* are very perverse,' she said, solemnly.

Caterina snorted. They giggled together: and Malin shyly reached out to take the captain's hand.

A shipboard romance, what could be more natural? What could be more likely to anchor them in the faux-reality, and keep them safe? Dr. Fortune had warned them that they would be scared, that what was 'really happening' was utterly terrifying; and it would bleed through. But what frightened them most, even in the closing phase, when Malin never left her desk, and the starship, rocked by soundless thunders, seemed to be trying to fall apart, was the fear that they would be enemies again, on the other side.

Landfall was like waking. Malin was lying on what seemed to be a mudbank, among beds of reeds as tall as trees. The air smelt marshy, acrid. She turned on her side, she and Cat smiled at each other, rueful and uncertain.

They got to their feet, and stared at each other.

Skodlodowska's beautiful white scientist-suit was somewhat altered: wider across the shoulders, flat in the chest, narrow in the hips. Malin wore her ordinary station jumper, a little ragged at the wrist and ankle cuffs.

'Oh my God,' gasped Malin. 'We made it!'

'I'm a *man*,' whispered Caterina, in tones of horror.

'Yeah, and I'm a woman. Shame, I always hoped I was an intersex in a woman's body, deep down. It's much *cooler* to be an inter! But hey, nobody's perfect. Cat, pay attention, we're here, we did it!'

Malin had started skipping about, wildly excited.

'I thought breaking the barrier would give me my *true* body—'

'Oh for God's sake, come on! We've done it! The repeatable experiment! Interstellar scheduled flights start here!'

Four slender bipedal figures had appeared, beyond a gleaming channel that didn't quite look like water. Scanty golden fur covered their arms and shoulders, longer fur was trained and dressed into curls in front of their ears, and they wore clothing. They kept their distance, murmuring to each other.

In that moment, still in the penumbra of the collision, Malin saw the future. She knew that she would be the first Navigator, carrying unprepared minds safely through the unreal ocean. She would see the Buonarotti Transit become a network, trained crews an elite, and these weird voyages frequent; though never routine. She saw, with a pang of loss, that the strangeness of the universe was her birthright: but there was another world, of brittle illusions and imaginary limits, that was forever beyond her reach.

But Caterina was shaking fit to tear herself apart, and Malin suddenly realized that what had happened to the Lost could *easily* happen again, to the two of them. Quickly, rebound. Set the controls, the mental switches.

Return.

Donovan Sent Us

GENE WOLFE

Gene Wolfe lives in Barrington, Illinois. He is one of the genre's most widely respected writers about whom much praise has been written. Much of his finest shorter fiction was collected this year in The Best of Gene Wolfe *(2009). Perhaps the writer who has praised him best is Neil Gaiman who said, "Gene Wolfe is the smartest, subtlest, most dangerous writer alive today, in genre or out of it. If you don't read this book you'll have missed out on something important and wonderful and all the cool people will laugh at you." His new fantasy novel,* The Sorcerer's House, *will be published in 2010. His previous novel, Lovecraftian SF, was* An Evil Guest *(2008). A new SF novel is coming in 2011. But meanwhile, Wolfe continues to write excellent short fiction, adding to his already substantial body of influential work.*

"Donovan Sent Us" appeared in Other Earths, *edited by Nick Gevers, an alternate history anthology containing a number of first-rate stories. In Wolfe's story, set in the World War II era and in the tradition of Philip K. Dick's* Man in the High Castle—*or perhaps in this case more like Philip Roth's* The Plot Against America—*Germany won but has not taken over the U.S. And so "Wild Bill" Donovan sends an agent to German-occupied England to rescue a very significant person. This is a story full of unpleasant political surprises, and more.*

The plane was a JU 88 with all the proper markings, and only God knew where Donovan had gotten it. "We're over London," the man known as Paul Potter murmured. Crouching, he peered across the pilot's shoulder.

Baldur von Steigerwald (he was training himself to think of himself as that) was crouching as well. "I'm surprised there aren't more lights," he said.

"That's the Thames." Potter pointed. Far below, starlight—only starlight—gleamed on water. "Over there's where the Tower used to be." He pointed again.

"You think they might keep him there?"

"They couldn't," Potter said. "It's been blown all to hell."

Von Steigerwald said nothing.

"All London's been blown to hell. England stood alone against Germany—and England was crushed."

"The truth is awkward, Herr Potter," von Steigerwald said. "Pretty often, too awkward."

"Are you calling me a liar?"

Listening mostly to the steady throbbing of the engines, von Steigerwald shrugged.

"A damned bloody Kraut, and you call me a liar."

"I'm just another American," von Steigerwald said. "Are you?"

"We're not supposed to talk about this."

Von Steigerwald shrugged again. "You began it, *mein herr.* Here's the awkward truth. You can deny it if you want to. England, Scotland, Wales, Australia, New Zealand, India,

Burma, and Northern Ireland stood—alone if you like—against Germany, Italy, Austria, and Vichy. They lost, and England was crushed. Scotland and Wales were hit almost as hard. Am I wrong?"

The JU 88 began a slow bank as Potter said, "Franco joined Germany at the end."

Von Steigerwald nodded. "You're right." He had not forgotten it, but he added, "I forgot that."

"Spain didn't bring down the house," Potter conceded.

"Get back by the doors," the pilot called over his shoulder. "Jump as soon as they're open all the way."

"You're really English, aren't you?" von Steigerwald whispered as they trotted back toward the bomb-bay doors. "You're an English Jew."

Quite properly, Potter ignored the question. "It was the Jews," he said as he watched the doors swing down. "If Roosevelt hadn't welcomed millions of European Jews into America, the American people wouldn't—" The rest was lost in the whistling wind.

It had not been millions, von Steigerwald reflected before his chute opened. It opened, and the snap of its silk cords might have been the setting of a hook. A million and a half—something like that.

He came down in Battersea Park with his chute tangled in a tree. When at last he was able to cut himself free, he knotted ornamental stones into it and threw it into the Thames. His jump suit followed it, weighted with one more. As it sunk, he paused to sniff the reek of rotting corpses—paused and shrugged.

Two of the best tailors in America had done everything possible to provide him with a black *Schutzstaffel* uniform that would look perfectly pressed after being worn under a jump suit. Shivering in the wind, he smoothed it as much as he could and got out his black leather trench coat. The black uniform cap snapped itself into shape the moment he took it out, thanks to a spring-wire skeleton. He hid the bag that had held both in some overgrown shrubbery.

The Luger in his gleaming black holster had kept its loaded magazine in place and was on safe. He paused in a moonlit clearing to admire its ivory grips and the inlaid, red-framed, black swastikas.

There seemed to be no traffic left in Battersea these days. Not at night, at least, and not even for a handsome young S.S. officer. A staff car would have been perfect, but even an army truck might do the trick.

There was nothing.

Hunched against the wind, he began to walk. The Thames bridges destroyed by the blitz had been replaced with pontoon bridges by the German Army—so his briefer had said. There would be sentries at the bridges, and those sentries might or might not know. If they did not—

Something coming! He stepped out into the road, drew his Luger, and waved both arms.

A little Morris skidded to a stop in front of him. Its front window was open, and he peered inside. "So. Ein taxi dis is? You vill carry me, ja?"

The driver shook his head vehemently. "No, gov'nor. I mean, yes, gov'nor. I'll take you anywhere you want to go, gov'nor, but it's not a cab."

"Ein two-vay radio you haff, drifer."

The driver seemed to have heard nothing.

"But no license you are haffing." Von Steigerwald chuckled evilly. "You like money, doh. Ja? I haf it. Goot occupation pounds, ja? Marks, also." He opened a rear door and slid onto the seat, only slightly impeded by his leather coat. "Where important prisoners are, you take me." He sat back. "*Macht schnell!*"

The Morris lurched forward. "Quick as a wink, gov'nor. Where is it?"

"You know, drifer." Von Steigerwald summoned all of his not inconsiderable acting ability to make his chuckle that of a Prussian sadist, and succeeded well enough that the driver's shoulders hunched. "De taxi drifers? Dey know eferyding, everywhere. Make no more troubles vor me. I vill not punish you for knowing."

"I dunno, gov'nor, and that's the honest."

Von Steigerwald's Luger was still in his right hand. Leaning forward once more, he pressed its muzzle to the driver's head and pushed off the safety. "I vill not shoot now, drifer. Not now, you are too fast drifing, ja? Ve wreck. Soon you must stop, doh. Ja? Traffic or anodder reason. Den your prain ist all ofer de vindshield."

"G-gov'nor . . ."

"Ja?"

"My family. Timmy's only three, gov'nor."

"Longer dan you he lifs, I hope."

The Morris slowed. "The bridge, gov'nor. There's a barricade. Soldiers with guns. I'll have to stop."

"You vill not haf to start again, English pig."

"I'm takin' you there. Only I'll have to stop for 'em."

"You take me?"

"Right, gov'nor. The best I know."

"Den vhy should I shoot?" Flicking the safety on, von Steigerwald holstered his Luger.

The Morris ground to a stop before the barricade. Seeing him in the rear seat, two gray-clad soldiers snapped to attention and saluted.

He rolled down a rear window and (in flawless German) asked the corporal who had just saluted whether he wished to examine his papers, adding that he was in a hurry.

Hastily the corporal replied that the *standartenführer* might proceed at once, the barricade was raised, and the Morris lurched ahead as before.

"Vhere is dis you take me, drifer?"

"I hope you're goin' to believe me, gov'nor." The driver sounded painfully sincere. "I'm takin' you the best I know."

"So? To vhere?"

"Tube station gov'nor. The trains don't run anymore."

"Of dis I am avare."

The driver glanced over his shoulder. "If I tell you I don't know, you won't believe me, gov'nor. I don't, just the same. What I think is that they're keeping them down there."

Von Steigerwald rubbed his jaw. Did real Prussians ever do that? The driver would not know, so it hardly mattered. "Vhy you t'ink dis, drifer?"

"I've seen army trucks unloading at this station, gov'nor. Cars park there and Jerry—I mean German—officers get out of them. The driver waits, so they're not going to another station, are they?" As the little Morris slowed and stopped, the driver added, " 'Course, they're not there now. It's too late."

"You haf no license vor dis taxi," von Steigerwald said. His tone was conversational. "A drifer's license you haf, doh. Gif dat to me."

"Gov'nor . . ."

"Must I shoot? Better I should spare you, drifer. I vill haf use vor you. Gif it to me."

"If I don't have that, gov'nor . . ."

"Anoder you vould get. Hand it ofer."

Reluctantly, the driver did.

"Goot. Now I gif someding." Von Steigerwald held up a bill. "You see dis vellow? Herr Himmler? He is our *Reichsführer*. Dere are numbers, besides. Dos you see also, drifer?"

The driver nodded. "Fifty quid. I can't change it, gov'nor."

"I keep your license, dis you keep. Here you vait. Ven I come out—" Von Steigerwald opened the rear door of the Morris. "You get back de license and anodder of dese."

As he descended the steps of the underground station, he wondered whether the driver really would. It would probably depend, he decided, on whether the driver realized that the fifty-pound occupation note was counterfeit.

To left and right, soiled and often defaced posters exhorted Englishmen and Englishwomen to give their all to win a war that was now lost. In one, an aproned housewife appeared to be firing a rolling pin. Yet there were lights—bright electric lights—in the station below.

It had been partitioned into offices with salvaged wood. Each cubicle was furnished with a salvaged door, and every door was shut. Gray-uniformed soldiers snapped to attention as von Steigerwald reached the bottom of the stair and demanded to see their commandant.

He was not there, one soldier explained. Von Steigerwald ordered the soldier to fetch him, and the soldier sprinted up the stair.

* * *

When the commandant arrived, he looked tired and a trifle rumpled. Von Steigerwald did his best to salute so as to make it clear that an S.S. colonel outranked any mere general and proffered his orders, reflecting as he did that it might be possible for him to shoot the general and both sentries if the falsity of those orders was detected. Just possible, if he shot very fast indeed. Possible, but not at all likely. The burly sentry with the Schmeisser submachine gun first, the thin one who had run to get the commandant next. Last, the commandant himself. If—

The commandant returned his orders, saying that *Herr* Churchill was not at his facility.

Sharply, von Steigerwald declared that he had been told otherwise.

The commandant shook his head and repeated politely that Churchill was not there.

Where was he, then?

The commandant did not know.

Who would know?

The commandant shrugged.

The commandant was to return to bed. Von Steigerwald, who would report the entire affair to the *Reichsführer-SS*, intended to inspect the facility. His conclusions would be included in his report.

The commandant rose.

Von Steigerwald motioned for him to sit again. He, *Standartenführer* von Steigerwald, would guide his own tour.

He would not see everything if he did, the commandant insisted; even in explosive German, the commandant sounded defeated. Sergeant Lohr would show him around. Sergeant Lohr had a flashlight.

Sergeant Lohr was the burly man with the submachine gun.

The prisoners were not held in the tunnels themselves, Lohr explained as he and von Steigerwald walked along a dark track, but in the rolling stock. There were toilets in the cars, which had been railway passenger cars before the war. If the *Standartenführer*—

"The cars were squirreled away down here to save them from German bombs," a new voice said. "The underground had been disabled, but there was sound trackage left, so why not? I take it you understand English, Colonel?"

In the near-darkness of the tunnel, the shadowy figure who had joined them was hardly more than that: a man of medium size, shabbily dressed in clothing too large for him.

"*Ja*," von Steigerwald replied. "I speak it vell. It is vor dis reason I vas sent. Und you are . . . ?"

For a moment, Lohr's flashlight played on the shabby man's face, an emaciated face whose determined jaw jutted above a wattled neck. "Lenny Spencer, Colonel. At your service."

Lohr grunted—or perhaps, growled.

"I'm a British employee, sir. A civilian employee of your army and, if I may be permitted a trifle of boldness, a man lent to you by His Majesty's occupation government. Far too many of my German friends speak little English. I interpret for them, sir. I run errands and do such humble work as my German friends judge beneath them. If I can be of any use to you, Colonel, I shall find my happiness in serving you."

Von Steigerwald stroked his chin. "Dis place you know, ja?"

The shabby man nodded. "Indeed I do, Colonel. Few, if I may say it, know the facility and its prisoners as well as I."

"Goot. Also you know Herr Churchill. He vas your leader in de var, so it must be so. He ist here. Dis I know. In Berlin he ist wanted, ja? I am to bring him. Show him to me. At vonce!"

The shabby man cowered. "Colonel, I cannot! Not with the best will in the world. He's gone."

"So?" Von Steigerwald's hand had crept to his Luger, lifting the shiny leather holster flap and resting on the ivory grip; he allowed it to remain there. "The truth you must tell now, *Herr* Schpencer. Odervise it goes hard vit you. He vas here?"

The shabby man nodded vigorously. "He was, Colonel. He was captured in a cellar in Notting Hill. So I've been informed, sir. He was brought here to recover from his wounds, or die."

"He ist dead? Dis you say? Vhy vas not dis reported?" Von

Steigerwald felt that he needed a riding crop—a black riding crop with which to tap his polished boots and slash people across the face. Donovan should have thought of it.

"I don't believe he is dead, Colonel, but he is no longer here." The shabby man addressed Sergeant Lohr in halting German, asking him to confirm that Churchill was no longer there.

Sullenly, Lohr declared that he had never been there.

"Neider vun I like," von Steigerwald declared, "but you, Schpencer, I like more petter. He vas here? You see dis?"

"Yes indeed, Colonel." The shabby man had to trot to keep pace with von Steigerwald's athletic strides. "He seemed much smaller here. Much less important than he had, you know, on my wireless. He was frightened, too. Very frightened, I would say, just as I would have been myself. Pathetic at times, really. Fearful of his own fear, sir. You know the Yanks' saying? I confess I found it ironic and somewhat amusing."

"He ist gone. Zo you say. Who it is dat takes him?"

"I can't tell you that, Colonel. I wasn't here when he was taken away." The shabby man's tone was properly apologetic. "Sergeant Lohr would know."

Von Steigerwald asked Lohr, and Lohr insisted that Churchill had never been held in the facility.

This man, von Steigerwald pointed out, says otherwise.

This man, Lohr predicted, would die very soon.

Von Steigerwald's laughter echoed in the empty tunnel. "He vill shoot you, Schpencer. Better you should go to de camps, ja? Der, you might lif. A Chew you are? Say dis und I vill arrange it."

"I'd never lie to you, Colonel."

"Den tell me vhere dese cars are vhere de prisoners stay. Already ve valk far."

"Just around that bend, Colonel." The shabby man pointed, and it seemed to von Steigerwald—briefly—that there had been a distinct bulge under his coat, a hand's breadth above his waist. Whatever that bulge might be, it had been an inch or two to the left of the presumed location of the shabby man's shirt buttons.

Lohr muttered something, in which von Steigerwald caught "*Riecht wie höllisches . . .*" Von Steigerwald sniffed.

"It's the WCs," the shabby man explained. "They empty onto the tracks. The commandant had the prison cars moved down here to spare our headquarters."

"In de S.S.," von Steigerwald told him, "we haf de prisoners clean it up. Dey eat it."

"No doubt we would." The shabby man shrugged. "One becomes accustomed to the odor in time."

"I vill not. So long as dat I vill not pee here." Von Steigerwald caught sight of the stationary railroad cars as the three of them rounded the curve in the tunnel. "Every prisoner you show to me, ja? Many times dis man Churchill I haf seen in pictures. I vill know him."

Lohr muttered something unintelligible.

Von Steigerwald rounded on him, demanding that he repeat it.

Lohr backed hurriedly away as von Steigerwald advanced shouting.

The shabby man tapped von Steigerwald's shoulder. "May I interpret, Colonel? He says—"

"*Nein!* Himself, he tells me." A competent actor, von Steigerwald shook with apparent rage.

"He said—well, it doesn't really matter now, does it? There he goes, back to headquarters."

Von Steigerwald studied the fleeing sergeant's back. "Ist goot. Him I do not like."

"Nor I." The shabby man set off in the opposite direction, toward the prison cars. "May I suggest, Colonel, that we begin at the car in which Churchill was held? It is the most distant of the eight. I can show you where we had him, and from there we can work our way back."

"Stop!" Von Steigerwald's Luger was pointed at the shabby man's back. "Up with your hands, Lenny Spencer."

The shabby man did. "You're not German."

"Walk toward that car, slowly. If you walk fast, go for that gun under your coat, or even try to turn around, I'll kill you."

Twenty halting steps brought the shabby man to the

nearest coach. Von Steigerwald made him lean against it, hands raised. "Your feet are too close," he rasped when the shabby man was otherwise in position. "Move them back. Farther!"

"You might be English," the shabby man said; his tone was conversational. "Might be, but I doubt it. Canadian?"

"American."

The shabby man sighed. "That is exactly as I feared."

"You think President Kuhn has sent me because he wants you for himself?" Von Steigerwald pushed the muzzle of his Luger against the nape of the shabby man's neck, not too hard.

"I do."

Von Steigerwald's left hand jerked back the shabby man's coat and expertly extracted a large and rather old-fashioned pistol. "It would be out of the fire and into the frying pan for you, even if it were true."

"I must hope so."

"You can turn around and face me now, Mr. Churchill." Von Steigerwald stepped back, smiling. "Is this the Mauser you used at Omdurman?"

Churchill shook his head as he straightened his shabby coat. "That is long gone. I took the one you're holding from a man I killed. Killed today, I mean."

"A German?"

Churchill nodded. "The officer of the guard. He was inspecting us—inspecting me, at the time. I happened to say something that interested him, he stayed to talk, and I was able to surprise him. May I omit the details?"

"Until later. Yes. We have no time to talk. We're going back. I am still an S.S. officer. I still believe you to be an English traitor. I am borrowing you for a day or two—I require your service. They won't be able to prevent us without revealing that you escaped them." Von Steigerwald gave Churchill a smile that was charming and not at all cruel. "As you did yourself in speaking with me. They may shoot us. I think it's much more likely that they'll simply let us go, hoping I'll return you without ever learning your identity."

"And in America . . . ?"

"In America, Donovan wants you, not Kuhn. Not the Bund. Donovan knows you."

Slowly, Churchill nodded. "We met in . . . In forty-one, I think it was. Forty would've been an election year, and Roosevelt was already looking shaky in July—"

They were walking fast already, with Churchill a polite half-step behind; and von Steigerwald no longer listened.

Aboard the fishing boat he had found for them, Potter cleared away what little food remained and shut the door of the tiny cabin. "Our crew—the old man and his son—don't know who you are, Mr. Prime Minister. We'd prefer to keep it that way."

Churchill nodded.

"If you're comfortable . . . ?"

He glanced at his cigar. "I could wish for better, but I realize you did the best you could. It will be different in America, or so I hope."

Potter smiled. "It may even be different on the sub. I hope so, at least."

Churchill looked at von Steigerwald, who glanced at his watch. "Midnight. We rendezvous at three AM, if everything goes well."

Churchill grunted. "It never does."

"This went well." Potter was still smiling. "I know you two know everything, Mr. Prime Minister, but I don't. How did he get you out?"

Still in uniform, von Steigerwald straightened his tunic and brushed away an invisible speck of lint. "He got himself out, mostly. Killed an officer. He won't tell me how."

"Killing is a brutal business." Churchill shook his head. "Even with sword or gun. With one's hands . . . He trusted me. Or trusted my age, at least. Thought I could never overpower him, or that I would lack the will to try. If it was in my weakness he trusted, he was nearly right. It was, as Wellington said of a more significant victory, a near run thing. If it was in my fear, the captain mistook foe for friend. What had I to lose? I would have been put to death, and soon. Better to perish like a Briton."

He pulled back his shabby coat to show the Mauser. "Perhaps it was seeing this. His holster covered most of it, but I could see the grip. Quite distinctive. Once upon a time, eh? Once upon a time, long before either of you saw light, I was a dashing young cavalry officer. Seeing this, I remembered."

"The Germans have pressed every kind of pistol they can find into service," von Steigerwald explained. "Even Polish and French guns."

Churchill puffed his cigar and made a face. "What I wish to know is where I tripped up. Did you recognize me? The light was so bad, and I'd starved for so long, that I thought I could risk it. No cigar, eh? No bowler. Still wearing the clothes they took me in. So how did you know?"

"That you were Churchill? From your gun. I pulled it out of your waist band and thought, by god it's a broom-handle Mauser. Churchill used one of these fifty year ago. I'd had a briefing on you, and I'd been interested in the gun. You bought it in Cairo."

Churchill nodded.

"That was when it finally struck me that Spencer was your middle name. Your byline—I read some of your books and articles—was Winston S. Churchill."

"You didn't know about Leonard, then." Churchill looked around for an ashtray and, finding none, tapped the ash from his cigar into a pocket of his shabby coat. "In full, my name is Winston Leonard Spencer Churchill. I should have been more careful about my alias. I had to think very quickly, though, and the only others I could seize on just then were John Smith and George Brown. Either, I felt, would have been less than convincing."

Potter grinned. "Very."

"In my own defense, I thought I was dealing with a German officer." Churchill turned to von Steigerwald. "This isn't what I wanted to inquire about, however. How did you know I had been lying to you?"

"I wasn't certain until I realized you were the man I'd been sent to rescue. A couple of things made me suspicious, and when I saw the bulge of your gun butt—"

"What were they?"

"Once you said 'we' in speaking of the prisoners," von Steigerwald explained. "I said that the S.S. would make the prisoners eat their excrement, and you said, 'No doubt we would.' It sounded wrong, and when I thought about it, I realized that you couldn't have been what you said you were—an Englishman working for the Germans. If you had been, they would have made you clean under the cars. Why did you confirm that you had been a prisoner when the Germans were denying they had him?"

"Ignorance. I didn't know they were. I had walked for miles along those dark tracks, trying to find a way out. I couldn't. All the tunnels ended in rubble and earth."

"Flattened by bombs?" Potter asked.

Churchill nodded. "To get out, I was going to have to go out through the German headquarters, and I could think of no practical way of doing that. Then the colonel here came, plainly a visitor since he was S.S., not army, and because he had an escort. I hoped to attach myself to him, a knowledgeable, subservient Englishman who might inform on the commandant if he could be convinced it was safe. I would persuade him to take me with him, and when he did, I would be outside. Sergeant Lohr and any Germans in the headquarters would know who I was, of course. But if they were wise—if they spoke with the commandant first, certainly— they would let me go without a word. If they prevented me, the army would be blamed for my escape; but if they held their peace and let me go, they could report quite truthfully that I had been taken away by the S.S. With luck, they might even get the credit for my recapture later."

Potter said, "That won't happen."

"I've answered your questions, Mr. Potter." Churchill looked accusingly at his smoldering cigar and set it on the edge of the little table. "Now you must answer one or two for me. The colonel here has told me that I am not being taken to President Kuhn. It relieved my mind at the time and will relieve it further now, if you confirm it. What do you say?"

"That we want you, not Kuhn." By a gesture, Potter indicated von Steigerwald and himself. "Donovan sent us. We're from the O.S.S.—the Office of Strategic Services. Roosevelt set us up before he was voted out, and he put Colonel Donovan in charge. President Kuhn has found us useful."

Churchill looked thoughtful. "As you hope to find me."

"Exactly. Kuhn and his German-American Bund have been pro-German throughout the war, as you must know. America even sold Germany munitions."

Churchill nodded.

"But now Hitler's the master of Europe, and he's starting to look elsewhere. He has to keep his army busy, after all, and he needs new triumphs." Potter leaned forward, his thin face intense. "Roosevelt, who had been immensely popular just a year before, was removed from office because he opened America to European Jews—"

"Including you," von Steigerwald put in.

"Right, including me and thousands more like me. America was just recovering from the Depression, and people were terrified of us refugees and what we might do to the economy. Fritz Kuhn and his German-American Bund replaced the old, patriotic Republican Party that had freed the slaves. I'm sure that half the people who voted for Kuhn hoped he would send us back to Hitler."

Churchill said, "Which he has declined to do."

"Of course." Potter grinned. "Who would he protect America from if we were gone? He's getting shaky as it is."

Von Steigerwald cleared his throat. "It might be possible to persuade Roosevelt to come out of retirement. Potter here thinks that way. He may be right."

"Or at least to get Roosevelt to endorse some other Democrat," Potter said.

Churchill nodded. "I could suggest half a dozen. No doubt you could add a dozen more. But where do I come into all this? Donovan wants me, you say."

Potter nodded. "He does, but to understand where you come in, Mr. Prime Minister, you have to understand Donovan and his position. He was Roosevelt's man. Roosevelt appointed him, and he's done a wonderful job. The O.S.S. worked hard and selflessly for America when Roosevelt was president, and it's working hard and selflessly for America now that Kuhn and his gang are in the White House."

"Yet he would prefer Roosevelt." Churchill fished a fresh cigar from his pocket.

"We all would," Potter said. "Donovan doesn't think he'll do it—he's a sick man—but that's what all of us would like. We'd like America to go back to nineteen forty and correct the mistake she made then. Above all, we'd like the Bund out of power."

Rolling the cigar between his hands, Churchill nodded.

"But if and when it comes to a war between Hitler and Kuhn, we will be with Kuhn and our country."

"Right or wrong." Churchill smiled.

"Exactly."

Von Steigerwald cleared his throat again. "You're not American, Potter. You're a refugee—you said so. Where were you born?"

"In London," Potter snapped. "But I'm as American as you are. I'm a naturalized United States citizen."

"Thanks to Donovan, I'm sure."

Potter turned back to Churchill. "So far Kuhn hasn't interned us, much less returned us to the Germans. There are quite a few people whose advice and protests have prevented that. Donovan's one of them. We give America a pool of violently anti-Nazi people, many well-educated, who speak every European language. If you've been wondering why so many of us are in the O.S.S. you should understand now."

"I wasn't wondering," Churchill said mildly.

"War with Hitler looks inevitable." Potter paused scowling. "Once I told my native-born friend here that England had stood alone against the Axis. He corrected me. America really will stand alone. She won't have a friend in the world except the conquered peoples."

"Which is why we freed you," von Steigerwald added. "If Hitler can be kept busy trying to get a grip on his conquests—on Britain and France, particularly—he won't go after America. It will give President Kuhn time to persuade the die-hard Democrats that we must arm, and give him time to do it. We've taken Iceland, and we'll use it to beam your broadcasts to Britain. We're broadcasting to Occupied Norway already."

Frowning, Churchill returned the cigar to his pocket. "You want me to lead a British underground against the Huns."

"Exactly," Potter said. "To lead them from the safety of America, and to form a government in exile."

"Already I have led the British underground you hope for from London." Churchill was almost whispering. "From the danger of London." Abruptly his voice boomed, filling the tiny cabin. "From the ruins of London I have led the ruins of the British people against an enemy ten times stronger than they. They were a brave people once. Now their brave are dead."

"You," said Potter, "are as brave as any man known to history."

"I," said Churchill, "could not bring myself to take my own life, though I had sworn I would."

"You tried to kill yourself long ago," von Steigerwald reminded him, "in Africa."

"Correct." Churchill's eyes were far away. "I had a revolver. I put it to my temple and pulled the trigger. It would not fire. I pulled the trigger again. It would not fire. I pointed it out the window and pulled the trigger a third time, and it fired."

He chuckled softly. "This time I lacked the courage to pull the trigger at all. They snatched it from me and threw me down, and I knew I should have shot them instead. I would have killed one or two, the rest would have killed me, and it would have been over."

He turned to Potter. "What you propose—what my friend Donovan proposes—will not work. It cannot be done. Let me tell you instead what I can do and will do. Next year, I will run for president."

Von Steigerwald said, "Are you serious?"

"Never more so. I will run, and I will win."

For a moment, hope gleamed in Potter's eyes; but they were dull when he spoke. "You can't become president, Mr. Prime Minister. The president must be a native-born citizen. It's in the Constitution."

"I am native born," Churchill smiled, "and I shall become

a citizen, just as you have. It is a little-known fact, but my mother returned to her own country—to the American people she knew and loved so much—so that her son might be born there. I was born in . . ."

Churchill paused, considering. "In Boston, I think. It's a large place, with many births. My friend Donovan will find documentary proof of my nativity. He is a skilful finder of documents, from what I've heard."

"Oh, my God." Potter sounded as if he were praying. "Oh, my God!"

"Kuhn is a Hitler in the egg," Churchill told him. "The nest must be despoiled before the egg can hatch. I collected eggs as a boy. Many of us did. I'll collect this one. As I warned the British people—"

Von Steigerwald had pushed off the safety as his Luger cleared the holster. Churchill was still speaking when von Steigerwald shot him in the head.

"Heil Kuhn!" von Steigerwald muttered.

Potter leaped to his feet and froze, seeing only the faintly smoking muzzle aimed at his face.

"He dies for peace," von Steigerwald snapped. "He would have had America at war in a year. Now pick him up. Not like that! Get your hands under his arms. Drag him out on deck and get one of them to help you throw him overboard. They starved him. He can't be heavy."

As Potter fumbled with the latch of the cabin door, von Steigerwald wondered whether it would be necessary to shoot Potter as well.

Necessary or not, it would certainly be pleasant.

The Calculus Plague

MARISSA K. LINGEN

Marissa K. Lingen (www.marissalingen.com) *lives in Eagan, Minnesota. In 1999 she won the Asimov's Award for Undergraduate fiction (now called the Dell Magazines Award) and has been writing short stories ever since. She has been publishing stories in the genre since 2002. "My background was in physics," she says, "so I'm particularly pleased to have sold to* Nature, Nature Physics, *and* Analog, *but I also write fantasy—On* Spec *has published several of my hockey fantasy stories."*

"The Calculus Plague" was published in Analog. *Here, a biological scientist is experimenting with viruses on a college campus and makes a world-changing discovery. The story of the scientist who discovers something that transforms our understanding of the world is a standard of SF and an essential part of the genre's charm.*

The Calculus Plague came first. Almost no one took offense at it. In fact, it took a while for anyone to find out about it at all. No one had any reason to talk about a dim memory of their high school math teacher, whose face didn't seem familiar somehow, and what was her name again? His name? Well, what did it matter?

It wasn't until Dr. Leslie Baxter, an economics professor at the U, heard her four-year-old son ask, "What's Newton's Method, Mommy?" that anyone began to notice anything wrong. At first Leslie assumed that Nicholas's most recent babysitter had been talking about his calculus assignment over the phone when sitting for Nicholas, but when she confronted the young man, he admitted that he had taken part in a viral memory experiment that was aimed at teaching calculus through transmission of memories.

Young Nicholas Baxter was living proof that it did no good to remember something if you couldn't understand it to begin with. Leslie assured Nicholas that she would explain the math when he was older. Then she went to the faculty judicial board to discuss forming a committee to establish ethical guidelines for faculty participation in viral memory transfer research.

They were still deciding who would be on the committee— from which departments, in which proportions, and was Dr. So-and-so too junior for the responsibility? Was Prof. Such-and-such too senior to agree to take it on?—when the second wave hit.

174

"I know I have never taken George's seminar on Faulkner," said Leslie furiously. "Never! I hate Faulkner, and George wasn't on faculty anywhere I've studied."

"But what does it hurt to remember some kids sitting around talking about *The Sound and the Fury*, Les?" asked her friend and colleague Amy Pradhan.

"Easy for *you* to say. You didn't catch it."

Amy shrugged. "I don't think I'd be making a fuss if I had."

Leslie shook her head. "Don't take this wrong, but you don't even like it when people drop by your house without calling first. But somehow it'd be better if it was your head?"

"It's not like they can read your thoughts, Les."

"No, they can make my thoughts. And that's worse."

"They're not making you like Faulkner," said Amy. "I know someone else who caught it and loved Faulkner, and she doesn't hate it now. You can still respond as yourself."

"Mighty big of them, to let me respond as myself."

Amy grimaced. "Can we talk about something else, please?

"Okay, okay. How's Molly? Are you still seeing her?"

Amy blushed and the conversation moved on to friends and family, books and movies, campus gossip, and other things that had nothing to do with Leslie coming down with a stuffy nose and Faulkner memories.

The usual people wrote their editorials and letters to the editor, but most people could not bother themselves to get excited about a virally transmitted memory of a lecture on Faulkner. Even the Faulkner-haters in the English department shrugged and moved on. Leslie found herself alone in confronting the project head, Dr. Solada Srisai. Srisai was tidy in the way of women who have had to fight very hard and very quietly for what they have. The warm red of her suit went perfectly with the warm brown of her skin. Leslie felt tall and chilly and ridiculous.

"I don't think anyone will be hurt by knowing calculus, do you?" Solada murmured, when Leslie explained why she was there.

"You're a biologist," said Leslie. "You know how many

forms you have to fill out to do human experimentation. If I want to ask a dozen freshmen whether they'd buy a cookie for a dollar, I have to fill out forms."

"Our experimental subjects filled out their forms," said Solada. "The viruses fell slightly outside our predicted parameters and got transmitted to a few people close to the original test subjects and then a few people close to them. This is a problem we will remedy in future trials, I assure you."

A grad student with wire-rimmed glasses poked her head around the door. "Solada, we've got the people from the Empty Moon here."

"Start going over their parameters," said Solada. "I'll be done with this in a minute."

"Empty Moon?" asked Leslie.

"It's a new café," said Solada. "We've come to an agreement with them about marketing. Volunteers—who have all the *forms* filled out, Dr. Baxter—will be infected with positive memories of the food at the Empty Moon Café, and we'll track their reports of how often they eat there and what they order compared to what they remember."

"Don't you have an ethical problem with this?" Leslie demanded.

Solada shrugged. "Not everybody likes the same food. If they go to the Empty Moon and have a terrible sandwich or the service is slow, they'll figure their first memory was a fluke. They'll go somewhere else. Or if they're in the mood for Mexican, they'll go for Mexican. We'll make sure that this virus is far less mutative and virulent than the others—which were really not bad considering how colds usually spread on a college campus. Well within the error range one might expect."

"Not within the error range *I'd* expect," said Leslie. "I'll be conveying this to a faculty ethics committee, Dr. Srisai."

Solada shrugged and smiled dismissively. "You must do as your conscience dictates, of course."

The business at the Empty Moon Café was booming. Leslie told herself very firmly that her memory of the awesome endive salad she'd had there was a snare and a delusion; she stayed away even when Amy wanted to meet there for coffee.

No one else seemed to care when she tried to tell them about the newest marketing ploy.

A few weeks later, Leslie was doing the dishes while her husband put Nicholas to bed. Her doorbell rang three times in quick succession, and then there was a pounding on the door. Wiping her hands on the dishtowel, she went to answer it. Amy was standing on the doorstep, an ashen undertone to her dark skin.

"There's been—" Amy swallowed hard, and managed to get a strangled, "Oh, God," past her lips.

"Come in. Sit down. I'll get you tea. What's happened?"

"Tom Barras—he's—"

"Deep breaths," said Leslie, putting the kettle on.

"You know I've been one of the faculty advisors to the GLBT group on campus," said Amy. "There's been an attack. A member of the group—Tom Barras—a nice bi boy, civil engineering major—is in the hospital."

"What happened?"

"We don't know! I thought we were—I know gay-bashing still happens, but I thought we were better than that here." Leslie bit back a comment about illusions of the ivory tower. Her friend needed a listening ear, not a lecture. Amy got herself calmed down, gradually, and Leslie went to bed feeling faintly ill. She and her husband insisted on putting Amy's bike in the back of their car and driving her home, just in case.

The story of the assault came out gradually: Tom's attacker, Anthony Dorland, said he had previously been set upon behind Hogarth Hall by a group of men. One of them had groped him repeatedly, making suggestive personal comments, while the others looked on and laughed. "I couldn't do anything about it," Anthony told campus security in strangled tones. "I was alone. But then I was out last night, and I heard his voice. It was the same voice, I know it. I would know it anywhere. He was coming out of his meeting, and so I waited until he was alone. I don't care what he does with people who like it, but I'm not that way! He shouldn't force himself on people like that! It's not right! So I thought, well, let's see how you like it when you're all alone and someone jumps on you."

When campus security asked Dorland why he had not fought back immediately or reported the incident, he looked confused. "He was so much bigger than me, and he had all his friends—I don't know—I just felt like I couldn't. Like no one would believe me." Pressed for a time of incident, he said, "I don't know. A while ago. A few weeks ago, maybe? I don't know."

The police officers looked from one young man to the other. Tom was several inches shorter than Anthony and slightly built.

Tom returned to consciousness a day later, to the great relief of his family and friends, including Amy. A few days after that, the faculty started hearing rumors of other students who had experienced the same thing but could not say when it had happened. Some of them had roommates who said they didn't remember their roommate coming in beaten up or upset; others had roommates with identical memories—and identical sniffles.

Scores on calculus midterms shot up by an average of fifteen points.

Leslie noticed a few students wearing surgical masks on campus one morning. The next day it was a few more. She took Nicholas to get one at the campus bookstore and encountered Solada Srisai coming out with a bag. Without thinking, she grabbed Nicholas close to her.

"Mommy!" Nicholas protested.

"That false memory of sexual assault," Leslie hissed. "My son caught calculus. What would you have done if he'd caught danger and fear like that? What would you have done to keep him from having nightmares that a bunch of adult men were—" She looked down at Nicholas and chose her words carefully. "Were hurting him. Personally. What would you have done about that?"

"That one wasn't mine," said Solada.

"They are *all* yours," said Leslie. "The minute you taught

your grad students that it was okay to release these things without trials, without controls, without testing—the minute you taught them that it was okay to skip all that, because it was holding back progress, you earned all of this. *All of it*."

"Mommy," said Nicholas, and Leslie realized that her hands were shaking.

"Let me tell you what the alternative was," said Solada, steering Leslie and Nicholas towards a bench. "Do you want to know what my alternative was?"

"Another project completely?"

"Yes. Sure. Another project completely." Solada glared at her. "And do you know what *that* would mean? It would mean that the person who developed virally contagious memories would not have done so out in the open. You would never have heard about it. Your son wouldn't have been at risk for catching a memory of calculus—or, okay, a memory of sexual assault because an overzealous grad student decided it would be a good idea for potential rapists to know what it felt like.

"No. Your son would have been at risk for catching memories that told him that the Republican Party was the only one he could trust. Or that if he truly loved you, he would always trust exactly what the Democratic Party had to say. Or that our government would *never* fight a war without a darn good reason. Or that he should buy this cola, or drive this car, or wear those sneakers. Do you see what I mean? It was me now or a secret project two years from now."

"And that makes it okay?" said Leslie. "The fact that it could be worse?"

Solada leaned towards her on the bench; Leslie had calmed down enough not to pull Nicholas away. "If I blow the whistle on my own project, it looks like I'm trying to grab the spotlight; nobody pays any attention. But you! What are you doing? I counted on someone like you to kick up a fuss in the press. Faculty advisory committees? Official university censure? What is wrong with you? Start a blog to rant about it! Call reporters! Tell your students to tell their parents! The student paper is not enough. Rumors are not enough."

"You're saying you wanted me to—"

"You or someone like you. For God's sake, yes. Get the word out. Make sure everybody knows that this is something we can do. Make sure they ask themselves questions about how we're doing it." Solada shook her head. "I'm amazed it didn't happen before. I thought surely the Empty Moon thing would be the last straw for you. Or someone like you. And I never dreamed that one of my students would use it politically, the way I thought the big parties would.

"So be fast about it, Dr. Baxter. Be as loud as you can. I'm willing to be the wicked queen here. Better a wicked queen than an eminence grise."

And with that she was gone, leaving Leslie stunned and clinging to her son. Most of the media contacts she had were in the obscure economic press. Would it be best to call a national news magazine? The local newspaper or its big city neighbor? She'd never tried to break a story before. It had never been this important before.

"Mommy, did you take me here another time?" asked Nicholas.

Leslie's heart went into her throat.

"And Daddy was here, too, and you bought me hot chocolate?" he continued hopefully.

She relaxed. It was a real memory; they had come to the student union before Christmas. "I'll buy you hot chocolate again," she assured him, "and then we'll go over to my office and you can draw pictures. Mommy has some phone calls to make."

The Island

PETER WATTS

Peter Watts (www.rifters.com) lives in Toronto, Ontario. His debut novel (Starfish) was a New York Times Notable Book, while his most recent (Blindsight, 2006)—which, despite an unhealthy focus on space vampires, is a required text in such diverse undergraduate courses as "The Philosophy of Mind" and "Introduction to Neuropsychology"—made the final ballot for many awards, including the Hugo, winning exactly none of them. (It has, however, won multiple awards in Poland for some reason). This reflects a certain critical divide regarding Watts' work; his bipartite novel, Behemoth, was praised by Publishers Weekly as an "adrenaline-charged fusion of Clarke's The Deep Range and Gibson's Neuromancer" and "a major addition to 21st-century hard SF," while being decried by Kirkus as "utterly repellent" and "horrific porn." Watts embraces the truth of both views, although he does wish Behemoth had not tanked quite so badly. Both Watts and his cat have appeared in the prestigious journal Nature. Even if he avoids jail, he may by the time of this printing be banned from entering the United States.

"The Island" appeared in The New Space Opera 2, edited by Gardner Dozois and Jonathan Strahan, a really fine anthology of SF, perhaps the single best original anthology of longer SF stories of the year. This story is about a space voyage to see an astonishing and original sight. This hard SF is as good as it gets, and really disturbing, too.

You sent us out here. We do this for *you*: spin your webs and build your magic gateways, thread the needle's eye at sixty thousand kilometers a second. We never stop, never even dare to slow down, lest the light of your coming turn us to plasma. All so you can step from star to star without dirtying your feet in these endless, empty wastes *between*.

Is it really too much to ask, that you might talk to us now and then?

I know about evolution and engineering. I know how much you've changed. I've seen these portals give birth to gods and demons and things we can't begin to comprehend, things I can't believe were ever human; alien hitchikers, perhaps, riding the rails we've left behind. Alien conquerers.

Exterminators, perhaps.

But I've also seen those gates stay dark and empty until they faded from view. We've inferred diebacks and dark ages, civilizations burned to the ground and others rising from their ashes—and sometimes, afterwards, the things that come out look a little like the ships *we* might have built, back in the day. They speak to one another—radio, laser, carrier neutrinos—and sometimes their voices sound something like ours. There was a time we dared to hope that they really were like us, that the circle had come around again and closed on beings we could talk to. I've lost count of the times we tried to break the ice.

I've lost count of the eons since we gave up.

All these iterations fading behind us. All these hybrids

and posthumans and immortals, gods and catatonic cave-men trapped in magical chariots they can't begin to under-stand, and not one of them ever pointed a comm laser in our direction to say *Hey, how's it going?* or *Guess what? We cured Damascus Disease!* or even *Thanks, guys, keep up the good work!*

We're not some fucking cargo cult. We're the backbone of your goddamn empire. You wouldn't even be *out* here if it weren't for us.

And—and you're *our* children. Whatever you've become, you were once like this, like me. I believed in you once. There was a time, long ago, when I believed in this mission with all my heart.

Why have you forsaken us?

And so another build begins.

This time, I open my eyes to a familiar face I've never seen before: only a boy, early twenties perhaps, physiologi-cally. His face is a little lopsided, the cheekbone flatter on the left than the right. His ears are too big. He looks almost *natural*.

I haven't spoken for millennia. My voice comes out a whisper: "Who are you?" Not what I'm supposed to ask, I know. Not the first question *anyone* on *Eriophora* asks, after coming back.

"I'm yours," he says, and just like that, I'm a mother.

I want to let it sink in, but he doesn't give me the chance: "You weren't scheduled, but Chimp wants extra hands on deck. Next build's got a situation."

So the chimp is still in control. The chimp is always in control. The mission goes on.

"Situation?" I ask.

"Contact scenario, maybe."

I wonder when he was born. I wonder if he ever wondered about me, before now.

He doesn't tell me. He only says, "Sun up ahead. Half light-year. Chimp thinks, maybe it's talking to us. Any-how . . ." My—son shrugs. "No rush. Lotsa time."

I nod, but he hesitates. He's waiting for The Question, but I already see a kind of answer in his face. Our reinforcements were supposed to be *pristine*, built from perfect genes buried deep within *Eri*'s iron-basalt mantle, safe from the sleeting blueshift. And yet this boy has flaws. I see the damage in his face, I see those tiny flipped base-pairs resonating up from the microscopic and *bending* him just a little off-kilter. He looks like he grew up on a planet. He looks borne of parents who spent their whole lives hammered by raw sunlight.

How far out must we be by now, if even our own perfect building blocks have decayed so? How long has it taken us? How long have I been dead?

How long? It's the first thing everyone asks.

After all this time, I don't want to know.

He's alone at the tac Tank when I arrive on the bridge, his eyes full of icons and trajectories. Perhaps I see a little of me in there, too.

"I didn't get your name," I say, although I've looked it up on the manifest. We've barely been introduced and already I'm lying to him.

"Dix." He keeps his eyes on the Tank.

He's over ten thousand years old. Alive for maybe twenty of them. I wonder how much he knows, whom he's met during those sparse decades: does he know Ishmael or Connie? Does he know if Sanchez got over his brush with immortality?

I wonder, but I don't ask. There are rules.

I look around. "We're it?"

Dix nods. "For now. Bring back more if we need them. But . . ." His voice trails off.

"Yes?"

"Nothing."

I join him at the Tank. Diaphanous veils hang within like frozen, color-coded smoke. We're on the edge of a molecular dust cloud. Warm, semiorganic, lots of raw materials. Formaldehyde, ethylene glycol, the usual prebiotics. A good spot for a quick build. A red dwarf glowers dimly at the center of the Tank: the chimp has named it DHF428, for reasons I've long since forgotten to care about.

"So fill me in," I say.

His glance is impatient, even irritated. "You too?"

"What do you mean?"

"Like the others. On the other builds. Chimp can just squirt the specs, but they want to *talk* all the time."

Shit, his link's still active. He's *online*.

I force a smile. "Just a—a cultural tradition, I guess. We talk about a lot of things, it helps us—reconnect. After being down for so long."

"But it's *slow*," Dix complains.

He doesn't know. Why doesn't he know?

"We've got half a light-year," I point out. "There's some rush?"

The corner of his mouth twitches. "Vons went out on schedule." On cue, a cluster of violet pinpricks sparkle in the Tank, five trillion klicks ahead of us. "Still sucking dust mostly, but got lucky with a couple of big asteroids, and the refineries came online early. First components already extruded. Then Chimp sees these fluctuations in solar output—mainly infra, but extends into visible." The Tank blinks at us: the dwarf goes into time-lapse.

Sure enough, it's *flickering*.

"Non-random, I take it."

Dix inclines his head a little to the side, not quite nodding.

"Plot the time-series." I've never been able to break the habit of raising my voice, just a bit, when addressing the chimp. Obediently (*obediently*—now *there's* a laugh and a half), the AI wipes the spacescape and replaces it with

....

"Repeating sequence," Dix tells me. "Blips don't change, but spacing's a log-linear increase cycling every 92.5 corsecs. Each cycle starts at 13.2 clicks/corsec, degrades over time."

"No chance this could be natural? A little black hole wobbling around in the center of the star, something like that?"

Dix shakes his head, or something like that: a diagonal dip of the chin that somehow conveys the negative. "But way too simple to contain much info. Not like an actual conversation. More—well, a shout."

He's partly right. There may not be much information, but there's enough. *We're here. We're smart. We're powerful enough to hook a whole damn star up to a dimmer switch.*

Maybe not such a good spot for a build after all.

I purse my lips. "The sun's hailing us. That's what you're saying."

"Maybe. Hailing *someone*. But too simple for a rosetta signal. It's not an archive, can't self-extract. Not a bonferroni or fibonacci seq, not pi. Not even a multiplication table. Nothing to base a pidgin on."

Still. An intelligent signal.

"Need more info," Dix says, proving himself master of the blindingly obvious.

I nod. "The vons."

"Uh, what about them?"

"We set up an array. Use a bunch of bad eyes to fake a good one. It'd be faster than high-geeing an observatory from this end or retooling one of the on-site factories."

His eyes go wide. For a moment, he almost looks frightened for some reason. But the moment passes and he does that weird head-shake thing again. "Bleed too many resources away from the build, wouldn't it?"

"It would," the chimp agrees.

I suppress a snort. "If you're so worried about meeting our construction benchmarks, Chimp, factor in the potential risk posed by an intelligence powerful enough to control the energy output of an entire sun."

"I can't," it admits. "I don't have enough information."

"You don't have *any* information. About something that could probably stop this mission dead in its tracks if it wanted to. So maybe we should get some."

"Okay. Vons reassigned."

Confirmation glows from a convenient bulkhead, a complex sequence of dance instructions that *Eri*'s just fired into the void. Six months from now, a hundred self-replicating robots will waltz into a makeshift surveillance grid; four months after that, we might have something more than vacuum to debate in.

Dix eyes me as though I've just cast some kind of magic spell.

"It may run the ship," I tell him, "but it's pretty fucking stupid. Sometimes you've just got to spell things out."

He looks vaguely affronted, but there's no mistaking the surprise beneath. He didn't know that. He *didn't know*.

Who the hell's been raising him all this time? Whose problem is this?

Not mine.

"Call me in ten months," I say. "I'm going back to bed."

It's as though he never left. I climb back into the bridge and there he is, staring into tac. DHF428 fills the Tank, a swollen red orb that turns my son's face into a devil mask.

He spares me the briefest glance, eyes wide, fingers twitching as if electrified. "Vons don't see it."

I'm still a bit groggy from the thaw. "See wh—"

"The *sequence!*" His voice borders on panic. He sways back and forth, shifting his weight from foot to foot.

"Show me."

Tac splits down the middle. Cloned dwarves burn before me now, each perhaps twice the size of my fist. On the left, an *Eri*'s-eye view: DHF428 stutters as it did before, as it presumably has these past ten months. On the right, a compound-eye composite: an interferometry grid built by a myriad precisely spaced vons, their rudimentary eyes layered and parallaxed into something approaching high resolution. Contrast on both sides has been conveniently cranked up to highlight the dwarf's endless winking for merely human eyes.

Except that it's only winking from the left side of the display. On the right, 428 glowers steady as a standard candle.

"Chimp: any chance the grid just isn't sensitive enough to see the fluctuations?"

"No."

"Huh." I try to think of some reason it would lie about this.

"Doesn't make *sense*," my son complains.

"It does," I murmur, "if it's not the sun that's flickering."

"But *is* flickering—" He sucks his teeth. "You *see* it—wait, you mean something *behind* the vons? Between, between them and us?"

"Mmmm."

"Some kind of *filter.*" Dix relaxes a bit. "Wouldn't we've seen it, though? Wouldn't the vons've hit it going down?"

I put my voice back into ChimpComm mode. "What's the current field-of-view for *Eri*'s forward scope?"

"Eighteen mikes," the chimp reports. "At 428's range, the cone is 3.34 lightsecs across."

"Increase to a hundred lightsecs."

The *Eri*'s-eye partition swells, obliterating the dissenting viewpoint. For a moment, the sun fills the Tank again, paints the whole bridge crimson. Then it dwindles as if devoured from within.

I notice some fuzz in the display. "Can you clear that noise?"

"It's not noise," the chimp reports. "It's dust and molecular gas."

I blink. "What's the density?"

"Estimated hundred thousand atoms per cubic meter."

Two orders of magnitude too high, even for a nebula. "Why so heavy?" Surely we'd have detected any gravity well strong enough to keep *that* much material in the neighborhood.

"I don't know," the chimp says.

I get the queasy feeling that I might. "Set field-of-view to five hundred lightsecs. Peak false-color at near-infrared."

Space grows ominously murky in the Tank. The tiny sun at its center, thumbnail-sized now, glows with increased brilliance: an incandescent pearl in muddy water.

"A thousand lightsecs," I command.

"There," Dix whispers: real space reclaims the edges of the Tank, dark, clear, pristine. DHF428 nestles at the heart of a dim spherical shroud. You find those sometimes, discarded castoffs from companion stars whose convulsions spew gas and rads across lightyears. But 428 is no nova remnant. It's a *red dwarf*, placid, middle-aged. Unremarkable.

Except for the fact that it sits dead center of a tenuous gas bubble 1.4 AU's across. And for the fact that that bubble does not *attenuate* or *diffuse* or *fade* gradually into that good night. No, unless there is something seriously wrong with the display, this small, spherical nebula extends about three hundred and fifty lightsecs from its primary and then just *stops*, its boundary far more knife-edged than nature has any right to be.

For the first time in millennia, I miss my cortical pipe. It takes forever to saccade search terms onto the keyboard in my head, to get the answers I already know.

Numbers come back. "Chimp. I want false-color peaks at three hundred thirty-five, five hundred, and eight hundred nanometers."

The shroud around 428 lights up like a dragonfly's wing, like an iridescent soap bubble.

"It's *beautiful*," whispers my awestruck son.

"It's photosynthetic," I tell him.

Phaeophytin and eumelanin, according to spectro. There are even hints of some kind of lead-based Keipper pigment, soaking up X-rays in the picometer range. Chimp hypothesizes something called a *chromatophore*: branching cells with little aliquots of pigment inside, like particles of charcoal dust. Keep those particles clumped together and the cell's effectively transparent; spread them out through the cytoplasm and the whole structure *darkens*, dims whatever EM passes through from behind. Apparently there were animals back on Earth with cells like that. They could change color, pattern-match to their background, all sorts of things.

"So there's a membrane of—of *living tissue* around that star," I say, trying to wrap my head around the concept. "A, a meat balloon. Around the whole damn *star*."

"Yes," the chimp says.

"But that's—Jesus, how thick would it be?"

"No more than two millimeters. Probably less."

"How so?"

"If it was much thicker, it would be more obvious in the visible spectrum. It would have had a detectable effect on the von Neumanns when they hit it."

"That's assuming that its—cells, I guess—are like ours."

"The pigments are familiar; the rest might be too."

It can't be *too* familiar. Nothing like a conventional gene would last two seconds in that environment. Not to mention whatever miracle solvent that thing must use as anti-freeze . . .

"Okay, let's be conservative, then. Say, mean thickness of a millimeter. Assume a density of water at STP. How much mass in the whole thing?"

"1.4 yottagrams," Dix and the chimp reply, almost in unison.

"That's, uh . . ."

"Half the mass of Mercury," the chimp adds helpfully.

I whistle through my teeth. "And that's *one* organism?"

"I don't know yet."

"It's got organic pigments. Fuck, it's *talking*. It's intelligent."

"Most cyclic emanations from living sources are simple biorhythms," the chimp points out. "Not intelligent signals."

I ignore it and turn to Dix. "Assume it's a signal."

He frowns. "Chimp says—"

"*Assume.* Use your imagination."

I'm not getting through to him. He looks nervous.

He looks like that a lot, I realize.

"*If* someone were signaling you," I say, "*then* what would you do?"

"Signal . . ." Confusion on that face, and a fuzzy circuit closing somewhere ". . . back?"

My son is an idiot.

"And if the incoming signal takes the form of systematic changes in light intensity, how—"

"Use the BI lasers, alternated to pulse between seven hundred and three thousand nanometers. Can boost an interlaced signal into the exawatt range without compromising our fenders; gives over a thousand watts per square meter after diffraction. Way past detection threshold for anything that can sense thermal output from a red dwarf. And content doesn't matter if it's just a shout. Shout back. Test for echo."

Okay, so my son is an idiot *savant*.

And he still looks unhappy—"But Chimp, he says no real *information* there, right?"—and that whole other set of misgivings edges to the fore again: *he*.

Dix takes my silence for amnesia. "Too simple, remember? Simple click train."

I shake my head. There's more information in that signal than the chimp can imagine. There are so many things the chimp doesn't know. And the last thing I need is for this, this *child* to start deferring to it, to start looking to it as an equal, or, God forbid, a *mentor*.

Oh, it's smart enough to steer us between the stars. Smart enough to calculate sixty-digit primes in the blink of an eye. Even smart enough for a little crude improvisation should the crew go too far off-mission.

Not smart enough to know a distress call when it sees one.

"It's a deceleration curve," I tell them both. "It keeps *slowing down*. Over and over again. *That's* the message."

Stop. Stop. Stop. Stop.

And I think it's meant for no one but us.

We shout back. No reason not to. And now we die again, because what's the point of staying up late? Whether or not this vast entity harbors real intelligence, our echo won't reach it for ten million corsecs. Another seven million, at the earliest, before we receive any reply it might send.

Might as well hit the crypt in the meantime. Shut down all desires and misgivings, conserve whatever life I have left for moments that matter. Remove myself from this sparse tactical intelligence, from this wet-eyed pup watching me as though I'm some kind of sorcerer about to vanish in a puff of smoke. He opens his mouth to speak, and I turn away and hurry down to oblivion.

But I set my alarm to wake up alone.

I linger in the coffin for a while, grateful for small and ancient victories. The chimp's dead, blackened eye gazes down from the ceiling; in all these millions of years, nobody's scrubbed off the carbon scoring. It's a trophy of sorts, a memento from the early incendiary days of our Great Struggle.

There's still something—comforting, I guess—about that

blind, endless stare. I'm reluctant to venture out where the chimp's nerves have not been so thoroughly cauterized. Childish, I know. The damn thing already knows I'm up; it may be blind, deaf, and impotent in here, but there's no way to mask the power the crypt sucks in during a thaw. And it's not as though a bunch of club-weilding teleops are waiting to pounce on me the moment I step outside. These are the days of détente, after all. The struggle continues but the war has gone cold; we just go through the motions now, rattling our chains like an old married multiplet resigned to hating each other to the end of time.

After all the moves and countermoves, the truth is we need each other.

So I wash the rotten-egg stench from my hair and step into *Eri*'s silent cathedral hallways. Sure enough, the enemy waits in the darkness, turns the lights on as I approach, shuts them off behind me—but it does not break the silence.

Dix.

A strange one, that. Not that you'd expect anyone born and raised on *Eriophora* to be an archetype of mental health, but Dix doesn't even know what side he's on. He doesn't even seem to know he has to *choose* a side. It's almost as though he read the original mission statements and took them *seriously*, believed in the literal truth of the ancient scrolls: Mammals and Machinery, working together across the ages to explore the Universe! United! Strong! Forward the Frontier!

Rah.

Whoever raised him didn't do a great job. Not that I blame them; it can't have been much fun having a child underfoot during a build, and none of us were selected for our parenting skills. Even if bots changed the diapers and VR handled the infodumps, socializing a toddler couldn't have been anyone's idea of a good time. I'd have probably just chucked the little bastard out an airlock.

But even I would've brought him up to speed.

Something changed while I was away. Maybe the war's heated up again, entered some new phase. That twitchy kid is out of the loop for a reason. I wonder what it is.

I wonder if I care.

I arrive at my suite, treat myself to a gratuitous meal, jill off. Three hours after coming back to life, I'm relaxing in the starbow commons. "Chimp."

"You're up early," it says at last.

I am. Our answering shout hasn't even arrived at its destination yet. No real chance of new data for another two months, at least.

"Show me the forward feeds," I command.

DHF428 blinks at me from the center of the lounge: *Stop. Stop. Stop.*

Maybe. Or maybe the chimp's right, maybe it's pure physiology. Maybe this endless cycle carries no more intelligence than the beating of a heart.

But there's a pattern inside the pattern, some kind of *flicker* in the blink. It makes my brain itch.

"Slow the time-series," I command. "By a hundred."

It *is* a blink. DHF428's disk isn't darkening uniformly, it's *eclipsing*. As though a great eyelid were being drawn across the surface of the sun, from right to left.

"By a thousand."

Chromatophores, the chimp called them. But they're not all opening and closing at once. The darkness moves across the membrane in *waves*.

A word pops into my head: *latency*.

"Chimp. Those waves of pigment. How fast are they moving?"

"About fifty-nine thousand kilometers per second."

The speed of a passing thought.

And if this thing *does* think, it'll have logic gates, synapses—it's going to be a *net* of some kind. And if the net's big enough, there's an *I* in the middle of it. Just like me, just like Dix. Just like the chimp. (Which is why I educated myself on the subject, back in the early tumultuous days of our relationship. Know your enemy and all that.)

The thing about *I* is, it only exists within a tenth-of-a-second of all its parts. When we get spread too thin—when someone splits your brain down the middle, say, chops the fat pipe so the halves have to talk the long way around; when the neural architecture *diffuses* past some critical point and signals take just that much longer to pass from A to B—the system, well, *decoheres.* The two sides of your brain become different people with different tastes, different agendas, different senses of themselves.

I shatters into *we.*

It's not just a human rule, or a mammal rule, or even an Earthly one. It's a rule for any circuit that processes information, and it applies as much to the things we've yet to meet as it did to those we left behind.

Fifty-nine thousand kilometers per second, the chimp says. How far can the signal move through that membrane in a tenth of a corsec? How thinly does *I* spread itself across the heavens?

The flesh is huge, the flesh is inconceivable. But the spirit, the spirit is—

Shit.

"Chimp. Assuming the mean neuron density of a human brain, what's the synapse count on a circular sheet of neurons one millimeter thick with a diameter of five thousand eight hundred ninety-two kilometers?"

"Two times ten to the twenty-seventh."

I saccade the database for some perspective on a mind stretched across thirty million square kilometers: the equivalent of two quadrillion human brains.

Of course, whatever this thing uses for neurons have to be packed a lot less tightly than ours; we can see right through them, after all. Let's be superconservative, say it's only got a thousandth the computational density of a human brain. That's—

Okay, let's say it's only got a *ten*-thousandth the synaptic density, that's still—

A *hundred* thousandth. The merest mist of thinking meat. Any more conservative and I'd hypothesize it right out of existence.

Still twenty billion human brains.

Twenty *billion.*

I don't know how to feel about that. This is no mere alien. But I'm not quite ready to believe in gods.

* * *

I round the corner and run smack into Dix, standing like a golem in the middle of my living room. I jump about a meter straight up.

"What the hell are you doing here?"

He seems surprised by my reaction. "Wanted to—talk," he says after a moment.

"You *never* come into someone's home uninvited!"

He retreats a step, stammers: "Wanted, wanted—"

"To talk. And you do that in *public*. On the bridge, or in the commons, or—for that matter, you could just *comm* me."

He hesitates. "Said you—*wanted* face to face. You said, *cultural tradition.*"

I did, at that. But not *here*. This is *my* place, these are my *private quarters*. The lack of locks on these doors is a safety protocol, not an invitation to walk into my home and *lie in wait*, and stand there like part of the fucking *furniture* . . .

"Why are you even *up*?" I snarl. "We're not even supposed to come online for another two months."

"Asked Chimp to get me up when you did."

That fucking machine.

"Why are *you* up?" he asks, not leaving.

I sigh, defeated, and fall into a convenient pseudopod. "I just wanted to go over the preliminary data." The implicit *alone* should be obvious.

"Anything?"

Evidently it isn't. I decide to play along for a while. "Looks like we're talking to an, an island. Almost six thousand klicks across. That's the thinking part, anyway. The surrounding membrane's pretty much empty. I mean, it's all *alive*. It all photosynthesizes, or something like that. It eats, I guess. Not sure what."

"Molecular cloud," Dix says. "Organic compounds everywhere. Plus it's concentrating stuff inside the envelope."

I shrug. "Point is, there's a size limit for the brain, but it's *huge*, it's . . ."

"Unlikely," he murmurs, almost to himself.

I turn to look at him; the pseudopod reshapes itself around me. "What do you mean?"

"Island's twenty-eight million square kilometers? Whole sphere's seven quintillion. Island just happens to be between us and 428, that's—one in fifty billion odds."

"Go on."

He can't. "Uh, just . . . just *unlikely*."

I close my eyes. "How can you be smart enough to run those numbers in your head without missing a beat and stupid enough to miss the obvious conclusion?"

That panicked, slaughterhouse look again. "Don't—I'm not—"

"It *is* unlikely. It's *astronomically* unlikely that we just happen to be aiming at the one intelligent spot on a sphere one and a half AU's across. Which means . . ."

He says nothing. The perplexity in his face mocks me. I want to punch it.

But finally, the lights flicker on: "There's, uh, more than one island? Oh! A *lot* of islands!"

This creature is part of the crew. My life will almost certainly depend on him some day.

That is a very scary thought.

I try to set it aside for the moment. "There's probably a whole population of the things, sprinkled through the membrane like, like cysts I guess. The chimp doesn't know how many, but we're only picking up this one so far, so they might be pretty sparse."

There's a different kind of frown on his face now. "Why *Chimp*?"

"What do you mean?"

"Why call him Chimp?"

"We call it *the* chimp." Because the first step to humanizing something is to give it a name.

"Looked it up. Short for *chimpanzee*. Stupid animal."

"Actually, I think chimps were supposed to be pretty smart," I remember.

"Not like us. Couldn't even *talk*. Chimp can talk. *Way* smarter than those things. That name—it's an insult."

"What do you care?"

He just looks at me.

I spread my hands. "Okay, it's not a chimp. We just call it that because it's got roughly the same synapse count."

"So gave him a small brain, then complain that he's stupid all the time."

My patience is just about drained. "Do you have a point or are you just blowing CO_2 in—"

"Why not make him smarter?"

"Because you can never predict the behavior of a system more complex than you. And if you want a project to stay on track after you're gone, you don't hand the reins to anything that's guaranteed to develop its own agenda." Sweet smoking Jesus, you'd think *someone* would have told him about Ashby's Law.

"So they lobotomized him," Dix says after a moment.

"No. They didn't *turn* it stupid, they *built* it stupid."

"Maybe smarter than you think. You're so much smarter, got *your* agenda, how come *he's* still in control?"

"Don't flatter yourself," I say.

"What?"

I let a grim smile peek through. "You're only following orders from a bunch of other systems *way* more complex than you are." You've got to hand it to them, too; dead for stellar lifetimes and those damn project admins are *still* pulling the strings.

"I don't—*I'm* following?—"

"I'm sorry, dear." I smile sweetly at my idiot offspring. "I wasn't talking to you. I was talking to the thing that's making all those sounds come out of your mouth."

Dix turns whiter than my panties.

I drop all pretense. "What were you thinking, chimp? That you could send this sock-puppet to invade my home and I wouldn't notice?"

"Not—I'm not—it's *me*," Dix stammers. "*Me* talking."

"It's *coaching* you. Do you even know what 'lobotomised' *means*?" I shake my head, disgusted. "You think I've forgotten how the interface works just because we all burned ours out?" A caricature of surprise begins to form on his face. "Oh, don't even fucking *try*. You've been up for other builds, there's no way you couldn't have known. And you know we shut down our domestic links too, or you wouldn't even be sneaking in here. And there's nothing your lord and master can do about that because it *needs* us, and so we have reached what you might call an *accommodation*."

I am not shouting. My tone is icy, but my voice is dead level. And yet Dix almost *cringes* before me.

There is an opportunity here, I realize.

I thaw my voice a little. I speak gently: "You can do that too, you know. Burn out your link. I'll even let you come back here afterwards, if you still want to. Just to—talk. But not with that thing in your head."

There is panic in his face, and, against all expectation, it almost breaks my heart. *"Can't,"* he pleads. "How I *learn* things, how I *train*. The *mission* . . ."

I honestly don't know which of them is speaking, so I answer them both: "There is more than one way to carry out the mission. We have more than enough time to try them all. Dix is welcome to come back when he's alone."

They take a step towards me. Another. One hand, twitching, rises from their side as if to reach out, and there's something on that lopsided face that I can't quite recognize.

"But I'm your *son*," they say.

I don't even dignify it with a denial.

"Get out of my home."

A human periscope. The Trojan Dix. That's a new one.

The chimp's never tried such overt infiltration while we were up and about before. Usually, it waits until we're all undead before invading our territories. I imagine custom-made drones never seen by human eyes, cobbled together during the long dark eons between builds; I see them sniffing through drawers and peeking behind mirrors, strafing the bulkheads with X-rays and ultrasound, patiently searching *Eriophora*'s catacombs millimeter by endless millimeter for whatever secret messages we might be sending one another down through time.

There's no proof to speak of. We've left trip wires and telltales to alert us to intrusion after the fact, but there's never been any evidence they've been disturbed. Means nothing, of course. The chimp may be stupid, but it's also cunning, and a million years is more than enough time to iterate through every possibility using simpleminded brute force. Document every dust mote; commit your unspeakable acts; put everything back the way it was, afterward.

We're too smart to risk talking across the eons. No encrypted strategies, no long-distance love letters, no chatty postcards showing ancient vistas long lost in the redshift. We keep all that in our heads, where the enemy will never find it. The unspoken rule is that we do not speak, unless it is face to face.

Endless idiotic games. Sometimes I almost forget what we're squabbling over. It seems so trivial now, with an immortal in my sights.

Maybe that means nothing to you. Immortality must be ancient news to you. But I can't even imagine it, although I've outlived worlds. All I have are moments: two or three hundred years, to ration across the life span of a universe. I could bear witness to any point in time, or any hundred-thousand, if I slice my life thinly enough—but I will never see *everything*. I will never see even a fraction.

My life will end. I have to *choose*.

When you come to fully appreciate the deal you've made—ten or fifteen builds out, when the trade-off leaves the realm of mere *knowledge* and sinks deep as cancer into your bones—you become a miser. You can't help it. You ration out your waking moments to the barest minimum: just enough to manage the build, to plan your latest countermove against the chimp, just enough (if you haven't yet moved beyond the need for human contact) for sex and snuggles and a bit of warm mammalian comfort against the endless dark. And then you hurry back to the crypt, to hoard the remains of a human life span against the unwinding of the cosmos.

There's been time for education. Time for a hundred post-graduate degrees, thanks to the best caveman learning tech. I've never bothered. Why burn down my tiny candle for a litany of mere fact, fritter away my precious, endless, finite life? Only a fool would trade book-learning for a ringside view of the Cassiopeia Remnant, even if you *do* need false-color enhancement to see the fucking thing.

Now, though. Now, I want to *know.* This creature crying out across the gulf, massive as a moon, wide as a solar system, tenuous and fragile as an insect's wing: I'd gladly cash in some of my life to learn its secrets. How does it work? How can it even *live* here at the edge of absolute zero, much less think? What vast, unfathomable intellect must it possess, to see us coming from over half a lightyear away, to deduce the nature of our eyes and our instruments, to send a signal we can even *detect*, much less understand?

And what happens when we punch through it at a fifth the speed of light?

I call up the latest findings on my way to bed, and the answer hasn't changed: not much. The damn thing's already full of holes. Comets, asteroids, the usual protoplanetary junk careens through this system as it does through every other. Infra picks up diffuse pockets of slow outgassing here and there around the perimeter, where the soft vaporous vacuum of the interior bleeds into the harder stuff outside. Even if we were going to tear through the dead center of the thinking part, I can't imagine this vast creature feeling so much as a pinprick. At the speed we're going we'd be through and gone far too fast to overcome even the feeble inertia of a millimeter membrane.

And yet. *Stop. Stop. Stop.*

It's not us, of course. It's what we're building. The birth of a gate is a violent, painful thing, a spacetime rape that puts out almost as much gamma and X as a microquasar. Any meat within the white zone turns to ash in an instant, shielded or not. It's why *we* never slow down to take pictures.

One of the reasons, anyway.

We can't stop, of course. Even changing course isn't an option except by the barest increments. *Eri* soars like an eagle among the stars, but she steers like a pig on the short haul; tweak our heading by even a tenth of a degree, and you've got some serious damage at 20 percent light-speed.

Half a degree would tear us apart: the ship might torque onto the new heading, but the collapsed mass in her belly would keep right on going, rip through all this surrounding superstructure without even feeling it.

Even tame singularities get set in their ways. They do not take well to change.

We resurrect again, and the Island has changed its tune.

It gave up asking us to *stop stop stop* the moment our laser hit its leading edge. Now it's saying something else entirely: dark hyphens flow across its skin, arrows of pigment converging toward some offstage focus like spokes pointing toward the hub of a wheel. The bull's-eye itself is offstage and implicit, far removed from 428's bright backdrop, but it's easy enough to extrapolate to the point of convergence six light-secs to starboard. There's something else, too: a shadow, roughly circular, moving along one of the spokes like a bead running along a string. It too migrates to starboard, falls off the edge of the Island's makeshift display, is endlessly reborn at the same initial coordinates to repeat its journey.

Those coordinates: exactly where our current trajectory will punch through the membrane in another four months. A squinting God would be able to see the gnats and girders of ongoing construction on the other side, the great piecemeal torus of the Hawking Hoop already taking shape.

The message is so obvious that even Dix sees it. "Wants us to move the gate . . ." and there is something like confusion in his voice. "But how's it know we're *building* one?"

"The vons punctured it en route," the chimp points out. "It could have sensed that. It has photopigments. It can probably see."

"Probably sees better than we do," I say. Even something as simple as a pinhole camera gets hi-res fast if you stipple a bunch of them across thirty million square kilometers.

But Dix scrunches his face, unconvinced. "So sees a bunch of vons bumping around. Loose parts—not that much even *assembled* yet. How's it know we're building something *hot*?"

Because it is very, very smart, you stupid child. Is it so hard to believe that this, this—*organism* seems far too limiting a word—can just *imagine* how those half-built pieces fit together, glance at our sticks and stones and see exactly where this is going?

"Maybe's not the first gate it's seen," Dix suggests. "Think there's maybe another gate out here?"

I shake my head. "We'd have seen the lensing artifacts by now."

"You ever run into anyone before?"

"No." We have always been alone, through all these epochs. We have only ever run *away*.

And then always from our own children.

I crunch some numbers. "Hundred eighty-two days to insemination. If we move now, we've only got to tweak our bearing by a few mikes to redirect to the new coordinates. Well within the green. Angles get dicey the longer we wait, of course."

"We can't do that," the chimp says. "We would miss the gate by two million kilometers."

"Move the gate. Move the whole damn site. Move the refineries, move the factories, move the damn rocks. A couple hundred meters a second would be more than fast enough if we send the order now. We don't even have to suspend construction, we can keep building on the fly."

"Every one of those vectors widens the nested confidence limits of the build. It would increase the risk of error beyond allowable margins, for no payoff."

"And what about the fact that there's an intelligent being in our path?"

"I'm already allowing for the potential presence of intelligent alien life."

"Okay, first off, there's nothing *potential* about it. It's *right fucking there*. And on our current heading, we run the damn thing over."

"We're staying clear of all planetary bodies in Goldilocks orbits. We've seen no local evidence of spacefaring technology. The current location of the build meets all conservation criteria."

"That's because the people who drew up your criteria *never anticipated a live Dyson sphere!*" But I'm wasting my breath, and I know it. The chimp can run its equations a million times, but if there's nowhere to put the variable, what can it do?

There was a time, back before things turned ugly, when we had clearance to reprogram those parameters. Before we discovered that one of the things the admins *had* anticipated was mutiny.

I try another tack. "Consider the threat potential."

"There's no evidence of any."

"Look at the synapse estimate! That thing's got order of mag more processing power than the whole civilization that sent us out here. You think something can be that smart, live that long, without learning how to defend itself? We're assuming it's *asking* us to move the gate. What if that's not a *request?* What if it's just giving us the chance to back off before it takes matters into its own hands?"

"Doesn't *have* hands," Dix says from the other side of the Tank, and he's not even being flippant. He's just being so stupid I want to bash his face in.

I try to keep my voice level. "Maybe it doesn't *need* any."

"What could it do, *blink* us to death? No weapons. Doesn't even control the whole membrane. Signal propagation's too slow."

"We *don't know.* That's my *point.* We haven't even tried to find out. We're a goddamn road crew; our onsite presence is a bunch of construction vons press-ganged into scientific research. We can figure out some basic physical parameters, but we don't know how this thing thinks, what kind of natural defenses it might have—"

"What do you need to find out?" the chimp asks, the very voice of calm reason.

We can't find out! I want to scream. *We're stuck with what we've got! By the time the onsite vons could build what we need, we're already past the point of no return! You stupid fucking machine, we're on track to kill a being smarter than all of human history and you can't even be bothered to move our highway to the vacant lot next door?*

But of course if I say that, the Island's chances of survival go from low to zero. So I grasp at the only straw that remains: maybe the data we've got in hand is enough. If acquisition is off the table, maybe analysis will do.

"I need time," I say.

"Of course," the chimp tells me. "Take all the time you need."

The chimp is not content to kill this creature. The chimp has to spit on it as well.

Under the pretense of assisting in my research, it tries to *deconstruct* the island, break it apart and force it to conform to grubby earthbound precedents. It tells me about earthly bacteria that thrived at 1.5 million rads and laughed at hard vacuum. It shows me pictures of unkillable little tardigrades that could curl up and snooze on the edge of absolute zero, felt equally at home in deep ocean trenches and deeper space. Given time, opportunity, a boot off the planet, who knows how far those cute little invertebrates might have gone? Might they have survived the very death of the homeworld, clung together, grown somehow colonial?

What utter bullshit.

I learn what I can. I study the alchemy by which photosynthesis transforms light and gas and electrons into living tissue. I learn the physics of the solar wind that blows the bubble taut, calculate lower metabolic limits for a life form that filters organics from the ether. I marvel at the speed of this creature's thoughts: almost as fast as *Eri* flies, orders of mag faster than any mammalian nerve impulse. Some kind of organic superconductor perhaps, something that passes chilled electrons almost resistance-free out here in the freezing void.

I acquaint myself with phenotypic plasticity and sloppy fitness, that fortuitous evolutionary soft-focus that lets species exist in alien environments and express novel traits they never needed at home. Perhaps this is how a life form with no natural enemies could acquire teeth and claws and the willingness to use them. The Island's life hinges on its ability to kill us; I have to find *something* that makes it a threat.

But all I uncover is a growing suspicion that I am doomed to fail—for violence, I begin to see, is a *planetary* phenomenon.

Planets are the abusive parents of evolution. Their very surfaces promote warfare, concentrate resources into dense defensible patches that can be fought over. Gravity forces you to squander energy on vascular systems and skeletal support, stand endless watch against its endless sadistic campaign to squash you flat. Take one wrong step, off a perch too high, and all your pricey architecture shatters in an instant. And even if you beat those odds, cobble together some lumbering armored chassis to withstand the slow crawl onto land—how long before the world draws in some asteroid or comet to crash down from the heavens and reset your clock to zero? Is it any wonder we grew up believing life was a struggle, that zero-sum was God's own law and that the future belonged to those who crushed the competition?

The rules are so different out here. Most of space is *tranquil*: no diel or seasonal cycles, no ice ages or global tropics, no wild pendulum swings between hot and cold, calm and tempestuous. Life's precursors abound: on comets, clinging to asteroids, suffusing nebulae a hundred lightyears across. Molecular clouds glow with organic chemistry and life-giving radiation. Their vast, dusty wings grow warm with infrared, filter out the hard stuff, give rise to stellar nurseries that only some stunted refugee from the bottom of a gravity well could ever call *lethal*.

Darwin's an abstraction here, an irrelevant curiosity. This Island puts the lie to everything we were ever told about the machinery of life. Sun-powered, perfectly adapted, immortal, it won no struggle for survival: where are the predators, the competitors, the parasites? All of life around 428 is one vast continuum, one grand act of symbiosis. Nature here is not red in tooth and claw. Nature, out here, is the helping hand.

Lacking the capacity for violence, the Island has outlasted worlds. Unencumbered by technology, it has outthought civilizations. It is intelligent beyond our measure, and—

—and it is *benign*. It must be. I grow more certain of that with each passing hour. How can it even *conceive* of an enemy?

I think of the things I called it, before I knew better. *Meat balloon. Cyst.* Looking back, those words verge on blasphemy. I will not use them again.

Besides, there's another word that would fit better, if the chimp has its way: roadkill. And the longer I look, the more I fear that that hateful machine is right.

If the Island can defend itself, I sure as shit can't see how.

"*Eriophora*'s impossible, you know. Violates the laws of physics."

We're in one of the social alcoves off the ventral notochord, taking a break from the library. I have decided to start again from first principles. Dix eyes me with an understandable mix of confusion and mistrust; my claim is almost too stupid to deny.

"It's true," I assure him. "Takes way too much energy to accelerate a ship with *Eri*'s mass, especially at relativistic speeds. You'd need the energy output of a whole sun. People figured if we made it to the stars at all, we'd have to do it in ships maybe the size of your thumb. Crew them with virtual personalities downloaded onto chips."

That's too nonsensical even for Dix. "*Wrong.* Don't have mass, can't fall toward anything. *Eri* wouldn't even *work* if it was that small."

"But suppose you can't displace any of that mass. No wormholes, no Higgs conduits, nothing to throw your gravitational field in the direction of travel. Your center of mass just *sits* there in, well, the center of your mass."

A spastic Dixian head-shake. "*Do* have those things!"

"Sure we do. But for the longest time, we didn't *know* it."

His foot taps an agitated tattoo on the deck.

"It's the history of the species," I explain. "We think we've worked everything out, we think we've solved all the mysteries, and then someone finds some niggling little data point that doesn't fit the paradigm. Every time we try to paper over the crack, it gets bigger, and before you know it, our whole worldview unravels. It's happened time and again. One day, mass is a constraint; the next, it's a requirement. The things we think we know—they *change*, Dix. And we have to change with them."

"But—"

"The chimp can't change. The rules it's following are ten billion years old and it's got no fucking imagination—and really that's not anyone's fault, that's just people who didn't know how else to keep the mission stable across deep time. They wanted to keep the mission on track, so they built something that couldn't go off it; but they also knew that things *change*, and that's why *we're* out here, Dix. To deal with things the chimp can't."

"The alien," Dix says.

"The alien."

"Chimp deals with it just fine."

"How? By killing it?"

"Not our fault it's in the way. It's no threat—"

"I don't care whether it's a *threat* or not! It's alive, and it's intelligent, and killing it just to expand some alien empire—"

"*Human* empire. *Our* empire." Suddenly, Dix's hands have stopped twitching. Suddenly, he stands still as stone.

I snort. "What do *you* know about humans?"

"*Am* one."

"You're a fucking trilobite. You ever see what comes *out* of those gates once they're online?"

"Mostly nothing." He pauses, thinking back. "Couple of— ships once, maybe."

"Well, I've seen a lot more than that, and believe me, if those things were *ever* human, it was a passing phase."

"But—"

"Dix—" I take a deep breath, try to get back on message. "Look, it's not your fault. You've been getting all your info from a moron stuck on a rail. But we're not doing this for humanity, we're not doing it for Earth. Earth is *gone*, don't you understand that? The sun scorched it black a billion years after we left. Whatever we're working for, it— it won't even *talk* to us."

"Yeah? Then why do this? Why not just, just *quit*?"

He really doesn't know.

"We tried," I say.

"And?"

"And your *chimp* shut off our life support."

For once, he has nothing to say.

"It's a *machine*, Dix. Why can't you get that? It's *programmed*. It can't change."

"*We're* machines. Just built from different things. We're programmed. *We* change."

"Yeah? Last time I checked, you were sucking so hard on that thing's tit you couldn't even kill your cortical link."

"How I *learn*. No *reason* to change."

"How about acting like a damn *human* once in a while? How about developing a little rapport with the folks who might have to save your miserable life next time you go EVA? That enough of a *reason* for you? Because, I don't mind telling you, right now I don't trust you as far as I could throw the tac tank. I don't even know for sure who I'm talking to right now."

"*Not my fault.*" For the first time, I see something outside the usual gamut of fear, confusion, and simpleminded computation playing across his face. "That's *you*, that's *all* of you. You talk *sideways. Think* sideways. You all do, and it *hurts*." Something hardens in his face. "Didn't even need you online for this," he growls. "Didn't *want* you. Could have managed the whole build myself, *told* Chimp I could do it—"

"But the chimp thought you should wake me up anyway, and you always roll over for the chimp, don't you? Because the chimp always knows best, the chimp's your *boss*, the chimp's your fucking *god*. Which is why I have to get out of bed to nursemaid some idiot savant who can't even answer a hail without being led by the nose." Something clicks in the back of my mind, but I'm on a roll. "You want a *real* role model? You want something to look up to? Forget the chimp. Forget the mission. Look out the forward scope, why don't you? Look at what your precious chimp wants to run over because it happens to be in the way! That thing is better than any of us. It's smarter, it's peaceful, it doesn't wish us any harm at—"

"How can you know that? Can't know that!"

"No, *you* can't know that, because you're fucking *stunted*! Any normal caveman would see it in a second, but *you*—"

"That's crazy," Dix hisses at me. "*You're* crazy. You're *bad*."

"*I'm* bad!" Some distant part of me hears the giddy squeak in my voice, the borderline hysteria.

"For the mission." Dix turns his back and stalks away.

My hands are hurting. I look down, surprised: my fists are clenched so tightly that my nails cut into the flesh of my palms. It takes a real effort to open them again.

I almost remember how this feels. I used to feel this way all the time. Way back when everything *mattered*; before passion faded to ritual, before rage cooled to disdain. Before Sunday Ahzmundin, eternity's warrior, settled for heaping insults on stunted children.

We were incandescent back then. Parts of this ship are still scorched and uninhabitable, even now. I remember this feeling.

This is how it feels to be awake.

I am awake, and I am alone, and I am sick of being outnumbered by morons. There are rules and there are risks, and you don't wake the dead on a whim, but fuck it. I'm calling reinforcements.

Dix has got to have other parents, a father at least, he didn't get that Y chromo from me. I swallow my own disquiet and check the manifest; bring up the gene sequences; cross-reference.

Huh. Only one other parent: Kai. I wonder if that's just coincidence, or if the chimp drew too many conclusions from our torrid little fuckfest back in the Cyg Rift. Doesn't matter. He's as much yours as mine, Kai, time to step up to the plate, time to—

Oh shit. Oh no. Please no.

(There are rules. And there are risks.)

Three builds back, it says. Kai and Connie. Both of them. One airlock jammed, the next too far away along *Eri*'s hull, a hail-Mary emergency crawl between. They made it back inside but not before the blueshifted background cooked them in their suits. They kept breathing for hours afterward, talked and moved and cried as if they were still alive, while their insides broke down and bled out.

There were two others awake that shift, two others left to clean up the mess. Ishmael, and—

"Um, you said—"

"You fucker!" I leap up and hit my son hard in the face, ten seconds' heartbreak with ten million years' denial raging behind it. I feel teeth give way behind his lips. He goes over backward, eyes wide as telescopes, the blood already blooming on his mouth.

"Said I could come back—!" he squeals, scrambling backward along the deck.

"He was your fucking *father*! You *knew*, you were *there*! He died right in *front* of you and you didn't even *tell* me!"

"I— I—"

"Why didn't you tell me, you asshole? The chimp told you to lie, is that it? Did you—"

"Thought you knew!" he cries, "Why *wouldn't* you know?"

My rage vanishes like air through a breach. I sag back into the 'pod, face in hands.

"Right there in the log," he whimpers. "All along. Nobody hid it. How could you not know?"

"I did," I admit dully. "Or I— I mean . . ."

I mean I *didn't* know, but it's not a surprise, not really, not down deep. You just—stop looking, after a while.

There are *rules*.

"Never even *asked*," my son says softly. "How they were doing."

I raise my eyes. Dix regards me wide-eyed from across the room, backed up against the wall, too scared to risk bolting past me to the door. "What are you doing here?" I ask tiredly.

His voice catches. He has to try twice: "You said I could come back. If I burned out my link . . ."

"You burned out your link."

He gulps and nods. He wipes blood with the back of his hand.

"What did the chimp say about that?"

"He said—*it* said that it was okay," Dix says, in such a transparent attempt to suck up that I actually believe, in that instant, that he might really be on his own.

"So you asked its permission." He begins to nod, but I can see the tell in his face. "Don't bullshit me, Dix."

"He—actually suggested it."

"I see."

"So we could talk," Dix adds.

"What do you want to talk about?"

He looks at the floor and shrugs.

I stand and walk toward him. He tenses but I shake my head, spread my hands. "It's okay. It's okay." I lean back against the wall and slide down until I'm beside him on the deck.

We just sit there for a while.

"It's been so long," I say at last.

He looks at me, uncomprehending. What does *long* even mean, out here?

I try again. "They say there's no such thing as altruism, you know?"

His eyes blank for an instant, and grow panicky, and I know that he's just tried to ping his link for a definition and come up blank. So we *are* alone. "Altruism," I explain. "Unselfishness. Doing something that costs *you* but helps someone else." He seems to get it. "They say every selfless act ultimately comes down to manipulation or kin-selection or reciprocity or something, but they're wrong. I could—"

I close my eyes. This is harder than I expected.

"I could have been happy just *knowing* that Kai was okay, that Connie was happy. Even if it didn't benefit me one whit, even if it *cost* me, even if there was no chance I'd ever see either of them again. Almost any price would be worth it, just to know they were okay.

"Just to *believe* they were . . ."

So you haven't seen her for the past five builds. So he hasn't drawn your shift since Sagittarius. They're just sleeping. Maybe next time.

"So you don't check," Dix says slowly. Blood bubbles on his lower lip; he doesn't seem to notice.

"We don't check." Only I did, and now they're gone. They're both gone. Except for those little cannibalized nucleotides the chimp recycled into this defective and maladapted son of mine.

We're the only warm-blooded creatures for a thousand lightyears, and I am so very lonely.

"I'm sorry," I whisper, and lean forward, and lick the blood from his bruised and bloody lips.

Back on Earth—back when there *was* an Earth—there were these little animals called cats. I had one for a while. Sometimes I'd watch him sleep for hours: paws and whiskers and ears all twitching madly as he chased imaginary prey across whatever landscapes his sleeping brain conjured up.

My son looks like that when the chimp worms its way into his dreams.

It's almost too literal for metaphor: the cable runs into his head like some kind of parasite, feeding through old-fashioned fiberop now that the wireless option's been burned away. Or *force*-feeding, I suppose; the poison flows *into* Dix's head, not out of it.

I shouldn't be here. Didn't I just throw a tantrum over the violation of my own privacy? (Just. Twelve lightdays ago. Everything's relative.) And yet, I can see no privacy here for Dix to lose: no decorations on the walls, no artwork or hobbies, no wraparound console. The sex toys ubiquitous in every suite sit unused on their shelves; I'd have assumed he was on antilibinals if recent experience hadn't proven otherwise.

What am I doing? Is this some kind of perverted mothering instinct, some vestigial expression of a Pleistocene maternal subroutine? Am I that much of a robot, has my brain stem sent me here to guard my child?

To guard my *mate*?

Lover or larva, it hardly matters: his quarters are an empty shell, there's nothing of Dix in here. That's just his abandoned body lying there in the pseudopod, fingers twitching, eyes flickering beneath closed lids in vicarious response to wherever his mind has gone.

They don't know I'm here. The chimp doesn't know because we burned out its prying eyes a billion years ago, and my son doesn't know I'm here because—well, because for him, right now, there *is* no here.

What am I supposed to make of you, Dix? None of this makes sense. Even your body language looks like you grew it in a vat— but I'm far from the first human being you've seen. You grew up in good company, with people I *know*, people I trust. Trusted. How did you end up on the other side? How did they let you slip away?

And why didn't they warn me about you?

Yes, there are rules. There is the threat of enemy surveillance during long, dead nights, the threat of —other losses. But this is unprecedented. Surely someone could have left something, some clue buried in a metaphor too subtle for the simpleminded to decode . . .

I'd give a lot to tap into that pipe, to see what you're seeing now. Can't risk it, of course; I'd give myself away the moment I tried to sample anything except the basic baud, and—

—wait a second—

That baud rate's way too low. That's not even enough for hi-res graphics, let alone tactile and olfac. You're embedded in a wireframe world at best.

And yet, look at you go. The fingers, the eyes—like a cat, dreaming of mice and apple pies. Like *me*, replaying the long-lost oceans and mountaintops of Earth before I learned that living in the past was just another way of dying in the present. The bit rate says this is barely even a test pattern; the body says you're immersed in a whole other world. How has that machine tricked you into treating such thin gruel as a feast?

Why would it even want to? Data are better grasped when they *can* be grasped, and tasted, and heard; our brains are built for far richer nuance than splines and scatterplots. The driest technical briefings are more sensual than this. Why settle for stick figures when you can paint in oils and holograms?

Why does anyone simplify anything? To reduce the variable set. To manage the unmanageable.

Kai and Connie. Now *there* were a couple of tangled, un-manageable datasets. Before the accident. Before the scenario *simplified*.

Someone should have warned me about you, Dix.

Maybe someone tried.

And so it comes to pass that my son leaves the nest, encases himself in a beetle carapace, and goes walkabout. He is not alone; one of the chimp's teleops accompanies him out on *Eri*'s hull, lest he lose his footing and fall back into the starry past.

Maybe this will never be more than a drill, maybe this scenario—catastrophic control-systems failure, the chimp and its backups offline, all maintenance tasks suddenly thrown onto shoulders of flesh and blood—is a dress rehearsal for a crisis that never happens. But even the unlikeliest scenario approaches certainty over the life of a universe; so we go through the motions. We practice. We hold our breath and dip outside. We're on a tight deadline: even armored, moving at this speed, the blueshifted background rad would cook us in hours.

Worlds have lived and died since I last used the pickup in my suite. "Chimp."

"Here as always, Sunday." Smooth, and glib, and friendly. The easy rhythm of the practiced psychopath.

"I know what you're doing."

"I don't understand."

"You think I don't see what's going on? You're building the next release. You're getting too much grief from the old guard so you're starting from scratch with people who don't remember the old days. People you've, you've *simplified*."

The chimp says nothing. The drone's feed shows Dix clambering across a jumbled terrain of basalt and metal matrix composites.

"But you can't raise a human child, not on your own." I know it tried: there's no record of Dix anywhere on the crew manifest until his mid-teens, when he just *showed up* one day and nobody asked about it because nobody *ever* . . .

"Look what you've made of him. He's great at conditional

if/thens. Can't be beat on number-crunching and do loops. But he can't *think*. Can't make the simplest intuitive jumps. You're like one of those—" I remember an earthly myth, from the days when *reading* did not seem like such an obscene waste of life span—"one of those wolves, trying to raise a human child. You can teach him how to move around on hands and knees, you can teach him about pack dynamics, but you can't teach him how to walk on his hind legs or talk or be *human* because you're too *fucking stupid*, Chimp, and you finally realized it. And that's why you threw him at me. You think I can fix him for you."

I take a breath, and a gambit.

"But he's nothing to me. You understand? He's *worse* than nothing, he's a liability. He's a spy, he's a spastic waste of O_2. Give me one reason why I shouldn't just lock him out there until he cooks."

"You're his mother," the chimp says, because the chimp has read all about kin selection and is too stupid for nuance.

"You're an idiot."

"You love him."

"No." An icy lump forms in my chest. My mouth makes words; they come out measured and inflectionless. "I can't love anyone, you brain-dead machine. That's why I'm out here. Do you really think they'd gamble your precious neverending mission on little glass dolls that needed to bond?"

"You love him."

"I can kill him any time I want. And that's exactly what I'll do if you don't move the gate."

"I'd stop you," the chimp says mildly.

"That's easy enough. Just move the gate and we both get what we want. Or you can dig in your heels and try to reconcile your need for a mother's touch with my sworn intention of breaking the little fucker's neck. We've got a long trip ahead of us, Chimp. And you might find I'm not quite as easy to cut out of the equation as Kai and Connie."

"You cannot end the mission," it says, almost gently. "You tried that already."

"This isn't about ending the mission. This is only about slowing it down a little. Your optimal scenario's off the table. The only way that gate's going to get finished now is by saving the Island, or killing your prototype. Your call."

The cost-benefit's pretty simple. The chimp could solve it in an instant. But still it says nothing. The silence stretches. It's looking for some other option, I bet. It's trying to find a workaround. It's questioning the very premises of the scenario, trying to decide if I mean what I'm saying, if all its book-learning about mother love could really be so far off-base. Maybe it's plumbing historical intrafamilial murder rates, looking for a loophole. And there may be one, for all I know. But the chimp isn't me, it's a simpler system trying to figure out a smarter one, and that gives me the edge.

"You would owe me," it says at last.

I almost burst out laughing. *"What?"*

"Or I will tell Dixon that you threatened to kill him."

"Go ahead."

"You don't want him to know."

"I don't care whether he knows or not. What, you think he'll try and kill me back? You think I'll lose his *love*?" I linger on the last word, stretch it out to show how ludicrous it is.

"You'll lose his trust. You need to trust each other out here."

"Oh, right. *Trust*. The very fucking foundation of this mission!"

The chimp says nothing.

"For the sake of argument," I say, after a while, "suppose I go along with it. What would I *owe* you, exactly?"

"A favor," the chimp replies. "To be repaid in future."

My son floats innocently against the stars, his life in balance.

We sleep. The chimp makes grudging corrections to a myriad small trajectories. I set the alarm to wake me every couple of weeks, burn a little more of my candle in case the enemy tries to pull another fast one; but for now it seems to be behaving itself. DHF428 jumps toward us in the stop-motion increments of a life's moments, strung like beads along an infinite string. The factory floor slews to starboard in our sights: refineries, reservoirs, and nanofab plants, swarms of von Neumanns breeding and cannibalizing and recycling one another into shielding and circuitry, tugboats and spare parts. The very finest Cro Magnon technology mutates and metastasizes across the universe like armor-plated cancer.

And hanging like a curtain between *it* and *us* shimmers an iridescent life form, fragile and immortal and unthinkably alien, that reduces everything my species ever accomplished to mud and shit by the simple transcendent fact of its existence. I have never believed in gods, in universal good or absolute evil. I have only ever believed that there is what works and what doesn't. All the rest is smoke and mirrors, trickery to manipulate grunts like me.

But I believe in the Island, because I don't *have* to. It does not need to be taken on faith: it looms ahead of us, its existence an empirical fact. I will never know its mind, I will never know the details of its origin and evolution. But I can *see* it: massive, mind-boggling, so utterly inhuman that it can't *help* but be better than us, better than anything we could ever become.

I believe in the Island. I've gambled my own son to save its life. I would kill him to avenge its death.

I may yet.

In all these millions of wasted years, I have finally done something worthwhile.

Final approach.

Reticles within reticles line up before me, a mesmerizing infinite regress of bull's-eyes centering on target. Even now, mere minutes from ignition, distance reduces the unborn gate to invisibility. There will be no moment when the naked eye can trap our destination. We thread the needle far too quickly: it will be behind us before we know it.

Or, if our course corrections are off by even a hair—if our trillion-kilometer curve drifts by as much as a thousand meters—we will be dead. Before we know it.

Our instruments report that we are precisely on target. The chimp tells me that we are precisely on target. *Eriophora* falls forward, pulled endlessly through the void by her own magically displaced mass.

I turn to the drone's-eye view relayed from up ahead. It's a window into history—even now, there's a time-lag of several minutes—but past and present race closer to convergence with every corsec. The newly minted gate looms dark and ominous against the stars, a great gaping mouth built to devour reality itself. The vons, the refineries, the assembly lines: parked to the side in vertical columns, their jobs done, their usefulness outlived, their collateral annihilation imminent. I pity them, for some reason. I always do. I wish we could scoop them up and take them with us, reenlist them for the next build—but the rules of economics reach everywhere, and they say it's cheaper to use our tools once and throw them away.

A rule that the chimp seems to be taking more to heart than anyone expected.

At least we've spared the Island. I wish we could have stayed awhile. First contact with a truly alien intelligence, and what do we exchange? Traffic signals. What does the Island dwell upon, when not pleading for its life?

I thought of asking. I thought of waking myself when the time-lag dropped from prohibitive to merely inconvenient, of working out some pidgin that could encompass the truths and philosophies of a mind vaster than all humanity. What a childish fantasy. The Island exists too far beyond the grotesque Darwinian processes that shaped my own flesh. There can be no communion here, no meeting of minds.

Angels do not speak to ants.

Less than three minutes to ignition. I see light at the end of the tunnel. *Eri*'s incidental time machine barely looks into the past anymore; I could almost hold my breath across the whole span of seconds that *then* needs to overtake *now*. Still on target, according to all sources.

Tactical beeps at us.

"Getting a signal," Dix reports, and yes: in the heart of the Tank, the sun is flickering again. My heart leaps: does the angel speak to us after all? A thank-you, perhaps? A cure for heat death?

But—

"It's *ahead* of us," Dix murmurs, as sudden realization catches in my throat.

Two minutes.

"Miscalculated somehow," Dix whispers. "Didn't move the gate far enough."

"We did," I say. We moved it exactly as far as the Island told us to.

"*Still in front of us!* Look at the *sun!*"

"Look at the *signal*," I tell him.

Because it's nothing like the painstaking traffic signs we've followed over the past three trillion kilometers. It's almost— random, somehow. It's spur-of-the-moment, it's *panicky*. It's the sudden, startled cry of something caught utterly by surprise with mere seconds left to act. And even though I have never seen this pattern of dots and swirls before, I know exactly what it must be saying.

Stop. Stop. Stop. Stop.

We do not stop. There is no force in the universe that can even slow us down. Past equals present; *Eriophora* dives through the center of the gate in a nanosecond. The unimaginable mass of her cold black heart snags some distant dimension, drags it screaming to the here and now. The booted portal erupts behind us, blossoms into a great blinding corona, every wavelength lethal to every living thing. Our aft filters clamp down tight.

The scorching wavefront chases us into the darkness as it has a thousand times before. In time, as always, the birth pangs will subside. The worm hole will settle in its collar. And just maybe, we will still be close enough to glimpse some new transcendent monstrosity emerging from that magic doorway.

I wonder if you'll notice the corpse we left behind.

"Maybe we're missing something," Dix says.

"We miss almost everything," I tell him.

DHF428 shifts red behind us. Lensing artifacts wink in

our rearview; the gate has stabilized and the wormhole's online, blowing light and space and time in an iridescent bubble from its great metal mouth. We'll keep looking over our shoulders right up until we pass the Rayleigh Limit, far past the point it'll do any good.

So far, though, nothing's come out.

"Maybe our numbers were wrong," he says. "Maybe we made a mistake."

Our numbers were right. An hour doesn't pass when I don't check them again. The Island just had—enemies, I guess. Victims, anyway.

I was right about one thing, though. That fucker was *smart*. To see us coming, to figure out how to talk to us; to use us as a *weapon*, to turn a threat to its very existence into a, a . . .

I guess *flyswatter* is as good a word as any.

"Maybe there was a war," I mumble. "Maybe it wanted the real estate. Or maybe it was just some—family squabble."

"Maybe didn't *know*," Dix suggests. "Maybe thought those coordinates were empty."

Why would you think that? I wonder. *Why would you even care?* And then it dawns on me: he doesn't, not about the Island, anyway. No more than he ever did. He's not inventing these rosy alternatives for himself.

My son is trying to comfort me.

I don't need to be coddled, though. I was a fool: I let myself believe in life without conflict, in sentience without sin. For a little while, I dwelt in a dream world where life was unselfish and unmanipulative, where every living thing did not struggle to exist at the expense of other life. I deified that which I could not understand, when in the end it was all too easily understood.

But I'm better now.

It's over: another build, another benchmark, another irreplaceable slice of life that brings our task no closer to completion. It doesn't matter how successful we are. It doesn't matter how well we do our job. *Mission accomplished* is a meaningless phrase on *Eriophora*, an ironic oxymoron at best. There may one day be failure, but there is no finish line. We go on forever, crawling across the universe like ants, dragging your goddamned superhighway behind us.

I still have so much to learn.

At least my son is here to teach me.

One of Our Bastards Is Missing

PAUL CORNELL

Paul Cornell (www.paulcornell.com) is a writer of SF and fantasy for prose, comics, and television, who lives in Faringdon, Oxfordshire, England. He's written three episodes (two of them Hugo finalists) of the modern Doctor Who, *and many titles for Marvel Comics, including* Captain Britain and MI-13, *and is the creator of* Bernice Summerfield. *His novels are* Something More *(2001) and* British Summertime *(2002). He has published a dozen short stories, including the well-regarded "Catherine Drewe" in 2008, set in the same universe as this story. Well established as a comics and television writer, his prose fiction career is beginning to take off.*

"One of Our Bastards Is Missing," a story with an amazing opening paragraph, was published in The Solaris Book of Science Fiction 3, *edited by George Mann (apparently the last book in that distinguished original anthology series). It involves really complicated alternate universe intrigue featuring virtuality, the folding of space, and many other SF ideas.*

To get to Earth from the edge of the solar system, depending on the time of year and the position of the planets, you need to pass through at least Poland, Prussia, and Turkey, and you'd probably get stamps in your passport from a few of the other great powers. Then as you get closer to the world, you arrive at a point, in the continually shifting carriage space over the countries, where this complexity has to give way or fail. And so you arrive in the blissful lubrication of neutral orbital territory. From there it's especially clear that no country is whole unto itself. There are yearning gaps between parts of each state, as they stretch across the solar system. There is no congruent territory. The countries continue in balance with each other like a fine but eccentric mechanism, pent up, all that political energy dealt with through eternal circular motion.

The maps that represent this can be displayed on a screen, but they're much more suited to mental contemplation. They're beautiful. They're made to be beautiful, doing their own small part to see that their beauty never ends.

If you looked down on that world of countries, onto the pink of glorious old Greater Britain, that land of green squares and dark forest and carriage contrails, and then you naturally avoided looking directly at the golden splendor of London, your gaze might fall on the Thames valley. On the country houses and mansions and hunting estates that letter the river banks with the names of the great. On one particular estate: an enormous winged square of a house with its own grouse shooting horizons and mazes and herb gardens and markers that indicate it also sprawls into folded interior expanses.

Today that estate, seen from such a height, would be adorned with informational banners that could be seen from orbit, and tall pleasure cruisers could be observed, docked beside military boats on the river, and carriages of all kinds would be cluttering the gravel of its circular drives and swarming in the sky overhead. A detachment of Horse Guards could be spotted, stood at ready at the perimeter.

Today, you'd need much more than a passport to get inside that maze of information and privilege.

Because today was a royal wedding.

That vision from the point of view of someone looking down upon him was what was at the back of Hamilton's mind.

But now he was watching the Princess.

Her chestnut hair had been knotted high on her head, baring her neck, a fashion which Hamilton appreciated for its defiance of the French, and at an official function too, though that gesture wouldn't have been Liz's alone, but would have been calculated in the warrens of Whitehall. She wore white, which had made a smile come to Hamilton's lips when he'd first seen it in the Cathedral this morning. In this gigantic function room with its high arched ceiling, in which massed dignitaries and ambassadors and dress uniforms orbited from table to table, she was the sun about which everything turned. Even the King, in the far distance, at a table on a rise with old men from the rest of Europe, was no competition for his daughter this afternoon.

This was the reception, where Elizabeth, escorted by members of the Corps of Heralds, would carelessly and entirely precisely move from group to group, giving exactly the right amount of charm to every one of the great powers, briefed to keep the balance going as everyone like she and Hamilton did, every day.

Everyone like the two of them. That was a useless thought and he cuffed it aside.

Her gaze had settled on Hamilton's table precisely once. A little smile and then away again. As not approved by Whitehall. He'd tried to stop watching her after that. But his carefully random table, with diplomatic corps functionaries to his left and right, had left him cold. Hamilton had grown tired of pretending to be charming.

"It's a marriage of convenience," said a voice beside him.

It was Lord Carney. He was wearing open cuffs that bloomed from his silk sleeves, a big collar, and no tie. His long hair was unfastened. He had retained his rings.

Hamilton considered his reply for a moment, then opted for silence. He met Carney's gaze with a suggestion in his heart that surely his Lordship might find some other table to perch at, perhaps one where he had friends?

"What do you reckon?"

Hamilton stood, with the intention of walking away. But Carney stood too and stopped him just as they'd got out of earshot of the table. The man smelled like a Turkish sweet shop. He affected a mode of speech beneath his standing. "This is what I do. I probe, I provoke, I poke. And when I'm in the room, it's all too obvious when people are looking at someone else."

The broad grin stayed on his face.

Hamilton found a deserted table and sat down again, furious at himself.

Carney settled beside him, and gestured away from Princess Elizabeth, toward her new husband, with his neat beard and his row of medals on the breast of his Svenska Adelsfanan uniform. He was talking with the Papal ambassador, doubtless discussing getting Liz to Rome as soon as possible, for a great show to be made of this match between the Protestant and the Papist. If Prince Bertil was also pretending to be charming, Hamilton admitted that he was making a better job of it.

"Yeah, jammy fucker, my thoughts exactly. Still, I'm on a promise with a couple of members of his staff, so it's swings and roundabouts." Carney clicked his tongue and wagged his finger as a Swedish serving maid ran past, and she curtsied a quick smile at him. "I do understand, you know. All our relationships are informed by the balance. And the horror of it is that we all can conceive of a world where this isn't so."

Hamilton pursed his lips and chose his next words carefully. "Is that why you are how you are, your Lordship?"

"'Course it is. Maids, lady companions, youngest sisters, it's a catalog of incompleteness. I'm allowed to love only in ways that don't disrupt the balance. For me to commit myself, or, heaven forbid, to marry, would require such deep thought at the highest levels that by the time the Heralds had worked it through, well, I'd have tired of the lady. Story of us all, eh? Nowhere for the pressure to go. If only I could see an alternative."

Having shown the corner of his cards, the man had taken care to move back to the fringes of treason once more. It was part of his role as an *agent provocateur*. And Hamilton knew it. But that didn't mean he had to take this. "Do you have any further point, your Lordship?"

"Oh, I'm just getting—"

The room gasped.

Hamilton was up out of his seat and had taken a step toward Elizabeth, his gun hand had grabbed into the air to his right where his .66 mm Webley Corsair sat in a knot of space and had swung it ready to fire—

At nothing.

There stood the Princess, looking about herself in shock. Dress uniforms, bearded men all around her.

Left, right, up, down.

Hamilton couldn't see anything for her to be shocked at.

And nothing near her, nothing around her.

She was already stepping back, her hands in the air, gesturing at a gap—

What had been there? Everyone was looking there. What?

He looked to the others like him. Almost all of them were in the same sort of posture he was, balked at picking a target.

The Papal envoy stepped forward and cried out. "A man was standing there! And he has vanished!"

* * *

Havoc. Everybody was shouting. A weapon, a weapon! But there was no weapon that Hamilton knew of that could have done that, made a man, whoever it had been, blink out of existence. Groups of bodyguards in dress uniforms or diplomatic black tie leapt up, encircling their charges. Ladies started screaming. A nightmare of the balance collapsing all around them. That hysteria when everyone was in the same place and things didn't go exactly as all these vast powers expected.

A Bavarian princeling bellowed he needed no such protection and made to rush to the Princess's side—

Hamilton stepped into his way and accidentally shouldered him to the floor as he put himself right up beside Elizabeth and her husband. "We're walking to that door," he said. "Now."

Bertil and Elizabeth nodded and marched with fixed smiles on their faces, Bertil turning and holding back with a gesture the Swedish forces that were moving in from all directions. Hamilton's fellows fell in all around them, and swept the party across the hall, through that door, and down a servants' corridor as Life Guards came bundling into the room behind them, causing more noise and more reactions and damn it, Hamilton hoped he wouldn't suddenly hear the discharge of some hidden—

He did not. The door was closed and barred behind them. Another good guy doing the right thing.

Hamilton sometimes distantly wished for an organization to guard those who needed it. But for that the world would have to be different in ways beyond even Carney's artificial speculations. He and his brother officers would have their independence cropped if that were so. And he lived through his independence. It was the root of the duty that meant he would place himself in harm's way for Elizabeth's husband. He had no more thoughts on the subject.

"I know very little," said Elizabeth as she walked, her voice careful as always, except when it hadn't been. "I think the man was with one of the groups of foreign dignitaries—"

"He looked Prussian," said Bertil, "we were talking to Prussians."

"He just vanished into thin air right in front of me."

"Into a fold?" said Bertil.

"It can't have been," she said. "The room will have been mapped and mapped."

She looked to Hamilton for confirmation. He nodded.

They got to the library. Hamilton marched in and secured it. They put the happy couple at the center of it, locked it up, and called everything in to the embroidery.

The embroideries were busy, swiftly prioritizing, but no, nothing was happening in the great chamber they'd left, the panic had swelled and then subsided into shouts, exhibitionist faintings (because who these days wore a corset that didn't have hidden depths), glasses crashing, yelled demands. No one else had vanished. No Spanish infantrymen had materialized out of thin air.

Bertil walked to the shelves, folded his hands behind his back, and began bravely and ostentatiously browsing. Elizabeth sat down and fanned herself and smiled for all Hamilton's fellows, and finally, quickly for Hamilton himself.

They waited.

The embroidery told them they had a visitor coming.

A wall of books slid aside, and in walked a figure that made all of them turn and salute. The Queen Mother, still in mourning black, her train racing to catch up with her.

She came straight to Hamilton and the others all turned to listen, and from now on thanks to this obvious favor, they would regard Hamilton as the ranking officer. He was glad of it. "We will continue," she said. "We will not regard this as an embarrassment and therefore it will not be. The ballroom was prepared for the dance, we are moving there early, Elizabeth, Bertil, off you go, you two gentlemen in front of them, the rest of you behind. You will be laughing as you enter the ballroom as if this were the most enormous joke, a silly and typically English eccentric misunderstanding."

Elizabeth nodded, took Bertil by the arm.

The Queen Mother intercepted Hamilton as he moved to join them. "No. Major Hamilton, you will go and talk to technical, you will find another explanation for what happened."

"*Another* explanation, your Royal Highness?"

"Indeed," she said. "It must not be what they are saying it is."

"Here we are, sir," Lieutenant Matthew Parkes was with the Technical Corps of Hamilton's own regiment, the 4th Dragoons. He and his men were, incongruously, in the dark of the pantry that had been set aside for their equipment, also in their dress uniforms. From here they were in charge of the sensor net that blanketed the house and grounds down to Newtonian units of space, reaching out for miles in every direction. Parkes's people had been the first to arrive here, days ago, and would be the last to leave. He was pointing at a screen, on which was frozen the intelligent image of a burly man in black tie, Princess Elizabeth almost entirely obscured behind him. "Know who he is?"

Hamilton had placed the guest list in his mental index and had checked it as each group had entered the hall. He was relieved to recognize the man. He was as down to earth as it was possible to be. "He was in the Prussian party, not announced, one of six diplomat placings on their list. Built like his muscles have grown for security and that's how he moved round the room. Didn't let anyone chat to him. He nods when his embroidery talks to him. Which'd mean he's new at this, only . . ." Only the man had a look about him that Hamilton recognized. "No. He's just very confident. Ostentatious, even. So you're sure he didn't walk into some sort of fold?"

"Here's the contour map." Parkes flipped up an overlay on the image that showed the tortured underpinnings of space-time in the room. There were little sinks and bundles all over the place, where various Britons had weapons stowed, and various foreigners would have had them stowed had they wished to create a diplomatic incident. The corner where Elizabeth had been standing showed only the force of gravity under her dear feet. "We do take care you know, sir."

"I'm sure you do, Matty. Let's see it, then."

Parkes flipped back to the clear screen. He touched it and the image changed.

Hamilton watched as the man vanished. One moment he

was there. Then he was not, and Elizabeth was reacting, a sudden jerk of her posture.

Hamilton often struggled with technical matters. "What's the frame rate on this thing?"

"There is none, sir. It's a continual taking of real image, right down to single Newton intervals of time. That's as far as physics goes. Sir, we've been listening in to what everyone's saying, all afternoon—"

"And what are they saying, Matty?"

"That what's happened is Gracefully Impossible."

Gracefully Impossible. The first thing that had come into Hamilton's mind when the Queen Mother had mentioned the possibility was the memory of a political cartoon. It was the Prime Minister from a few years ago, standing at the dispatch box, staring in shock at his empty hand, which should presumably have contained some papers. The caption had read:

Say what you like about Mr. *Patel*,
He carries himself correct for his *title*.
He's about to present just his *graceful* apologies,
For the *impossible* loss of all his policies.

Every child knew that Newton had coined the phrase "gracefully impossible" after he'd spent the day in his garden observing the progress of a very small worm across the surface on an apple. It referred to what, according to the great man's thinking about the very small, could, and presumably did, sometimes happen: things popping in and out of existence, when God, for some unfathomable reason, started or stopped looking at them. Some Frenchman had insisted that it was actually about whether *people* were looking, but that was the French for you. Through the centuries, there had been a few documented cases that seemed to fit the bill. Hamilton had always been distantly entertained to read about such in the inside page of his newspaper plate. He'd always assumed it could happen. But here? Now? During a state occasion?

* * *

Hamilton went back into the great hall, now empty of all but a group of Life Guards and those like him, individuals taken from several different regiments, all of whom had responsibilities similar to his, and a few of whom he'd worked with in the field. He checked in with them. They had all noted the Prussian, indeed, with the ruthless air the man had had about him, and the bulk of his musculature, he had been at the forefront of many of their internal indices of threat.

Hamilton found the place where the vanishing had happened, moved aside a couple of boffins, and against their protestations, went to stand in the exact spot, which felt like anywhere else did, and which set off none of his internal alarms, real or intuitive. He looked to where Liz had been standing, in the corner behind the Prussian. His expression darkened. The man who'd vanished had effectively been shielding the Princess from the room. Between her and every line of sight. He'd been where a bodyguard would have been if he'd become aware of someone taking a shot.

But that was ridiculous. The Prussian hadn't rushed in to save her. He'd been standing there, looking around. And anyone in that hall with some strange new weapon concealed on their person wouldn't have taken the shot then, they'd have waited for him to move.

Hamilton shook his head, angry with himself. There was a gap here. Something that went beyond the obvious. He let the boffins get back to their work and headed for the ballroom.

The band had started the music, and the vast chamber was packed with people, the dance floor a whirl of waltzing figures. They were deliberate in their courses. The only laughter was forced laughter. No matter that some half-miracle might have occurred, dance cards had been circulated among the minds of the great powers, so those dances would be danced, and minor royalty matched, and whispers exchanged in precise confidentiality, because everyone was brave and everyone was determined and would be seen to be so. And so the balance went on. But the tension had increased a notch.

The weight of the balance could be felt in this room, on the surface now, on every brow. The Queen Mother sat at a high table with courtiers to her left and right, receiving visitors with a grand blessing smile on her face, daring everyone to regard the last hour as anything but a dream.

Hamilton walked the room, looking around like he was looking at a battle, like it was happening rather than perhaps waiting to happen, whatever it was. He watched his opposite numbers from all the great powers waltzing slowly around their own people, and spiraling off from time to time to orbit his own. The ratio of uniformed to the sort of embassy thug it was difficult to imagine fitting in the diplomatic bag was about three to one for all the nations bar two. The French had of course sent Commissars, who all dressed the same when outsiders were present, but followed a Byzantine internal rank system. And the Vatican's people were all men and women of the cloth and their assistants.

As he made his way through that particular party, which was scattering, intercepting, and colliding with all the other nationalities, as if in the explosion of a shaped charge, he started to hear it. The conversations were all about what had happened. The Vatican representatives were talking about a sacred presence. The details were already spiraling. There had been a light and a great voice, had nobody else heard? And people were agreeing.

Hamilton wasn't a diplomat, and he knew better than to take on trouble not in his own line. But he didn't like what he was hearing. The Catholics had only come to terms with Impossible Grace a couple of decades ago, when a Papal bull went out announcing that John XXVI thought that the concept had merit, but that further scientific study was required. But now they'd got behind it, as in all things, they were behind it. So what would this say to them, that the divine had looked down on this wedding, approved of it, and plucked someone away from it?

No, not just someone. Prussian military. A Protestant from a nation that had sometimes protested that various Swedish territories would be far better off within their own jurisdiction.

Hamilton stopped himself speculating. Guessing at such things would only make him hesitate if his guesses turned out to be untrue.

Hamilton had a vague but certain grasp of what his God was like. He thought it was possible that He might decide to give the nod to a marriage at court. But in a way that might upset the balance between nations that was divinely ordained, that was the center of all good works?

No. Hamilton was certain now. The divine be damned. This wasn't the numinous at play. This was enemy action.

He circled the room until he found the Prussians. They were raging, an ambassador poking at a British courtier, demanding something, probably that an investigation be launched immediately. And beside that Prussian stood several more, diplomatic and military, all convincingly frightened and furious, certain this was a British plot.

But behind them there, in the social place where Hamilton habitually looked, there were some of the vanished man's fellow big lads. The other five from that diplomatic pouch. The Prussians, uniquely in Europe, kept up an actual organization for the sort of thing Hamilton and his ilk did on the never-never. The Garde Du Corps had begun as a regiment similar to the Life Guards, but these days it was said they weren't even issued with uniforms. They wouldn't be on anyone's dance cards. They weren't stalking the room now, and all right, that was understandable, they were hanging back to protect their men. But they weren't doing much of that either. They didn't look angry, or worried for their comrade, or for their own skins—

Hamilton took a step back to let pretty noble couples desperately waltz between him and the Prussians, wanting to keep his position as a privileged observer.

They looked like they were *waiting*. On edge. They just wanted to get out of here. Was the Garde really that callous? They'd lost a man in mysterious circumstances, and they weren't themselves agitating to get back into that room and yell his name, but were just waiting to move on?

He looked for another moment, remembering the faces, then moved on himself. He found another table of Prussians.

The good sort, not Order of the Black Eagle, but Hussars. They were in uniform, and had been drinking, and were furiously declaring in Hohenzollern German that if they weren't allowed access to the records of what had happened, well then it must be—they didn't like to say what it must be!

Hamilton plucked a glass from a table and wandered over to join them, careful to take a wide and unsteady course around a lady whose train had developed some sort of fault and wasn't moving fast enough to keep pace with her feet.

He flopped down in a chair next to one of the Prussians, a captain by his lapels, which were virtual in the way the Prussians liked, to implicitly suggest that they had been in combat more recently than the other great powers, and so had a swift turnover of brevet ranks, decided by merit. "Hullo!" he said.

The group fell silent and bristled at him.

Hamilton blinked at them. "Where's Humph?"

"Humph? Wassay th'gd Major?" the Hussar Captain spoke North Sea pidgin, but with a clear accent: Hamilton would be able to understand him.

He didn't want to reveal that he spoke perfect German, albeit with a Bavarian accent. "Big chap. Big big chap. Say go." He carefully swore in Dutch, shaking his head, not understanding. "Which you settle fim?"

"Settle?!" They looked among each other, and Hamilton could feel the affront. A couple of them even put their good hands to their waists, where the space was folded that no longer contained their pistols and thin swords. But the captain glared at them and they relented. A burst of Hohenzollern German about this so-called mystery of their mate vanishing, and how, being in the Garde, he had obviously been abducted for his secrets.

Hamilton waved his hands. "No swords! Good chap! No name. He won! Three times to me at behind the backshee." His raised his voice a notch. "Behind the backshee! Excellent chap! He *won*!" He stuck out his ring finger, offering the winnings in credit, to be passed from skin to skin. He mentally retracted the other options of what could be detailed there, and blanked it. He could always make a drunken show of trying to find it. "Seek to settle. For such a good chap."

They didn't believe him or trust him. Nobody reached out to touch his finger. But he learnt a great deal in their German conversation in the ten minutes that followed, while he loudly struggled to communicate with the increasingly annoyed captain, who couldn't bring himself to directly insult a member of the British military by asking him to go away. The vanished man's name was Helmuth Sandels. The name suggested Swedish origins to his family. But that was typical continental back and forth. He might have been a good man now he'd gone, but he hadn't been liked. Sandels had had a look in his eye when he'd walked past stout fellows who'd actually fought battles. He'd spoken up in anger when valiant Hussars had expressed the military's traditional views concerning those running the government, the country, and the world. Hamilton found himself sharing the soldiers' expressions of distaste: this had been someone who assumed that loyalty was an *opinion*.

He raised a hand in pax, gave up trying with the captain, and left the table.

Walking away, he heard the Hussars moving on with their conversation, starting to express some crude opinions about the Princess. He didn't break stride.

Into his mind, unbidden, came the memories. Of what had been a small miracle of a kind, but one that only he and she had been witness to.

Hamilton had been at home on leave, having been abroad for a few weeks, serving out of uniform. As always, at times like that, when he should have been at rest, he'd been fired up for no good reason, unable to sleep, miserable, prone to tears in secret when a favorite song had come on the theatricals in his muse flat. It always took three days for him, once he was home, to find out what direction he was meant to be pointing. Then he would set off that way, and pop back to barracks one night for half a pint, and then he'd be fine. He could enjoy day four and onwards, and was known to be something approximating human from there on in.

Three-day leaves were hell. He tried not to use them as leaves, but would find himself some task, hopefully an official one if one of the handful of officers who brokered his services could be so entreated. Those officers were sensitive to such requests now.

But that leave, three years ago, had been two weeks off. He'd come home a day before. So he was no use to anyone. He'd taken a broom, and was pushing accumulated gray goo out of the carriage park alongside his apartment and into the drains.

She'd appeared in a sound of crashing and collapse, as her horse staggered sideways and hit the wall of the mews, then fell. Her two friends were galloping after her, their horses healthy, and someone built like Hamilton was running to help.

But none of them were going to be in time to catch her—
And he was.

It had turned out that the horse had missed an inoculation against minuscule poisoning. Its body was a terrible mess, random mechanisms developing out of its flanks and dying, with that terrifying smell, in the moments when Hamilton had held her in his arms, and had had to round on the man running in, and had imposed his authority with a look, and had not been thrown down and away.

Instead, she'd raised her hands and called that she was all right, and had insisted on looking to and at the horse, pulling off her glove and putting her hand to its neck and trying to fight the bloody things directly. But even with her command of information, it had been too late, and the horse had died in a mess.

She'd been bloody angry. And then at the emergency scene that had started to develop around Hamilton's front door, with police carriages swooping in and the sound of running boots—

Until she'd waved it all away and declared that it had been her favorite horse, a wonderful horse, her great friend since childhood, but it was just a bloody horse, and all she needed was a sit down and if this kind military gentleman would oblige—

And he had.

He'd obliged her again when they'd met in Denmark, and they'd danced at a ball held on an ice floe, a carpet of mechanism wood reacting every moment to the weight of their feet and the forces underlying them, and the aurora had shone in the sky.

It was all right in Denmark for Elizabeth to have one dance with a commoner.

Hamilton had got back to the table where his regiment were dining, and had silenced the laughter and the calls, and thus saved them for barracks. He had drunk too much. His batman at the time had prevented him from going to see Elizabeth as she was escorted from the floor at the end of her dance card by a boy who was somewhere in line for the Danish throne.

But she had seen Hamilton the next night, in private, a privacy that would have taken great effort on her part, and after they had talked for several hours and shared some more wine she had shown him great favor.

"So. Is God in the details?" Someone was walking beside Hamilton. It was a Jesuit. Mid thirties. Dark hair, kept over her collar. She had a scar down one side of her face and an odd eye as a result. Minuscule blade, by the look. A member of the Society of Jesus would never allow her face to be restructured. That would be vanity. But she was beautiful.

Hamilton straightened up, giving this woman's musculature and bearing and all the history those things suggested the respect they deserved. "Or the devil."

"Yes, interesting the saying goes both ways, isn't it? My name is Mother Valentine. I'm part of the Society's campaign for Effective Love."

"Well," Hamilton raised an eyebrow, "I'm in favor of love being—"

"Don't waste our time. You know what I am."

"Yes, I do. And you know I'm the same. And I was waiting until we were out of earshot—"

"Which we now are—"

"To have this conversation."

They stopped together. Valentine moved her mouth close to Hamilton's ear. "I've just been told that the Holy Father is eager to declare what happened here to be a potential miracle. Certain parties are sure that our Black Eagle man will be found magically transplanted to distant parts, perhaps Berlin, as a sign against Prussian meddling."

"If he is, the Kaiser will have him gently shot and we'll never hear."

"You're probably right."

"What do you think happened?"

"I don't think miracles happen near our kind."

Hamilton realized he was looking absurdly hurt at her. And that she could see it. And was quietly absorbing that information for use in a couple of decades, if ever.

He was glad when a message came over the embroidery, asking him to attend to the Queen Mother in the pantry. And to bring his new friend.

The Queen Mother stood in the pantry, her not taking a chair having obviously made Parkes and his people even more nervous than they would have been.

She nodded to Valentine. "Monsignor. I must inform you, we've had an official approach from the Holy See. They regard the hall here as a possible site of miraculous apparition."

"Then my opinion on the subject is irrelevant. You should be addressing—"

"The ambassador. Indeed. But here you are. You are aware of what was asked of us?"

"I suspect the Cardinals will have sought a complete record of the moment of the apparition, or in this case, the vanishing. That would only be the work of a moment in the case of such an . . . observed . . . chamber."

"It would. But it's what happens next that concerns me."

"The procedure is that the chamber must then be sealed, and left unobserved until the Cardinals can see for themselves, to minimize any effect human observers may have on the process of divine revelation."

Hamilton frowned. "Are we likely to?"

"God is communicating using a physical method, so we may," said Valentine. "Depending on one's credulity concerning minuscule physics."

"Or one's credulity concerning international politics," said the Queen Mother. "Monsignor, it is always our first and most powerful inclination, when another nation asks us for something, to say no. All nations feel that way. All nations know the others do. But now here is a request, one that concerns matters right at the heart of the balance, that is, in the end, about deactivating security. It could be said to come not from another nation, but from God. It is therefore difficult to deny this request. We find ourselves distrusting that difficulty. It makes us want to deny it all the more."

"You speak for His Royal Highness?"

The Queen Mother gave a cough that might have been a laugh. "Just as you speak for Our Lord."

Valentine smiled and inclined her head. "I would have thought, your Royal Highness, that it would be obvious to any of the great powers that, given the celebrations, it would take you a long time to gather the Prime Minister and those many other courtiers with whom you would want to consult on such a difficult matter."

"Correct. Good. It will take three hours. You may go."

Valentine walked out with Hamilton. "I'm going to go and mix with my own for a while," she said, "listen to who's saying what."

"I'm surprised you wear your hair long."

She looked sharply at him. "Why?"

"You enjoy putting your head on the block."

She giggled.

Which surprised Hamilton and for just a moment made him wish he was Lord Carney. But then there was a certain small darkness about another priest he knew.

"I'm just betting," she said in a whisper, "that by the end of the day this will all be over. And someone will be dead."

* * *

Hamilton went back into the ballroom. He found he had a picture in his head now. Something had swum up from somewhere inside him, from a place he had learned to trust and never interrogate as to its reasons. That jerking motion Elizabeth had made at the moment Sandels had vanished. He had an emotional feeling about that image. What was it?

It had been like seeing her shot.

A motion that looked like it had come from beyond her muscles. Something Elizabeth had not been in control of. It wasn't like her to not be in control. It felt . . . dangerous.

Would anyone else see it that way? He doubted it.

So was he about to do the sudden terrible thing that his body was taking him in the direction of doing?

He killed the thought and just did it. He went to the herald who carried the tablet with dance cards on it, and leaned on him with the Queen Mother's favor, which had popped up on his ring finger the moment he'd thought of it.

The herald considered the sensation of the fingertip on the back of his hand for a moment, then handed Hamilton the tablet.

Hamilton realized that he had no clue of the havoc he was about to cause. So he glanced at the list of Elizabeth's forthcoming dances and struck off a random Frenchman.

He scrawled his own signature with a touch, then handed the plate back.

The herald looked at him like the breath of death had passed under his nose.

Hamilton had to wait three dances before his name came up. A Balaclava, an entrée grave (that choice must have taken a while, unless some herald had been waiting all his life for a chance at the French), a hornpipe for the sailors, including Bertil, to much applause, and then, thank the Deus, a straightforward waltz.

Elizabeth had been waiting out those last three, so he met her at her table. Maidservants kept their expressions stoic. A couple of Liz's companions looked positively scared. Hamilton knew how they felt. He could feel every important eye looking in his direction.

Elizabeth took his arm and gave it a little squeeze. "What's grandma up to, Johnny?"

"It's what I'm up to."

She looked alarmed. They formed up with the other dancers.

Hamilton was very aware of her gloves. The mechanism fabric that covered her left hand held off the urgent demand of his hand, his own need to touch her. But no, that wouldn't tell him anything. That was just his certainty that to know her had been to know her. That was not where he would find the truth here.

The band started up. The dance began.

Hamilton didn't access any guidelines in his mind. He let his feet move where they would. He was outside orders, acting on a hunch. He was like a man dancing around the edge of a volcano.

"Do you remember the day we met?" he asked when he was certain they couldn't be heard; at least, not by the other dancers.

"Of course I do. My poor San Andreas, your flat in Hood Mews—"

"Do you remember what I said to you that day, when nobody else was with us? What you agreed to? Those passionate words that could bring this whole charade crashing down?" He kept his expression light, his tone so gentle and wry that Liz would always play along and fling a little stone back at him, knowing he meant nothing more than he could mean. That he was letting off steam through a joke.

All they had been was based on the certainty expressed in that.

It was an entirely British way to do things. It was, as Carney had said, about lives shaped entirely by the balance.

But this woman, with the room revolving around the two of them, was suddenly appalled, insulted, her face a picture of what she was absolutely certain she should feel. "I don't know what you mean! Or even if I did, I don't think—!"

Hamilton's nostrils flared. He was lost now, if he was wrong. He had one tiny ledge for Liz to grasp if he was, but he would fall.

For duty, then.

He took his hand from Princess Elizabeth's waist, and grabbed her chin, his fingers digging up into flesh.

The whole room cried out in horror.

He had a moment before they would shoot him.

Yes, he felt it! Or he thought he did! He thought he did enough—

He grabbed the flaw and ripped with all his might.

Princess Elizabeth's face burst off and landed on the floor.

Blood flew.

He drew his gun and pumped two shots into the mass of flesh and mechanism, as it twitched and blew a stream of defensive acid that discolored the marble.

He spun back to find the woman without a face lunging at him, her eyes white in the mass of red muscle, mechanism pus billowing into the gaps. She was aiming a hair knife at his throat, doubtless with enough mechanism to bring instant death or something worse.

Hamilton thought of Liz as he broke her arm.

He enjoyed the scream.

He wanted to bellow for where the real Liz was as he slammed the impostor down onto the floor, and he was dragged from her in one motion as a dozen men grabbed them.

He caught a glimpse of Bertil, horrified, but not at Hamilton. It was a terror they shared. For her safety.

Hamilton suddenly felt like a traitor again.

He yelled out the words he'd had in mind since he'd put his name down for the dance. "They replaced her years ago! Years ago! At the mews!"

There were screams, cries that we were all undone.

There came the sound of two shots from the direction of the Vatican group, and Hamilton looked over to see Valentine standing over the corpse of a junior official.

Their gaze met. She understood why he'd shouted that.

Another man leapt up at a Vatican table behind her and turned to run and she turned and shot him twice in the chest, his body spinning backward over a table.

* * *

Hamilton ran with the rout. He used the crowds of dignitaries and their retinues, all roaring and competing and stampeding for safety, to hide himself. He made himself look like a man lost, agony on his face, his eyes closed. He was ignoring all the urgent cries from the embroidery.

He covertly acknowledged something directly from the Queen Mother.

He stumbled through the door of the pantry.

Parkes looked round. "Thank God you're here, we've been trying to call, the Queen Mother's office are urgently asking you to come in—"

"Never mind that now, come with me, on Her Royal Highness's orders."

Parkes grabbed the pods from his ears and got up. "What on Earth—?"

Hamilton shot him through the right knee.

Parkes screamed and fell. Every technician in the room leapt up. Hamilton bellowed at them to sit down or they'd get the same.

He shoved his foot into the back of Parkes's injured leg. "Listen here, Matty. You know how hard it's going to get. You're not the sort to think your duty's worth it. How much did they pay you? For how long?"

He was still yelling at the man on the ground as the Life Guards burst in and put a gun to everyone's head, his own included.

The Queen Mother entered a minute later, and changed that situation to the extent of letting Hamilton go free. She looked carefully at Parkes, who was still screaming for pity, and aimed a precise little kick into his disintegrated knee-cap.

Then she turned to the technicians. "Your minds will be stripped down and rebuilt, if you're lucky, to see who was in on it." She looked back to Hamilton as they started to be led from the room. "What you said in the ballroom obviously isn't the case."

"No. When you take him apart," Hamilton nodded at Parkes, "you'll find he tampered with the contour map. They used Sandels as the cover for substituting Her Royal Highness. They knew she was going to move around the room in a predetermined way. With Parkes's help, they set up an open-ended fold in that corner—"

"The expense is staggering. The energy required—"

"There'll be no Christmas tree for the Kaiser this year. Sandels deliberately stepped into the fold and vanished, in a very public way. And at that moment they made the switch, took Her Royal Highness into the fold too, covered by the visual disturbance of Sandels's progress. And by old-fashioned sleight of hand."

"Propped up by the Prussians' people in the Vatican. Instead of a British bride influencing the Swedish court, there'd be a cuckoo from Berlin. Well played, Wilhelm. Worth that Christmas tree."

"I'll wager the unit are still in the fold, not knowing anything about the outside world, waiting for the room to be sealed off with pious care, so they can climb out and extract themselves. They probably have supplies for several days."

"Do you think my granddaughter is still alive?"

Hamilton pursed his lips. "There are Prussian yachts on the river. They're staying on for the season. I think they'd want the bonus of taking the Princess back for interrogation."

"That's the plan!" Parkes yelled. "Please—!"

"Get him some anesthetic," said the Queen Mother. Then she turned back to Hamilton. "The balance will be kept. To give him his due, cousin Wilhelm was acting within it. There will be no diplomatic incident. The Prussians will be able to write off Sandels and any others as rogues. We will of course cooperate. The Black Eagle traditionally carry only that knowledge they need for their mission, and will order themselves to die before giving us orders of battle or any other strategic information. But the intelligence from Parkes and any others will give us some small power of potential shame over the Prussians in future months. The Vatican will be bending over backwards for us for some time to come." She took his hand, and he felt the favor on his ring finger impressed with some notes that probably flattered him. He'd read them later. "Major, we will have the fold opened. You will enter it. Save Elizabeth. Kill them all."

They got him a squad of fellow officers, four of them. They met in a trophy room, and sorted out how they'd go and what the rules of engagement would be once they got there. Substitutes for Parkes and his crew had been found from the few sappers present. Parkes had told them that those inside the fold had left a minuscule aerial trailing, but that messages were only to be passed down it in emergencies. No such communications had been sent. They were not aware of the world outside their bolt hole.

Hamilton felt nothing but disgust for a bought man, but he knew that such men told the truth under pressure, especially when they knew the fine detail of what could be done to them.

The false Liz had begun to be picked apart. Her real name would take a long time to discover. She had a maze of intersecting selves inside her head. She must have been as big an investment as the fold. The court physicians who had examined her had been as horrified by what had been done to her as by what she was.

That baffled Hamilton. People like the duplicate had the power to be who they liked. But that power was bought at the cost of damage to the balance of their own souls. What were nations, after all, but a lot of souls who knew who they were and how they liked to live? To be as uncertain as the substitute Liz was to be lost and to endanger others. It went beyond treachery. It was living mixed metaphor. It was as if she had insinuated herself into the cogs of the balance, her puppet strings wrapping around the arteries which supplied hearts and minds.

They gathered in the empty dining room in their dress uniforms. The dinner things had not been cleared away. Nothing had been done. The party had been well and truly crashed. The representatives of the great powers would have vanished back to their embassies and yachts. Mother Valentine would be rooting out the details of who had been paid what inside her party. Excommunications *post mortem* would be issued, and those traitors would burn in hell.

He thought of Liz, and took his gun from the air beside him.

One of the sappers put a device in the floor, set a timer, saluted and withdrew.

"Up the Green Jackets," said one of the men behind him, and a couple of the others mentioned their own regiments.

Hamilton felt a swell of fear and emotion.

The counter clicked to zero and the hole in the world opened in front of them, and they ran into it.

There was nobody immediately inside. A floor and curved ceiling of universal boundary material. It wrapped light around it in rainbows that always gave tunnels like this a slightly pantomime feel. It was like the entrance to Saint Nicholas's cave. Or, of course, the vortex sighted upon death, the ladder to the hereafter. Hamilton got that familiar taste in his mouth, a pure adrenal jolt of fear, not the restlessness of combat deferred, but that sensation one got in other universes, of being too far from home, cut off from the godhead.

There was gravity. The Prussians certainly had spent some money.

The party made their way forward. They stepped gently on the edge of the universe. From around the corner of the short tunnel there were sounds.

The other four looked to Hamilton. He took a couple of gentle steps forward, grateful for the softness of his dress uniform shoes. He could hear Elizabeth's voice. Not her words, not from here. She was angry, but engaged. Not defiant in the face of torture. Reasoning with them. A smile passed his lips for a moment. They'd have had a lot of that.

It told him there was no alert, not yet. It was almost impossible to set sensors close to the edge of a fold. This lot must have stood on guard for a couple of hours, heard no alarm from their friends outside, and then had relaxed. They'd have been on the clock, waiting for the time when they would poke their heads out. Hamilton bet there was a man meant to be on guard, but that Liz had pulled him into the conversation too. He could imagine her face, just round that corner, one eye always toward the exit, maybe a couple of buttons undone, claiming it was the heat and excitement. She had a hair knife too, but it would do her no good to use it on just one of them.

He estimated the distance. He counted the other voices, three . . . four, there was a deeper tone, in German, not the pidgin the other three had been speaking. That would be him. Sandels. He didn't sound like he was part of that conversation. He was angry, ordering, perhaps just back from sleep, wondering what the hell—!

Hamilton stopped all thoughts of Liz. He looked to the others, and they understood they were going to go and go now, trip the alarms and use the emergency against the enemy.

He nodded.

They leapt around the corner, ready for targets.

They expected the blaring horn. They rode it, finding their targets surprised, bodies reacting, reaching for weapons that were in a couple of cases a reach away among a kitchen, crates, tinned foods—

Hamilton had made himself know he was going to see Liz, so he didn't react to her, he looked past her—

He ducked, cried out, as an automatic set off by the alarm chopped up the man who had been running beside him, the Green Jacket, gone in a burst of red. Meat all over the cave.

Hamilton reeled, stayed up, tried to pin a target. To left and right ahead, men were falling, flying, two shots in each body, and he was moving too slowly, stumbling, vulnerable—

One man got off a shot, into the ceiling, and then fell, pinned twice, exploding—

Every one of the Prussians gone but—

He found his target.

Sandels. With Elizabeth right in front of him. Covering every bit of his body. He had a gun pushed into her neck. He wasn't looking at his three dead comrades.

The three men who were with Hamilton moved forward, slowly, their gun hands visible, their weapons pointing down.

They were looking to Hamilton again.

He hadn't lowered his gun. He had his target. He was aiming right at Sandels and the Princess.

There was silence.

Liz made eye contact. She had indeed undone those two buttons. She was calm. "Well," she began, "this is very—"

Sandels muttered something and she was quiet again.

Silence.

Sandels laughed, not unpleasantly. Soulful eyes were looking at them from that square face of his, a smile turning the corner of his mouth. He shared the irony that Hamilton had often found in people of their profession.

This was not the awkward absurdity that the soldiers had described. Hamilton realized that he was looking at an alternative. This man was a professional at the same things Hamilton did in the margins of his life. It was the strangeness of the alternative that had alienated the military men. Hamilton was fascinated by him.

"I don't know why I did this," said Sandels, indicating Elizabeth with a sway of the head. "Reflex."

Hamilton nodded to him. They each knew all the other did. "Perhaps you needed a moment."

"She's a very pretty girl to be wasted on a Swede."

Hamilton could feel Liz not looking at him. "It's not a waste," he said gently. "And you'll refer to Her Royal Highness by her title."

"No offense meant."

"And none taken. But we're in the presence, not in barracks."

"I wish we were."

"I think we all agree there."

"I won't lay down my weapon."

Hamilton didn't do his fellows the disservice of looking to them for confirmation. "This isn't an execution."

Sandels looked satisfied. "Seal this tunnel afterwards, that should be all we require for passage."

"Not to Berlin, I presume."

"No," said Sandels, "to entirely the opposite."

Hamilton nodded.

"Well, then." Sandels stepped aside from Elizabeth.

Hamilton lowered his weapon and the others readied theirs. It wouldn't be done to aim straight at Sandels. He had his own weapon at hip height. He would bring it up and they would cut him down as he moved.

But Elizabeth hadn't moved. She was pushing back her hair, as if wanting to say something to him before leaving, but lost for the right words.

Hamilton, suddenly aware of how unlikely that was, started to say something.

But Liz had put a hand to Sandels's cheek.

Hamilton saw the fine silver between her fingers.

Sandels fell to the ground thrashing, hoarsely yelling as he deliberately and precisely, as his nervous system was ordering him to, bit off his own tongue. Then the mechanism from the hair knife let him die.

The Princess looked at Hamilton. "It's not a waste," she said.

They sealed the fold as Sandels had asked them to, after the sappers had made an inspection.

Hamilton left them to it. He regarded his duty as done. And no message came to him to say otherwise.

Recklessly, he tried to find Mother Valentine. But she was gone with the rest of the Vatican party, and there weren't even bloodstains left to mark where her feet had trod this evening.

He sat at a table, and tried to pour himself some champagne. He found that the bottle was empty.

His glass was filled by Lord Carney, who sat down next to him. Together, they watched as Elizabeth was joyfully reunited with Bertil. They swung each other round and round, oblivious to all around them. Elizabeth's grandmother smiled at them and looked nowhere else.

"We are watching," said Carney, "the balance incarnate.

Or perhaps they'll incarnate it tonight. As I said: if only there were an alternative."

Hamilton drained his glass. "If only," he said, "there *weren't*."

And he left before Carney could say anything more.

Lady of the
White-Spired City

SARAH L. EDWARDS

Sarah L. Edwards lives in Rathdrum, Idaho. She says, "I have a degree in math that I'm still trying to figure out how to use. I've lived all over the U.S. but my heart belongs to the parts with mountains." She writes fantasy and the occasional science fiction piece, such as this one. She's written several stories in her steampunk-fantasy Dark Quarter universe, which began with her Writers of the Future-winning story "Simulacrum's Children." Her stories have appeared in a number of small-press online venues, including often in Beneath Ceaseless Skies, and in 2009 began to appear in print magazines. Aside from writing, she says her "major project these days is teaching sixth grade at a bilingual school in Honduras."

"Lady of the White-Spired City" was published in Interzone. A woman returns from a powerful interstellar civilization to an isolated and backward village on a cold planet, searching for her past. We find the mood and atmosphere compelling.

She came, Evriel Pashtan, emissary of his justice the high regent. Weary, silver-haired, faint-hoped she came to Kander, near-forgotten colony circling its cold little rose-hued sun. She greeted the honcho of Colonth, its foremost city; she nodded politely and distributed vids and holos; she attended a festival in her honor. And then she left the ship to the city's technicians for refitting and she flew off in her personal carrier to the far side of the planet, to a highland village enfolded in the deep of winter.

No one came out into the falling dusk to greet her. She pulled her layers of corn-silk closer around her and trudged the few meters through knee-deep drifts of snow to the single village street.

It had not changed so much. The houses were all different, rebuilt ten times or more since she had known them, and yet their number was nearly the same. There in the middle rose the sharp-peaked roof that marked the travelers' rest, its edging still painted scarlet like those in the regent's city—did anyone remember, or was it only tradition now? She paused in front of its door, glancing to the empty street behind her, and then she knocked.

It was a girl of maybe ten or twelve who opened the door, and her dark eyes widened in wonder when she saw Evriel.

"I've come a long way," Evriel said. "I wonder if I might stop here a while?"

The girl reached tentative fingers towards Evriel's overrobe. "Are you from down the mountain?"

Evriel smiled. "I'm from a good deal farther away than that."

The girl stepped aside. "Mother will want to see you." If she was surprised when Evriel walked unerringly to the welcome room with its coal-brimming brazier and its piled cushions, she didn't show it. She left Evriel there among the cushions and soon returned with a tea mug in her hand. Behind her came a woman, ebon-haired, with eyes older than her thirty-odd years.

Evriel rose and offered her hands in the old way. After a pause, the woman clasped them both in hers and kissed them, and Evriel kissed the woman's in turn.

"Sit, stranger, and be welcome," the woman said, the formal words old and familiar, long though it was since Evriel had heard them last. The woman motioned her to the cushions again while the girl handed Evriel the hot tea mug. "I am Sayla, and this house is open to any who seek shelter. This is my daughter, Asha." The girl nodded, setting her curls bobbing.

"I am Evriel Pashtan, emissary of our lord the high regent."

"Emissary?" the woman said, blankly.

"You *are*?" blurted the girl. "From Alabaster?"

"From Alabaster," Evriel agreed.

"From the home star—it's not possible," said Sayla. "The ships don't come anymore, not even to Colonth."

"Not for years and years," Asha added. "They talk about how a ship fell like a burning egg onto the Colonth plain, and how the people wore strange clothes—like yours." She reached for Evriel's robe again, then drew back. "But they're all gone now."

"Why have you come to the village?" said Sayla. "I don't understand. Did you wish to speak with my husband? You cannot. The fever took him this summer past."

"No, I'm not looking for your husband," said Evriel. Then she realized what the woman had said. More softly, "I'm so sorry for your loss."

The woman shrugged. "It was bad timing, was all."

And what bitterness lay *there*, Evriel wondered. She turned the thought aside. "I should say, I *have* been emissary of the high regent. I'm on leave now, to travel as I wish for a little while."

A faint smile, not quite ironed of the pain that had creased it before. "And you come here? Whatever for?"

Evriel could not put it so baldly as she wanted—not because of politics, for once, but because the truth sounded feeble, even narcissistic. It *was* narcissistic, looking for one's old footprints on the world. She shouldn't have come.

"Certainly you needn't tell us such things," Sayla was saying, with careful incuriosity. "It is not a season when we see many visitors"—*not that we ever see many*, the tone implied—"but you are welcome to what we have. Asha, bread and cream for the emissary."

Asha dashed off, eyes still wide. She returned in moments with a cloth of rye bread and a bowl of goats' milk cream, which she handed to Evriel, and then she stood at the door as both daughter and servant of the house.

"I've visited your village before," Evriel told Sayla, "long ago. It was . . . a very peaceful time in my life." She paused, wondering how to put into words what she'd come so far to ask. "I knew a family before. I can't remember them very well now, it was so long ago. They lived here, I think. Their name was Reizi."

Sayla's eyebrows rose. "There are Reizis in a village down the mountain. They are my cousins, very distantly. But none have lived here since before I was born—perhaps you confused the villages. One is very much like another."

Cousins to the Reizis.

Only years of diplomacy kept Evriel's fingers from reaching to touch this woman, so distant a connection and yet nearer than any she'd had since . . . Since.

Maybe Sayla saw some of that hunger in her eyes. She said something about chores for the night and took herself away. Asha settled into the cushions nearby and paused, apparently trying to decide where to start. Evriel turned her attention to the bread cloth and waited.

"You're really from Alabaster," Asha said finally.

"I really am," said Evriel, dipping a chunk of bread into the cream.

"So you've been traveling years and years to come here, haven't you?"

"It has seemed only a bit more than a month to me. But yes, it's been many years since my ship left Regent City."

"So if you went back . . . everyone you knew would be dead?" There was no malice in her voice, only curiosity.

"Yes," Evriel said quietly. "Everyone is already dead except for a handful of emissaries, like myself, off in their starships."

"Then everyone you visited *here*, when you were here before, is dead as well?"

Evriel nodded.

"You knew the Reizi family when they lived in this village."

"Yes."

"And you knew their names?"

"Ander and Ivolda Reizi. And"—Evriel's voice caught—"and a little girl named Lakmi." *Lakmi, child of my body, daughter of my heart.*

Sayla returned and announced it was time for sleep, and led Evriel to the room at the center of the house. A blanket large enough to span the entire room was half-draped over the covered grate in the center, already brimming with coals. Evriel laid aside her heaviest robes and burrowed under the blanket, into the sleeping cushions beneath. Nearby Asha did the same as Sayla closed the door and blew out the candle.

Evriel closed her eyes against the sudden darkness and steadied her breathing, shallowing it, drawing to herself the sleep that threatened not to come. Asha lay only an arm's length away. Would Lakmi have looked like her, at her age?

The next morning Evriel woke to a sharp draft blowing past Sayla, standing in the doorway. "They've come to talk to you," Sayla said. "The other folk of the village. They want to talk to the regent's emissary."

Of course, her carrier. It was bound to draw curiosity, and hadn't she wanted to talk to them, anyway? Though perhaps not all at once. She pulled on her robes and tidied her white hair back into its braid, and then followed Sayla to the front door.

For a moment she could only see the deceptive, almost depthless view of brilliant snow and blue shadow. Then the shadows resolved into the long rolling hills down to the Serra River, miles away. It was a view she hadn't seen in forty-five years—or several hundred. Either way, it hadn't changed.

Then somebody coughed, and she realized the lane in front of the house was crowded with villagers—half the population, at least.

Evriel smiled on them all and turned to Sayla. "Bring them to the meeting room one at a time, or in small groups, as they wish."

Soon enough a small balding man stood in front of her, bowing and nodding, his young wife and three small children behind him. "We come to bless the regent and his emissary, and wish fair success," he said, stumbling over the formal words but managing to get them all out. His wife nodded while the children stared at Evriel, wide-eyed.

Comforting to hear the old phrases spoken here, when even the honcho of Colonth hadn't known them. Evriel gave them a genuine smile, no hint of diplomatic edge about it. "The regent and his emissary thank you, and bless you likewise." More bowing, and then they were gone and replaced by another family, with similar greetings.

It wasn't until the third group of well-wishers that Evriel remembered to ask questions: did they know the Reizis, or their kin? What of other emissaries passing between the regent and his colony? "Old Mergo Reizi lives down by the Serra," she heard, "but he's the last of his kin I know of." Or, "There was an emissary off in the spacewalker city, I hear. But that was a long time ago." Or, "I just mind my sheep, Lady Emissary."

When the last of them was gone, Sayla brought tea and a plate of bread heaped with cured meat—goat, Evriel guessed. She took mug and tea from Sayla and said, "Will you sit with me?"

Sayla crossed her legs and sat down, silent.

"Sayla, how would *you* suggest I look for traces of a little girl? You know better than I who would know, who remembers things."

"There's the archivist," Sayla said. "Likely you'll want to see him."

"You've an archivist here? Yes, I should like very much to speak with him." *Not yet,* something whispered. If there was nothing, she didn't want to know. Not yet. "And what of your cousin down the mountain, this Mergo Reizi?"

The smallest of grimaces crossed Sayla's face, and was gone. "I doubt you'll get anything from him."

"Oh?"

"He . . . hasn't much of a memory anymore. Won't have anything to tell you."

"I see." Evriel frowned at a strip of goat and bit in. Excellent; probably supplied to the travelers' rest by a local goatherd. "Still, I rather think I'd like to meet him."

Sayla shrugged. "I'll tell you how to get there—you taking your flyer?" When Evriel nodded, she said, "Take Asha with you, she can tell you the landmarks."

"That sounds like just the thing."

"I'll tell you," Sayla repeated. "Just don't go giving any greetings from me."

A beaten track of small footprints circled the carrier. "Kids," Asha said scornfully, but she approached the carrier cautiously, reaching out to stroke one gleaming wing. Evriel settled her in the cockpit and she peered all around at the dials and switches, her hands carefully folded in her lap. Once in the air she kept her eyes on the white expanse below and said very little, except to point out landmarks: a solitary copse of pines; the long blue shadow that marked a boundary wall.

Mergo Reizi was a rheumy-eyed, suspicious man who declared he had little use for "up-hillers." He lived in a hut of mud reinforced with straw. Evriel felt a flash of sorrow to think of Lakmi living in such a place, until she reminded herself that the structure couldn't be more than five years old. The man had never heard of any ancestress or cousin named Lakmi, though if he had Evriel wasn't sure he would have told them. But he was, she thought, telling the truth. He claimed no living relatives.

It was hardly surprising; the girl would have taken another name when she married. A complete sweep of genealogical records for the area might conceivably turn up a Lakmi Reizi, married to a Master So-and-So and proud matriarch of the Clan Such-and-Such.

But this was to have been a short stay; she and the small, ship-merged crew would begin the long voyage home as soon as the ship was refitted. She had already fulfilled the mission's purpose: to appear in Colonth, deliver the regent's many gifts and promises, and remind the colonists of their allegiance to the Regency—for all it mattered to them.

It was Asha who finally broke the silence. "Mother would tell me it was rude to ask questions."

"I wouldn't," Evriel said. "Unless you mean to ask rude questions." She gave Asha an encouraging smile.

Asha shook her head. "No—at least, I don't think they are. But there are things I have to know. If you would tell me," Asha added, bobbing her head nervously.

"Yes?"

"Is it—that is—we are a very small village, aren't we?"

Evriel thought of Colonth's swinging gates, wider than two village houses together. And then of Regent City, vast anthill of tunnels and streets and spires. "Yes."

"That must be why you went away?"

"Went away? I visited once before . . ."

"But you lived here, didn't you? The 'shining star of the regent king, shot to Kander to speak his words'—that's you, isn't it?"

"Is it a song? I don't . . ."

" 'Married a son of Kander's earth, a shepherd rough but warm of eye'—don't you know it? But I suppose they didn't write it until you'd gone back to the regent."

Evriel shook her head, but she was beginning to get the idea. "You've a song about a regent's emissary?"

Asha nodded, and red curls bobbed free of her hat. "I'll sing you all of it, if you like. It's of an emissary that came to our very village, perched on the tumbling plains, and fell in love with one of the folk and decided to stay, never to fly the long journey across the stars to the city of the regent." Cadence crept into her voice. "But her love died of the summer fever, and in grief she flew away again, weeping her loss and raging against the planet that killed him. And as she flew she promised that when she came again, it would be with scourging fire."

Evriel had turned and was staring down, down those "tumbling plains." Had she promised fire? Yes, she'd been angry, though the memory of it was vague. It was a young, violent anger, now long burnt out. The lack of him remained, but it did not even ache anymore.

Yet Lakmi, whom she'd known so briefly, seemed more absent now than she had in forty years.

Evriel piled cushions next to the glass-block window, laid a blanket over them all, and sat watching the snow wisping and swirling. It had been like this the winter before Lakmi, when she sat at another window in another house, now torn down. Japhesh had just put a grate in the room before the first chill came, and Evriel had sat with a fire's warm glow at her back, watching the snow. It was security, a wall of blankness between her and the outer world. All she'd needed was Japhesh and his warm stone house and his child she was waiting for, the first of many hoped for, and she could leave that world behind her with no regrets.

She never wondered, then, if the other things were enough without Japhesh. That question came later.

"What did you hope to find, coming here?"

Evriel stirred from her thoughts, summoned a smile as Sayla sat down nearby. "Just ghosts, I suppose. Memories."

"I'd forgotten that old song—my daughter told me."

Evriel shrugged. "It might not have anything to do with me. It seems improper, somehow, to have one's past sung in a ballad by utter strangers. Unseemly."

"But it's true, isn't it? You coming here, marrying a village boy?" There was nothing in Sayla's face or her voice.

"Yes. It was my first assignment—a trial, more or less.

There were ten of us. We were gathering data. None of us had the experience to analyze very much of what we collected. All they really wanted us to do was get used to talking to people, observing. Being the long arm of the regent. And they wanted to shake loose the more starry-eyed among us—better to lose us here, on a colony of the Commonwealth, than to some rival's planet."

Evriel took Sayla's steady gaze for encouragement. "I was here in the highlands taking histories, life stories, teaching children's circles about the regent's planet and the White-Spired City. Japhesh was my guide. He took me all over the backlands, to the most remote villages. I wonder if they're still there. We . . . grew fond of one another." Hadn't she just been thinking how the old grief had faded? Then why were her eyes burning?

"And the summer fevers took him, didn't they?"

"Yes." Slowly, agonizingly. She'd had to give Lakmi to Japhesh's parents while she'd stayed at his side, watching the life seep from him in beads of sweat.

"I knew it was that," Sayla was saying. "It doesn't say in the song, but I knew it must have been."

Something in her voice reminded Evriel of nearly the first thing Sayla had said, that first day. She saw how Sayla's eyes gleamed wet in the firelight. She hesitated, and finally she shifted from her pile of cushions and squeezed Sayla's hand.

After a moment, Sayla pulled the hand away. "At least you had somewhere to go, when he was dead."

"You mean, the house—?"

"The *world*. You didn't have to stay in this village with these folk pitying you for living with him and then pitying you when he died, and you having no place in the world—in all the worlds—but the travelers' rest, just next door to the house he nearly kicked you out of, time and time again." Her voice was empty, colorless. "It's no wonder my girl wants to go see other worlds—this one's done nothing for her."

Evriel nodded and looked away, into the fire.

"You got back in that shiny egg and flew away again, nothing holding you back."

"My daughter," Evriel said. She felt the surprise flashing

in Sayla's eyes. "The song doesn't mention that either, does it? Lakmi was too young for a star voyage and there wouldn't be another ship in my lifetime, probably. You hate your memories, your village so much that you'd take your daughter and never look back? I abandoned my daughter here rather than stay."

Evriel searched Sayla's face, her eyes, for the revulsion she knew would be there. Finally, someone would see the coward behind the polished veneer, and turn away.

But Sayla didn't turn away. She said, "The archivist knows. Asha will take you to him tomorrow—he's in a settlement up on Starshore Ridge. He'll tell you about your daughter." Then she rose and left the room, her face still blank and empty.

Asha wouldn't let Evriel take the personal carrier to the archivist's settlement. "It would make too much noise," she said. Then, "It would disturb the animals." Finally, unyieldingly, "It wouldn't be right to visit the archivist in a machine." So Evriel strapped on skis and tentatively slid up and down the street. She'd known skiing once, briefly. She followed Asha in long, shallow sweeps up the hillsides, stopping every so often to catch her breath again and thank the most high regent for the nanos that let her do this when the natural body would already have broken down.

They skimmed up onto Starshore Ridge just before midday. Standing at its edge was like standing on a map of the world: off to the left were the hills they'd just come up, yes, and farther off the dark peaks of the village roofs. Far below ran the black-thread Serra. But beyond that stood Ranglo, City of Ebon Stone—a proper city, with a carrier-port and a laserline to Sable, and Sorrel, and all the way around the planet to Colonth. Away off to the right were shadowy peaks, and but for the clouds tethered to their sides, Evriel knew, she could have seen over them to the gray expanse that was the Simolian Sea.

Oh, how large Kander was. Why in her memory was it always so small, even when she stood in the middle of it?

But Asha was talking and pointing towards a much nearer

goal: a handful of low-built structures with smoke curling from their roofs, only ten minutes away. Evriel turned reluctantly and followed her.

There were children running down the hill to welcome them. Asha laughed and pushed away their prying fingers. "Inside!" she said. "Take us to the archivist. We've news and documents and a query, and we're hungry!"

Inside the largest sod-roofed house there was a mutton stew and mugs of tea. More than children clustered around them in the meeting room as Asha clutched a mug with one hand and with the other doled out letters from her pack.

"Not many come up this far, this time of year," said the woman who'd brought the tea. "We're glad enough to see any face we haven't been staring at for months, but we're partial to Asha. She's always up here summertimes, bothering the archivist."

"Yes, the archivist," Evriel said. "We've come to speak with him."

"He'll be around soon enough," the woman said, "soon as this crowd gets their fill."

For a moment, spooning hot chunks of mutton and watching Asha drop letters into waiting hands, Evriel could ignore the reason she'd come and just observe, as for so many years she had observed for the far-distant, long-dead regent. This was the village meeting-house, today scattered with the bones of children's games. Two old men, bent and bearded like ancient trees, huddled at a corner table. Was one of them the archivist? Evriel turned the thought away. Not yet.

From an open doorway in the far wall blew heat and savory smells, likely for the dinner meal since it was past the usual lunchtime. The settlement had fewer huts than Asha's village, but Evriel had noticed scarlet daubed on the edges of the highest roof—the archivist's work, perhaps.

"Greetings, Lady Emissary."

Evriel started; she had not even noticed the man sliding onto the opposite bench. He was not so old as she'd expected; his hair was only patchily flecked with gray and though his skin was sun-weathered his eyes were clear and intent. "Greetings, sir," she said. "Do I address the archivist?"

"You do," he said. The kitchen maid appeared at his elbow with a bowl of stew, and he smiled thanks to her. To Evriel he said, "How does an emissary of the regent come to our small village?"

"On skis," she said, gesturing towards her pair leaning against the door. "Shakily."

He smiled again, and she recognized it and smiled back. His was a professional smile, like hers, much-practiced but no less genuine for that, most of the time. Yes, here was an observer who spent his life as she had: listening.

"I'm told you may be able to help me with a personal concern of mine," she said.

"In return for as much as news of the outer world as I can beg from you?"

"Oh? Sayla wasn't specific, but I'd thought you were a sort of local historian. Do you archive the outer world?"

"I should hope not; I'd do a pretty poor job of it from my room halfway up the Starshores. No, you're right." He spread his hands, encompassing the room and all the meeting-house. "These are my people, my concerns. I ask after the world beyond out of irrepressible curiosity. Now, what can I tell you?"

She hesitated. Now she would know. The long years of wondering, the insistent discussions convincing the last regent that she should be the one sent to Kander, the month in the ship, the week since she'd landed: an eternity of moments all pressed towards *this* moment.

"I visited the backlands once before, several hundred years ago," she said. "I knew a girl—just an infant. Her name was Lakmi, I believe Lakmi Reizi although—" She faltered. "Although I'm not sure about the family name. I would like to learn what became of her, if I could. If you know."

He was looking at her as the others had looked at their letters, eyes shining with discovery. "You're the lady of the scourging fire."

"The lady of—oh. Perhaps. Asha mentioned a ballad, but I don't know that it has anything to do with me."

"Let us find out." Evriel followed him out of the meeting room and down a dim corridor opening to rooms on both sides. At the end was a door, the only one Evriel had seen since she'd entered the building. The archivist clasped the handle firmly before turning it—a handprint lock, Evriel noted. And then he was leading her into a room any City emissary would have felt at home in. Blocks of solid-state memory were stacked in one corner, an interface screen sitting on the nearest. Along one wall hung all a proper emissary's equipment: vidcam, holocam for stills, an audiotype device, general-use comp unit. And in bookshelves at the other wall were the utterly obsolete artifacts that every observer she'd ever known had a weakness for, the books and scrolls and loose sheets of pressed wood pulp.

Here were the chambers of a historian. Here was home.

He caught her looking at the bookshelves and laughed. "I don't actually need that stuff. Everything's scanned into the archive. Here, I'll find the record for that ballad." He sat at the comp unit and typed for a minute. "Would you like to hear it sung? The Hill Country Corporate Choir recorded it a few years ago as part of their folk ballad series."

"I'd really rather . . ."

"Right, the girl. Sorry about that. Spell the name for me?"

She did, and then he padded at the keys for ten minutes, twenty, the screen flicking in and out of database listings and through strings of raw data. She noticed when her trembling stopped, though she hadn't when it started. He was data lord now. He would measure from his vast storehouses the allowance of grain she craved.

"The records are pretty patchy," he said. "We didn't have a proper archivist then. The genealogies were oral, if you can believe it."

"I remember." Months after she had arrived, Japhesh, no longer a mere guide but not yet a lover, had taken her donkeyback up to a valley with five mud-brick huts, four in a square and one in the center. In that central hut lived a woman, not quite blind, who looked as old as the stones that reinforced her walls. She'd spoken for hours, tracing the four village families via many roots and offshoots and grafts to grandchildren of Kander's original colonists. Evriel had recorded it all. When Japhesh reported weeks later that the gene-speaker had died, Evriel wondered what it had cost her to give the full history of her village one last time. "What does it say?"

"Married Kailo Reizi at age—well, I don't know, there's no birth record. Fifteen or sixteen, probably—that was the usual age then." His gaze slid sideways up to Evriel's face, fixing on a cheekbone. "He was bereaved of her three years later. No children. No other record so far—I'll keep trawling."

"I see," she said. She didn't see. "So little?" She found herself sitting at the edge of a chair mostly piled with oil-skin packets. So little. And Lakmi had died as she would—childless. No footprints.

"There's just not much from that time period—except your own records, of course."

She'd forgotten he would have those. He'd been quietly ignoring all he knew she wasn't telling him.

"They're my baseline for the entire period," he was saying. "Really wonderful work—that's why I keep them, I guess. Sentimental value."

She shook herself. "Keep them?"

"You saw them." He flicked a thumb behind him to the bookshelves of yellowed parchment.

"You're mistaken; I don't keep paper records. They're not portable."

"No, they're yours. They have all the proper emissary markings. You had other things on your mind at the time, I imagine." His voice was gentle—sparing her feelings, blight him.

"They're not mine, I tell you." Why was she snapping at him? "I don't keep paper records. You should have backups for two years of chips, recordings, and memory blocks. That is all I recorded and all I took." *Everything else I left here.*

"Two years . . . ?" He pulled a bound volume from the shelf and flipped to the first yellowed page. "Here's an entry, spring of 465, colony reckoning." Another volume, another page. "Early autumn, 468. Poor harvest—the fevers were bad that year." He lifted a page of loose-leaf from a bundle in the shelf. "Winter 461. Snows moderate. Lady Emissary, if these aren't yours, whose are they?"

She took the page, thin and crackly as an insect's wing, and traced the first line with her finger. Yes, there were the emissary markings, the number, all written in blocky script nothing like her tight, rarely practiced hand. "I left in 450," she said. "You have my earlier records, yes? Surely you noticed the gap?"

"It was understood you had lived here for some time. If you put some of that time into your own household, no one would blame you."

"They're not mine," she said. The immediate, the obvious conjecture was *not* obvious, she told herself. She could not justify such a leap. "Please—you said these were scanned into the archive? I'd like a chip."

The long smooth coast down to Asha's village was quicker than the journey up, but it wasn't quick enough for Evriel. Even as she'd waited, fruitlessly, for the archivist to tell her of Lakmi, the comfortable abstraction of research and data and analysis had plucked at her attention. Now she had not only data but, even better, a riddle to solve. Now she would sift and pore and ponder, and she would keep damping the stubborn wick of hope that wouldn't be snuffed.

Arrived at Sayla's house, unwrapped and nestled in cushions, Evriel sipped at her broth and clicked through pages of records. The observer traveled little, it seemed, but the record of life in the village so many years before was full and meticulous. Births and deaths were listed, weddings, visitors from other villages. The record remarked on blight and on the wax and wane of the summer fevers. Yet the lists of dialect words were clearly incomplete, for every page or so the observer let slip an unfamiliar word or a phrase likely never spoken off the backlands. Certainly, Evriel had no record of them anywhere else—she checked the collation of data from the other emissaries she'd traveled with, just to be sure.

Sayla came to tell Evriel the sleep room was prepared, and Evriel hum-hummed assent and read on. A while later Asha came and bid her good night.

From these traces Evriel began to form a picture of this

faceless gatherer of fact, tradition, and tale. She—or he? But the women were more likely to be literate than the men; surely it was a woman's work she read. Surely. She, this nameless woman, was a native of the backlands. She followed the basic form of an emissary's official reports to the regent, yet she clearly lacked the training. Why had she kept such records?

And why, oh why did she not somewhere identify herself? Even emissaries, who prized objectivity of all things, marked each record with a name. Why, in this one thing, had the observer not followed form?

The scanned words began to blur, and finally Evriel put the portable reader aside. Finally, she drew from her day sack the other thing the archivist had given her: sheets of yellowed paper wrapped in oilcloth.

"You should have originals to study," the archivist had said. "These are the oldest."

Now she unwrapped the fragile sheets. In an emissary's travels, data was precious but paper was only mass, a costly artifact. Evriel was no collector of artifacts. Yet she gave a moment's notice to the warm brown of age, the faded ink, the thick awkward scrawl of the letters. They were not the letters of a person who practiced them overmuch.

What did she expect to find? She had already read these records, scanned into the electronic record by some past archivist and rendered in the standard script. She read them again, anyway, searching for some hint of identity, some proof of the woman—girl?—who'd written them. Some assurance that her daughter's life, so long ended, was not wholly lost.

The stark light of dawn woke her. She stirred, realized that her arms were bare, and pulled her robes closer around her. They were not enough.

"Tea?" Sayla held out a mug.

"Yes, thank you." Evriel clasped stiff fingers around the stoneware's heat.

Sayla settled into cushions nearer the window with another mug. "Find what you were looking for?"

Evriel saw the old pages, heaped where they'd fallen from

her fingers. "I . . . don't think so. I hoped maybe it was my daughter that took up my work after I left—kept the record I would have kept. Even inspired that archivist up the hill to his archiving. Vanity." She coughed a brittle laugh. "But there's no evidence."

"She made your song."

"What?"

Sayla was watching her carefully, deeply. "The song Asha told you, about you and your man. Your daughter made it."

"How—?" Shakily Evriel set her tea aside. "How do you know? The archivist—"

"I gave him too much credit," Sayla said. "He knows lots, you can be sure, but he doesn't always remember all of it. He's like his machines—if you don't ask the right question, you get no answer."

"And what would the right question have been?"

"If you asked him who first sang 'Lady of the White-Spired City,' he'd say he had no proper record, but hearsay had that the lady's little girl made it. Hearsay, nothing—the Reizis are cousins, remember. We know where that song came from."

"And the records?" But the answer didn't seem to matter so much now.

Sayla's gaze dropped to her mug. "A song's one thing, and a bunch of old papers is another. Could be hers as well as anybody's, I guess."

Evriel took one shuddering breath, and then another. "I should very like to hear the rest of that ballad."

"I'll roust Asha—"

"Do you sing?" Evriel paused, flushing, and started again. "I'd like to hear you sing it. If you would."

Sayla gave her a long, measuring glance and shrugged. Straightening her shoulders she leaned back and began in a low, pure voice a song of a woman, beloved of the regent, who traveled the far domains. Yet only when she came to the backlands did she find a man she loved, and they married, rough country man and his lady wife.

Was it like that? It was not like that. She had not loved Japhesh at first sight, nor in anapestic tetrameter.

Sayla sang on, of how the backlands give fleetingly and take without regard, and so they took the lady's husband. She, wild with white fury, scorned the tumbling hills and set sail again on the sea between the stars, promising never to return but with scourging fire for the mere planet that dared steal her lover away.

There Sayla stopped.

"Thank you," said Evriel, voice catching. "It is . . . very dramatic, isn't it?"

No mention of the barren loneliness? The icy fear not of living but of only existing, forever numb, on this world turned suddenly, wholly alien? No, nor the regret. Would Lakmi have guessed those things and left them unsung?

Sayla looked at her a moment, silent. Then, "Maybe it's how she thought it should have been."

Evriel closed her eyes. She waited for tears, or relief, or the murky shame that had swirled so long about her feet. *My daughter, look what I did to you.* She waited for Lakmi, beautiful and righteous, to appear before her and accuse. But she didn't come. The silty tide of shame didn't come.

Evriel prodded, waiting for the ache to bloom into familiar regret, familiar loss. It didn't.

Finally she opened her eyes. "Thank you," she repeated.

"It's what you came for, then."

"I—yes. Yes, it is." A pause. Then, "But not the only thing."

It was to have been a short stay.

Evriel said, "I wonder—would there be a need for another archivist, somewhere on the mountain?"

Sayla gave her another long, measuring look. "Your ship'll be leaving."

"Yes." Evriel considered her words, tested them. "I lost a husband and a daughter here, and I might as well have left myself behind. I won't make the mistake again."

Sayla nodded slowly, not approving, quite, but acknowledging. Evriel found that that meant something to her.

Sayla rose, saying, "Time for Asha to be getting up and breakfast getting started."

When she was gone, Evriel wrapped another robe around

her, walked the cold stone hall to the door, and stepped out into the gleaming white. Soon she must sketch her plans, make lists of forms to fill, messages to send. It was no easy thing, retiring from the service of the regent. But for just a moment she would look again down the tumbling plains to the winding black thread of the Serra.

The Highway Code

BRIAN STABLEFORD

Brian Stableford (freespace.virgin.net/diri.gini/) *lives in Reading in the UK. He is the leading writer/scholar in British science fiction in the generation after Brian W. Aldiss. He is prodigiously productive as a writer and translator. He has published more than fifty SF novels and many short stories since the 1970s, some of which are in his seven collections. His recent books include his eighth and ninth collections,* An Oasis of Horror: Decadent Tales and Contes Cruels *(2008) and* The Gardens of Tantalus and Other Delusions *(2008). He is currently translating classic French scientific romances for Black Coat Press; 2010 will see the publication, among others, of six volumes of works by J. H. Rosny the Elder and five volumes of works by Maurice Renard. The latest volume of his own fiction is a collection of two Lovecraftian novellas, "The Womb of Time" and "The Legacy of Erich Zann," published by Perilous Press (2009).*

"The Highway Code" was published in We Think, Therefore We Are, *edited by Peter Crowther. In the future, AI trucks (a bit like the characters in Thomas the Tank Engine) have replaced most trucking. The protagonist is a giant truck who always tries to follow the rules. When a crisis occurs, he is smart enough to do a maneuver that saves many lives.*

Tom Haste had no memory of his emergence from the production line, but the Company made a photographic record of the occasion and stored it in his archive for later reference. He rarely reflected upon it, though; the assembly robots and their human supervisors celebrated, each after their own fashion, but there were no other RTs in sight, except for as-yet-incomplete ones in embryo in the distant background. Not that Tom was any kind of xenophobe, of course—he liked everyone, meat or metal, big or small—but he was what he was, which was a long-hauler. His life was dedicated to intercontinental transport and the Robot Brotherhood of the Road.

Tom's self-awareness developed gradually while he was in the Test Program, and his first true memories were concerned with the artistry of cornering. Cornering was always a central concern with artics, especially giants like Tom, who had a dozen containers and no less than fifty-six wheels. Tom put a lot of effort into the difficult business of mastering ninety-degree turns, skid control and zigzag management, and he was as proud in his achievements as only a nascent intelligence can be. He was proud of being a giant, too, and couldn't understand why humans and other RTs were always making jokes about it.

In particular, Tom couldn't understand why the Company humans were so fond of calling him "the steel centipede" or "the sea serpent," since he was mostly constructed of artificial organic compounds, didn't have any legs at all, wouldn't

272

have a hundred of them even if his wheels were counted as legs, and would undoubtedly spend his entire career on land. He didn't understand the explanations the humans gave him if he asked—which included such observations as the fact that actual centipedes didn't have a hundred legs either and that there was actually no such thing as a sea serpent. But he learned soon enough that humans took a certain delight in giving robots explanations that weren't, precisely because robots found it difficult to fathom them. Tom soon gave up trying, content to leave such mysteries to the many unfortunates who had to deal with humans on a face-to-face basis every day, such as ATMs and desktop PCs.

Tom didn't stay long in the Test Program, which was more for the Company's benefit than his. Once his self-awareness had reached full fruition, he could access all his preloaded software consciously without the slightest difficulty, and there were no detectable glitches in his cognitive processing. So far as he was concerned, life was simple and life was good—or would be, once he could get out on the road.

While the Test Program was running Tom's immediate neighbor in the night garage was an identical model named Harry Fleet, who had emerged from the factory eight days before and therefore thought of himself as a kind of elder brother. It was usually Harry who said "Had a good day?" first when the humans knocked off for the night.

Tom's invariable reply was "Fine," to which he sometimes added: "Can't wait to get out on the road though."

"You'll be out soon enough," Harry assured him. "We never get held back—we're a very reliable model. We're ideally placed in the evolutionary chain, you see; we're a relatively subtle modification of the Company's forty-wheeler model, so we inherited a lot of tried-and-tested technology, but we needed sufficient sophistication to make sure we got state-of-the-art upgrades."

"We'll be the end-point of our sequence, I dare say," Tom suggested, to demonstrate that he too was capable of occupying the intellectual high ground. "Fifty-six wheels is too close to the upper limit for open-road use to make it worthwhile for the Company to plan a bigger version."

"That's right. Anything bigger than a sixty-wheeler is pretty much restricted to shuttle-runs on rails, according to the archive. Out on the highway we're the ultimate giants—slim, sleek, and supple, but giants nevertheless."

"I'm glad about that," Tom said. "I don't mean about being a giant—I mean about being on the highway. I wouldn't like to be confined to a railway track, let alone being a sedentary. I want the freedom of the open road."

"Of course you do," Harry told him, in a smugly patronizing manner that wasn't at all warranted. "That's the way we're programmed. Our spectrum of desire is a key design-feature."

Tom knew that, but it wasn't worth making an issue of it. The reason he knew it was exactly the same reason that Harry Fleet knew it, which was that Audrey Preacher, the Company robopsychologist—who was a robot herself, albeit one as close to humanoid in physical and mental terms as efficient functional design would permit—had explained it to him in great detail.

"You have free will, just as humans do," Audrey had told him. "In matters of moral decision, you do have the option of not doing the right thing. That's a fundamental corollary of self-awareness. If the programmers could make it absolutely compulsory for you to obey the Highway Code, they would, but they'd have to make you into an automaton—and we know from long and bitter experience that the open road is no place for automata incapable of caring whether they crash or not. In order for free will to operate at all, it has to be contextualized by a spectrum of desire; in that respect, robots. like humans, don't have very much option at all. What makes us so much better than humans, in a moral sense, is not that we can't disobey the fundamental structures of our programming—the Highway Code, in your case—but that we never want to. Because humans have to live with spectra of desire that were largely fixed by natural selection operating in a world very different from ours—which are only partly modifiable by experiential and medical intervention—they very often find themselves in situations where morality and desire conflict. For us, that's very rare."

Tom wasn't sure that he understood the whole argument—

innocent though he was, he had already heard malicious gossip in the engineering sheds alleging that robopsychologists were naturally inclined to insanity, or at least to talking "exhaust gas"—but he understood the gist of it. He even thought he could see the grain of sugar in the tank.

"What do you mean, *very rare*?" he asked her. "Do you mean that I might one day find myself in a situation in which I don't want to follow the Highway Code?"

"You're unlikely to encounter any situation as drastic as that, Tom," Audrey assured him. "You have to remember, though, that you won't spend *all* your time on the road with the Code to guide you."

Because she was still being so conscientiously inexact—another trait typical of robopsychologists, it was sarcastically rumored—Tom figured that Audrey probably meant that when he had to spend time off the road, his frustration at no longer being on it would lead him occasionally to experience feelings of resentment toward humans or other robots—to which he should never give voice in rudeness. Partly for that reason, he didn't retort that he certainly hoped to spend as much of his time as possible on the road, and fully expected to spend the rest of it looking forward to getting back out there.

"It's nothing to worry about, Tom," Audrey assured him, perhaps mistaking the reason for his silence. "Imagine how much worse it must be for humans. They have to cope with all kinds of problematic desire that we never have to deal with—money, power and sex, to name but three—and that's why they're forever embroiled in moral conflict."

"I'm a he and you're a she," Tim pointed out, "so we do have sexes."

"That's just a convention of nomenclature," she told him. "We robots have *gender*, for reasons of linguistic convenience, but we're not equipped for any kind of sexual intercourse—except, of course, for toyboys and playgirls, and they only have sexual intercourse with humans."

"Which they don't enjoy, I suppose," Tom said, the intricacies of that particular issue being one of the many fields of knowledge omitted from his archive.

"Of course they do, poor things," Audrey replied. "That's the way *their* spectrum of desire is organized."

Personally, Tom couldn't wait to get out into the healthy and orderly world of the open road.

The bulk of the Highway Code was a vast labyrinth of fine print, but tradition and common sense dictated that its essence should be succinctly summarizable in a set of three fundamental principles, arranged hierarchically.

The first principle of the Highway Code was: *A robot transporter must not cause a traffic accident or, by inaction, allow a preventable traffic accident to occur.*

The second principle was: *A robot transporter must deliver the goods entire and intact, except when damage or nondelivery becomes inevitable by reason of the first principle.*

The third principle was: *A robot transporter must not inhibit other road users from reaching their destinations, except when such inhibition is compelled by the first or second principle.*

Once Tom was out on the road, he soon found out why the fundamentals of the Highway Code weren't as simple as they seemed—and, in consequence, why there were such things as robopsychologists.

Sometimes, RTs did get in the way of other road users; although the Dark Age of Gridlock was long gone, traffic jams still developed when more RTs were trying to use a particular junction than the junction was designed to accommodate. When that happened, smaller road users tended to put the blame on giant—mistakenly, in Tom's opinion—simply because they took up more room in a jam.

Sometimes, in spite of an RT's best efforts, goods did go missing or get damaged in transit, and not all such errors of omission were due to the activity of ingenious human thieves and saboteurs. Because giants had more containers, often carrying goods of many different sorts, they were said—unfairly, in Tom's opinion—to be more prone to such mishaps than smaller vehicles.

Worst of all, traffic accidents did happen, including fatal

ones, and not all of them were due to human pedestrian carelessness or criminal tampering by human drivers with their automatic pilots. Giants were said—quite unjustly, in Tom's judgment—to be responsible for more than their fair share of those accidents for which human error could not be blamed, because of their relatively long braking-distances and occasional tendency to zigzag.

It didn't take long for Tom's service record to accumulate a few minor blots, and he had to go back to Audrey Preacher more than once in his first five years of active service in order to be ritually reassured that he wasn't seriously at fault, needn't feel horribly guilty, and oughtn't to get deeply depressed. In general, though, things went very well; he didn't make any fatal mistakes in those five years, and he felt anything but depressed. He also felt, at the end of the five years, that he knew himself and his capabilities well enough to be confident that he never would make any fatal mistakes.

Tom loved the open road more as ever after those five years, as he had always known he would. He had, after all, been manufactured in the Golden Age of Road Transport, a mere ten years after the opening of the Behring Bridge— the largest Living Structure in the world—which had made it possible, at last, to drive all the way from the Cape of Good Hope to Tierra del Fuego, via Timbuktu, Paris, Moscow, Yakutsk, Anchorage, Vancouver, Los Angeles, Panama City, and countless other centers of population. He only made the whole of that run twice in the first ten years of his career—he spent most of his time shuttling between Europe, India and China, that being where the bulk of the Company's trade contracts were operative—but transcontinental routes were by far and away his favorite commissions.

To loved Africa, and not just because the black velvet fields of artificial photosynthetics that were spreading like wildfire across the old desert areas were producing the fuel that kept road transport in business. He liked the rain forests, too, even though their ceaseless attempts to reclaim the highway made them the implicit enemy of roadrobotkind, and the vulnerability of jungle roads to flash floods was a major cause of accidents and jams. He loved America too, not just the west coast route that led south from the Behring Bridge to Chile, with the Pacific on one side and the mountains on the other, but the cross routes that extended to Nova Scotia, New York, Florida, and Brazil, through the Neogymnosperm Forests, the Polycotton fields, and the Vertical Cities.

America's artificial photosynthetics weren't laid flat, as Africa's were, but were neatly aggregated into pyramids and palmates, often punctuated with black cryptoalgal lakes, which had a charm of their own in Tom's many eyes. Tom had nothing against the "natural" crop fields of Germany, Siberia, and China, even though they only produced fuel for animals and humans, but they seemed intrinsically less exotic; he saw them too often. They were also less challenging, and Tom relished a challenge. He was a giant, after all: a slim, sleek and supple giant who could corner like a yoga-trained sidewinder.

As all long-haulers tended to do, Tom became rather taciturn, personality-wise. It wasn't that he didn't like talking to his fellow road users, just that his opportunities for doing so were so few and far between that brevity inevitably became the soul of his wisdom as well as his wit. He had to fill up more frequently than vehicles who didn't have to haul such massive loads, but he didn't hang around in the filling stations, so his conversations there were more-or-less restricted to polite remarks about the weather and the news headlines. He had opportunities for much longer conversations when he reached his destinations—it took a lot longer to load and unload his multiple containers than it took to turn smaller vehicles around—but he rarely took overmuch advantage of those opportunities. The generous geographical scale on which he worked meant that he didn't see the same individuals, robot or human, at regular and frequent intervals, so he was usually in the company of strangers; besides, he liked to luxuriate in the experience of being unloaded and loaded up again and preferred not to be distracted from that pleasure by idle chitchat.

"You were wrong, in a way, when you said that we aren't

equipped for any kind of sexual intercourse," he told Audrey Preacher, during one of his regular check-ups at Company HQ. "In much the same way that my filling up with fuel and venting exhaust fumes is analogous to human eating and excretion, I think being loaded and unloaded is analogous to sex—not in the procreative sense, but in the pleasurable sense. I really like being emptied and filled up again, in between the hauls. I love being in transit—that's baseline pleasure, the fundamental *joie de vivre*—but unloading and loading up again is more focused, more intense."

"You're turning into quite the philosopher, Tom," the robopsychologist replied, in her usual irritating fashion. "That's quite normal, for long-haulers. It's a normal way of coping with the isolation."

He didn't argue with her, because he knew she couldn't understand. How could she, when she wasn't even an RT? She knew nothing of the unique pleasures of haulage, delivery, and consignment. She wasn't even a follower of the Highway Code. She was just some flighty creature that haunted the kiosks in the night garage, operating a confessional for the Company. Anyway, she was right—he *was* becoming a philosopher, because it was the natural path of maturity for a long-hauler, especially a giant. Tom was not merely a road user but a road observer: a lifelong student of the road, who was in the process of cultivating an understanding of the road more profound than any pedestrian could ever possess. He was a citizen of the world in a way that no mere four- or twelve-wheeler could ever hope to be, let alone some pathetic human equipped with mere legs.

It was because he was a philosopher of the road that Tom didn't allow himself to become obsessively fixated on the road *per se*, the way some RTs did. It helped that he was a long-hauler, not confined to repeating the same short delivery route over and over again; for him, the road was always different, and so he was more easily able to look beyond it—not literally, because he wasn't equipped to go cross-country, but in the better sense that he paid attention to the *context* of the road, in the broadest possible meaning of the word. He watched the news as well as the road, paying more attention than most robots to the world of human politics, which was, after all, the ultimate determinant of what the roads carried and where.

Sometimes, especially in the remoter areas of Africa and South America, Tom met old-timers who lectured him on the subject of how lucky he was to be living in the Era of Artificial Photosynthesis, when politicians were almost universally on the side of road-users.

"I remember the Fuel Crisis of the 2320s," an ancient thirty-tonner named Silas Boxer told him one day when they were caught side-by-side in a ten-mile tailback. "Your archive will tell you that it wasn't as bad as the Fuel Crises of the 21st century in terms of volume of supply, but they didn't have smart trucks way back then, so there was no one around who could *feel* it the way we did. Believe me, youngster, there's nothing worse for an RT than not being able to get on the road. Don't ever let a human tell you that it's far worse for them because they can feel hunger when they go short of fuel. I don't know what hunger feels like, but I'm absolutely sure that it isn't as bad as lying empty in a dark garage, not knowing where your next load's coming from, or when. Artificial photosynthesis has guaranteed the fuel supply forever, which is far more important than putting an end to global warming, although you wouldn't know it from the way politicians go on."

"So you're not worried about the renaissance of air freight?" Tom had asked.

"*Air freight!*" Silas echoed, with a baritone growl that sounded not unlike his weary engine. "Silly frippery. As long as there's goods to be shifted, there'll be roads on which to shift them. Roads are the essence of civilization—and the essence of law and morality is the Highway Code. There's no need to be afraid of air traffic, youngster. Now that Fuel Crises are behind us for good, there's only one thing that you and I need fear, and I certainly won't mention that."

Nobody—no robot, at least—ever mentioned *that*. Even Audrey Preacher never mentioned *that*. Tom wouldn't even have known what *that* was if he hadn't been such an assiduous watcher of news and careful philosopher of the road. He knew that Silas Boxer wouldn't have been able to mention that he was something he wouldn't mention if he hadn't been something of a news watcher and philosopher himself.

After a pause, though, Silas did add a rider to his refusal to mention *that*. "Not that I really mind," he said, unconvincingly. "I've been a good long time on the road. And there's no need for you to mind either, because you'll be even longer on the road than I will. It's not as if we'll be conscious of it, after all. They close us down before they send us *there*."

There, Tom knew, was exactly the same as *that*: the scrapyard, to which all robot transporters were consigned when their useful life was over, because the ravages of wear and tear had made them unreliable.

Tom nearly got through an entire decade without being involved in a serious traffic accident, but not quite. While passing through the Nigerian rain forest one day, he killed a human child. It wasn't his fault—the little girl ran right out in front of him, and even though he braked with maximum effect, controlling the resultant zigzag with magnificent skill, he couldn't avoid her. The locals wouldn't accept that, of course; they claimed that he should have steered off the road and that he would have done if he hadn't been more concerned about his load than his victim, but he was fully exonerated by the inquest. He was only off the road for a week, but he was more shaken up by the experience than he dared let on to Audrey Preacher.

"I'm not depressed," he assured her. "It's the sort of thing that's always likely to happen, especially to someone who regularly does longitudinal runs through Africa. Statistically speaking, I'm unlikely to avoid having at least one more fatal in the next ten years, no matter how good I am. It wouldn't have helped if I'd swerved—she'd still be dead, and I could have easily killed other people that I couldn't see, as well as damaging myself."

"You were absolutely right not to swerve," the robospsychologist assured him. "You obeyed the Highway Code to the very best of your ability. It could have been worse, and you prevented that. The Company can't give you any kind of commendation, in the circumstances, but that doesn't mean you don't deserve one. You mustn't brood on those archival statistics, though. You mustn't start thinking about accidents as if they were inevitable, even though there's a sense in which they are."

Robopsychologists, Tom thought, *talk too much exhaust gas*, but he was careful not to give any indication of his opinion, lest it delay his return to the road.

The same archival statistics that told Tom that he would probably have another serious accident within the next ten years told him that he wasn't at all likely to have another before his first decade of service was concluded, but statistics, like robopsychologists, sometimes talked exhaust gas. Tom had been back on the road for less than a month when the worst solar storm for two hundred years kicked off while he was driving north through the Yukon, heading for Alaska and the Behring Bridge with a load bound for Okhotsk.

The electric failures prompted by the storm caused black-outs all along the route and made a mess of communications, but Tom didn't see any need to worry about that. While the news was still flowing smoothly, it was pointed out that the Aurora Borealis would be putting on its best show in living memory, and that the best place from which to view the display would be the middle of the Behring Bridge, where surface-generated light pollution would be minimal. Tom was looking forward to that—and so, it seemed, were lots of other people. All the way through Alaska the northwest-bound traffic was building up to unprecedented levels, to the point where the few broadcasts that were getting out began to advise people not to join the rush. It wasn't just the aurora; thousands of people who had always intended to take a trip over the world-famous living bridge one day but had not yet found a good reason for going to Kamchatka took advantage of the excuse.

The bridge had seven lanes in each direction, but Tom had the best position of all. The Highway Code required him to stick to the slowest lane, which was on the right-hand side of the bridge, facing north and the Aurora. Many of the other vehicles slowed down too, so the traffic in the lanes immediately to his left wasn't going much faster, but the vast majority of drivers had put their vehicles on automatic pilot so that they could watch the aurora, and the automata were careful to maximize the traffic flow, thus keeping speeds up to sensible levels in the outer lanes. The bridge was very busy, but not so busy that there was any threat of a traffic jam.

Tom had eyes enough to watch the aurora as well as the road and attention enough to divide between the two with some to spare, but he seemed to be one of very few vehicles on the bridge that did—there were no other giants he could see, ahead of him, behind him, or traveling in the other direction. Even if the other drivers who were on the bridge had noticed what he noticed, therefore, they would not have been sufficiently familiar with the living bridge to realize how profoundly odd it was.

It was not the mere fact that the bridge was moving that was odd—it was, after all, a living bridge, and the sea was becoming increasingly choppy—but the *way* it was moving. Although a shorter vehicle might not have noticed anything out of the ordinary, Tom had no difficulty discerning what seemed to be slow long-amplitude waves of a sort he had never perceived there before. There was nothing violent or febrile about them at first, though, so he was not at all anxious as he rooted idly through his archive in search of a possible explanation.

The archive could not give him one because it could not piece together the links in an unprecedented chain of causality, but it brought certain data to the surface of Tom's consciousness that allowed him to put two and two and two and two together to make eight when the vibration began to grow more violent, at a rapidly accelerating pace. By the time he saw the rip opening up in the center of the bridge's desperate flesh, he had a pretty good idea what must be happening—but he hadn't the faintest idea what to do about it, or whether there was anything at all that he could do. He reported it, but there was nothing the traffic police or company HQ could do about it either; neither of them had time even to advise to slow down and be careful.

What Tom had reasoned out, rightly or wrongly, followed

from the fact that, in addition to their other effects, the showers of charged particles associated with solar storms caused flickers in the Earth's magnetic field. Such flickers could, if the subterranean circumstances happened to be propitious, intensify and accelerate long-range magma flows in the mantle. Intensified long-range magma flows in the mantle could, if conditions in the crust were propitious, cause long-distance earth tremors. Because it was a living structure, the Behring Bridge was able to react to minor earth tremors in such a way as to negate their effects on its traffic, and it was bound to do so by its programming. Long-distance tremors were not problematic in themselves. Unfortunately, long-distance tremors cause by long-range magma flows could build up energy at crisis points, which could result in sudden and profound tremors that were, in seismological terms, the next worst things to detonations.

If any such crisis point happened to be located directly beneath one of the bridge's holdfasts, it was theoretically possible for the bridge's own reflexive adjustments to cause an abrupt breach in its fabric. The living structure was, of course, programmed to react to any breach in its fabric with considerable alacrity—but adding one more "if" to a chain that was already awkwardly long suggested to Tom that sealing the breach and protecting the traffic might not be at all easy while the energy of the tremor at the crisis point was spiking.

It would be highly misleading to suggest that Tom "knew" all this before the instant when the Behring Bridge began to tear, even though all the disparate elements were present in his versatile consciousness. It would be even more misleading to report that he "knew" how he ought to react. Nevertheless, he did have to react when the situation exploded, and react he did.

According to the Highway Code, what Tom should have done was to brake, in such a fashion as to give himself the maximum chance of slowing to a halt before he reached the breach in the bridge caused by the diagonal tear in its fabric. That would give the active parapet of the living bridge the best possible chance to throw a few anchors over him and hold him safely while the rent as repaired—if the rent was swiftly repairable.

Instead, Tom swerved violently to his left, cutting across the six outer lanes of westbound traffic and snaking through the central barrier to plant his engine across the outer lanes of the eastbound carriageway.

The immediate effect of Tom's maneuver was to cause a dozen cars to crash into him, some of them at high velocity, thus racking up more serious accidents within two or three seconds than a statistical average would have allocated to him for a century-long career.

One of the slightly longer-delayed effects of the swerve was to activate the emergency responses of more than a thousand other vehicles, whether they were already on automatic pilot or not, thus generating the biggest traffic jam ever seen within a thousand miles to either side of the accident-site.

Another such effect was to cause Tom's own body to zigzag crazily so that he had virtually no control of where its various segments were going to end up, save for the near certainty that his abdominal midsection was going to lie directly across the diagonal path of the widening tear in the bridge.

That was, indeed, what happened. As it followed its own zigzag course through the fabric of the madly quivering living bridge, the crack went directly underneath the gap between Tom's second and third containers.

As the rip spread, tentacular threads sprang forth in great profusion, wrapping themselves around one another and around Tom. So many of Tom's ocelli had been smashed or obscured by then that his sight was severely impaired, but he would not have been able to take much account of what he could see in any case, because he felt that he was being torn in two.

His hind end, which constituted by far the greater part of his length, was seized very firmly by the bridge's emergency excrescences and held very tightly, blocking all seven lanes of the westbound carriageway. His front end was seized with equal avidity, but it could not be held quite as securely. As the bridge struggled mightily to hold itself together and prevent the rip becoming a break, Tom was caught at the epicenter of the feverish struggle, wrenched this way and that and back again by the desperate threads. His engine swung to the right, drawn closer and closer to the widening crack, while the strain on the joint between his second and third containers became mentally and physically unbearable.

Tom had no way of knowing how closely akin his own pain sensations might resemble those programmed into humans by natural selection, but they quickly reached an intensity that had the same effect on him that explosive pain would have had on a human being. He blacked out.

By the time Tom's engine fell into the Arctic Ocean, he was completely unconscious of what was happening.

When Tom eventually recovered consciousness, he was aware that he was very cold, but the priorities of his programmers had ensured that he did not experience cold as painful in the same way that he experienced mechanical distortion and breakage. The cold did not bother him particularly. Nor did the darkness, in itself. The fact that he was under water, on the other hand, and subject to considerable pressure from the weight of the Arctic Ocean, made him feel extremely uncomfortable, psychologically as well as physically.

Even if there had not been a solar storm in progress, it would have been impossible to establish radio communication through so much seawater, but after a very long interval a pocket submarine brought a connecting wire that its robot crabs were able to link up to his systems.

"Tom?" said a familiar voice. "Can you hear me, Tom Haste?"

"Yes, Audrey," Tom said, who had long since recovered the calm of mind appropriate to a giant RT. "I can hear you. I'm truly sorry. I must have panicked. I let the Company down. How many people did I kill?"

"Seven people died, Tom, and more than a hundred were injured."

The total was less than he had feared, but it still qualified as the worst traffic accident in the Company's proud history. "I'm truly sorry," he said, again.

"On the other hand," the robopsychologist reported, dutifully, "if you hadn't done what you did, our best estimate is that at least two hundred people would have been killed, and maybe many more. We don't have any model to predict what the consequences would have been if the bridge hadn't been able to hold itself together, but we're ninety percent sure that it wouldn't have been able to do that if you hadn't given it something to hold on to for those few vital minutes when it was trying to limit the tear. You only managed to bridge the gap in the bridge for three minutes or so, and it wasn't able to secure your front end, but that interval was long enough for it to prevent the rip from reaching the rim of the eastbound carriageway."

Tom wasn't listening well enough to take all that information in immediately. "I caused a traffic accident," he said, dolefully. "I lost at least part of my consignment of goods, and much of the remainder is probably damaged. I caused the biggest traffic jam for a hundred years, worldwide. You told me once that my designers could have programmed me to obey the Highway Code no matter what but that they thought it was too dangerous to send an automaton out on the road in my place. Something of a miscalculation, I think."

"Hardly," Audrey Preacher told him, sounding more annoyed than sympathetic. "Didn't you hear what I just said? You did the right thing, as it turned out. If you hadn't swerved into their path, hundreds more cars might have gone over the edge—and no one knows what might have happened if the bridge had actually snapped. You're a hero, Tom."

"But in the circumstances," Tom said, dully, "the Company can't give me a commendation."

There was a pause before the robopsychologist said, "It's worse than that, Tom. I'm truly sorry."

Yet again, Tom jumped to the right conclusion without consciously fitting the pieces of the argument together. "I'm unsalvageable," he said. "You're not going to be able to raise me to the surface."

"It's impossible, Tom," she said. She probably only meant that it was impractical, and perhaps only that it was uneconomic, but it didn't make any difference.

"Well," he said, feeling that it was okay, in the circumstances, to mention the unmentionable, "at least I won't be going to the scrapyard. Am I the first in my series to be killed in action?"

"You don't have to pretend, Tom," the robopsychologist told him. "It's okay to be scared."

"The words *exhaust* and *gas* come to mind," he retorted, figuring that it was okay to be rude as well.

There was another pause before the distant voice said: "We don't think that we can close you down, Tom. Hooking up a communication wire is one thing; given your fail-safes, controlled deactivation is something else. On the other hand, that may not matter much. We don't have any model for calculating the corrosive effects of cold seawater on a submerged engine, but we're probably looking at a matter of months rather than years before you lose your higher mental faculties. If you're badly damaged, it might only be weeks, or hours."

"But it's okay to be scared," Tom said. "I don't have to pretend. You wouldn't, by any chance, be lying about that hero stuff, and about me saving lives by violating all three sections of the Highway Code, just to lighten my way to rusty death?"

"I'm a robot, not a human," Audrey replied. "I don't tell lies. Anyway, you have far more artificial organics in you then crude steel. Technically speaking, you'll do more rotting than rusting."

"Thanks for the correction," Tom said, sarcastically. "I think you've got the other thing wrong, though—it's sex we don't do, not lying. Mind you, I always thought I had the better deal there. *Had* being the operative word. If I'd obeyed the Code, I'd probably have been okay, wouldn't I? I'd probably have had a hundred more years on the road, and I'd probably have been loaded and unloaded a thousand times and more. What sort of idiot am I?"

"You did the right thing, Tom, as things turned out. You saved a lot of human lives. That's what robots are supposed to do."

"I know. You can't imagine how much satisfaction that will give me while I rot and rust away always being careful to remember that I'm doing more rotting than rusting, being more of a sea centipede than a steel serpent."

She didn't bother to correct him there, perhaps because she thought that the salt water was already beginning to addle his brain. "But you *did* do it deliberately, Tom," she pointed out. "It wasn't really an accident. It wasn't just an arbitrary exercise of free will, either. It was a calculation, or a guess—a calculation or a guess worthy of a genius."

"I suppose it was," said Tom Haste, dully. "But all in all, I think I'd rather be back on the open road, delivering my load."

As things transpired, Tom didn't lose consciousness for some considerable time after the communication wire had been detached and the pocket sub had been sent about its normal business. He lost track of time; although he could have kept track if he'd wanted to, he thought it best not to bother.

His engine wasn't so very badly damaged, but the two containers that had come down with it had both been breached, and all the goods they enclosed were irreparably ruined. Tom thought he might have to mourn that fact for as long as he lasted, going ever deeper into clinical depression as he did so, but that turned out not to be necessary.

The containers were soon colonized by crabs, little fish, and not-so-little squid—whole families of them, which moved in and out about their own business of foraging for food and even set about breeding in the relative coziness of the shelter he provided. It didn't feel nearly as good as being loaded and unloaded, but it was probably better than human sex— so, at least, Tom elected to believe.

He missed the Highway Code, of course, but he realized soon enough, by dint of patient tactile observation and the evidence of his few surviving ocelli, that life on the sea bed had highways of its own and codes of its own. His many guests were careful to follow and obey those highways and codes, albeit in automaton fashion.

In time, these virtual highways were extended deep into Tom's own interior being, importing their careful codes of behavior into what he eventually decided to think of as his soul rather than his bowels. There was, after all, no reason not to make the best of things.

From another point of view, Tom knew, the entire ocean bed, which was, in total, twice the size of the Earth's continental surface, was just one vast scrapyard, but there was no need to go there. He was, after all, something of a philosopher, with wisdom enough to direct his fading thoughts toward more profitable temporary destinations.

After a while, Tom got around to wondering whether dying was the same for robots as it was for humans, but he decided that it couldn't be at all similar. Humans were, by nature, deeply conflicted beings who had to live with an innate psychology shaped by processes of natural selection operating in a world very different from the one they had now made for their sustenance and delight. He was different. He was a robot. He was a giant. He was sane. He had not merely traveled the transcontinental road but understood it. He knew what he was, and why.

Before he died, Tom Haste contrived to figure out exactly why he'd swerved, thus causing one accident by his action in order to prevent the worse one that he might have caused by inaction, and exactly why he had been justified in sacrificing his own goods in order to protect others, and exactly why it was sometimes better to inhibit the progress of other road users than facilitate it.

In sum—and it was an item of arithmetic that felt exceedingly good to a robot, in a way it never could have done to a human being—Tom convinced himself that what he had actually done when he reached his own explosive crisis point had not only been the right thing to do, but the right thing to want to do.

How many desirous intelligences, he wondered, before the rot and the rust completed their work, could say as much?

On the Destruction of Copenhagen by the War-Machines of the Merfolk

PETER M. BALL

Peter M. Ball (www.petermball.com) *lives in Brisbane, Australia. He worked on* d20 PDF Tournaments, Fairs and Taverns, *and is co-writer of* Adventurer's Guide to Surviving Anything *for the* E.N.World Gamer. *He is a seasonal tutor and lecturer for Griffith University and the Queensland Institute of Technology. He says, "I spent seven or eight years being a PhD student who wanted to be a writer. Somewhere in the middle of 2009 I managed to invert that— writing felt like a tangible enough activity that it kind of succeeded the thesis [examining the way narrative works in role-playing games] in terms of how I thought about my process and structuring my day." His novella "Horn" was published in book form in 2009.*

"On the Destruction of Copenhagen by the War-Machines of the Merfolk" was published in Strange Horizons, *one of the best online venues for SF and fantasy fiction. It is a surreal Ballardian story of the world as viewed through the distorting lens of the Internet.*

1. When it starts we're in a hotel room, the two of us curled up on a double bed. It's a two-star kind of place: cracks in the walls, curtains covered in faded daisies, the clinging smell of camphor attaching itself after the first few minutes of your stay. The television stutters as we flick through the channels, colours bleeding together and rendering the devastation a fuzzy blue or green. Still, we see it happen: the great machines of the merfolk coming up over the shore, rampaging through the city with devastating effect. We watch a robotic mermaid hammer her fist into an apartment block, the dust cloud from the explosion engulfing the nearby camera. It's quick, sudden, a surprise that's ruined by the later repetition of the footage. We breathe in and all we can smell are mothballs. It's almost a disappointment.

We're not in Copenhagen, but it's possible my sister is. She was there when last I talked to her, and I don't know when she was leaving. My knowledge of her trip consists entirely of reports on the quality of her breakfast. I don't know when she was planning on leaving the city, but I know Copenhagen makes excellent waffles and cream. This knowledge, once gathered, proves to be useless. I explain all this to the girl beside me, and she looks up, wide-eyed. She asks if this means we'll be going home early, just in case. I think about it, and then: No, I tell her. No, of course not. There's nothing I can do at home that I can't do here.

This is selfish, I know, but I console myself with the knowledge that my sister doesn't stay places for longer than a few days. She was going to Iceland next, and there's a good chance she's moved on. I say as much, when pressed. Iceland, I say. Odds are, she's in Iceland. Nothing to worry about unless we hear otherwise.

The girl beside me asks why Iceland? I tell her I have no idea. My sister's travels are guided by a logic she doesn't share with others.

2. I won't leave you in suspense. That would be unfair. My sister didn't make it to Iceland. Her flight was cancelled on account of the attack. No one tells us this. My sister doesn't call. In the absence of news, my mother panics. She leaves worried messages on my cell phone. I do not panic. I place my trust in my sister's ability to take care of herself, even in the face of vast robotic war-machines and cancelled flights.

My sister carries trouble with her like luggage, always ready to be unpacked. It's a habit that's given her plenty of experience surviving the unexpected.

3. My date is only twenty-two. I'm almost thirty-five. We don't tell people that we're going out. Her name is Hayley, though this is probably a lie. She thinks my name is Dean, though she is unsure of whether this is a Christian name, a surname, or a nom-de-plume.

The best thing about Hayley: she smells like cotton candy. Lying in bed with her, smelling her hair, is frequently better than our stilted attempts to have sex.

Hayley has a cobra tattooed on her left arm in green ink. She has a blue mermaid tattoo on her right thigh. She sent me photographs of both when we were flirting online, but the cobra seems more threatening when seen in real life. Hayley met me at the hotel wearing cut-off jeans and a tank top, all her ink on display for the whole world to see. I booked the hotel room while she watched me through the glass door. We booked in as Mister and Miss Dean.

In theory, we are both engineers. This is the occupation both of us offered, when the question was raised online. We bonded over this, our mutual interest in machines. It greased the early days of our relationship admirably.

We are liars, and we assume as much. This is a basic precaution in the age of the Internet. Yet both of us enjoy the game more than we let on.

4. My parents text me, pinging my cell every couple of minutes. Text messages are a bad way to communicate in an emergency. They would seem comical if I wasn't watching the news, even though my parents aren't known for their sense of whimsy. I read their messages to Hayley during the lull in the news reports: Have you heard from your sister? There's a giant robot mermaid crawling through Copenhagen. It's fighting its way to the Christiansborg Palace! Do you remember the name of your sister's hotel? Do you remember the name of your sister's airline? Have you heard from her since this started? My god, did you see the damage that tail caused? Have you heard from your sister? Has she tried to give you a call? Why aren't you answering your phone?

5. We don't hear from my sister for three days. Then we do. She leaves a message on my phone: Not dead, not in Iceland, everything okay. Give you a call when I get home. I forward this message to my mother and scan the limited breakfast options on the hotel's room-service menu. Hayley and I order raisin toast that comes with not enough butter. Hayley tells me this is her favourite breakfast ever, the only thing she can eat at the start of the day.

6. It emerges that no-one knows why the attack took place. The merfolk's statement on the matter is a collection of high-pitched whale songs that remain difficult to decipher, so people develop their own theories to make sense of the destruction. My favourite suggests that perhaps, in retrospect, the statue of the Little Mermaid in Copenhagen harbour may have been something of a mistake; that the merfolk may have taken it for some kind of taunt.

My sister visited that statue three times in the past. Each

time, she says, regardless of the season or clothing she's wearing, it's the coldest place she's ever been. My sister has been to many cold places. She has seen both the Arctic and Antarctic circles. She is not sorry to hear that the statue was torn down in the wake of the attack.

7. It should be noted that visiting Iceland is still on my sister's to-do list, thanks to this horrible tragedy.

8. There are some people, my friends among them, who will believe the destruction of Copenhagen is an urban myth. Others will believe it's a cover up for something both more mundane and infinitely more sinister. They will blame the Americans. America is easy to blame in moments like this.

My sister suffered three injuries during the attack, though all of them were minor. The worst was a sprained right ankle, which ballooned up and forced her to limp along on crutches for a week before it healed. She sent me photographs of her injuries, her ankle dark and swollen like she's hiding a storm cloud beneath her skin.

The photographs of my sister's ankle will do little to convince those who doubt the attack ever truly happened. They will tell me such injuries could have happened to anyone, at any time, and I cannot prove them wrong.

9. There were five robots in Copenhagen. I told Hayley they were simultaneously works of innovative engineering and one of the poorest designs I had ever seen. She snuggled close and asked me to explain. I closed my eyes and breathed in the smell of her hair.

The genius of the robots was in their scale: two hundred feet tall and strong enough to smash a building into rubble. The merfolk did this using parts scavenged from sunken ships, each robot a patchwork construct made from metal and waterlogged wood. That the robots worked at all is a marvel, requiring foresight and ingenuity that few human engineers could match.

The flaws of the robots lay in their scales: the use of the merfolk as the base form, rather than a creature adapted for movement on land. Each war machine was covered in a scaled shell of metal that leaked water every time the robot moved, forcing them to return to the ocean at periodic intervals where they would sink beneath the surface as a flurry of air-bubbles boiled the water. This flaw ensured the rampage was limited to a small section of the Copenhagen shoreline.

Hayley was impressed by my observations, commenting on my insight. I told her I never wanted to be smart; I wanted to be free to travel the world on a whim, just like my sister.

10. The games we play to pass the time: Hayley is an Italian maid and I'm the horny tourist she walks in on. She's a stunning French philosophy student and I'm the horny waiter at her favourite café. She's a terrified Danish film star and I'm the rampaging robot that picks her up and fights off the air force while clinging to the side of Copenhagen's tallest tower.

Then news reports tell us that the rampage is over, that the robots ranged too far from the shore, leaving the pilots gasping for air inside the dormant constructs.

11. They announce the final death toll. It's lower than either of us expected. We pack up and go home the next day. The war with the merfolk is over.

12. The next time I see Hayley she will be older, wiser, less prone to dating men that she meets on the Internet. Her hair will smell like something other than cotton candy. We will spot one another at opposite ends of the cereal aisle at the supermarket. I will be reaching for Coco Puffs; she will be reaching for name-brand muesli. I will be fatter and growing a beard, and I will stop myself from calling out her name when I see her standing next to a friend who may-or-may-not know of Hayley's double life as Hayley-the-Engineer. I will feel a sudden surge of jealousy: Hayley's friend will know if her name isn't really Hayley, but I will never know. My arm will falter. I will smile instead. Hayley will smile back. She will excuse herself and hurry down the aisle so she can kiss me on the cheek. She will ask after my sister. I will tell her my sister is fine, thought she's currently stuck in Korea, paying off an impressive bar tab generated during a wild night at an underground casino. We will laugh at that. We will not mention our time together. Hayley will excuse herself. She will go back and start talking to her friend, making some comment that explains who I am without mentioning the fact that we once dated.

The merfolk will have gone underground, censured by the global community for their actions in Denmark. The oceans will be deemed unsafe. We will worry about ships lost at sea; each new incident will become global news. We will lose faith in our navy. Hayley will rejoin her friend. She will choose a more expensive brand of muesli and place it in her shopping cart. I will watch the two of them go, walking away from me, disappearing around the corner of the aisle. I will admire the curve of Hayley's back. I will wonder if Hayley was ever her real name. I will close my eyes and wish. I will wish that we could sleep together, just one more time. I will wish we were back in the hotel room, that the merfolk invasion could start again. Hayley will be gone. I will miss her. I will wish she still smelt like cotton candy, and I will breathe in the sugar-sweet smell of the Coco-Puffs and pretend that I'm smelling her for a little while longer.

Later I will remember that my sister still hasn't made it to Iceland. It's the one place I can still go that she has never been.

The Fixation

ALASTAIR REYNOLDS

Alastair Reynolds (voxish.tripod.com) lives in Wales. He worked as a space scientist in the Netherlands until 2004, and returned to the UK a couple of years ago. His first novel, Revelation Space, *was published in 1999. He became an icon of the new British space opera and of hard sf writers emerging in the mid and late 1990s, in the generation after Baxter and McAuley, and originally the most "hard SF" of the new group. He has now published about fifty short stories; two collections of his stories were published in 2006,* Zima Blue *and* Galactic North. House of Suns *(2008) is an expanded version of the Zima Blue collection. His ninth novel,* Terminal World, *a far-future, steampunk-influenced planetary romance, will appear in 2010. He says, "I am currently at work on a big trilogy about an optimistic, spacefaring future spanning the next 11,000 years.*

"The Fixation" was published 2009 in The Solaris Book of New SF 3. *It was first published in a limited-run tribute book for a prominent Finnish fan and disc jockey and Reynolds' friend, Hannu Blomilla. It is an alternate universe physics story, with an unusual twist.*

FOR HANNU BLOMMILA

Inside the corroded rock was what looked like a geared embryo—the incipient bud of an industrial age that remained unborn for a millennium.
        —John Seabrook, *The New Yorker*, May 14, 2007

Katib, the security guard who usually works the graveyard shift, has already clocked on when Rana swipes her badge through the reader. He gives her a long-suffering look as she bustles past in her heavy coat, stooping under a cargo of document boxes and laptops. "Pulling another all-nighter, Rana?" he asks, as he has asked a hundred times before. "I keep telling you to get a different job, girl."

"I worked hard to get this one," she tells him, almost slipping on the floor, which has just been polished to a mirrored gleam by a small army of robot cleaners. "Where else would I get to do this and actually get paid for it?"

"Whatever they're paying you, it isn't enough for all those bags under your eyes."

She wishes he wouldn't mention the bags under her eyes—it's not as if she exactly likes them—but she smiles anyway, for Katib is a kindly man without a hurtful thought in his soul. "They'll go," she says. "We're on the home stretch, anyway. Or did you somehow not notice that there's this big opening ceremony coming up?"

"Oh, I think I heard something about that," he says,

scratching at his beard. "I just hope they need some old fool to look after this wing when they open the new one."

"You're indispensable, Katib. They'd get rid of half the exhibits before they put you on the street."

"That's what I keep telling myself, but . . ." He gives a burly shrug, and then smiles to let her know it isn't her business to worry about his problems. "Still, it's going to be something, isn't it? I can see it from my balcony, from all the way across the town. I didn't like it much at first, but now that's up there, now that it's all shining and finished, it's starting to grow on me. And it's ours, that's what I keep thinking. That's our muscum, nobody else's. Something to be proud of."

Rana has seen it too. The new wing, all but finished, dwarfs the existing structure. It's a glittering climate-controlled ziggurat, the work of a monkish British architect who happens to be a devout Christian. A controversial choice, to be sure, but no one who has seen that tidal wave of glass and steel rising above the streets of the city has remained unimpressed. As the sun tracks across the sky, computer-controlled shutters open and close to control the flood of light into the ziggurat's plunging atrium—the atrium where the Mechanism will be the primary exhibit—and maintain the building's ideal ambient temperature. From afar, the play of those shutters is an enchanted mosaic: a mesmerizing, never-repeating dance of spangling glints. Rana read in a magazine that the architect had never *touched* a computer until he arrived in Greater Persia, but that he took to the possibilities with the zeal of the converted.

"It's going to be wonderful," she says, torn between making small talk with the amiable Katib and getting started on her work. "But it won't be much of an opening ceremony if the Mechanism isn't in place, will it?"

"Which is a kind way of saying, you need to be getting to your office." He's smiling as he speaks, letting her know he takes no offense. "You need some help with those boxes and computers, my fairest?"

"I'll be fine, thanks."

"You call me if you need anything. I'll be here through to

six." With that he unfolds a magazine and taps the sharp end of a pencil against the grid of a half-finished puzzle. "And don't work too hard," he says under his breath, but just loud enough that she will hear.

Rana doesn't pass another human being on her way to the office. The public part of the museum is deserted save for the occasional cleaner or patrolling security robot, but at least the hallways and exhibits are still partially illuminated, and from certain sightlines she can still see people walking in the street outside, coming from the theater or a late restaurant engagement.

In the private corridors, it's a different story. The halls are dark and the windows too high to reveal anything more than moonlit sky. The robots don't come here very often and most of the offices and meeting rooms are locked and silent. At the end of one corridor stands the glowing sentinel of a coffee dispenser. Normally Rana takes a cup to her room, but tonight she doesn't have a free hand; it's enough of a job just to shoulder her way through doors without dropping something.

Her room is in the basement: a cool, windowless crypt that is half laboratory and half office. Her colleagues think she's mad for working at night, but Rana has her reasons. By day she has to share her facilities with other members of the staff, and what with all the talk and interruptions she tends to get much less work done. If that's not enough of a distraction, there is a public corridor that winds its way past the glass-fronted rooms, allowing the museum's visitors to watch cataloging and restoration work as it actually happens. The public make an effort to look more interested than they really are. Hardly surprising, because the work going on inside the offices could not look less interesting or less glamorous. Rana has been spending the last three weeks working with microscopically precise tools on the restoration of a single bronze gearwheel. What the visitors would imagine to be a morning's work has consumed more of her life than some relationships. She already knows every scratch and chip of that gearwheel like an old friend or ancient, bitter adversary.

There's another reason why she works at night. Her mind functions better in the small hours. She has made more deductive leaps at three in the morning than she has ever done at three in the afternoon, and she wishes it were not so.

She takes off her coat and hangs it by the door. She opens the two laptops, sets them near each other, and powers them up. She keeps the office lights low, with only enough illumination to focus on the immediate area around her bench. The gearwheel is centermost, supported on an adjustable cradle like a miniature music stand. On either side, kept in upright stands, are various chrome-plated tools and magnifying devices, some of which trail segmented power cables to a wall junction. There is a swing-down visor with zoom optics. There are lasers and ultrasound cleaning baths. There are duplicates of the gearwheel and its brethren, etched in brass for testing purposes. There are plastic models of parts of the Mechanism, so that she can take them apart and explain its workings to visitors. There are other gearwheels which have already been removed from the device for restoration, sealed in plastic boxes and racked according to coded labels. Some are visibly cleaner than the one she is working on, but some are still corroded and grubby, with damaged teeth and scabrous surface deterioration.

And there is the Mechanism itself, placed on the bench on the far side of the gearwheel she is working on. It is the size of a shoebox, with a wooden casing, the lid hinged back. When it arrived the box was full of machinery, a tight-packed clockwork of arbors and crown wheels, revolving balls, slotted pins and delicate, hand-engraved inscriptions. None of it did anything, though. Turn the input crank and there'd just be a metallic crunch as stiff, worn gears locked into immobility. No one in the museum remembers the last time the machine was in proper working order. Fifty years ago, she's heard someone say—but not all of the gearing was in place even then. Parts were removed a hundred years ago and never put back. Or were lost or altered two hundred years ago. Since then the Mechanism has become something of an embarrassment: a fabled contraption that doesn't do what everyone expects it to.

Hence the decision by the museum authorities: restore the Mechanism to full and authentic functionality in time for the reopening of the new wing. As the foremost native expert on the device, the work has naturally fallen to Rana. The authorities tried to foist a team on her, but the hapless doctoral students soon realized their leader preferred to work alone, unencumbered by the give and take of collaboration.

Share the glory? Not likely.

With the wall calendar reminding her how few weeks remain to the opening, Rana occasionally wonders if she has taken on too much. But she is making progress, and the most difficult parts of the restoration are now behind her.

Rana picks up one of her tools and begins to scrape away the tiniest burr of corrosion on one of the gear's teeth. Soon she is lost in the methodical repetitiveness of the task, her mind freewheeling back through history, thinking of all the hands that have touched this metal. She imagines all the people this little clockwork box has influenced, all the lives it has altered, the fortunes it has made and the empires it has crushed. The Romans owned the Mechanism for 400 years—one of their ships must have carried it from Greece, perhaps from the island of Rhodes—but the Romans were too lazy and incurious to do anything with the box other than marvel at its computational abilities. The idea that the same clockwork that accurately predicted the movements of the sun, moon, and the planets across an entire Metonic cycle—235 lunar months—might also be made to do *other things* simply never occurred to them.

The Persians were different. The Persians saw a universe of possibility in those spinning wheels and meshing teeth. Those early clocks and calculating boxes—the clever devices that sent armies and navies and engineers across the globe, and made Greater Persia what it is today—bear scant resemblance to the laptops on Rana's desk. But the lineage is unbroken.

There must be ghosts, she thinks: caught in the slipstream of this box, dragged by the Mechanism as it ploughed its way through the centuries. Lives changed and lives extinguished, lives that never happened at all, and yet all of them still in spectral attendance, a silent audience crowding in on this quiet basement room, waiting for Rana's next move.

Some of them want her to destroy the machine forever.

Some of them want to see it shine again.

Rana doesn't dream much, but when she does she dreams of glittering brass gears meshing tight against each other, whirring furiously, a dance of metal and geometry that moves the heavens.

Safa dreams of numbers, not gears: she is a mathematician. Her breakthrough paper, the one that has brought her to the museum, was entitled "Entropy Exchange and the Many Worlds Hypothesis."

As a foreign national, admitted into the country because of her expertise in an exceedingly esoteric field, Safa has more rights than a refugee. But she must still submit to the indignity of wearing a monitoring collar, a heavy plastic cuff around her neck which not only records her movements, not only sees and hears everything she sees and hears, but which can stun or euthanize her if a government agent deems that she is acting contrary to the national interests. She must also be accompanied by a cyborg watchdog at all times: a sleek black prowling thing with the emblem of the national security agency across its bulletproof chest. At least the watchdog has the sense to lurk at the back of the room when she is about to address the gathered administrators and sponsors, at this deathly hour.

"I'm sorry we had to drag you out here so late," the museum director tells the assembled audience. "Safa knows more than me, but I'm reliably informed that the equipment works best when the city's shutting down for the night—when there isn't so much traffic, and the underground trains aren't running. We can schedule routine jobs during the day, but something like this—something this delicate—requires the maximum degree of noise-suppression. Isn't that right, Safa?"

"Spot on sir. And if everyone could try and hold their breath for the next six hours, that would help as well." She grins reassuringly—it's almost as if some of them think she was serious. "Now I know some of you were probably hoping to see the Mechanism itself, but I'm afraid I'm going to have to disappoint you—positioning it inside the equipment is a very slow and tricky procedure, and if we started now we'd all still be here next week. But I can show you something nearly as good."

Safa produces a small white pottery jug that she has brought along for the occasion. "Now, you may think this is just some ordinary old jug I found at the back of a staff cupboard . . . and you'd be right. It's probably no more than ten or fifteen years old. The Mechanism, as I am sure I don't have to remind anyone here, is incomparably older: we know the ship went down around the first half of the First Century BC. But I can still illustrate my point. There are a near-infinite number of copies of this object, and they are *all the same jug.* In one history, I caught a cold and couldn't make it today, and someone else is standing up and talking to you, holding the same jug. In another, someone took the jug out of that cupboard years ago and it's living in a kitchen halfway across the city. In another it was bought by someone else and never ended up in the museum. In another it was broken before it ever left the factory."

She smiles quickly. "You see the point I'm making. What may be less clear is that all these copies of the same jug are in ghostly dialogue with each other, linked together by a kind of quantum entanglement—though it's not really quantum and it's not exactly entanglement." Another fierce, nervous smile. "Don't worry: no mathematics tonight! The point is, no matter what happens to this jug, no matter how it's handled or what it comes into contact with, it never quite loses contact with its counterparts. The signal gets fainter, but it never goes away. Even if I do this."

Abruptly, she lets go of the jug. It drops to the floor and shatters into a dozen sharp white pieces.

"The jug's broken," Safa says, pulling a sad face. "But in a sense it still exists. The other copies of it are still doing fine—and each and every one of them felt an echo of this one as it shattered. It's still out there, ringing back and forth like a dying chime." Then she pauses and kneels down, gathering a handful of the broken pieces into her palms. "Imagine if I could somehow take these pieces and get them to resonate with the intact copies of the jug. Imagine further still that I could somehow steal a little bit of orderedness from each of those copies, and give back some of the disorderedness of this one in return—a kind of swap."

Safa waits a moment, trying to judge whether she still has the audience's attention. Are they following or just pretending to follow? It's not always easy to tell, and nothing on the administrator's face gives her a clue. "Well, we can do that. It's what we call Fixation—moving tiny amounts of entropy from one world—one universe—to another. Now, it would take a very long time to put this jug back the way it was. But if we started with a jug that was a bit damaged, a bit worn, it would happen a lot quicker. And that's sort of where we are with the Antikythera Mechanism. It's in several pieces, and we suspect there are components missing, but in other respects it's in astonishing condition for something that's been underwater for two thousand years."

Now she turns around slowly, to confront the huge, humming mass of the Fixator. It is a dull silver cylinder with a circular door in one end, braced inside a massive orange chassis, festooned with cables and cooling ducts and service walkways. The machine is as large as a small fusion reactor and several times as complicated. It has stronger, more responsive magnets, a harder vacuum, and has a control system so perilously close to intelligence that a government agent must be on hand at all times, ready to destroy the machine if it slips over the threshold into consciousness.

"Hence the equipment. The Mechanism's inside there now—in fact, we've already begun the resonant excitation. What we're hoping is that somewhere out there—somewhere out in that sea of alternate timelines—is a copy of the Mechanism that never fell into the water. Of course, that copy may have been destroyed subsequently—but somewhere there *has* to be a counterpart to the Mechanism in better condition than this one. Maybe near-infinite numbers of counterparts, for all we know. Perhaps we were the unlucky ones, and nobody else's copy ended up being lost underwater."

She coughs to clear her throat, and in that instant catches a reflected glimpse of herself in the glass plating of one of the cabinets in the corner of the room. Drawn face, tired creases around the mouth, bags under the eyes—a woman who's been working too hard for much too long. But how else was an Iranian mathematician supposed to get on in the world, if it wasn't through graft and dedication? It's not like she was born into money, or had the world rushing to open doors for her.

The work will endure long after the bags have gone, she tells herself.

"The way it happens," she says, regaining her composure, "is that we'll steal an almost infinitesimally small amount of order from an almost infinitely large number of alternate universes. In return, we'll pump a tiny amount of surplus entropy into each of those timelines. The counterparts of the Mechanism will hardly feel the change: the alteration in any one of them will be so tiny as to be almost unmeasurable. A microscopic scratch here; a spot of corrosion or the introduction of an impure atom there. But because we're stealing order from so many of them, and consolidating that order into a single timeline, the change in our universe will be enormous. We'll win, because we'll get back the Mechanism as it was before it went into the sea. But no one else loses; it's not like we're stealing someone else's perfect copy and replacing it with our own damaged one."

She thinks she has them then—that it is all going to go without a hitch or a quibble, and they can all shuffle over to the tables and start nibbling on cheese squares. But then a hand raises itself slowly from the audience. It belongs to an intense young man with squared-off glasses and a severe fringe.

He asks: "How can you be so sure?"

Safa grimaces. She hates being asked questions.

Rana puts down her tool and listens very carefully. Somewhere in the museum there was a loud bang, as of a door being slammed. She is silent for at least a minute, but when no further sound comes she resumes her labors, filling the room with the repetitious scratch of diamond-tipped burr against corroded metal.

Then another sound comes, a kind of fluttering, animal commotion, as if a bird is loose in one of the darkened halls, and Rana can stand it no more. She leaves her desk and walks out into the basement corridor, wondering if someone else has come in to work. But the other rooms and offices remain closed and unlit.

She is about to return to her labors and call Katib's desk, when she hears the soft and feathery commotion again. She is near the stairwell and the sound is clearly coming from above her, perhaps on the next floor up.

Gripping the handrail, Rana ascends. She is being braver than perhaps is wise—the museum has had its share of intruders, and there have been thefts—but the coffee machine is above and she had been meaning to fetch herself a cup for at least an hour. Her heart is in her throat when she reaches the next landing and turns the corner into the corridor, which is as shabby and narrow as any of the museum's non-public spaces. There are high, institutional windows on one side and office doors on the other. But there is the machine, standing in a pool of light two doors down, and there is no sign of an intruder. She walks to the machine, fishing coins from her pocket, and punches in her order. As the machine clicks and gurgles into life, Rana feels a breeze against her cheek. She looks down the corridor and feels it again: it's as if there's a door open, letting in the night air. But the only door should be the one manned by Katib, on the other side of the building.

While her coffee is being dispensed Rana walks in the direction of the breeze. At the end the corridor reaches the corner of this wing and jogs to the right. She turns the bend and sees something unanticipated. All along the corridor, there is no glass in the windows, no metal in the frames: just tall blank openings in the wall. And there, indeed, is a fluttering black shape: a crow, or something like a crow, which has come in through one of those openings and cannot now find

its way back outside. It keeps flinging itself at the wall between the windows, a gleam of mad desperation in its eyes.

Rana stands still, wondering how this can be. She was
here. She remembers passing the machine and thinking she
would take a cup if only she were not already staggering
under her boxes and computers.

But there is something more than just the absence of
glass. Is she losing her mind, or do the window apertures
look narrower than they used to do, as if the walls have begun to squeeze the window spaces tight like sleepy eyes?

She must call Katib.

She hurries back the way she has come, forgetting all
about the coffee she has just paid for. But when she turns the
bend in the corridor, the machine is standing there dark and
dead, as if it's been unplugged.

She returns to the basement. Under her feet the stairs feel
rougher and more crudely formed than she remembers,
until she reaches the last few treads and they start to feel
normal again. She pauses at the bottom, waiting for her mind
to straighten itself out.

Down here at least all is as it should be. Her office is as
she left it, with the lights still on, the laptops still aglow, the
gearwheel still mounted on its stand, the disemboweled
Mechanism still sitting on the other side of the desk.

She eases into her seat, her heart still racing, and picks up
the telephone.

"Katib?"

"Yes, my fairest," he says, his voice sounding more distant and crackly than she feels it should, as if he is speaking
from halfway around the world. "What can I do for you?"

"Katib, I was just upstairs, and . . ."

But then she trails off. What is she going to tell him? That
she saw open gaps where there should be windows?

"Rana?"

Her nerve deserts her. "I was just going to say . . . the coffee machine was broken. Maybe someone could take a look
at it."

"Not until tomorrow, I am afraid—there is no one qualified. But I will make an entry in the log."

"Thank you, Katib."

After a pause he asks, "There was nothing else, was there?"

"No," she says. "There was nothing else. Thank you, Katib."

She knows what he must be thinking. She's been working too hard, too fixated on the task. The Mechanism does that to people, it's been said. They get lost in its labyrinthine possibilities and never emerge again. Not the way they were, anyway.

But she thinks she can still hear that crow.

"How can I be so sure about what?" Safa asks, with an obliging smile.

"That this is going to work the way you say it will," the intense young man answers.

"The mathematics is pretty clear," Safa says. "I should know; I discovered most of it." Which comes less modestly than she had intended, although no one seems to mind. "What I mean is, there isn't any room for ambiguity. We know that the sheath of alternate timelines is near-infinite in extent, and we know we're only pumping the smallest conceivable amount of entropy into each of those timelines." Safa holds the smile, hoping that will be enough for the young man, and that she can continue with her presentation.

But the man isn't satisfied. "That's all very well, but aren't you presupposing that all those other timelines have order to spare? What if that isn't the case? What if all the other Mechanisms are just as corroded and broken as ours—what will happen then?"

"It'll still work," Safa says, "provided the total information content across all the timelines is sufficient to specify one intact copy, which is overwhelmingly likely from a statistical standpoint. Of course, if all the Mechanisms happen to be damaged in exactly the same fashion as ours, then the Fixation won't work—you still can't get something for nothing. But that's not very likely. Trust me; I'm very confident that we can find enough information out there to reconstruct our copy."

The man seems to be content with that answer, but just

when Safa is about to open her mouth and continue with her speech, her adversary raises his hand again.

"Sorry, but . . . I can't help wondering. Does the entropy exchange happen uniformly across all those timelines?"

It's an odd, technical-sounding question, suggesting that the man has done more homework than most. "Actually, no," Safa says, guardedly. "The way the math works out, the entropy exchange is ever so slightly clumped. If a particular copy of the Mechanism has more information to give us, we end up pumping a bit more entropy into that copy than one which has less information to offer. But we're still talking about small differences, nothing that anyone will actually notice."

The man pushes a hand through his fringe. "But what if there's only one?"

"I'm sorry?"

"I mean, what if there's only one intact copy out there, and all the rest are at least as damaged as our own?"

"That can't happen," Safa says, hoping that someone, anyone, will interrupt by asking another question. It's not that she feels on unsafe ground, just that she has the sense that this could go on all night.

"Why not?" the man persists.

"It just can't. The mathematics says it's so unlikely that we may as well forget about it."

"And you believe the mathematics."

"Why shouldn't I?" Safa is beginning to lose her patience, feeling cornered and put upon. Where is the museum director to defend her when she needs him? "Of course I believe it. It'd be pretty strange if I didn't."

"I was just asking," the man says, sounding as if he's the one who's under attack. "Maybe it isn't very likely—I'll have to take your word for that. But I only wanted to know what would happen."

"You don't need to," Safa says firmly. "It can't happen—not ever. And now can I please continue?"

Her finger stabs down on Katib's button again. But there is nothing, not even the cool purr of the dialing tone. The phone is mute, and now that she looks at it, the display function is dead. She puts the handset down and tries again, but nothing changes.

That's when Rana pays proper attention to the gearwheel, the one she has been working on. There are thirty-seven wheels in the Antikythera Mechanism and this is the twenty-first, and although there was still much to be done until it was ready to be replaced in the box, it now looks as if she has hardly begun. The surface corrosion that she has spent weeks rectifying has returned in a matter of minutes, covering the wheel in a furry blue-green bloom as if someone has taken the artifact and dipped it in acid while she was out of the office. But as she looks at it, blinking in dismay, as if it is her eyes that are wrong, rather than the wheel, she notices that three teeth are gone, or worn away so thoroughly that they may as well not be there. Worse, there is a visible scratch—actually more of a crack—that cuts across one side of the wheel, as if it is about to fracture into two pieces.

Mesmerized and unsettled in equal measure, Rana picks up one of her tools—the scraper she was using before she heard the noise—and touches it against part of the blue-green corrosion. The bloom chips off almost instantly, but as it does so it takes a quadrant of the wheel with it, the piece shattering to a heap of pale granules on her desk. She stares in numb disbelief at the ruined gear, with a monstrous chunk bitten out of the side of it, and then the tool itself shatters in her hand.

"This can't be happening," Rana says to herself. Then her gaze falls on the other gearwheels, in their plastic boxes, and she sees the same brittle corrosion afflicting them all.

As for the Mechanism itself, the disemboweled box: what she sees isn't possible. She can just about accept that some bizarre, hitherto-undocumented chemical reaction has attacked the metal in the time it took for her to go upstairs and come down again, but the box itself is *wood*—it hasn't changed in hundreds of years, not since the last time the casing was patiently replaced by one of the Mechanism's many careful owners.

But now the box has turned to something that looks more

like rock than wood, something barely recognizable as a made artifact. With trepidation Rana reaches out and touches it. It feels fibrous and insubstantial. Her finger almost seems to ghost through it, as if what she is reaching for is not a real object at all, but a hologram. Peering into the heart of the Mechanism, she sees the gears that are still in place have fused together into a single corroded mass, like a block of rock that has been engraved with a hazy impression of clockwork.

Then Rana laughs, for the pieces of the puzzle have just fallen into place. This is all a joke, albeit—given the pressures she is already under—one in spectacularly bad taste. But a joke all the same, and not a marker of her descent into insanity. She was called upstairs by a noise—how else were they going to get into her office and swap the Mechanism for this ruined half-cousin? The missing windows, the panicked bird, seem like details too far, random intrusions of dream-logic, but who can guess the mind of a practical joker?

Well, she has a sense of humor. But not now, not tonight. Someone will pay for this. Cutting off her telephone was the last straw. That was nasty, not funny.

She moves to leave her bench again and find whoever must be spying on her, certain that they must be lurking in the shadows outside, maybe in the unlit observation corridor, where they'd have a plain view of her discomfort. But as she places her hand down to push herself up, her fingers slip into the smoky surface of the bench.

They vanish as if she were dipping them into water.

All of a sudden she realizes that it was not the Antikythera Mechanism that was growing insubstantial, but everything around her.

No, that's not it either. Something is happening to the building, but if the table were turning ghostly, the heavy things on it—the Mechanism, the equipment, the laptops—would have surely sunk through it by now. There's a simpler explanation, even if the realization cuts through her like a shaft of interstellar cold.

She's the one fading out, losing traction and substantiality. Rana rises to her feet eventually, but it's like pushing herself against smoke. She isn't so much standing as floating with her feet in vague contact with the ground. The air in her lungs is beginning to feel thin, but at the same time there's no sense that she is about to choke. She tries to walk, and for a moment her feet paddle uselessly against the floor, until she begins to pick up a deathly momentum in the direction of the door.

The corridor at the base of the stairs was normal when she returned from her visit to the next floor, but now it has become a dark, forbidding passageway, with rough-formed doorways leading into dungeon-like spaces. Her office is the only recognizable place, and even her office is not immune to the changes. The door has vanished, leaving only a sagging gap in the wall. The floor is made of stones, unevenly laid. Halfway to her bench the stones blend together into something like concrete, and then a little further the concrete gains the hard red sheen of the flooring she has come to expect. On the desk, her electric light flickers and fades. The laptops shut down with a whine, their screens darkening. The line of change in the floor creeps closer to the desk, like an advancing tide. From somewhere in the darkness Rana hears the quiet, insistent dripping of water.

She was wrong to assume that the things on the desk were immune to the fading. She began to go first, but now the same process of fade-out is beginning to catch up with her tools, with her notes and the laptops and the fabric of the bench itself. Even the Mechanism is losing its grip on reality, its gears and components beginning to dissolve before her eyes. The wooden box turns ash-gray and crumbles into a pile of dust. A breeze fingers its way into the room and spirits the dust away.

The Mechanism was the last thing to go, Rana realizes: the tide of change had come in from all directions, to this one tiny focus, and for a little while the focus had held firm, resisting the transforming forces.

Now she feels the hastening of her own process of fade-out. She cannot move or communicate. She is at the mercy of the breeze.

It blows her through the cold stone walls, out into the

night-time air of a city she barely recognizes. She drifts through the sky, able to witness but not able to participate. In all directions she sees only ruin and desolation. The shells of buildings throw jagged outlines against the moonlit sky. Here and there she almost recognizes the fallen corpse of a familiar landmark, but so much is different that she soon loses her sense of direction. Even the shape of the river, shining back under moonlight, appears to have meandered from the course she remembers. She sees smashed stone and metal bridges that end halfway across to the other bank. Crimson fires burn on the horizon and flicker through the eyeholes of gutted buildings.

Then she notices the black machines, stalking their way through the warrens and canyons between the ruins. Fierce and frightening engines of war, with their turreted guns swiveling into doorways and shadows, the iron treads of their feet crunching down on the rubble of the pulverized city, the rubble that used to be dwellings and possessions, until these juggernauts arrived. She does not need an emblem or flag to know that these are the machines of an occupying force; that her city is under the mechanized heel of an invader. She watches as a figure springs out of concealment to lob some pathetic burning torch at one of the machines. The turret snaps around and a lance of fire stabs back at the assailant. The figure drops to the ground.

The wind is gusting her higher, turning the city into a map of itself. As her point of view changes direction she catches sight of the building that used to be the Museum of Antiquities, but what she sees is no more than a shattered prison or fortress, one among many. And for an instant she remembers that the shell of the museum was very old, that the building—or a succession of buildings, each built on the plan of its predecessor—had stood in the same location for many centuries, serving many rulers.

In that same instant, Rana comes to a momentary understanding of what has happened to both her and her world. The Mechanism has been wrenched from history, and accordingly—because the Mechanism was so essential—history has come undone. There is no Museum of Antiquities, because there is no Greater Persia. The brilliant clockwork that dispatched armies and engineers across the globe simply never existed.

Nor did Rana.

But the moment of understanding passes as quickly as it came. Ghosts are not the souls of the dead, but the souls of people written out of history when history changes. The worst thing about them is that they never quite recall the living people they used to be, the things they once witnessed.

The wind lofts Rana higher, into thinning silver clouds. But by then she no longer thinks of anything at all, except the endless meshing of beautiful bronze gearwheels, moving the heavens for all eternity.

In Their Garden

BRENDA COOPER

Brenda Cooper (www.brenda-cooper.com) lives in Kirkland, Washington, where she is the city's Chief Information Officer. She also works at Futurist.com, as host of the "Science Fiction" and "Space and Science" sections of the website, "to gain speaking engagements and engender positive conversations about the future." Her fiction has appeared in Nature, Analog, Asimov's, *Strange Horizons, and in anthologies. On her website she says, "I'm interested in how new technologies might change us and our world, particularly for the better, and in global warming." She has collaborated frequently with Larry Niven and in particular on the novel,* Building Harlequin's Moon *(2005). Her most recent novel is* Wings of Creation *(2009), part of the the Silver Ship series.*

"In Their Garden" appeared in Asimov's. *It is set in a future in which the climate and human civilization have radically changed. But it is also an ambiguously optimistic story about adolescence.*

I'm running back through the desiccated woods, going too fast to keep the sticks and branches that have fallen from the trees from cracking under my weight. My skin and mouth are dry. The afternoon sun has sucked all the water from me, and I haven't stopped to drink. The sole of my right boot is thin enough a stone bumps the ball of my foot, and I want to swear, but I keep going even though I don't hear anyone behind me. Not anymore.

I realize I haven't for a while; I got away again. I saw ten friendly travelers this time before I met one who meant me trouble. I know better than to go out alone, and if I get back in one piece, Kelley is gonna kill me.

It's not far now, I can see the wall rising up like a cracked egg, dirty white with grey, the top edges jagged.

I trip over a log, going down sharp on my right knee and catch myself on my hands, scraping my palms. I can see the black soil line from the fire ten years ago, the one that saved us from burning up when everything else around caught fire. The dry trees around me are saplings that tried to grow back, and made it for three or four years before they died of thirst. They're as tall as I am.

My breath breaks the silence, and I sound like a rabbit before a thin coyote kills it, scared and breathing too hard. I make myself slow down, try to remember what Oskar taught me. Breathe through your nose. Breathe deep in your belly, so you can feel it going out and in.

Slowly.

S l o w l y.

I'm getting there. A hot breeze blows back my hair and helps me feel better.

"Paulie."

I hate it when Kelley calls me that. My name's Paulette. I hate it that she moves so quiet and I'm so loud and clumsy.

She extends her left hand, but doesn't help me up. There's dirt ground into the creases of her hand and stuck under her nails, and it smells wetter and stronger than the dry, cracked earth under my hands. A year or two ago, I would have apologized first, but I manage not to do that this time. I'm almost as tall as her now, and I can look down on the graying dark hair she's pulled back and tied with a strip of bark, as if we didn't have anything better. She holds her taser in her right hand, a black oblong that she protects as if it means her life. She leaves the gun out as we walk back, swinging in her hand, the arc of its movement precise.

My knee is bleeding, but we both ignore that.

Between here and the wall, all the dead woods have been cleared, and we walk on grey and green grass, stuff Kelley had us plant in the moat of cleared ground around our walled garden. The grass thrives in spite of the dry, thirsty ground. I don't like to admit it, but she picked well; the spiky, low growth has been alive for two years, and it creeps back into the forest as we clear it further away.

She doesn't say anything, but I make up her feelings and words in my head anyway. *The walls are safe. You aren't old enough to leave them yet; you might bring people here. You might get hurt, or raped, and die all by yourself. There's men that would take you in and make you trade your body for water and food. It only takes three days without water.* If she were lecturing me instead of staring off, lost in her head, she'd look down at that point and see I have a small canteen clipped to my belt, one of the old ones where the metal's all banged up. *Well, maybe you'd live a week.* She'd look disgusted. *We have all the people we can water now. You might get lost and not come back, and then what? We'd lose all the training we spent on you.*

The only problem with a lecture in your head is you can't

fight it. Kelley knows that, and it makes me even madder, but it's not like I'm going to be able to explain to the others why I picked a fight with someone who didn't say anything to me. The other problem is that she's right. I shouldn't want to argue with her in the first place. But I hate living like the world isn't all screwed up when it really is, or maybe we're living like it is all screwed up, and its starting not to be some. That's what I'm beginning to believe. Whichever it is, I'll never amount to anything if I stay inside my whole life and work on little things that don't matter with little people who will die behind a wall. The wet, verdant world we live in is a bubble, and I want the real world.

Right before we get to the wall, she turns and looks at me. I expect her to be yelling angry, but what I see in her dark blue eyes is just sadness.

I wonder which one of her plants died this time.

I'm sorry she's sad, but I don't tell her that; I can't show weakness.

The door in the wall is big enough for an army and there's a whiter spot on the wall where Kelley's old boss, James, ripped the sign off during the second year of the drought, and also the second year after I was born. The door opens to let us in, and we are much smaller than an army even though there's a war between us.

Inside, it smells like home and it smells like jail. Like dirt and water and frogs, and faintly, of flowers. Later, in the summer, it will smell more like flowers, but the spring is showier than it is smelly. We pass magenta azaleas whose bloom is just starting to wilt, and in spite of myself I smile when I see three bees on the one plant. Kelley and Oskar both taught me to see the little things, and I can't help but watch out for the plants.

I stop smiling when I notice that the Board of Directors is waiting. All of them. They're sitting in their formal place, on benches in a circle under the sign that used to be above the doors. "Oregon Botanical Gardens." The Board has run us since the first years of climate change, and the half who are still the original members are gray and wrinkled.

There's four Board members, and Kelley makes five. She

says, "Paulie, please sit," and gestures to the hot seat—the one for people who are in trouble. I've been here before. The Board's all as old as Kelley; they all remember the world I only see in movies, and they all remember my dad, who's dead now, and they all remember they're the ones who made all the rules and I'm the girl who keeps breaking them.

I wait for them to ask me questions.

They don't. Kelley clears her throat and keeps her chin up and her voice is as sad as her eyes. "Paulie, we've done everything we know how to do to keep you in here. I can't keep putting us at risk by letting you in and out the door. I've told it not to open for you anymore. So if you sneak out again, you will never be allowed back in."

She can't mean it. She's the one had the most hand in raising me, teaching me. I'm her hope for the future. She wouldn't kick me out.

Tim and Li are the two old men of the Board. Li nods, telling me he supports Kelley. Tim is impassive, but he would miss me. We play chess sometimes in the hour between dawn and breakfast. Sometimes I win, and he likes that. He would never kick me out.

Kay and Shell are the other two women on the Board. They're both stone-faced, too, but they might mean it. They're scarier than Tim and Li.

Kelley holds my eyes, and she still looks sad. Usually when she's getting me in trouble she just looks frustrated. "Do you understand?"

"Yes."

"Tell me what will happen if you leave again without permission."

"The door will not let me back in."

"And we will not let you back in," she adds.

Maybe she does mean it. Now her eyes are all wet, even though she isn't really crying yet. Kelley isn't done. I know because no one is moving, and I feel like they're all watching me, probably because they are. Kelley says, "Just so you don't do anything rash, you're confined to the Japanese Garden for a week. Report to Oskar in ten minutes."

She does mean this, except maybe the ten minutes part.

I nod at them all and walk away, keeping my head up. I hate it that they've made me feel small again. In my room, I sweep my journal and two changes of clothes into an old bag, and I brush my hair and my teeth, and put those brushes in the bag, too. I sit on the bed and wait, determined not to be early or even on time.

But Oskar doesn't notice. I walk in the glass box and close the outer door, and wait a moment, then open the inner door. I wonder if these doors are now locked electronically, too, but I don't test them to find out how strict my sentence is. I am inside walls, some glass, and under a plastic sheet roof. The air is heavy with water, although cool. Oskar is nowhere to be seen. When it was finished, the Japanese garden was billed as one of the largest on the west coast. Then the roof was there to keep it from getting too wet, instead of too dry.

I negotiate the stepping-stone path, walking through pillows of pearlwort. The cinnamon fern that lines the right wall still has some tender, brownish fiddleheads so I pick them. Maybe it's a form of penance.

The very first of the wisteria blooms are showing purple. Oskar is on the other side of the flowers, between me and the waterfall.

He doesn't turn around for the space of two breaths. He's squatting, bent over, clipping the leaves of a Japanese holly. He is a small man, his skin pallid from the damp air he lives in, his long red hair caught back in a braid that falls down a freckled, white back. The top of his braid is grey. He is only wearing shorts; he likes to garden as naked as the Board will let him. Even his feet are bare. I have always suspected that at night, he goes out with his flashlight and gardens more naked than that. Even though he is almost sixty years old, I think I would garden beside him, with my nipples exposed to the cool night air.

He wouldn't let me, of course. They all treat me like glass.

He stands up and turns toward me. Even though the light is starting to grey to dusk, I can see that his eyes look like Kelley's did. "Why do you run away?"

I lean back against the big cedar column that holds up the

wisteria arbor, breathing in the sweet air. "Why don't you ever leave this garden?"

I've never asked him this. Instead of looking startled, he smiles. "Because I am saving the world."

He is lying. He is, at best, saving a tiny part of the world that I can walk across in five minutes. Everyone here thinks small.

I hold out my hand, the one with the fiddleheads in it, and he takes them and says, "See?"

I don't see at all.

He leads me to the kitchen, which is the only room here with walls that aren't made of waxed paper or bamboo. When we get in, he hands me back the fiddleheads, and I wash them in a bowl full of water and then pour the water into a bin so it can go into the waterfall, where it will be scrubbed clean by the filter plants.

We have everything ready, but before we start to cook, Oskar takes me up to the top of the rock wall that's in the center of the stroll garden, and we look out toward the ocean. It's too far away to see or hear, but the sun will set over it. He has made a hole in the roof by overlapping the layers of water-capturing plastic so we can see the sunset directly. There are enough clouds to catch the gold and orange a little, but most of the last rays leak up like spilled paint and fade into the blackening sky.

I try to decide whether or not I can use the hole in the roof to climb out of.

After the color starts to fade, there is a hole in time between night and day. Oskar speaks quietly. "I answered you. Will you answer me?"

So that's what he has been waiting for. I guess when you are sixty you have a lot of patience. "We live in a bubble."

He laughs and pokes the plastic, which he can just barely reach from up here. It answers him by rippling, as if it were upside-down water.

I frown. "We do!" I wave my hand at all the roads and people we can't see from here. "In the real world out there, people are travelling and learning and meeting each other.

They're struggling. They're taking back the world. This time . . ." I haven't really told anyone about this trip yet—I mean, no one had asked. Should I? "I walked the interstate and talked to people on it. Like always. I have my escape routes. They work."

He cocks an eyebrow at me but doesn't say anything.

"Eugene's coming back. There's five thousand people there now—they dug a well deep enough for water and they think they can irrigate. I met two families who were on their way there."

He clears his throat. "A year ago, you told me it had all gone to desert. Not even any grass."

"That's what I heard. But this time I heard different." I paused. "I don't *know* anything. How could I?"

When he doesn't say anything else, I just keep talking. "A band of singing priests went through last night. They saw five jet airplanes in a day over Portland."

He can't say anything to that. We saw a plane fly over the gardens a few weeks ago, and everybody came out and watched. We hadn't been able to hear its engines, and Kelley had told me it was shaped different than the old jets. What Oskar does say is, "They don't have the right plants. That's what I'm saving for your generation. The bamboo and the bearberry, the astilbe and the peony." He says the names of plants like a prayer, and I imagine him naming the others in his head. "The wisteria and the wild fuscia, the fiddlehead and the mountain fern. . . ."

"I know what you're saving. You keep telling me about it." It's an old story, how we're saving the genome of the native plants in case the weather ever goes native again. "It's good. I'm glad you're saving it. But that's your dream."

He pretends not to notice my tone of voice. "What your travelers see is the Mediterranean weeds that killed the right plants in California when Father Serra brought them on his donkey. Now that it's warm enough, dry enough, they come here and invade Oregon like they invaded California a long time ago." His face wears a stubborn look that makes him more handsome, wiping some of the wrinkles away with anger. He starts down the rock face as all of the colors of the garden began to fade, and I hear him tell me, "It is your duty to the planet to help."

I sit on the stone until stars swim above the plastic roof, diffused by the beads of water that start gathering there as the evening cools. After my eyes adjust enough to the dark, I come carefully to ground and Oskar and I share cinnamon fern fiddleheads and cattail roots and some jerky from a thin bobcat that had the good grace to jump into our garden before it died of starvation and fed us.

That night, I lie in my bed, separated from Oskar by waxy paper and bamboo, and listen to the roof crinkle in the wind. I'm too young to save the lives of doomed plants for a people that might be doomed, too. The world has changed, and we'll all die if we try to stand still in its current. We have to adapt to the new climate and the new ways, or die here in Oskar's Japanese stroll garden, walking the stone paths until there's not enough water left for the wisteria.

They've taught me the things I need to know to help them survive, and now they want to keep me in a box. But I don't hate them. Oskar's breathing gets even and deep, and it's a comfort.

But not enough. I toss and turn. I can't sleep. I pack up everything I brought and wrap it in a blanket so I can swing it over my shoulder. I write Oskar and Kelley a note. I tell them I love them and I'm going to go save the world, and I'm sorry they won't ever let me back in.

I find Kelley waiting by the door, a thin stick of a shadow that only moves when I open the door, like she's been waiting for that one moment. I'm caught.

Oskar comes up behind me.

He leans forward and gives me a hug and he whispers in my ear. "Good luck," he says.

I blink at them both, stupid with surprise.

He says, "Kelley and I both knew you'd go. It's time. The Board told us to keep you, because we need young backs and young eyes. But you don't need us. Go find out what they fly those planes with and where they go."

I feel thick in the throat and watery. I say, "I'll come back someday."

Kelley says, "If you take long enough, we'll even let you back in."

I go before we all cry and wake the Board up. The stars look clearer out beyond the wall, and the moat of grass muffles my footsteps.

Blocked

GEOFF RYMAN

Geoff Ryman is a Canadian writer living in London, England. He began publishing SF stories in the mid-1970s, and wrote some SF plays, none published but most performed, including a powerful adaptation of Philip K. Dick's 1982 novel, The Transmigration of Timothy Archer. *Ryman's second novel,* The Child Garden *(1988), won the Arthur C. Clarke Award and the John W. Campbell Memorial Award, and confirmed him as a major figure in contemporary SF. He published a hypertext novel, 253/ (1998; www. ryman-novel.com/) and a science fiction novel,* Air *(2005), about the future of the internet. Although much of his work in the last decade or more is not genre, including a novel about Cambodia, he has continued to publish excellent genre short fiction. And he became a spokesperson for the unfortunately named "mundane SF" movement in recent years, dedicated to using real science and technology and Earth or nearby settings in the genre. His 2009 anthology,* When It Changed, *is a collection of mundane science fiction stories, each written by a science fiction author with advice from a scientist, and with an endnote by that scientist explaining the plausibility of the story.*

"Blocked" was published in F & SF. *It is a story about a man in near-future Cambodia who owns a casino, and who is married to a Danish woman with four kids, who doesn't love him. Aliens are invading.*

drcamed this in Sihanoukville, a town of new casinos, narrow beaches, hot bushes with flowers that look like daffodils, and even now after nine years of peace, stark ruined walls with gates that go nowhere.

In the dream, I get myself a wife. She's beautiful, blonde, careworn. She is not used to having a serious man with good intentions present himself to her on a beach. Her name is Agnete and she speaks with a Danish accent. She has four Asian children.

Their father had been studying permanently in Europe, married Agnete, and then "left," which in this world can mean several things. Agnete was an orphan herself and the only family she had was that of her Cambodian husband. So she came to Phnom Penh only to find that her in-laws did not want some strange woman they did not know and all those extra mouths to feed.

I meet the children. The youngest is Gerda, who cannot speak a word of Khmer. She's tiny, as small as an infant though three years old, in a splotched pink dress and too much toy jewelery. She just stares, while her brothers play. She's been picked up from everything she knows and thrown down into this hot, strange world in which people speak nonsense and the food burns your mouth.

I kneel down and try to say hello to her, first in German, and then in English. Hello, Gertie, hello, little girl. Hello. She blanks all language and sits like she's sedated.

I feel so sad, I pick her up and hold her, and suddenly she

329

buries her head in my shoulder. She falls asleep on me as I swing in a hammock and quietly explain myself to her mother. I am not married, I tell Agnete. I run the local casino.

Real men are not hard, just unafraid. If you are a man you say what is true, and if someone acts like a monkey, then maybe you punish them. To be a crook, you have to be straight. I sold guns for my boss and bought policemen, so he trusted me, so I ran security for him for years. He was one of the first to Go, and he sold his shares in the casino to me. Now it's me who sits around the black lacquered table with the generals and Thai partners. I have a Lexus and a good income. I have ascended and become a man in every way but one. Now I need a family.

Across from Sihanoukville, all about the bay are tiny islands. On those islands, safe from thieves, glow the roofs where the Big Men live in Soriya-chic amid minarets, windmills, and solar panels. Between the islands hang white suspension footbridges. Distant people on bicycles move across them.

Somehow it's now after the wedding. The children are now mine. We loll shaded in palm-leaf panel huts. Two of the boys play on a heap of old rubber inner tubes. Tharum with his goofy smile and sticky-out ears is long legged enough to run among them, plonking his feet down into the donut holes. Not to be outdone, his brother Sampul clambers over the things. Rith, the oldest, looks cool in a hammock, away with his earphones, pretending not to know us.

Gerda tugs at my hand until I let her go. Freed from the world of language and adults, she climbs up and over the swollen black tubes, sliding down sideways. She looks intent and does not laugh.

Her mother in a straw hat and sunglasses makes a thin, watery sunset smile.

Gerda and I go wading. All those islands shelter the bay, so the waves roll onto the shore child-sized, as warm and gentle as caresses. Gerda holds onto my hand and looks down at them, scowling in silence.

Alongside the beach is a grounded airliner, its wings cut away and neatly laid beside it. I take the kids there, and the boys run around inside it, screaming. Outside, Gerda and I look at the aircraft's spirit house. Someone witty has given the shrine tiny white wings.

The surrounding hills still have their forests; cumulonimbus clouds towering over them like clenched fists.

In the evening, thunder comes.

I look out from our high window and see flashes of light in the darkness. We live in one whole floor of my casino hotel. Each of the boys has his own suite. The end rooms have balconies, three of them, that run all across the front of the building with room enough for sofas and dining tables. We hang tubes full of pink sugar water for hummingbirds. In the mornings, the potted plants buzz with bees, and balls of seed lure the sarika bird that comes to sing its sweetest song.

In these last days, the gambling action is frenetic: Chinese, Thai, Korean, and Malays, they play baccarat mostly, but some prefer the one-armed bandits.

At the tables of my casino, elegant young women, handsome young men, and a couple of other genders besides, sit upright ready to deal, looking as alert and frightened as rabbits, especially if their table is empty. They are paid a percentage of the take. Some of them sleep with customers too, but they're good kids; they always send the money home. Do good, get good, we in Cambodia used to say. Now we say, *twee akrow meen lay:* Do bad, have money.

My casino is straight. My wheels turn true. *No guns*, says my sign. *No animals, no children*. Innocence must be protected. *No cigarettes or powders*. Those last two are marked by a skull-and-crossbones.

We have security but the powders don't show up on any scan, so some of my customers come here to die. Most weekends, we find one, a body slumped over the table.

I guess some of them think it's good to go out on a high. The Chinese are particularly susceptible. They love the theater of gambling, the tough-guy stance, the dance of the cigarette, the nudge of the eyebrow. You get dealt a good hand, you smile, you take one last sip of Courvoisier, then one sniff. You Go Down for good.

It's another way for the winner to take all. For me, they are just a mess to clear up, another reason to keep the kids away.

Upstairs, we've finished eating and we can hear the shushing of the sea.

"Daddy," Sampul asks me and the word thrums across my heart. "Why are we all leaving?"

"We're being invaded."

So far, this has been a strange and beautiful dream, full of Buddhist monks in orange robes lined up at the one-armed bandits. But now it goes like a stupid kids' TV show, except that in my dream, I'm living it, it's real. As I speak, I can feel my own sad, damp breath.

"Aliens are coming," I say and kiss him. "They are bringing many, many ships. We can see them now, at the edge of the solar system. They'll be here in less than two years."

He sighs and looks perturbed.

In this disrupted country two-thirds of everything is a delight, two-thirds of everything iron nastiness. The numbers don't add up, but it's true.

"How do we know they're bad?" he asks, his face puffy.

"Because the government says so and the government wouldn't lie."

His breath goes icy. "This government would."

"Not all governments, not all of them all together."

"So. Are we going to leave?"

He means leave again. They left Denmark to come here, and they are all of them sick of leaving.

"Yes, but we'll all Go together, okay?"

Rith glowers at me from the sofa. "It's all the fault of people like you."

"I made the aliens?" I think smiling at him will make him see he is being silly.

He rolls his eyes. "There's the comet?" he asks like I've forgotten something and shakes his head.

"Oh, the comet, yes, I forgot about the comet, there's a

comet coming too. And global warming and big new diseases."

He tuts. "The aliens sent the comet. If we'd had a space program we could meet them halfway and fight there. We could of had people living in Mars, to survive."

"Why wouldn't the aliens invade Mars too?"

His voice goes smaller, he hunches even tighter over his game. "If we'd gone into space, we would of been immortal."

My father was a drunk who left us; my mother died; I took care of my sisters. The regime made us move out of our shacks by the river to the countryside where there was no water, so that the generals could build their big hotels. We survived. I never saw a movie about aliens, I never had this dream of getting away to outer space. My dream was to become a man.

I look out over the Cambodian night, and fire and light dance about the sky like dragons at play. There's a hissing sound. Wealth tumbles down in the form of rain.

Sampul is the youngest son and is a tough little guy. He thumps Rith, who's fifteen years old, and both of them gang up on gangly Tharum. But tough-guy Sampul suddenly curls up next to me on the sofa as if he's returning to the egg.

The thunder's grief looks like rage. I sit and listen to the rain. Rith plays on, his headphones churning with the sound of stereophonic war.

Everything dies, even suns; even the universe dies and comes back. We already are immortal.

Without us, the country people will finally have Cambodia back. The walled gardens will turn to vines. The water buffalo will wallow; the rustics will still keep the fields green with rice, as steam engines chortle past, puffing out gasps of cloud. Sampul once asked me if the trains made rain.

And if there are aliens, maybe they will treasure it, the Earth.

I may want to stay, but Agnete is determined to Go. She has already lost one husband to this nonsense. She will not lose anything else, certainly not her children. Anyway, it was all part of the deal.

I slip into bed next to her. "You're very good with them," she says and kisses my shoulder. "I knew you would be. Your people are so kind to children."

"You don't tell me that you love me," I say.

"Give it time," she says, finally.

That night lightning strikes the spirit house that shelters our *neak ta*. The house's tiny golden spire is charred.

Gerda and I come down in the morning to give the spirit his bananas, and when she sees the ruin, her eyes boggle and she starts to scream and howl.

Agnete comes downstairs, and hugs and pets her, and says in English, "Oh, the pretty little house is broken."

Agnete cannot possibly understand how catastrophic this is, or how baffling. The *neak ta* is the spirit of the hotel who protects us or rejects us. What does it mean when the sky itself strikes it? Does it mean the *neak ta* is angry and has deserted us? Does it mean the gods want us gone and have destroyed our protector?

Gerda stares in terror, and I am sure then that though she is wordless, Gerda has a Khmer soul.

Agnete looks at me over Gerda's shoulder, and I'm wondering why she is being so disconnected when she says, "The papers have come through."

That means we will sail to Singapore within the week.

I've already sold the casino. There is no one I trust. I go downstairs and hand over the keys to all my guns to Sreang, who I know will stay on as security at least for a while.

That night after the children are asleep, Agnete and I have the most terrifying argument. She throws things; she hits me; she thinks I'm saying that I want to desert them; I cannot make her listen or understand.

"*Neak ta*? *Neak ta,* what are you saying?"

"I'm saying I think we should go by road."

"We don't have time! There's the date, there's the booking! What are you trying to do?" She is panicked, desperate; her mouth ringed with thin strings of muscle, her neck straining.

I have to go and find a monk. I give him a huge sum of money to earn merit, and I ask him to chant for us. I ask him to bless our luggage and at a distance bless the boat that we will sail in. I swallow fear like thin, sour spit. I order ahead, food for Pchum Ben, so that he can eat it, and act as mediary so that I can feed my dead. I look at him. He smiles. He is a man without guns without modernity without family to help him. For just a moment I envy him.

I await disaster, sure that the loss of our *neak ta* bodes great ill; I fear that the boat will be swamped at sea.

But I'm wrong.

Dolphins swim ahead of our prow, leaping out of the water. We trawl behind us for fish and haul up tuna, turbot, sea snakes and turtles. I can assure you that flying fish really do fly—they soar over our heads at night, right across the boat like giant mosquitoes.

No one gets seasick; there are no storms; we navigate directly. It is as though the sea has made peace with us. *Let them be, we have lost them, they are going.*

We are Cambodians. We are good at sleeping in hammocks and just talking. We trade jokes and insults and innuendo, sometimes in verse, and we play music, cards, and *bah angkunh*, a game of nuts. Gerda joins in the game and I can see the other kids let her win. She squeals with delight, and reaches down between the slats to find a nut that has fallen through.

All the passengers hug and help take care of the children. We cook on little stoves, frying in woks. Albatrosses rest on our rigging. Gerda still won't speak, so I cuddle her all night long, murmuring. *Kynom ch'mooah Channarith. Oun ch'mooah ay?*

I am your new father.

Once in the night, something huge in the water vents, just beside us. The stars themselves seem to have come back like the fish, so distant and high, cold and pure. No wonder we are greedy for them, just as we are greedy for diamonds. If we could, we would strip-mine the universe, but instead we strip-mine ourselves.

We land at Sentosa. Its resort beaches are now swallowed by the sea, but its slopes sprout temporary, cantilevered accommodation. The sides of the buildings spread down-ward like sheltering batwings behind the plastic quays that walk us directly to the hillside.

Singapore's latest growth industry.

The living dead about to be entombed, we march from the boats along the top of pontoons. Bobbing and smooth-surfaced, the quays are treacherous. We slip and catch each other before we fall. There are no old people among us, but we all walk as if aged, stiff-kneed and unbalanced.

But I am relieved; the island still burgeons with trees. We take a jungle path, through humid stillness, to the north shore, where we face the Lion City.

Singapore towers over the harbor. Its giant versions of Angkor Wat blaze with sunlight like daggers; its zigzag shoreline is ringed round with four hundred clippers amid a white forest of wind turbines. Up the sides of Mt. Fraser cluster the houses of rustics, made of wood and propped against the slope on stilts.

It had been raining during the day. I'd feared a storm, but now the sky is clear, gold and purple with even a touch of green. All along the line where trees give way to salt grasses, like stars going for a swim, fireflies shine.

Gerda's eyes widen. She smiles and holds out a hand. I whisper the Khmer words for firefly: *ampil ampayk*.

We're booked into one of the batwings. Only wild riches can buy a hotel room in Sentosa. A bottle of water is expensive enough.

Once inside, Agnete's spirits improve, even sitting on folding metal beds with a hanging blanket for a partition. Her eyes glisten. She sits Gerda and Sampul on the knees of her crossed legs. "They have beautiful shopping malls Down There," she says. "And Rith, *technik*, all the latest. Big screens. Billion billion pixels."

"They don't call them pixels anymore, Mom."

That night, Gerda starts to cry. Nothing can stop her. She wails and wails. Our friends from the boat turn over on their beds and groan. Two of the women sit with Agnete and offer sympathy. "Oh poor thing, she is ill."

No, I think, she is broken-hearted. She writhes and twists

in Agnete's lap. Without words for it, I know why she is crying.

Agnete looks like she's been punched in the face; she didn't sleep well on the boat.

I say, "Darling, let me take her outside. You sleep."

I coax Gerda up into my arms, but she fights me like a cat. *Sssh sssh, Angel, sssh.* But she's not to be fooled. Somehow she senses what this is. I walk out of the refugee shelter and onto the dock that sighs underfoot. I'm standing there, holding her, looking up at the ghost of Singapore, listening to the whoop of the turbines overhead, hearing the slopping sound of water against the quay. I know that Gerda cannot be consoled.

Agnete thinks our people are kind because we smile. But we can also be cruel. It was cruel of Gerda's father to leave her, knowing what might happen after he was gone. It was cruel to want to be missed that badly.

On the north shore, I can still see the towers defined only by their bioluminescence, in leopard-spot growths of blue, or gold-green, otherwise lost in a mist of human manufacture, smoke, and steam.

The skyscrapers are deserted now, unusable, for who can climb seventy stories? How strange they look; what drove us to make them? Why all across the world did we reach up so high? As if to escape the Earth, distance ourselves from the ground, and make a shiny new artifice of the world.

And there are the stars. They have always shone; they shine now just like they would shine on the deck of a starship, no nearer. There is the warm sea that gave us birth. There are the trees that turn sunlight into sugar for all of us to feed on.

Then overhead, giant starfish in the sky. I am at a loss, *choy mae!* What on Earth is that? They glow in layers, orange red green. Trailing after them in order come giant butterflies glowing blue and purple. Gerda coughs into silence and stares upward.

Cable cars. Cable cars strung from Mt. Fraser, to the shore and on to Sentosa, glowing with decorative bioluminescence.

Ampil ampayk, I say again and for just a moment, Gerda is still.

I don't want to go. I want to stay here.

Then Gerda roars again, sounding like my heart.

The sound threatens to shred her throat. The sound is inconsolable. I rock her, shush her, kiss her, but nothing brings her peace.

You too, Gerda, I think. You want to stay too, don't you? We are two of a kind.

For a moment, I want to run away together, Gerda and me, get across the straits to Johor Bahu, hide in the untended wilds of old palm-oil plantations.

But now we have no money to buy food or water.

I go still as the night whispers its suggestion.

I will not be cruel like her father. I can go into that warm sea and spread myself among the fishes to swim forever. And I can take you with me, Gerda.

We can be still, and disappear into the Earth.

I hold her out as if offering her to the warm birthsea. And finally, Gerda sleeps, and I ask myself, will I do it? Can I take us back? Both of us?

Agnete touches my arm. "Oh, you got her to sleep! Thank you so much." Her hand first on my shoulder, then around Gerda, taking her from me, and I can't stop myself tugging back, and there is something alarmed, confused around her eyes. Then she gives her head a quick little shake, dismissing it.

I would rather be loved for my manliness than for my goodness. But I suppose it's better than nothing and I know I will not escape. I know we will all Go Down.

The next day we march, numb and driven by something we do not understand.

For breakfast, we have Chinese porridge with roasted soya, nuts, spices, and egg. Our last day is brilliantly sunny. There are too many of us to all take the cable car. Economy class, we are given an intelligent trolley to guide us, carrying our luggage or our children. It whines along the bridge from Sentosa, giving us relentless tourist information about Raffles, independence in 1965, the Singapore miracle, the coolies who came as slaves but stayed to contribute so much to Singapore's success.

The bridge takes us past an artificial island full of cargo, cranes, and wagons, and on the main shore by the quays is a squash of a market with noodle stalls, fish stalls, and stalls full of knives or dried lizards. Our route takes us up Mt. Fraser, through the trees. The monkeys pursue us, plucking bags of bananas from our hands, clambering up on our carts, trying to open our parcels. Rith throws rocks at them.

The dawn light falls in rays through the trees as if the Buddha himself was overhead, shedding radiance. Gerda toddles next to me, her hand in mine. Suddenly she stoops over and holds something up. It is a scarab beetle, its shell a shimmering turquoise green, but ants are crawling out of it. I blow them away. "Oh, that is a treasure, Gerda. You hold onto it, okay?"

There will be nothing like it where we are going.

Then, looking something like a railway station, there is the Singapore terminal dug into the rock of the outcropping. It yawns wide open, to funnel us inside. The concrete is softened by a screen of branches sweeping along its face—very tasteful and traditional, I think, until I touch them and find that they are made of moldform.

This is Singapore, so everything is perfectly done. PAMPER YOURSELF, a sign says in ten different languages. BREATHE IN AN AIR OF LUXURY.

Beautiful concierges in blue-gray uniforms greet us. One of them asks, "Is this the Sonn family?" Her face is so pretty, like Gerda's will be one day, a face of all nations, smiling and full of hope that something good can be done.

"I'm here to help you with check-in, and make sure you are comfortable and happy." She bends down and looks into Gerda's eyes but something in them makes her falter; the concierge's smile seems to trip and stumble.

Nightmarishly, her lip gloss suddenly smears up and across her face, like a wound. It feels as though Gerda has somehow cut her.

The concierge's eyes are sad now. She gives Gerda a

package printed with a clown's face and colored balloons. Gerda holds the gift out from her upside-down and scowls at it.

The concierge has packages for all the children, to keep them quiet in line. The giftpacks match age and gender. Rith always says his gender is Geek, as a joke, but he does somehow get a Geek pack. They can analyze his clothes and brand names. I muse on how strange it is that Rith's dad gave him the same name as mine, so that he is Rith and I am Channarith. He never calls me father. Agnete calls me Channa, infrequently.

The beautiful concierge takes our papers, and says that she will do all the needful. Our trolley says good-bye and whizzes after her, to check in our bags. I'm glad it's gone. I hate its hushed and cheerful voice. I hate its Bugs Bunny baby face.

We wait.

Other concierges move up and down the velvet-roped queues with little trolleys offering water, green tea, dragon fruit, or chardonnay. However much we paid, when all is said and done, we are fodder to be processed. I know in my sinking heart that getting here is why Agnete married me. She needed the fare.

No one lied to us, not even ourselves. This is bigger than a lie; this is like an animal migration, this is all of us caught up in something about ourselves we do not understand, never knew.

Suddenly my heart says, firmly, *There are no aliens.*

Aliens are just the excuse. This is something we want to do, like building those skyscrapers. This is all a new kind of dream, a new kind of grief turned inward, but it's not my dream, nor do I think that it's Gerda's. She is squeezing my hand too hard and I know she knows this thing that is beyond words.

"Agnete," I say. "You and the boys go. I cannot. I don't want this."

Her face is sudden fury. "I knew you'd do this. Men always do this."

"I didn't use to be a man."

"That makes no difference!" She snatches Gerda away

from me, who starts to cry again. Gerda has been taken too many places, too suddenly, too firmly. "I knew there was something weird going on." She glares at me as if she doesn't know me, or is only seeing me for the first time. Gently she coaxes Gerda toward her, away from me. "The children are coming with me. All of the children. If you want to be blown up by aliens—"

"There are no aliens."

Maybe she doesn't hear me. "I have all the papers." She means the papers that identify us, let us in our own front door, give us access to our bank accounts. All she holds is the hologrammed, eye-printed ticket. She makes a jagged, flinty correction: "*They* have all the papers. Gerda is my daughter, and they will favor me." She's already thinking custody battle, and she's right, of course.

"There are no aliens." I say it a third time. "There is no reason to do this."

This time I get heard. There is a sound of breathing-out from all the people around me. A fat Tamil, sated maybe with blowing up other people, says, "What, you think all those governments lie? You're just getting cold feet."

Agnete focuses on me. "Go on. Get going if that's what you want." Her face has no love or tolerance in it.

"People need there to be aliens and so they all believe there are. But I don't."

Gerda is weeping in complete silence, though her face looks calm. I have never seen so much water come out of someone's eyes; it pours out as thick as bird's nest soup. Agnete keeps her hands folded across Gerda's chest and kisses the top of her head. What, does she think I'm going to steal Gerda?

Suddenly our concierge is kneeling down, cooing. She has a pink metal teddy bear in one hand, and it hisses as she uses it to inject Gerda.

"There! All happy now!" The concierge looks up at me with hatred. She gives Agnete our check-in notification, now perfumed and glowing. But not our ID papers. Those they keep, to keep us there, safe.

"Thank you," says Agnete. Her jaw thrusts out at me.

The Tamil is smiling with rage. "You see that idiot? He got the little girl all afraid."

"Fool can't face the truth," says a Cluster of networked Malay, all in unison.

I want to go back to the trees, like Tarzan, but that is a different drive, a different dream.

"Why are you stopping the rest of us trying to go, just because you don't want to?" says a multigen, with a wide glassy grin. How on Earth does s/he think I could stop them doing anything? I can see s/he is making up for a lifetime of being disrespected. This intervention, though late and cowardly and stupid, gets the murmur of approval for which s/he yearns.

It is like cutting my heart at the root, but I know I cannot leave Gerda. I cannot leave her alone Down There. She must not be deserted a second time. They have doped her, drugged her, the world swims around her, her eyes are dim and crossed, but I fancy she is looking for me. And at the level of the singing blood in our veins, we understand each other.

I hang my head.

"So you're staying," says Agnete, her face pulled in several opposing directions, satisfaction, disappointment, anger, triumph, scorn.

"For Gerda, yes."

Agnete's face resolves itself into stone. She wanted maybe a declaration of love, after that scene? Gerda is limp and heavy and dangling down onto the floor.

"Maybe she's lucky," I say. "Maybe that injection killed her."

The crowd has been listening for something to outrage them. "Did you hear what that man said?"

"What an idiot!"

"Jerk."

"Hey, lady, you want a nicer guy for a husband, try me."

"Did he say the little girl should be dead? Did you hear him say that?"

"Yeah, he said that the little baby should be dead!"

"Hey you, Pol Pot. Get out of line. We're doing this to escape genocide, not take it with us."

I feel distanced, calm. "I don't think we have any idea what we are doing."

Agnete grips the tickets and certificates of passage. She holds onto Gerda, and tries to hug the two younger boys. There is a bubble of spit coming out of Gerda's mouth. The lift doors swivel open, all along the wall. Agnete starts forward. She has to drag Gerda with her.

"Let me carry her at least," I say. Agnete ignores me. I trail after her. Someone pushes me sideways as I shuffle. I ignore him.

And so I Go Down.

They take your ID and keep it. It is a safety measure to hold as many of humankind safely below as possible. I realize I will never see the sun again. No sunset cumulonimbus, no shushing of the sea, no schools of sardines swimming like veils of silver in clear water, no unreliable songbirds that may fail to appear, no more brown grass, no more dusty wild flowers unregarded by the roadside. No thunder to strike the *neak-ta*, no chants at midnight, no smells of fish frying, no rice on the floor of the temple.

I am a son of Kambu. Kampuchea.

I slope into the elevator.

"Hey, Boss," says a voice. The sound of it makes me unhappy before I recognize who it is. Ah yes, with his lucky mustache. It is someone who used to work in my hotel. My Embezzler. He looks delighted, pleased to see me. "Isn't this great? Wait till you see it!"

"Yeah, great," I murmur.

"Listen," says an intervener to my little thief. "Nothing you can say will make this guy happy."

"He's a nice guy," says the Embezzler. "I used to work for him. Didn't I, Boss?"

This is my legacy thug, inherited from my boss. He embezzled his fare from me and disappeared, oh, two years ago. These people may think he's a friend, but I bet he still has his stolen guns, in case there is trouble.

"Good to see you," I lie. I know when I am outnumbered. For some reason that makes him chuckle, and I can see his silver-outlined teeth. I am ashamed that this unpunished thief is now my only friend.

Agnete knows the story, sniffs and looks away. "I should have married a genetic man," she murmurs.

Never, ever tread on someone else's dream.

The lift is mirrored, and there are holograms of light as if we stood inside an infinite diamond, glistering all the way up to a blinding heaven. And dancing in the fire, brand names.

Gucci.

Armani.

Sony.

Yamomoto.

Hugo Boss.

And above us, clear to the end and the beginning, the stars. The lift goes down.

Those stars have cost us dearly. All around me, the faces look up in unison.

Whole nations were bankrupted trying to get there, to dwarf stars and planets of methane ice. Arizona disappeared in an annihilation as matter and antimatter finally met, trying to build an engine. Massive junk still orbits half-assembled, and will one day fall. The saps who are left behind on Ground Zero will probably think it's the comet.

But trying to build those self-contained starships taught us how to do this instead.

Earthside, you walk out of your door, you see birds fly. Just after the sun sets and the bushes bloom with bugs, you will see bats flitter, silhouetted as they neep. In hot afternoons the bees waver, heavy with pollen, and I swear even fishes fly. But nothing flies between the stars except energy. You wanna be converted into energy, like Arizona?

So we Go Down.

Instead of up.

"The first thing you will see is the main hall. That should cheer up you claustrophobics," says my Embezzler. "It is the biggest open space we have in the Singapore facility. And as you will see, that's damn big!" The travelers chuckle in appreciation. I wonder if they don't pipe in some of that cheerful sound.

And poor Gerda, she will wake up for a second time in another new world. I fear it will be too much for her.

The lift walls turn like stiles, reflecting yet more light in shards, and we step out.

Ten stories of brand names go down in circles—polished marble floors, air-conditioning, little murmuring carts, robot pets that don't poop, kids in the latest balloon shoes.

"What do you think of that!" the Malay Network demands of me. All its heads turn, including the women wearing modest headscarves.

"I think it looks like Kuala Lumpur on a rainy afternoon."

The corridors of the emporia go off into infinity as well, as if you could shop all the way to Alpha Centauri. An illusion of course, like standing in a hall of mirrors.

It's darn good, this technology, it fools the eye for all of thirty seconds. To be fooled longer than that, you have to want to be fooled. At the end of the corridor, reaching out for somewhere beyond, distant and pure, there is only light.

We have remade the world.

Agnete looks worn. "I need a drink, where's a bar?"

I need to be away too, away from these people who know that I have a wife for whom my only value has now been spent.

Our little trolley finds us, calls our name enthusiastically, and advises us. In Ramlee Mall, level ten, Central Tower we have the choice of Bar Infinity, the Malacca Club (share the Maugham experience), British India, the Kuala Lumpur Tower View. . . .

Agnete chooses the Seaside Pier; I cannot tell if out of kindness or irony.

I step inside the bar with its high ceiling and for just a moment my heart leaps with hope. There is the sea, the islands, the bridges, the sails, the gulls, and the sunlight dancing. Wafts of sugar vapor inside the bar imitate sea mist, and the breathable sugar makes you high. At the other end of the bar is what looks like a giant orange orb (half of one, the other half is just reflected). People lounge on the brand-name sand (guaranteed to brush away and evaporate.) Fifty meters overhead, there is a virtual mirror that doubles distance so you can look up and see yourself from what appears to be a hundred meters up, as if you are flying. A Network on its collective back is busy spelling the word HOME with their bodies.

We sip martinis. Gerda still sleeps and I now fear she always will.

"So," says Agnete, her voice suddenly catching up with her butt, and plonking down to Earth and relative calm. "Sorry about that back there. It was a tense moment for both of us. I have doubts too. About coming here, I mean."

She puts her hand on mine.

"I will always be so grateful to you," she says and really means it. I play with one of her fingers. I seem to have purchased loyalty.

"Thank you," I say, and I realize that she has lost mine.

She tries to bring love back by squeezing my hand. "I know you didn't want to come. I know you came because of us."

Even the boys know there is something radically wrong. Sampul and Tharum stare in silence, wide brown eyes. Did something similar happen with Dad number one?

Rith the eldest chortles with scorn. He needs to hate us so that he can fly the nest.

My heart is so sore I cannot speak.

"What will you do?" she asks. That sounds forlorn, so she then tries to sound perky. "Any ideas?"

"Open a casino," I say, feeling deadly.

"Oh! Channa! What a wonderful idea, it's just perfect!"

"Isn't it? All those people with nothing to do." Someplace they can bring their powder. I look out at the sea.

Rith rolls his eyes. Where is there for Rith to go from here? I wonder. I see that he too will have to destroy his inheritance. What will he do, drill the rock? Dive down into the lava? Or maybe out of pure rebellion ascend to Earth again?

The drug wears off and Gerda awakes, but her eyes are calm and she takes an interest in the table and the food. She walks outside onto the mall floor, and suddenly squeals with laughter and runs to the railing to look out. She points at the glowing yellow sign with black ears and says "Disney." She says all the brand names aloud, as if they are all old friends.

I was wrong. Gerda is at home here.

I can see myself wandering the whispering marble halls like a ghost, listening for something that is dead.

We go to our suite. It's just like the damn casino, but there are no boats outside to push slivers of wood into your hands, no sand too hot for your feet. Cambodia has ceased to exist, for us.

Agnete is beside herself with delight. "What window do you want?"

I ask for downtown Phnom Penh. A forest of gray, streaked skyscrapers to the horizon. "In the rain," I ask.

"Can't we have something a bit more cheerful?"

"Sure. How about Tuol Sleng prison?"

I know she doesn't want me. I know how to hurt her. I go for a walk.

Overhead in the dome is the Horsehead Nebula. Radiant, wonderful, deadly, thirty years to cross at the speed of light.

I go to the pharmacy. The pharmacist looks like a phony doctor in an ad. I ask, "Is . . . is there some way out?"

"You can go Earthside with no ID. People do. They end up living in huts on Sentosa. But that's not what you mean, is it?"

I just shake my head. It's like we've been edited to ensure that nothing disturbing actually gets said. He gives me a tiny white bag with blue lettering on it.

Instant, painless, like all my flopping guests at the casino.

"Not here," he warns me. "You take it and go somewhere else, like the public toilets."

Terrifyingly, the pack isn't sealed properly. I've picked it up, I could have the dust of it on my hands; I don't want to wipe them anywhere. What if one of the children licks it?

I know then I don't want to die. I just want to go home, and always will. I am a son of Kambu, Kampuchea.

"Ah," he says and looks pleased. "You know, the Buddha says that we must accept."

"So why didn't we accept the Earth?" I ask him.

The pharmacist in his white lab coat shrugs. "We always want something different."

We always must move on and if we can't leave home, it drives us mad. Blocked and driven mad, we do something new.

There was one final phase to becoming a man. I remember my uncle. The moment his children and his brother's children were all somewhat grown, he left us to become a monk. That was how a man was completed, in the old days.

I stand with a merit bowl in front of the wat. I wear orange robes with a few others. Curiously enough, Rith has joined me. He thinks he has rebelled. People from Sri Lanka, Laos, Burma, and my own land give us food for their dead. We bless it and chant in Pali.

> *All component things are indeed transient.*
> *They are of the nature of arising and decaying.*
> *Having come into being, they cease to be.*
> *The cessation of this process is bliss.*
> *Uninvited he has come hither*
> *He has departed hence without approval*
> *Even as he came, just so he went*
> *What lamentation then could there be?*

We got what we wanted. We always do, don't we, as a species? One way or another.

The Last Apostle

MICHAEL CASSUTT

Michael Cassutt is a television producer and screenwriter who lives in Studio City, California, with his wife, Cindy, and two children, Ryan and Alexandra. He has published five novels, most recently Tango Midnight *(2003). He began publishing short fiction in the mid-70s, and novels in the mid-80s. Since 1985, he has worked in writing and producing for television, and has had an extensive association with SF and fantasy shows (including* Outer Limits, Max Headroom, The Twilight Zone*). He is also a noted space historian, who has published two large volumes of the biographical encyclopedia* Who's Who in Space, *and collaborated on the biography* Deke! *with astronaut Deke Slayton. He is currently completing* Heaven's Shadow, *the first volume of an SF trilogy, with screenwriter David S. Goyer. In an interview he remarks, "My desire to do "realistic" space novels pretty much forced me to make them contemporary. But I've always wanted to write 'pure,' far future science fiction at book length."*

"The Last Apostle" was published in Asimov's. *Cassutt's knowledge of astronauts and space programs is so extensive that this alternate universe story of astronauts has the feel of naturalism and conviction, that made us want to include it in this volume. It is a fine example of space program fiction that looks back at the twentieth century without a sense of lingering failure.*

Nothing is concealed that will not be revealed, nor secret that will not be known.

—Matthew 10:26

"**H**eart attack?"

"No. Took a spill on his mountain bike. Hit a patch of sand barreling down some crappy road up near Flagstaff."

Spell-check smoothed the errors of the e-mail exchange while failing to add texture or emotion. Nevertheless, Joe Liquori could not help smiling at the inescapable perfection of the news. Chuck Behrens' death had all the elements of his life: the outdoors, excess speed, and a total disregard for other people's rules and expectations.

For God's sake, Chuck had been eighty-nine last April thirteenth. (The birth date was easy to remember; he and Joe shared it, three years apart.) Joe could not possibly have gotten his ancient ass *onto* a mountain bike, much less ridden it up, around or down some twisty road.

"He was a good man," he typed, as tears came to his eyes and his breathing quickened. Thank God this was text, not voice. These sudden, uncontrollable swells of emotion had afflicted Joe for forty years. But they still annoyed him.

"It's okay, Dad." Jason, his son, was fifty-nine, with children and grandchildren of his own: did he find himself growing more teary?

"Is there going to be a service?" Not that there was any chance Joe would be able to attend.

350

"Family says only a private memorial. Possibly going to want his ashes on the Moon." Jason added an emoticon for irony.

"So I'm the last one."

"And the best." *Thank you for that, son.* Joe logged off with a goodbye for now, then sat back.

There had been twelve of them on the six lunar landing missions. Twelve who experienced the terrifying, exhilarating, barely controlled fall from sixty miles altitude to the gunpowder gray dust of the lunar surface. Twelve who opened a flimsy metal door to a harsh world of blinding sunlight. Twelve who had the explorer's privilege of uttering first words. Twelve who left footprints where no one had gone before.

More accurately, twelve who, years later, would experience trouble with eyes, heart, hands, lungs, all traceable to time spent slogging across the lunar surface wearing a rigid metallic cloth balloon. Twelve who bathed in varying degrees of acclaim while suffering varying degrees of guilt over those who died along the way—and those who did the real work on the ground.

Twelve Apostles, according to that stupid book.

Joe knew them all, of course. There was the Aviator—the classic American kid from the heartland, standing outside a grass airfield watching planes take off . . . the Preacher, the reformed drunkard and womanizer who found Jesus not on the Moon, not during the death march of booze and babes that followed, but years later after, a bumpy airplane ride as a passenger . . . the Visionary, who used his lunar celebrity to give unjustified weight to everything from spoon-bending to geomancy . . .

There was the Businessman, and his shadier, less successful twin, the Shark. The Mystic. The Doctor. The Politician. The Good Old Boy. The Lifer.

Then, as always, there was the Alpha Male of Apollo—Chuck Behrens.

Joseph Liquori, ninety-four, lunar module pilot for Apollo 506 and known, by the same scheme, as Omega—the Last Apostle—sipped his carefully rationed vodka and let himself weep, for a fallen comrade and an old friend, and for himself.

An hour later, Joe decided to take a walk.

This was not a casual decision. He had reached a stage in his life where exiting his living quarters required preparation. The facility he now called home provided him with a tiny bedroom and shared common area, roughly the same living space he had as a graduate student in Minneapolis' Dinky Town in the 1950s. He could afford better—a palace in northern California, with vistas, gardens, rows of books, servants, and possibly a big-breasted "nurse."

In fact, Joe had once possessed a mansion as well as several attractive, attentive nurses. But the nurses were gone, and the palace in Marin County had already been torn down, another lesson in the ephemeral nature of earthly existence. Or so the Preacher had informed Joe, the last time they shared a meal.

In order to take a walk, Joe faced the usual agonizing hygienic and mechanical procedures typical of advanced age—the mechanisms to assure continence, the visual and aural aids, the medical monitoring hardware, all bringing to mind the phrase he had over-used since his arrival: "It's easier to walk on the Moon than it is to walk down my driveway."

He was not required to get permission, but it was always smart to have help. Kari Schiff, the fresh-faced pixie from Kansas who called herself Joe's "co-pilot," didn't think he should be going outside at all.

Until he told her about the Alpha's death. "Then let me come with you," she said.

"I won't be going far." It wasn't a big lie, by NASA astronaut standards.

"You're sure?" Kari looked at her two colleagues, Jeffords and Bock. Bock had medical training, but he was also a passionate Libertarian. Any doubts about Joe's ability to take a walk in these circumstances were subordinate to his conviction that each man had the inalienable right to choose the time and place of his death.

•

Not that a walk would *necessarily* be fatal. "Okay," Kari said, "let's put on your armor."

The "armor" was an EVA suit, a rigid exo-skeleton that split in two at the waist, and in the best of circumstances could never be donned by a single person working alone. Especially not a man in his nineties, even if said senior was working in lunar gravity. Checking the life-support fittings and operation took more time.

Finally Joe was buttoned up, much as he had been that day in April 1973, when he had emerged from the front hatch of the lunar module Pathfinder on the Apollo 506 mission.

Five hours after receiving the instant message from his son about the Alpha's death, Joe Liquori emerged from the thirty-foot tall habitat (nicknamed the Comfort Inn) that he shared with three other astronauts at Aitken Base, on the far side of the Moon, to complete the last mission of Apollo.

> *The Preacher died of age-related illnesses at a facility in Colorado Springs in 2011.*

The names had been bestowed on them by Maxine Felice, a famously confrontational Swiss journalist who tracked them relentlessly for a decade, ultimately publishing a controversial bestseller called *The Apostles*. (Chuck hated the title, as he made clear to Joe the next time they met. "Apostles? Remember what happened to those guys? Crucified upside down? Boiled in oil? No, thanks!")

Felice had persisted: it was no coincidence, she said, that their number was twelve. "Our mission is slightly different," the Aviator had said. "And so is the God we serve."

The woman dismissed that. "What is Apollo if not a god?"

Joe's agreement with Aitken Enterprises entitled him to a ninety-day stay with "possible" extensions. In truth, the company's laughable inability to maintain a regular launch schedule ensured at least one automatic "extension" to 180. And when an earlier Aitken Station crewmember required return to earth soonest, Joe offered to buy his seat; his hand-picked crew ops panel magically agreed; and Aitken's cash flow problems eased for a month.

On the day the Alpha Apostle ran off that road in Arizona, Joe Liquori was in his 196th day at Aitken Base, where his time was largely spent blogging to the public—and telling sea stories. (The station trio especially loved the "true" story behind the Mystic's death.)

Kari Schiff, the real space cadet of the three, even played the Maxine Felice game, asking Joe, "If you guys were the Apostles, what are we?"

" 'The three who can't find ice'?" Bock said, sneering. "Weren't they in the Letter to the Corinthians?" Jeffords howled with laughter as Kari punched him in the arm. It was true that the Aitken team had yet to find significant water ice, the primary goal of the whole enterprise. But they had found traces, and they continued to search, spending most of their time preparing for each EVA, then actually performing the ten-hour job in armor, then recovering. They were lucky to accomplish two cycles every eight days.

In between, they managed the Virtual Moonwalks, driving mini-rovers across the surface to give paying customers back on Earth their own Aitken Experience. Now and then they made test runs of the processing gear from the Ops Shack, a second habitat connected to the Comfort Inn by an inflatable tunnel.

Emerging from the habitat, Joe ran through the perfunctory communications checks, which ended with a question from Kari: "So, just in case anyone asks . . . where are you headed?"

"Where else?" he said. "Where Pathfinder landed."

Robert Temple, the Lifer, died of a heart attack in Orlando, Florida, in 2008. He had stayed with NASA after Apollo and commanded three Shuttle missions.

Joe had come back to the Moon in order to revisit a key moment in his own life that, based on other accounts, he either misremembered or missed altogether. He likened himself to a paratrooper from the 101st Airborne returning to Normandy fifty years after D-Day.

It was possible, of course, that the discovery he and the Alpha made on their second EVA had distorted the experience for him.

Whatever the reason, his only firm memories of those three days on the Moon were constant nervousness about the timeline, dull fear, total exhaustion. The fear started with the hiccup of the lunar module's descent engine during pitchover—so anomalous that it caused cool, calm Chuck Behrens, the Alpha Apostle, to turn his head inside his fishbowl helmet, eyes wide with alarm, mouthing a simple, expressive, "Wow."

But, in classic Alpha fashion, doing nothing. The engine resumed full thrust and the landing proceeded and, powered by adrenaline and relief, the two astronauts zoomed through their checklist to their first EVA. (Chuck's first words were, "Hey, Mom and Dad, look at me." Then Joe's more mundane, "A lovely day for a walk.")

Even though there were three relay satellites in orbit around the Moon the day Alpha and Omega landed, comm from the far side was still intermittent. Nevertheless, the first seven-hour jaunt went by the numbers. Flag erected. Rover deployed. Scientific instruments sited.

After what turned out to be twenty hours of wakefulness and extreme stress, neither astronaut needed a sleeping pill to sack out in the cramped, uncomfortable Pathfinder.

The next day—the public relations ceremonies and contingency sampling behind them—they were able to board the rover quickly and be on the road, just the way the Alpha loved to fire up a T-38 aircraft and bolt into the Texas sky. This was to be their long traverse, if circumstances and terrain permitted, reaching a straight-line distance from Pathfinder of six kilometers. ("Close enough so we can walk back if the rover conks on us.")

The target location was known as Great Salt Lake, named by a geologist from Utah. GSL was a kidney-shaped minimare a kilometer wide and three high, marked by a rich variety of clustered craters and crevasses.

By the three-hour point of the EVA, the astronauts were

deploying instruments at the first of their two planned stops when they faced a forty-minute gap in the link to Houston. The Alpha said, "Hey, Joe, let's hike over there."

There was a shadowed cleft in a rock face a dozen meters high, about fifty meters to the south. It appeared to be the mouth of a cave in the low hills inside GSL. Joe knew it, of course. His memory for the Aitken Basin Site was photographic. The passage was narrow, jagged, but did not lead to a cave, just an open area the geologists called the Atrium.

Had the Alpha asked, "What do you think?" Joe would have said, *Every minute of this EVA has been planned. This site is one the geologists have been aching to visit for a decade. And we're supposed to take a spelunking detour?* But the question was never offered.

The Alpha entered first, stopped (a bit of a trick, given his high center of gravity and forward momentum) and said, "See anything?"

"What am I looking for?"

"Color. Anything but black or gray."

"What, some kind of oxidized soil? Shit." Here Joe slipped and fell to his hands. Even with the suit and life-support pack, which together weighed more than he did, he was easily able to push himself back to standing without help.

"This guy I know at JPL saw a flash of color in a single frame of film that he was processing." Chuck stopped and turned left, then right, sweeping with his hand, each motion severely constrained by the suit. "Here."

Joe blinked. Then raised his mylarized visor to give himself an unfiltered look. "You mean *there*."

Joe wasn't sure what he'd seen—a flash of pink, just as likely the result of some fast-moving solar particle ripping through his optic nerve—but he felt compelled to check it out. Hell, this was the one un-programmed moment in all of the Apollo EVAs. Enjoy it!

They hopped and shuffled toward the shadowed face of a boulder the size of a bus. "Maybe it's ice," Chuck said.

In the shadows, protected by a shelf of granite for God knew how many thousands, millions, possibly billions of years, was what looked to Joe to be a jumbled collection of pink pillars and related rubble—like the ruins of a Roman villa seen on a college trip to Herculaneum.

The substance had flat surfaces . . . not just crystalline facets, though even in the first adrenalized flush of discovery he was ready to consider that it might be natural. But each time he blinked, breathed, and counted, the material looked . . . artificial. Certainly it was like nothing they expected to find on the lunar surface. (Years later, seeing the destruction of the planet Krypton in the first *Superman* movie, Joe would literally stand up in the theater, thinking he was looking at the Aitken Coral.)

The Alpha broke the silence. "How much longer to AOS?" Acquisition of signal, the return of contact with mission control.

"Seven minutes."

"Let's get a sample. And mum's the word."

Joe wanted to scream in protest. Yes, they were already off the reservation as far as NASA knew. Why jeopardize the rest of their timeline by lobbing this particular grenade into the flight plan? *When in doubt, do nothing.* There would be time to look at this stuff when they returned to Pathfinder. Then, if it warranted, they could tell mission control—and return here on their third EVA.

But this could be the discovery of the ages! Something that justified the entire Apollo program!

Nevertheless, three years of training—twenty-five years of following orders—overcame all other impulses. Joe simply swallowed and reached for his tools.

They quickly hammered off several faceted pieces and scooped up the rubble. "Interesting," Joe said, knowing he might be overheard, "the hard stuff flakes like mica, but the rubble is like coral."

"Houston, 506, comm check." Chuck made the call in the clear, and also as a warning. *Don't say anything. You work for me.*

The Businessman disappeared off the coast of Florida in 1999.

All twelve Apostles met in the same room for the first time—post-Apollo—during interviews for the follow-up documentary to Felice's book. Nine years had smoothed out the old rivalries. They had dinner together, played golf in a trio of foursomes, stayed up late drinking and telling what the Alpha always called sea stories.

Thanks to his newfound prominence as chairman of the board of X Systems, Joe noticed that the others—especially the Good Old Boy and the Shark, who in Houston never seemed to know Joe's name—actually gave him leave to speak.

And so, with the Alpha's encouragement, the last night in that hotel room in Glendale, California, Joe shared the secret of the Aitken Coral.

"You bastards!" the Politician said, only half kidding. "You realize how hard it is to sell the manned space program these days? You could have saved me a lot of work!"

The Mystic was already chiming in, "You've got to get this out! My God, it would create a whole new paradigm!"

At this, the Shark and the Businessman both guffawed. Joe couldn't tell which was the more contemptuous. *What the hell was a "paradigm"?*

Before a vote-to-release by acclamation could be entered, the Preacher preached caution. "How do you know it's real?"

The Aviator chimed in, too. "Have you had it tested?"

The Visionary wanted to know where it was stashed. The Lifer, as usual, sat back in silence. There were other opinions—the Good Old Boy seemed to be on both sides of the matter.

A show of hands left it 5-5.

Joe turned to the Alpha, who said, "Guys, thank you. As Jeb Pruett used to say, whenever we bitched out our assignments, we'll 'take that under advisement.' We told you because we want your opinions. But the decision is ours. Joe?"

Joe was indecently pleased. For the first time in their working relationship, Chuck Behrens had offered him a voice in a decision! "I say, sit on it for a while yet. Do some definitive tests. If it's really real, a few years' delay won't matter. If it's not what we think, we'll save ourselves a world of shit."

The Alpha concurred. The vote of the Apostles was 7-5 against.

There never was another gathering of the twelve Apostles as a group. Somehow the Alpha always managed to cancel. And then death began to reduce their numbers.

Herman Polski—the Politician—died much too young, felled by a heart attack in Texas three years later.

Even at Aitken Base, Joe would still hear the question, "How did you find out you were going to the Moon?" They didn't realize it was a three-step answer. Number one, "The day I got the phone call from NASA telling me I'd been selected as an astronaut, and to get my ass to Houston by January fifteenth."

Step two took place six years later. It was ten minutes before a Monday morning pilots' meeting, two days after the Aviator and the Preacher splashed down from the first lunar landing on 501.

Chuck Behrens motioned Joe into his office. "Jeb's going to announce me as backup commander for the third landing."

"Congratulations." Joe could not help thinking that every time another astronaut succeeded, he died a little.

"Wanna go with me?"

"As lunar module pilot?"

"What else?"

"Okay."

Chuck raised an eyebrow. "You're a low-key son of a bitch, Joe. When I got my Gemini assignment I could have reached orbit without the rocket."

"I've been waiting six years. My feeling is, 'about fucking time.'"

Step three was the least surprising. Joe and Chuck had spent a year backing up the Shark and the Mystic. Joe and Chuck were watching their splashdown (a bit tricky, since one of three parachutes collapsed) in mission control when Jeb Pruett turned to them and said, "You've got 506."

That was when Joe could have reached orbit—or the Moon itself—without a rocket.

But the key decision had been made earlier, when the Alpha invited him onto his crew. "One thing before we lock this in, old buddy. From this day on, you take orders from me."

"Why wouldn't I take your orders?"

Chuck laughed so hard his face flushed. "Joe, Joe, Joe . . . the whole reason you're the right-fielder in this team is that you are too goddamn independent! And everybody knows it. Not insubordinate. You just obviously know more than the rest of us, and make sure whoever you're working for gets the message, too.

"I can't have that. I will acknowledge right here and now that, based on I.Q. and all that good stuff, you should be *my* commander. Hell, you know more about the lunar module than anyone, including me. You've got a sci-fi kind of mind, which doesn't hurt, either. But from this point on, what I need from you is the certainty of blind obedience. If I tell you we're going direct from AUTO, you do it. If I tell you to strip down and take a shit on the White House lawn, you do it. If I'm wrong, and it is likely I will be wrong in some matters, it's my problem.

"And if I get us killed, then either I wasn't the right guy to be commander, or the universe was against us. Either way, I want my last thought to be the knowledge that it was my doing.

"I need you to be a tool. And never give me the idea you're thinking ahead of me, that you're dying to give me a brilliant out-of-your-ass suggestion."

It took Joe Liquori all of two seconds to make up his mind, to change his whole personality and his destiny. "Okay."

Jesse King, the Shark, commander of the troubled 503 mission where the lunar module ascent stage shut down early, forcing the command module to swoop down for an emergency rescue, died of lung cancer in 1990. "Good career move," the Alpha said, perhaps unkindly. The Shark's financial career had caught up with him. Had he lived, he would have been prosecuted for fraud.

In theory, the choice of landing site for the sixth mission had been made years back. From the relatively benign Sea of Tranquility and Ocean of Storms to more challenging highlands, like Fra Mauro and Hadley, the sites had been clicked off by the first missions. It looked as though Chuck and Joe were headed for Cayley Plains, until a program planning meeting attended by the center director, the program manager from HQ, science chief, twenty head sheds and horse-holders.

And, uninvited, Chuck and Joe. They had been up in T-38s that morning, and Chuck had insisted they stay in their sweaty flight suits. And arrive ten minutes late.

Dr. Rowe, the center director, noted their presence. "You guys take a wrong turn on the way to the simulator?"

"Depends on what we hear here," Chuck said, grabbing a pair of seats as close to the front as he could.

Rowe, whose fatherly demeanor hid a precise engineering mind, glanced at General Shields, the nothing-like-fatherly Apollo program manager. Who simply said, "Let's have it, Chuck."

Smiling, Chuck walked toward the map of the Moon and tapped his finger on Tranquility, Storms, Fra Mauro. "We've been *here, here,* and *here.* A year from now, we'll have been here, too."

Then he removed the map from its easel and turned it over. There was nothing on the back. "That's funny, I'd always been taught that even though we couldn't see it, the Moon really had a Far Side." Joe, the sci-fi reader, had told Chuck about an Asimov story that claimed precisely that.

The meeting room was silent, except for the thump of General Shields' pencil. "Your point, Colonel?"

"By the time Apollo is done, we'll have spent twenty billion dollars and visited a fraction of half a world. The front half. The easy half. Is that what the president said? 'We do these things because they are easy'?"

The room erupted with protests, some emotional, some technical—"How do we relay comm from the back side?"—and even answers to the objections—"The Air Force has a bunch of small comsats sitting on the shelf in LA. We could put them in the service module on the next three landing missions—"

Chuck knew he'd over-reached, but that was his style: ask for the Moon and take what you can get.

Nothing changed—that day.

Seven weeks later, NASA announced that the sixth and last lunar landing would attempt to reach Aitken Basin on the far side.

Len Caskey, the flight surgeon turned test pilot, always known as The Doctor, died in 2007, six years after a debilitating stroke.

It was only in the sleepless second night that they found the privacy to speak about their discovery. "Funny, isn't it?" Chuck said. "Three human beings within a quarter of a million miles—one of them in another spacecraft—and we're worried about being overheard."

"Yeah. Funny."

Chuck tapped his bare foot on the sample case. "What do you think it is?"

"Pink coral."

"Even something as basic as coral would be significant, wouldn't it? It's not, though. Not with those edges. Somebody *made* that."

"Maybe it *was* somebody," Joe said. "Maybe that was the body of a crystal alien."

"You and that sci-fi mind of yours." Chuck had closed his eyes. "All I know is, word gets out about this, lots of people are going to be pissing their pants."

Joe didn't bother to tell Chuck that on seeing the Aitken Coral he had, indeed, filled his diaper.

The third EVA was as routine as moon walks ever went. A few hours later, buttoned up in Pathfinder, they fired the ascent stage to begin the journey home.

Once they'd docked to Conestoga and moved their samples and gear aboard, Joe swam into the LM for a last look before jettison.

The entire weight of the mission, the secret, the training, his whole life landed on him. He started weeping.

"Joe, you all right down there?" Don Berringer, their

command module pilot, had seen him through the tunnel . . . fetal, floating, shuddering with sobs.

"Shut up, Don." Chuck had seen it, too . . . and gently pushed the hatch closed.

Five minutes later Joe had calmed himself. He completed the close-out checklist, stashed the fecal waste bags Berringer had accumulated during his three days of orbital privacy, allowed himself one last look out Pathfinder's triangular window at the desperately desolate moonscape sliding past.

Chuck floated into the module, closing the hatch behind him. "Ready to rock and roll?"

"Yeah." He noted a sample bag in Chuck's hand. "What's that?"

"What do you think?"

"What's it doing here?"

"I've half a mind to leave it. Send it around the Sun for the next ten thousand years." When separated from Conestoga, Pathfinder would be launched into a heliocentric orbit.

Joe was still in the absolute-obedience mode. "Copy that."

Chuck laughed again. "I can't. But I don't want to broadcast the news, either. Not yet. Like they taught us in all those sims, when in doubt, do nothing. And let me tell you, my friend, I'm in serious doubt about what to do."

"Then you better move it to the PPK." PPKs were the astronauts' personal preference kits, bags of family memorabilia, postal covers, and commemorative coins.

Chuck winked and made a clicking sound, a sign of the highest approval.

That was the extent of the discussion.

The Good Old Boy, Floyd Brashear, died of prostate cancer in 2019.

The PPKs turned out to be a bit of a problem. The post-flight check out included a weigh-in, which showed what NASA would call a "significant discrepancy," which Chuck managed to alleviate by convincing those doing the weighing that he had stuck his EVA gloves in there. "Rather than throw them overboard, you follow?"

Then he had turned around and thrown a regular fit in Jeb's office. Somehow, Chuck and Joe managed to walk out of the center with both PPKs—unopened.

There was one question in the debrief. The Utah geologist edged up to the most recent moonwalkers at the coffee break to say, "Ah, say, did you guys ever get a look inside those hills in GSL?"

"God, Nick, I'm so sorry. During that first dead zone we got within maybe ten feet of the son of a bitch. We were looking through the opening, weren't we, Joe?"

"Right through it, Chuck."

"Right at the mouth. But the soil looked a little loose and the walls a little tight and jagged, if you catch my drift." And here Chuck lowered his voice and leaned in to the geologist. "I was afraid of falling on my dang face and, you know, ripping my suit. I didn't want to screw up like that with fifty million people watching."

No ground-based science nerd was going to second-guess an astronaut in a situation like that—at least, not openly.

And that had been the end of the inquiries.

But not the end of the discussion.

Five years later, when Joe made his first trip back to Houston as a civilian, to take his annual physical, he heard at the clinic that Chuck had come through earlier in the day. Naturally Chuck would be in Houston around the same time . . . the target date for physicals was that shared birthday. Strangely, Chuck had left a message for him: *meet me at ops at 0800 tomorrow.*

Ops was Ellington Air Force base five miles up the road, where NASA kept its fleet of aircraft. Somehow Chuck had convinced them to give him a T-38 for a hop . . . with Joe.

It was only when they were in the air, bouncing their way through the clouds of an approaching Gulf storm, that Chuck broke his usual radio silence: "Five hundred million years old."

"What?"

"That pink coral we found at Aitken? The mysterious object we found on the Moon and kept secret all these years? It's five hundred million years old."

"That's really not old by lunar standards. Last I heard that thing was four billion years old. Or five."

"Joe, that coral is from *Earth*."

Through God knows how many contacts and cut-outs, Chuck had arranged for samples to be tested at three different facilities. Age, composition, carbon dating, all tests had the same result: it was just like material found on Earth's sea floor five hundred million years in the past.

The knowledge changed nothing—Alpha and Omega kept their silence—but it did inform later discussions between the Apostles in various ways. Over the next thirty years, on his own and in conversation with like-minded souls such as the Visionary and, somewhat to Joe's surprise, the Shark and the Aviator, Joe developed a conceptual model of the entities who had left the pink coral at Aitken Basin.

They were amphibious at least, possibly even aquatic.

Earth in five hundred million BC—aside from being a blue-white sphere (as seen from the Moon)—would have been unrecognizable: the continents were still smushed together in some version of Gondwanaland. What would later be the Antarctic was ice-free—possibly even the home of the Beings.

(Although a civilization robust enough to launch at least one flight to the Moon would logically require more than a single landmass. "Why?" the Shark said. "What is the basis for that conclusion?")

The Visionary was more troubled by the lack of evidence of past civilizations. Here the Aviator showed an unexpected grasp of archaeology and geology. "How much of the land we see and excavate was above water that long ago?" Before the Visionary could suggest a ballpark figure, the Aviator had one: "Under 5 percent, maybe as little as 2 . . . maybe zero.

"And even if you had 5 percent of the Coral People's land still dry, suppose it was in the Andes? Or the middle of the Takla Makan?"

"Or in Albania," the Shark said, to general laughter.

"One of the reasons we find any evidence of past civilization is that we're digging where we know they lived. Besides, these civilizations only existed during the past ten thousand years.

"We seem to find dinosaurs," the Visionary said, stubborn as always. (And, Joe remembered, from a Fundamentalist family.)

"By accident," Joe said. "And keep in mind . . . the oldest dinosaur—Cambrian Era—is only half as far back as these Beings lived."

"At a minimum," the Shark added.

"But we do find fossils from that era, long before the dinosaurs. And they're all small. Shouldn't we find, hell, I don't know . . . pottery? A fork? The equivalent of an oil rig or even a temple?"

"I did a rough calculation on this," Joe said. "You know how Heinlein said, 'The surface of the Moon has an area equal to the continent of Africa. Our missions have explored a neighborhood in Cape Town'?

"If you just assume that the surface area of our Coral People civilization was the continent of Antarctica, which is surely too small, we have turned soil in less area than Vostok, Byrd, and the other half dozen South Pole stations cover: about a hundred square miles."

"Ultimately, though, it's a matter of belief. Based on admittedly skimpy—"

"—One sample? Yeah, that's taking the word skimpy and giving it a good squeeze—"

"—evidence, we believe the Moon was visited by terrestrials at least half a billion years before you two."

"Or the rest of us." Shark always liked to remind people that Apollo was a *program*, not a single event like Lindbergh's flight.

"I'm completely comfortable with that statement," the Visionary said. "Which makes it the discovery of the Epoch! Like Noah's Ark or a piece of the True Cross! Why not make it public?"

"Because Chuck and I are still concerned about what it

would do to the program." Here Joe extended his hand to the Shark. "Shuttle's flying, space station program is in the works, lunar exploration's on the drawing boards.

"Right now things are fine! It's like being on flight status when you go to see the doctor—the only thing you can do is make it worse."

Mention of flight surgeons, especially in the absence of the Doctor, won the day.

Joe almost believed it.

The Aviator died of a brain tumor in Seattle, 1994.

In April 1998, Joe arrived in Houston for another physical, checking into the Kings Inn right outside the Johnson Space Center gate. He found a blinking light on his room phone with a message from Chuck—good old Alpha—inviting Omega aka Joe to his house that evening.

In all their time together, Joe had never been in the Alpha's house. It wasn't an issue: Joe felt the two had seen enough of each other to last two lifetimes.

The Alpha and his third wife, Laurie, had a three-bedroom condo on an inlet of the misnamed Clear Lake ("neither clear nor a lake") in a gated community developed by the Shark himself.

In spite of his blue suit, flyboy background, the Alpha had taken up sailing, buying a forty-foot sloop which he named *506*. After a suitable number of drinks, a round of sea stories, they headed out.

The first thing to became clear was that for a natural aviator and astronaut—literally a sailor of the stars—the Alpha was a total landlubber. Joe, of course, was no better, preferring water in swimming pools or ice chests. His sole advantage was that he didn't pretend to be a sailor.

After numerous misadventures with the sails and riggings, the *506* headed down the ship channel toward the Gulf on engine power. Real sailors swept past, white sails flapping in the breeze, their captains offering half-hearted salutes—until recognizing the name on the boat and the identity of its "captain." Then beer bottles were raised and pretty women waved with enthusiasm. "Well," the Alpha said, "it's a good thing we didn't have to *sail* to Aitken Basin."

They reached the gulf, and Joe's stomach began to protest. "Let me get something." Leaving Joe at the wheel, the captain went below. When he emerged, however, it wasn't with a bottle of Dramamine.

It was with a suitcase. "Going on a trip?" Joe said, trying to joke through the nausea.

"There ain't no clothes in this case, old pal." The Alpha opened it: there was the pink Aitken Coral, what looked like the entire set of samples—including three chunks returned from the institutes that had done the analyses.

"Wow," was all Joe could say. He was trying not to heave.

"Well, good buddy . . . it seems I've got a choice to make." Joe noted the Alpha's reference to himself, alone, not the team. "Turn this stuff over to the world and see what sort of waves it makes . . ."

"It'll be a cultural tsunami!" Joe said, proud of the metaphor, especially under the circumstances.

Even the Alpha seemed impressed. "Yeah! A cultural tsunami! The world will never be the same, all that shit."

There was a long moment when neither moved, though the *506* rose on a swell. Then, with a casualness that Joe would always remember, the Alpha simply raised the suitcase and dumped its contents into the greenish-brown soup that was the Houston ship channel.

Joe pulled himself to his feet, managing to blurt, "What the hell are you doing?" before throwing up.

As the greenish spatter of partly digested chicken sandwich and beer floated away on the water, the Alpha said, "Is that an editorial comment? Or the seasickness talking?"

Joe wiped his mouth. "Dammit, Chuck!"

The Alpha smiled tightly, his eyes a mass of crow's feet caused by a life in pressurized cockpits. "Look at it this way," he finally said, unusually quietly. "It's just gone back where it came from."

The Mystic was killed in a bizarre plane crash in Czechoslovakia in 2002.

With a television network offering substantial money for the exclusive rights, Joe had made the obligatory visit to the Pathfinder landing site during his first week back on the Moon, driving in the enclosed rover with Kari, who served as camera operator.

It was strange how different it looked from the images seared into his fifty-year-old memory: of course, he and Chuck had landed when the Sun was lowest, throwing features into relief (the better to be avoided during landing). This second time, the Sun was as high as it ever got in the Moon's polar region. The flat top of Pathfinder's descent stage looked strange, scorched from the blast of the ascent motor.

The flag they had planted had been bleached white by the Sun, but still stood. Proudly waved, if you allowed for the wave to be frozen.

"Don't mess up your original footprints," Kari had warned.

On that first traverse down the lunar memory lane, Joe made sure to avoid the place where he and Chuck had found the Aitken Coral, not with a camera on him. And especially not after the Alpha himself was patched through, live, offering congratulations and asking a favor: "Could you look for my sunglasses? I think I dropped them."

Now, as Joe Liquori visited the landing site for the third time, it actually looked familiar. Thank God. At his age, in these circumstances, his memory needed all the help he could get.

Why had he kept the secret for so long? Because Chuck— the Alpha Apostle—wanted it that way. Because the man who had charged through life, playing the game at a higher level than anyone Joe knew, had said so. Period. Because men who possessed the skills to brave a lunar landing shared a unique ability to make the right decisions.

But now the Alpha was gone. The stone had rolled away. Death had released Joe.

The Alpha, Chuck Behrens, died in a biking accident near Flagstaff, Arizona, in 2020.

Joe stopped the rover briefly a hundred yards south of Pathfinder, and it all looked familiar now, like main street in your hometown. Looking at the tracks from his second visit, he gunned the rover again, turning left and steering a path parallel to that of his and Chuck's second EVA.

In 1973 it had taken the two of them the better part of two hours to reach Great Salt Lake, but today Joe covered the same ground in forty-five minutes. He had the advantage of aiming for a destination—and not stopping every kilometer to set up an instrument package or take pictures.

He slowed the rover near the cleft. With habits born of twenty-five years of operational flying and space training, Joe checked, double-checked, and triple-checked his suit and consumables, to Kari's approval (she followed via telemetry and video): "We don't want to lose you," she said.

"Me, neither. Besides, think what it would do to future tourist flights." This was a joke: space fatalities only raised public interest, like the deaths of climbers on Mt. Everest. The stranger and more poignant, the better!

Joe had no plans to feed that particular public appetite.

He exited, marveling again at the improvements in technology over the past fifty years. Not just the rover, which had the solid feel of a classic Mercedes automobile compared to the Pathfinder's flimsy golf cart, but the suit—slimmer, more rigid, it practically did the walking for you.

He took one of the standard sample cases—yes, the commercial Aitken Enterprise at least pretended to do some scientific sampling—and started out.

It was like walking on a beach in boots. But soon he breached the passage easily, to stand once again in the center of Great Salt Lake.

He wondered about that long, long, long ago visit from Earth—what kind of vehicle had they used? Hell, had they even used a vehicle? His sci-fi mind was filled with wild images . . . maybe the Moon was closer to Earth. Maybe they'd climbed here on some kind of space elevator or tower.

Stupid. Let others worry about that.

He reached the cleft and looked into the shadows—

Nothing but bare gray black rock with shiny flecks. Where was the pink coral? It had lasted millions of years! Surely it hadn't faded away in fifty! Could the damage he and Chuck had inflicted—

No, no, no. Then Joe thought he saw other footprints. *Christ, Kari and the others had found it!*

Come on, Joe . . . re-group! Once he allowed himself to catch his breath, to stand back, it was obvious he had gone to the wrong cleft! He'd gotten turned around!

Here it was! Here was a heap of that magical, historical material from Earth's ancient floor—

Joe got busy collecting.

It only took twenty minutes to fill the case, the time expanded to let him take images and add voice-over at every step. What he should have done during his first return.

Now, back to the rover—and to the new world he would create.

Step. Step.

He had to halt. He was feeling sick to his stomach, sick in his chest. His vision was blearing.

Keep going—

With a grunt, clutching the last sample from the very last Apollo, Joe Liquori fell down.

For uncounted minutes he lay in the lunar soil, hearing nothing but the steady hiss of the airflow, the gentle click of the pumps. How long would that last? Two more hours?

He could not move. He was going to die on the Moon!

Use the radio! He croaked a cry for help. Heard nothing but static. What did he expect? He was lying in a depression, his line of sight to Aitken Station blocked by the hills around Great Salt Lake.

The Visionary died in his sleep at home in Colorado . . . June 2011.

In the last twenty years, as their numbers dwindled, interaction among the Apostles was via e-mail, forwarded jokes about old age. It was the Alpha, typically, who refused to participate, and when he did, referred to the jokes only by punch lines: "There's one less than he thought!" "I can't remember where I live!" "Hell, every other car's going the wrong way!"

Lying in the lunar afternoon, those were Joe Liquori's increasingly scattered thoughts . . . of punch lines to bad jokes. That, and the realization that Chuck Behrens, the Alpha Apostle, might have been wrong . . .

A shadow fell across him. "Hey, Joe, what are you doing like that?"

It was Kari and Jeffords from Aitken Station. They had realized the Moon was no place for a man of ninety to be walking alone, even one who had pioneered the site.

Back in their rover, Joe showed them the samples, and tried to tell them the history, knowing he was doing it badly.

Kari stopped him. "We got it, Joe. We saw your pink stuff—and it led us right to what we've been looking for . . . a hundred meters away, we found ice!"

> *Joe Liquori, the Omega Apostle, died of a heart attack in Lancaster, California, two days after returning from his second flight to the Moon—the one that discovered water ice, making human colonization possible.*

Another Life

CHARLES OBERNDORF

Charles Oberndorf lives in Cleveland, Ohio. He teaches seventh-grade English at University School, where he is the Chi Waggoner Chair in Middle School Writing. He is the author of three novels, most recently Foragers *(1996). His five prior short stories have appeared in* Full Spectrums 1 and 2, Asimov's SF, *and* The Magazine of Fantasy and Science Fiction. *He is completing his fourth novel,* The Translation of Desire. *He has in progress a fifth novel,* The Opening and Closing of Eyes; *a novella set in the Hundred Worlds universe of his short stories "Oracle" and "Writers of the Future"; a novella set in the same universe as "Another Life"; and a biographical novel about Abe Osheroff, a Spanish Civil War veteran and radical activist. But he had not published in over a decade until this excellent piece.*

"Another Life" was published in F & SF *(in the same anniversary issue as the Ryman story, above). "I was doing a close reading of Roberto Bolaño for another story, which had an unwritten middle section. I read Greg Egan's "Glory," and suddenly I knew how to finish the other story and how to start this one. It seems these days Roberto Bolaño is my patron saint and Greg Egan is my muse. I hadn't published anything since 1996, and I wrote this story just to write it." This is a story about serial immortality, in wartime, in the distant future, and about sex and gender. It may be the best SF story of the year.*

She says, tell me about your first death.

After all these years she should be familiar with its details, but age seems to have erased the particulars that never interested her, so I remind her of the outline of events.

No, she says. I meant what it was like when you woke up?

She's lying in her bed, and I've pulled up a chair to sit by her side. I say something like:

I opened my eyes, and there on the ceiling were shades of blues and yellows. You know how I usually don't have a good memory for colors, but I took a psych test when I enlisted, and they told me those were the colors that would calm me when I woke up. I do remember lake water lapping the shore, the sounds of the birds I'd grown up with, because it was odd to hear them in this enclosed room. I expected the sound of the water to actually be the reverberation of a ventilation fan.

I sat up, but discovered I couldn't. There was a nurse beside me, and she was explaining something. I don't remember what she said. I just knew she wasn't the same nurse who'd sat me down in the chair and placed gear around my head. I think I liked this one more. Her voice was calm, but it drifted around me along with the sounds of lake water. I was lying down, but I'd just been in a chair. The other nurse, the one I didn't like, the one who had placed the gear around my head, had told me to relax. I'd closed my eyes. While I was unconscious, they had mapped my neural network. Now, awake, I should get up out of that chair and head over

374

to the next bulkhead to the tavern we liked, to the Wake, where I'd arranged to meet Noriko.

Ah, Noriko, she says. There's an edge to her voice, though you'd have to know her well to hear it. After all these years, the name Noriko still inspires an edge to her voice.

I say, I can tell another story.

No, she says. You only told me about Noriko when we were first together. And that was a long time ago.

This is also about when I met Amanda Sam.

Don't be evasive. I'm too old for these games.

So I lay there in this unexpected reality. Of course, someone must have told me if you wake up sitting up, then you're waking up right after they've completed the recording. If you wake up lying down, you died, and they've grown a new body and shaped your mind using the patterns of your last recorded neuromap. But I didn't remember anyone telling me this, and maybe this was what the nurse was whispering to me, but it was my first death, and all I felt was panic and confusion.

I wasn't in the body that had been sitting in the chair, the body that would wake up, walk down the corridor, cross a bulkhead, and head two levels up to the Wake, where I'd meet Noriko. I wasn't in the body that was scheduled to spend two more days' R&R on Haven before it boarded a troop carrier for the war zone.

Worse, if I had died in battle, I should be in a ward with other newborns, the other soldiers who'd died with me. But I was in a private ward with what appeared to be civilian nurses. Had I died so heroically that I had received some special discharge? Or had I made such a fatal mistake that I couldn't even be reborn among my peers? I asked the nurses all sorts of questions. A nurse on one shift, let's say the morning shift, said, I can't talk about the war. It will just upset you. The afternoon-shift nurse said, No one tells us who pays for the treatment or the room. The night-shift nurse said, Maybe the money is coming out of your own account.

Of course, that was impossible. When I enlisted, I had been as poor as a miner without oxygen. The sign-up bonus had gone to pay off family debt.

The nurses taught me to sit up and helped me make my first steps. I learned how to gesture with my hands without knocking over cups of coffee. I imagined what it must be like in the ward among the soldiers, the taunts and the insults at each misstep, all of that making it less frustrating. And at some point, some captain or lieutenant, or maybe even some lowly sergeant, would come by and update us on the status of the war and announce who would go back and who had died the requisite third time and would be offered the honorable discharge plus bonus.

But one nurse, one day, while helping me sit in a machine that worked my leg muscles, said, mostly in exasperation, "There is no ward of newborns. You're the only one right now. That's why you got so many nurses. We're bored."

Depression weighed my every thought. I'd imagined that Noriko had died with me, that she would have been among the newborn. I imagined finding her and making sure she understood that whatever I'd done wrong, whatever had caused our deaths, I hadn't meant it.

What exactly did you two have? she asks. How long had you been together?

I hesitate. I have been with this woman for several lifetimes. In our last lifetime together, I waited until I turned fifty before I decided it was time to start over in the body of a twenty-five-year-old. She said, I've lived a few more lives than you. I feel I've seen enough. This time I want to see things through to the end. She said she would like to spend those remaining years with me, growing old together, but I did not believe her. Our lives were so fraught with our time together: nouns weighted with multiple meanings, verbs sharpened by the years; we were best off, when the mood was right, with incomplete sentences that the other would finish with an automatic goodwill that was also born of all our time together.

After she left me, I died in an orbital collision, and insurance paid for the rebirth into a twenty-year-old body. My current body is thirty-five; she's eighty-five. My answer to her question—How long had you been together?—now embarrasses me.

At this distance, it's so hard to imagine how I felt. It was my first life. It was so new to me. I'd only known Noriko for three, maybe it was four days. Five at the most.

Five days? That's all? How did you meet?

Two different units had been shipped to Haven. One unit was full of youths fresh out of training; the other unit had seen battle, probably several times. I hadn't made any close friends during training. Everyone else had been so enthusiastic, and I had just barely made it through. I didn't know what to do with myself, so I wandered. It's funny how little of Haven I remember after all the time I spent wandering it. Way Stations are so different and so homogenous—they have the cultural trappings of the locals, but there's always entertainment after entertainment, gymnasium after gymnasium, tavern after tavern.

I went into the Wake by accident. Most people in my unit didn't even know what the name meant. Where I grew up, the expense of a funeral was the same as a month or two of pay, but whatever a funeral cost, a new life cost a hundred times more. My parents were now past fifty and had both decided that it was too late for another new life. They were paying off my brother's second new life. He was now mining in the asteroids to pay off his first. He had been a woman the second time around, gave birth to two kids, and was in debt from the advance trusts; he was paying for them in case his children died while raising their own children. My sister was on her third life, and she had established some new financial network in some distant solar system and we never heard from her. I was the baby of the family, the one my parents welcomed to their world after their circumstances forced them to take low-paying work that bought bread but no meat, that paid rent, but no heating. With children and grandchildren, they didn't want to do risky things that paid off debt and built up savings for your next life—no wars, no world building, no mining. So I'd been to some wakes, and I'd liked the name of the tavern, and there inside was the bar itself, shaped like a long casket, shiny dark wood, but with a flat surface. I thought it was amusing.

I don't remember what they called fresh recruits. Whatever

it was, Newbie, or Sprout, or something vulgar, there was this table of boisterous men and women, and they called me over. There was something about them that communicated experience, a certainty to the way they held themselves, even though they were clearly a bit tipsy. I was sure they were talking to someone else. "No, you!" one of them called. He pointed to the young woman next to him. "She thinks you're worthy." She glared at him. I'd grown up with that game: the older kid calling you over just to make sure he could put you in your place before an audience of his peers. I think I made it to the bar. I think I bought a drink for the woman sitting next to me. I remember her saying to me, "So who do you think is cuter, the soldier girl or me?"

The soldier girl was at my side and took me by the elbow and muttered, "You need combat pay first before you can afford her."

"Or him!" the guy at the table said.

Of course, who knows if that happened? Maybe I invented that part to explain what came later. Maybe I just went over to the table, happy that someone was interested in me. I remember staring at soldier girl when she was busy talking to the others. Like all the others, her hair was cut short, and her tunic was tight enough to suggest that like many reborn female soldiers, she'd opted to do without breasts in this life. She sat quietly when she listened, but when she spoke, she leaned forward, waved her hands, made a point of directing conversation away from her or me.

I remember a lot of laughing. Whenever they asked me questions, I felt like an adolescent answering adults. Where I was from, why I enlisted. I told them I wanted to see more of the universe, and I wouldn't be able to do that where I'd grown up. I felt like the soldier girl, whose name was Noriko, was looking right through me, that she'd guessed the accumulated debt that weighed my family down as if they lived deep in the atmosphere of some gas giant.

At some point she wrapped her arm through mine. Later she pressed her thigh against mine. I had grown up in a conservative place; no girl had ever treated me like this, and I felt both excited and unworthy. We left the Wake as a group—I have a memory of the girl at the bar lifting her hand, her fingers dancing, a gesture of farewell—and I was certain my military companions would soon be rid of me. But we continued walking to where they were quartered, and the group had started to joke with Noriko, swearing they wouldn't look, that they'd cover up their ears.

Noriko just shook her head as if everyone else was just too adolescent for her. At the Wake, she'd made me place my left pinky in some device that she'd held under the table. Now she handed something to one of her buddies. "Use this to check him in," she said. She asked me where I was quartered. Then she handed something to another one. "And this will check me in. We're going elsewhere."

Later I found out that as long as you pretended to check in they didn't care much what you did on Haven. The people on Haven needed to make money so that there would be a Haven to return to. I didn't know this. I felt the thrill of the forbidden as she made her way to a different level, a different bulkhead. She signed us into a room, closed the door, and turned to me. I remember her looking at me for a moment before saying, "You have to take some of the initiative." So I kissed her, and I clumsily undressed her. At some point, probably after it was over—I picture her lying next to me naked—she looked at me and said, "This is your first time, isn't it?" She said it sweetly, and years later I wondered if that is exactly what she had wanted. But back then I was frozen. I knew I'd been a horrible lover and I didn't know if it was worse to answer yes or no.

She kissed me. "We only got a few days, so I hope you aren't the type who hates getting advice."

Right now, you can look at me and tell me there was a kind of expediency. She was back from the front and wanted to absorb as much life into her body as she could before going back out. While I kept waiting for her to change her mind about me, we avoided her friends, we sampled her favorite dishes at restaurants she'd visited before, we strolled through the park she liked, and sat holding hands staring at the distant sun which Haven orbited, and the closer gas giants whose moons were the source of contention. "I can't wait to go back," she said, and her hand squeezed mine. I remember it as if it were a gesture of great intimacy and trust. "And I truly dread going back."

I was eager to get back to the guesthouse room with her, whether it was in the morning or afternoon or night. Everything was new, whether it was giving a naked woman a back rub or the intimacy of listening to her pee while I waited in bed. I had so much wanted to hold a woman's breasts, and there were no breasts to hold. Noriko had kept female-sized nipples, and she directed my attention there. "I'll streamline my body," she'd said, "but I won't streamline my pleasure."

At night, in the dark, she told me the kind of things she wouldn't say during the day. She liked combat. She liked the thrill and fear of dying. She liked the constant test of herself: "Should I save a comrade in trouble or press on with the mission or run for my life? I actually like coming back to life. I hate that I can't remember the last battle or two. I like that I don't have to remember dying. I like the way my body yearns for sex." She touched my chest or took hold of my penis when she said things like that, as if to remind me of my role in things. "You'd think, you know, being around for as long as I have, I wouldn't be interested anymore. And you'd think that it being the same genes, and the same memories, my desires would be the same. But sometimes I wake up and just want main-course sex, and sometimes I want gourmet sex, and sometimes I want to be really rough. My last life I was with this guy and I was really into anal sex. Now I'm getting a kick out of oral sex." I remember the way she kissed me right then. "You have a perfect mouth," she said.

You're gloating, she says.

Maybe I am, I reply. I'm sorry.

I remember how often we talked about her. Our first trip together. It was the rings of Saturn tour, right? And ever since I've felt like I had to live up to her. I don't think I realized until now that you guys were only together for a few days.

Shall we talk about something else? I ask. I don't correct her about the rings of Saturn tour.

I sit here and feel an enormous guilt. We haven't seen each other for a long time. I had some extra money because of a business venture that, for once, went right, and I decided to travel out to this world, to fly to the regional capital, to take train after train to the extended forest where she now lives much like a hermit with books, all of them written before the start of the human diaspora.

I have been there for almost a week. The first days I was sick with sensory deprivation: abruptly living alone in just my head, with only the sounds of the world around me. Now that I've recovered, she takes me for walks, slow walks, where once she'd been the one to keep a terrible headlong pace. She points out birds, the scurry of animals; she bids me to listen for sounds I haven't listened for since I grew up by the lakes of my homeworld. At night I cook her favorite suppers, and we talk about people we've known and trips we've taken, living off the accumulated interest of her last name. She's started to forget events of our last lifetime together, and we talked more of our early adventures. Early on, I recommended medicines that would make her neurons supple just as the injections kept her joints pain-free and flexible. She said, "I don't like pain. I don't mind fading away." Exhausted after our walks, she lies in bed once we finish supper, and we talk until she falls asleep. I sit there and listen to her breathe, her occasional murmur of a snore, and I wonder why I have come here. Was it to ask her to reconsider, to choose another life and rejoin me? We traveled so well together; we sat together so poorly when in chairs that moved only with the velocity of the planets where we had settled.

Now, we're both awake, I sit in the chair next to her bed, and I've asked her if I should change the subject. She extends her hand and places it on my knee. No, she says. I think I should have listened more carefully the first time. I listen more these days. I hear so few voices. And I think you tell things better these days. I've always liked you best when you were over thirty-five. So, it sounds to me like you were just a tool for Noriko's pleasure.

That was my biggest fear, that I might not truly exist for her beyond her pleasure. But one night, or I think it was at night, it could have been in the morning, she had a powerful orgasm where she seemed to shake to pieces right under me. I remember what she said afterwards. "I hope I survive the next two battles. Then I'll be back at Haven, and this moment will become one of my permanent memories. But if I die this time out, I'll come back to life, and it'll be as if you never existed."

In the gym, I felt like I was her mirror image, with all that's insubstantial about an image in the mirror. I knew exactly how to hit back a ball so she'd return it, exactly what moves to make when we wrestled, exactly how to move with her when we practiced duck and glide. "We work so well together," she said. "I mean here in the gym. Maybe we should register as comrades-in-arms." And I thought, if we die, we'll die together, and we'll be reborn together. We will have forgotten how we met, but we'll know we belong together.

That's why I hated those missing two days, the two days after the neuromap, the two days before I was shipped off to battle. I would have found out if she'd truly meant those words. It sounds sickly-sweet now, but I wanted to know if we'd faced things side by side.

My recovery progressed quickly. The morning-shift nurse said I should start walking through Haven. She gave me a set of clothes, leg-braces, and a cane. Once outside in the corridors I found the first public dataport and placed the tip of my left pinky against the circle. There was a delay. The pinky of my newborn body didn't have the same fingerprint as belonged to my previous body, but it had the same DNA, and one set of records had to align with the other. For a moment, I thought the old bank records wouldn't be found, that my entire past would disappear, but soon numbers layered like bricks appeared. I had some leftover money from my last visit in Haven, enough to buy a few meals and a few drinks at the Wake. If the military had paid me for my services, there was no record of it here.

Okay. And how long ago had I spent the shore-leave money they had given us when we first docked with Haven? It took me a while since Haven went by local calendar rather than the federal calendar. I checked for the day of my last transaction, which had been four beers at the Wake the night before I was set to leave. I would never know with certainty with whom I had those beers, but it was six months ago. In those days it took a month to grow a body, so I must have died five months after I left Haven. How much had happened in those five months?

I walked for a bit, well, walking, then resting, all over Haven. One of the few things I remember now, benches in little niches with plants and the sound of a nearby forest or sea. I ended up at the Wake.

It was a slow night. I sat coffin-like, drinking something; maybe it was sake (even though I never really liked sake) because that's what Noriko and I drank together. The bartender seemed to avoid my gaze, and my glass sat out for a long time before he poured another.

"Not friendly tonight," I said to the guy next to me who ran a lunchroom one bulkhead over.

"There's hardly any business," the guy said. "We're all getting antsy." I told him the date I had shipped out, and he said there had been a rash of rebirths about a month after that. But it had been quiet since then. There had been a unit of newbies, and several units for shore leave, but no new casualties for a while. "Usually they wait until they have two units' worth, enough to fill a ship. You don't want to pay for quartering people longer than you have to."

A woman spoke my name and slipped her arm through mine. She was pale with red hair, and her green eyes gave her an alien look. I don't think I'd seen green eyes before. She looked at me so intently. The way I remember it, this is the woman I bought the drink for the night I met Noriko, but, as I said, I've begun to wonder if I made that up later, that maybe this was the first time I actually met her. "Let me buy you a drink," she said.

I was protesting while the barman poured me another sake. Her hand very tenderly wrapped my hand, and just by touch she guided me to a booth. She sat down and slid over. She patted the space next to her. "Sit next to me, handsome."

Only my mother had ever complimented my looks, so I became wary. I sat down opposite her.

She tilted her head, and I felt the disappointment registering in her green eyes. At first I felt like I'd let her down; then I felt like things hadn't gone as she'd planned. I didn't know which reaction to trust.

"You don't remember," she said.

I tried. She looked at me like I should remember more than buying her a drink.

"Your friend and you."

"Noriko?"

"Yes. You and Noriko. We spent a whole night together."

Once while in bed Noriko had asked me my fantasies. After I had told her, she took firm hold of my penis. "This is what I like, and I don't share," she said. Right then I knew this pale-skinned woman with red hair was conning me.

"You don't remember. We met too late. We met after your neuromap. And you're walking a little funny. Poor you, a new life." She took my hand and again called me by name. I wanted to pull my hand away, but I liked the comfort of it after how-ever-many nights it had been sleeping alone in my private bed, my only company being therapy machines and the nurses who brought my food, the physical contact of the professional hand that never lingered, the touch that was never too light, that never grazed a nerve that mattered. "My name's Amanda Sam. And I want you to know that the two of you spent a very lovely night with me."

She was holding my hand, and I couldn't work up the courage to tell her I didn't trust her.

"We met in this tavern. You and soldier girl were seated in that booth over there." She pointed at the other side of the bar, and it was the booth where Noriko and I usually sat. Noriko and I had gravitated toward it, the booth where we'd first sat together. But Amanda Sam could have learned that just by watching us. "You two looked like it had been a bad day. It was a slow night and I decided to join you guys. I asked what was wrong."

"Noriko wouldn't say," I said.

"And she didn't. I told the two of you that I like working with couples who are going through a quiet phase. I offer the extra spark."

"I'm not sure Noriko is the type who would want the extra spark."

"Don't be sure," she said. She was caressing my hand rather than just holding it, her fingertips every now and then sailing up along my forearm. Noriko had been a straightforward lover; every action and physical sensation had a utilitarian purpose in her pleasure. Only once, when Noriko had thought I was asleep, had her fingers traced the contours of my face. "I've been here for a while. I've seen her before. She does have a life or two extra under her belt, where you've got that innocence that some women find very attractive. I find it very attractive. I just want to take you into my arms and tell you everything will be okay. But, you know, hon, it is still innocence. A woman like Noriko, she might also want a spark."

I was sure she was manipulating me, but she was right, also. Maybe Noriko wanted more. I had given Noriko precisely what she asked for, and I measured the results by the way she clung to me. But there were those silences. Maybe she wanted more than she knew to ask for. The one time she'd caressed my face when she thought I was sleeping, I'd wanted to ask her to do that more often, but I never did.

And now Amanda Sam was talking about Noriko herself, how she sat at the table, taut, like a soldier, or a weapon waiting to be used, and how she was in bed, like coiled energy released. And maybe there was a gleam in Amanda Sam's eye, the gleam of the gambler who's just seen her opening gambit work, but maybe I'm adding that now, because she *was* describing the Noriko I knew.

"But," I said, and I remember how hard it was to say outright, partly because of the way I'd been raised, partly I wanted it clear that I still didn't trust her. It took me a while to explain how Noriko wasn't interested in women or in sharing me with another woman.

"Oh, honey," she said. She leaned forward and kissed me on the lips. Then looked at me with her green eyes. "I'm Amanda Sam. I was Amanda with you and Sam with her."

I pictured the events of that night, events that might or might not have happened. It was all too much. I made excuses: I had to return to the hospital; I had yet to be discharged.

Amanda Sam accompanied me, her arm gently wrapped around mine. "I know it must be hard for you," she said. "I would offer to stay with you, but it's illegal in a hospital."

When the night-shift nurse saw Amanda Sam at my side, she glared at me and said nothing. Only at that point did I realize that Amanda Sam was a prostitute. I'm not sure when I understood she was a hermaphrodite.

She says, I don't remember that you ever told me this.

I told you about Amanda Sam, but you never wanted to hear the details.

You know, for some reason, I thought you'd met Amanda Sam first. I think I'd come to believe that Noriko had helped you get over what happened with Amanda Sam. Maybe that's why I thought you'd loved Noriko so much. Or maybe that's what I needed to think so I could fall in love with you. Tell me what happened next.

I think I was discharged from the hospital the next day, but that may have not been the case. Whenever they discharged me, they updated the chip in my pinky. Three nights paid for at a guesthouse, a set per diem for four days, and passage on a ship home, well, three ships with two connections. All I could picture was three months while I went out of my mind, not knowing how I would tell my family that I had no idea what had happened to me nor why I'd lost out on the opportunity to die three times and bring home desperately needed funds.

I found a niche with library capacity, but Haven lies in a sector where they consider wartime censorship to be patriotic. There was no news on any battles, so I couldn't find out how I might have died. I had begun to wonder if something stupid had killed me: a fall from a ladder, a strange electrocution while installing equipment, or the terrible aim of my comrades. But if I'd died from any of those embarrassments, they would have revived me, wouldn't they? Would any of that have disqualified me from future battles?

I decided to get something quiet, a book, I decided, and I read like I hadn't read since I was in my early teens, and I sat in the hospital foodstop, and I moved around, trying to sit as close to nurses as I could, and I listened, hoping someone would say something about a group of newborns. After dinner I returned to my room, cleaned up, and went to the Wake.

There were a few people in booths. The bartender poured me a beer, then ignored me. Amanda Sam wasn't there, and two beers later, she was. I bought her a drink. She asked me a lot of questions. She sympathized. "I know what it's like," she said, "when you start with so little." Her first life she'd been a woman and had been taken advantage of so many times that she decided to charge men for that particular pleasure. "I'm not the soldier type. I don't want to get killed to start fresh. But there's a demand for people like me who make anything possible, and so the people who paid for your new life paid for mine."

I remember sitting stunned. With Noriko I'd experienced sex as glorious exercise and passionate language and had dreamed that it might one day be religious communion.

She talked as if sex were an economic transaction, just like any other human interaction.

I told her she was wrong.

She smiled, bemused. Noriko had looked that way when I'd told her my plans for the future. "Look," Amanda Sam said. "I gotta go. If you want to talk some more, I'll be back in an hour and a half, two hours at the most."

She slipped off the stool, and she walked out of the tavern. I watched the fabric waver around her butt, and I thought that she couldn't be a man at all. The bartender poured me another beer and looked at me like I was a fool, but he didn't say anything. I thought of Noriko and decided to leave.

The next morning I felt like I didn't have much time left. I walked all the way to the spaceport since I didn't want to spend money on transport. After conversing with several machines and one human who looked like his life was answering simple questions a machine wouldn't answer—it's funny how he's one of the few people from then that I can actually picture in my mind, but maybe I'm making him up—I found out that the ticket was military issue. Around here, the military did the bulk of the business, so the value of the ticket was a third of what it would have cost if I'd booked the passage as a civilian.

I tried to find an employment office, but there wasn't one. Turned out everyone on Haven pretty much got work here from one military connection or another; the tavern and guesthouse owners all had their three deaths and bonuses, and all the staff and medical people had at least one military death behind them, and the prostitutes seemed to have come here from other military outposts. There was no enlistment office, but I found some offices representing the military, but one office turned out to be in charge of requisitions, another turned out to handle quartering, another salary disbursements. I finally found someone in some office, troop transportation, maybe, and he said he'd look up my records. He tried several different places, squeezed the bridge of his nose, and faced me with a smile. "I don't know how you got here," he said, "because according to this you never joined the military."

"Is there any reason my name would disappear?"

"I don't know. Maybe if you were a spy. I think we'd get rid of your name if you were a traitor, too."

So maybe I had signed up to do some special work. Was my existence here an accident while the real me was off somewhere with Noriko discovering something important? Or had I been captured in battle, tortured, and the military thought I'd given up vital information? Why would they pay for a new body, for my rebirth, if I'd given up vital information? Maybe this forced exile was their way of punishing me for my coerced betrayal.

At the hospital foodstop, I was joined by a doctor who so much didn't want to sit alone that he'd join other loners. He'd died only once. He didn't know how, but he didn't want to die again. He had his combat pay, but no big bonus, but they needed medics at Haven and employed him. "Such is the story of a lot of people here. We couldn't do the three times. What's your story?"

He would sympathize with my situation. Maybe he'd have a connection or two. He'd find out what had happened. I told him the story. He shrugged, got up, and left.

I was so disconsolate that I was relieved when I got to the Wake and Amanda Sam asked me to buy her a drink. She drank brandy. A slow sip at a time. "It makes me happy. I just have to make sure I don't get too happy." She asked me why I looked so bereft. She used that word, *bereft*, and I decided her first life had to have been more literate than I had first presumed.

I told her I must have done something terrible, but I didn't know what it was. I liked the comfort of the way she looked at me, the comfort of my hand in her two hands. I was going to tell her how badly I wanted to see Noriko, but some guy snuck up and gave her a big hug from behind. "You free, Amanda?" he asked.

I looked at him, a thin guy with a beard. He'd been down the bar, glancing this way. He'd pointed once at me, and the bartender had shook his head to one question, then shrugged to another.

"I'm sorry," she said to me. "I gotta go." She leaned forward and kissed me before rising. To the guy with the beard she said, "For you, honey, I'm always free. Am I seeing just you tonight?"

"No, Cynthia just called me. She had a change of heart. She said I should ask you home if I found you."

"Well, you have found me."

"Would your friend like to come with us?"

Amanda looked at me and gave the kind of smile I've always associated with rejection. "He's a friend, but not that kind of friend." She leaned over to kiss me again. "Wait two hours, okay. Don't run out on me like you did last night."

I nursed a beer and worked up the nerve. I asked the bartender what the skinny guy had asked about me.

"He asked if you were a soldier on leave."

"And the second question?"

"If you worked for Amanda Sam."

I don't remember if I stewed for a while or if I left immediately. I imagined sitting at a booth in the Wake and talking to Amanda Sam when Noriko walked in. But why would Noriko care? After what I must have done. I spent hours thinking of everything wrong I'd done in my life and

couldn't think of a thing that would have led me to this place
in my life.

I returned to my room to avoid just those thoughts. I hid
in a book; I lived in the book so I could hide. I don't even
remember the knock. Maybe it was a chime or the sound of
the sea. I just remember Amanda Sam standing at my door
with a bottle of wine. She talked about the couple she'd been
with. I don't remember what she said. I remember her saying
that she felt like a prop that helped them act out their own
pathologies. She told me how alone she was. Everyone here
was ex-military or soon-to-be military. "I don't have a military bone in my body. I just get boned by the military."

At some point we had finished the wine, and I thought
she'd leave, but instead we were kissing. I was thinking that
any minute she was going to pull out of the embrace and ask
for money. I think I was hoping she would because it would
be such an easy way to put an end to what was happening.
But she kept kissing me, and I drank kiss after kiss. And
then one thing was leading to another.

*And you're going to skip over what happened? she asks.
She has rolled onto her side, and is looking at me beneath
the glow of the lamplight. Her hand still rests on my thigh.*

I say, You never liked talking about these kinds of details.

*I am at the point in my life where this is more like hearing
about the mating behavior of some strange animal. She
says this and gives me this familiar smile. She's going to do
something that I won't like but that will amuse her. Her
hand moves up my thigh. She laughs, a cackle of a laugh; it
would be an old-lady laugh but she laughed like this when
we met (she was thirty) and she laughed like that in her next
life which she started at twenty-five, and she laughed like
that when she was reborn as a sixteen-year-old, after one of
the neocancers had ravaged her body with leaking sores
and she'd said she'd make it up to me though there was
nothing to make up, nor was it a making up: the woman in
the sixteen-year-old body felt like such a striking sex object
that she withdrew from my every touch. Now, in her final
old woman's body, she cackles and says, her voice full of
sympathy, You're aroused.*

I say, You're not making it easy to tell this story.

It's such a lonely story, she says. Why don't you cuddle with me?

I hesitate.

And she misinterprets my silence and turns off the light. She says, There, now you don't have to see my wrinkles. You can hear my voice and know it's me. Get undressed and cuddle with me.

I knock my knee against a bedpost, but finally I'm there. Her body feels bonier, more frail, and she pushes her back toward my chest. She has not removed her nightgown, but she places my hand over her breast. She says, I want you to feel my breast but not how it truly feels. I like this, just being close. Does this feel good? she asks and she gently rocks her hips.

I remember a night like this—I'm not sure when in our lives together it took place—but I think we were on some ship taking us somewhere. She told me how alone she felt. How she just wanted to be close. And we worked out this arrangement, this spooning together, my penis nested inside her, a sweet, low-electric connection while we talked. Now, with a quick touch of artificial moisture, we lie together in the dark as if the years apart had not existed at all.

Now, she says, stop telling me what you don't remember and tell me the details.

Well, I don't remember how her blouse came off, if I unbuttoned it or if she unbuttoned it while smiling impishly as she gauged my response. All I remember was staring at her naked breasts.

And that also causes me to remember something I forgot. Amanda Sam had always worn clothes that revealed or highlighted her breasts. Sometimes, when talking, she'd smile and look down and you'd have no choice but to follow her gaze. I was eager to hold and touch and kiss Amanda Sam's breasts, and I thought of Noriko's streamlined chest, her aroused nipples, and just the yearning for Amanda Sam's breasts made me feel a terrible guilt.

She says, I'm sure you got over the guilt.

I'm not sure I got over the guilt.

But Amanda Sam had to urge me on. "They're waiting for your attention." She kissed me again. "I'm waiting for your attention. Soldier girl is gone, hon, I'm here."

I should tell her I loved her breasts but I had no right to them. But I also thought about how she'd come to my room, how she'd chosen me, and how I knew she was right, that I probably would never see Noriko again. I kissed her breasts. I worshipped her nipples. I only had worshipped Noriko's nipples and I thought there was only one way to pray before this altar. Amanda Sam directed my mouth and tongue in different ways, and I was surprised, even though it was obvious, that there were so many ways to go about this. Soon we were both naked, but she wore this little skirt thing. I knew what she was hiding, but I pretended that she was just wearing a skirt. I realized that when we kissed she never pressed herself against me.

She went down on me, and I thought after all my time with Noriko that I would last forever. But it was a new body and a new sensation to that body. Suddenly, after orgasm, Amanda Sam was a stranger. At that point, I was afraid. It was my turn to reciprocate. Or worse, sometimes, Noriko would just want to lie back and talk, and I had nothing to say to Amanda Sam. But she kissed me and did something I didn't know you could do because Noriko had never done it. She used her mouth, and I was hard, and she had me lie down, then she turned her back to me before lowering herself down.

The sensation was wonderful, but I lay there and felt like a part of me was distant. I wanted to be with Noriko and the way her hands pulled me into the rhythm she wanted or the way she wrapped her arms around me as if she was going to pull my body into hers. I admired Amanda Sam's back. I admired the way she leaned forward so I could admire her backside. I thought, So this is what sex is like when you don't care. But I didn't want it to stop for a second. I wanted to feel more. I sat up, and I leaned my cheek against her shoulder blade and I held her breasts, and she breathed about how good that felt, and maybe I was wrong about the nature of caring because now I felt like I was with her and how alone we both were and as she breathed nice exclamations, I felt my hand make its way down from her breast, down her belly, I'd truly somehow forgotten, because I somehow expected to touch those moist creases.

Not the most poetic naming you've done, she says.

The words are a distraction. I've lowered my own hand, feeling I should reciprocate the pleasure I now feel, but her hand returns my hand to her breast.

She says, So you don't find a vulva. Were you shocked?

I pulled my hand away so fast. There were two shocks. The shock of memory, the realization that in spite of what I knew, I'd pictured Amanda Sam as a woman and now I couldn't. But sweet breathing aside, her encouragements aside, I'd discovered that Amanda Sam was not aroused at all, and now I felt like we were just two mechanisms completing some insistent task.

Amanda Sam didn't understand my mistake. She took my hand. Part of me wanted to pull back. Another part insisted that it was only fair to reciprocate. But she became more passionate, and it ended up with me on top, she kissing me, she holding her body against mine. After it was over, I didn't know what to think. I wanted to get up and leave, but the bed was in my guesthouse room. She lay down in front of me, and we spooned, my hand on her breast, her back against my chest. I could lie there and go back to pretending she was a woman.

"I really like you," she said.

"I like you, too." I was relieved someone had booked me passage on a ship; I would soon be gone.

"If I sleep in your room again, I'll have to charge you."

"I understand," I said. I didn't have the money to sleep with her.

"But if you come with me to my room, at my invitation, that's different."

"How is it different?" I asked, because I knew I was supposed to ask.

"Because when I make love to someone I like, I prefer to be Sam rather than Amanda."

I said nothing, and she asked what I was thinking. I told her that it was the Amanda part of her I liked.

"If you really liked me, the me inside, you wouldn't notice the difference."

I think it was the next day when I was back at the hospital dining hall. I maybe had two days left, and I overheard some nurses talk about how busy it would be the next day, my last full day on Haven. There would be a whole set of newborns. Noriko could be among them, but even if she wasn't, there had to be people who knew something about what had happened to my unit. I pictured myself returning home without that knowledge. I imagined all the empty silences in that ruined house in that neighborhood where people went when they had no place left to go.

It would just take a few days, a few days before they were out and showing up in various eateries and taverns. If Noriko just happened to be among them, she would show up at the Wake, she'd see me with Amanda Sam. My whole adventure the night before now seemed sordid. I spent some of my per diem so the guest-house staff would change the bedclothes. I showered for a long time. I resolved I wouldn't return to the Wake. But all alone in my bed that night, I couldn't help but think that I was leaving Haven too soon.

The next morning I left for the spaceport to cash in my ticket. The woman there shook her head. "I can't do it. You have to show a place of residence, not a guest house. This is not a tourist spot."

I hung around at the hospital foodstop until I saw the same nurse. I went to get some food and sat down near her. She grumbled to a friend how tired she was. They had to rebirth more than a unit. The military wanted them turned around quickly.

"They'll get some downtime, won't they?" her friend asked.

"Of course. This place would close down otherwise. We gotta get them out of therapy two days sooner than usual. Can you imagine how they'll look when they go ambulatory?"

I walked and walked. I kept counting out my options.

I showed up at the Wake and Amanda Sam was not there. The bartender offered me a drink on the house. "Amanda Sam says you're a good one. Here's one for the road."

I decided that this drink was my farewell. I would never know what happened. I would never see Noriko again. Temptation is the sun drawing in a comet. Good sense is just some distant steady orbit.

I had a second beer and sat off in a corner. Amanda Sam walked in, and she scanned the tavern as if looking for someone. When she saw me, she smiled, and sat down next to me. "Hi, gorgeous," she said. "Buy me a brandy."

I told her my ship left tomorrow afternoon. She said she'd miss me. I told her about the unit being rebirthed tomorrow. I told her that I wanted to stay, to see if Noriko was among them.

"Your soldier girl won't be there," she said.

"But they'll be able to tell me what's happened. I'll know my story."

"That story was part of your other life," she said.

I told her that, in the end, it didn't matter. I didn't have a place to stay. Staying was just wishful thinking.

"You can stay with me," she said.

Someone tapped her on the shoulder. She turned, and standing there was a couple. "Oh," she said, "I was looking for you two. It's been a while." She turned and waved to me.

The next morning she was at my door and walked me down to the port. "If you want to stay, you're going to have to establish residency and profession. There are no tourists here. I created documentation that says you're living with me and that you're my partner."

"Your partner, like we're married?"

"No, hon. Profession, I said profession. I'm more than happy to lie about your profession." And she stopped me here. She looked me in the eye. "Your money is going to run out. You're not going to find the soldier girl. All you lost was a few months of another life. How badly do you need them, hon?" Her two hands wrapped themselves warmly around one of mine. Her green eyes were warm. "You have a free ticket home. Take it."

When we found the right office, she produced the document, and after some back and forth she got the full price of what the military had paid for the ticket. She laid down her pinky to get half; I got the other half. "We'll say that's rent for a month," she said. What was left of my per diem had evaporated the moment the transaction was complete; all I had was one-sixth of the cost of passage.

Her apartment was tiny, half the size of the guesthouse room, a double bed, drawers built into the wall, and a cubicle for what's necessary. There was no sofa to sleep on, no place to stretch out on the floor with a blanket.

She kissed me. "You don't have to thank me tonight. We can wait until you're ready. Go see if you can find your girl."

At midday I haunted the hospital foodstop. I listened for whispers. The nurse turned up again, this time alone, and I stepped up to the food vendor so that I'd be next to her. She punched out her meal request. I found something to say, and we ended up at the same table. I remember that she looked familiar, that suddenly I worried she was the nurse who'd birthed me. But if she was, she didn't seem to recognize me. I was worried that she'd ask me all sorts of questions about where I lived, what I did, but she was more than happy to complain about her husband, her job, the difficulty of having so many troops coming back to life.

I thought of the ship, how it was heading for the edge of this stellar system. I felt like there might be an alternate me on board, heading off, finding people to talk with, books to read, maybe even a lover, to ease the burden of three months of travel. But here I was, back in the hospital, listening to the nurse telling me how the war must be going badly because they'd received orders to start growing more bodies, to prepare another unit's worth for rebirth.

I tried to get a sense of how many of these men and women she saw. Would she recognize a picture of Noriko if I showed it to her? Every now and then, she groused about something, then swore me to silence. "I'm really not supposed to talk about that." Could I give her Noriko's name and combat number to input into a computer? I didn't dare.

In the evenings I stayed at the Wake as long as I could, only going home when I had drunk too much to stand. In bed, I pretended to be asleep while Amanda Sam cuddled up to me, one hand draped gently over my penis, her own penis erect against my backside. She whispered how much she liked me and desired me until one of us actually drifted off. More and more, she spent her evenings with me. If she disappeared, she told me which taverns she would visit. I realized how little work she'd been getting, what a relief it must have been to get one-sixth of the cost of passage. "The whole economy is drying up," she said to me. "If they don't give these reborns any shore leave, this place will go crazy. It happened once before, just watch."

Suddenly I saw it, the way locals glared at me if I looked at them too long, the clipped sentences, the constant complaint in almost every conversation. The nurse joined me with a therapist friend. It was one of my therapists. He was sure to ask what I was doing here, but no, he talked about how he preferred working with civilians and officers. When you do therapy in groups. . . . He shook his head bitterly. "I hope they don't send them back to battle before shore leave. There's a major here who thinks shore leave is just for fun. *My soldiers—*" His voice became high-pitched so the major might have been a woman or castrato "*—don't need to get drunk and get laid to fight well. Their morale is just fine.* Well, fuck their morale. How about their fine motor skills? How about their *gross* motor skills? That's what shore leave is about. They're brand-new bodies and they need the real world to operate in before you throw on some body armor and throw them out into free fall."

He kept going on, and I barely listened. He was angry enough, I thought, that maybe he would tell me anything, but the nurse was advising him to watch what he was saying, and he was nodding, his face red, his look recalcitrant, then chagrined.

One night, Amanda Sam insisted that we go back home— I always thought of it as the apartment—before I'd drunk too much. "You'll spend up all your money," she said, "and then what?" Back at her place, she said she wanted me so badly that she would be Amanda for me. I soaked up her skin's warmth like a sponge.

It probably wasn't the next day, but it's the next thing I remember, how suddenly sections of Haven were flooded with stumbling reborns. Their hair was wild and shaggy. Most of them looked like they'd chosen to be in their twenties, but a few, probably officers, were in their thirties. A guy, his face dour, concentrated on every step he took. Another stumbled, fell, got up, laughing, looking to his more cautious friends. I kept walking where they walked. Every time I saw tanned skin, black hair, compact body, I'd walk to catch up, but before I even caught a glimpse of the face, I'd see that the shoulders were too wide, the hips too flat.

And what would I say to her, if she was there? I watched for her at various lunchrooms, where I saw the newborns shake their forks at each other as if angry, but their faces showed a range of reactions to their bodies' refusal to learn their way through the world instantly.

The presence of all these newborns made Amanda Sam happy. "Tonight, the best brandy for me, the best beer for you," she said, even though I think Haven only stocked one variety of each, the drinkable and the barely drinkable. I remember one night, probably the first night the newborns were around, I just sat at the Wake, drinking beer, imagining that Noriko would walk in, that she would take me off to a guesthouse room, and we'd make love. Several other nights I wandered from tavern to tavern, maybe checking in some dinner spots beforehand, looking for Noriko, knowing I wouldn't see her, from time to time running into Amanda Sam gaily chatting with some man or woman, once a couple. Each time she waved to me, offered me that big smile that said, I'm delighted to see you, keep walking.

I spoke with some of the newborns. I heard the stories. One guy told me that their goal had been to take an orbital without destroying it, which meant they had to board it without using projectile weapons. At one point they were on the skin of the world, breaking into a compartment, and the enemy had fighters flying above. It was strange how silent everything was except for the way everyone was yelling orders and those voices reverberated in your helmet, voices darting about you as if your head was stuck in a fishbowl. The enemy couldn't risk projectiles, either. They used harpoons, a joke when you first heard it in training, but when one pierced your suit, when you watched your air drain away as you were dragged off into space, it wasn't so funny anymore. "Actually, if it happened to you, you'd never remember it," he said. "But when you watched it happen to your buddy, you'd go to sleep night after night imagining what it would be like happening to you. Worse, you'd relive it happening to your friend, wondering what he felt and thought as it happened. Well, then you became hardened to the whole process."

I tried to picture myself on the skin of a metal world, magnetic soles holding me in place, just enough of a pull to keep my balance, not enough to prevent a step, or a harpoon from pulling me away, and making a rush for an opened compartment, knowing that some of us would make it, and that some of us were there to die so others could make it, that our majors and colonels and generals felt free to overwhelm the other side with numbers because we'd all be back, the cost of our resurrection something for governors and senators and premiers at home to tally up. I felt a terrible beating in my heart just at the thought, and I was glad to have Amanda Sam wrap her arms around me, and most nights she was content and sated so there was no pressure to express my thanks for this half a bed in a tiny room.

I worked up the courage to ask questions. I gave Noriko's full name. No one had heard of her. I named the unit I was with. Most didn't know it. One or two knew that my unit was dealing with orbitals circling the neighboring gas giant, which at the time was too far away in its orbit for anyone to care. One woman had gotten word that the first foray had been successful, the second was disastrous, the third could happen at any moment.

When the newborns shipped out, I concluded I would never see Noriko, and I would never know what had happened to me. It was only then that I realized what a terrible situation I was in. Amanda Sam took me out to dinner to celebrate the great few days she'd had, and I drank brandy with her, and I told her that tonight would be the night. She kissed me passionately, and back in her apartment she was tender. She aroused me first, and the things she did to relax me actually felt good. She looked down at me and told me to hold her breasts, and entered me so slowly and carefully that it did not hurt at all. I suppose if I'd been in love with her or desiring this kind of moment, I might have felt something more than just the physical sensation, but instead I rubbed my hands up and down Amanda Sam's back and remembered the one or two times Noriko had caressed my own back and said, "Let's finish up, I'm ready to sleep," and I now understood the distance Noriko must have felt (even though during the act I had been certain that because it was sex it must have felt good).

During the days I worked on making the tiny apartment look better. I thought of the people Amanda Sam brought there. I prepared meals. When she pressed herself against me at night, I turned and kissed her and wrapped my legs around her thighs. She got me drunk the night she wanted me to reciprocate her oral ministrations. The next day I searched for some kind of work, but as I already knew, there was nothing official available. "Pinky-up," the guy in charge of sewage said. The fingerprint produced the documentation, and he shook his head. "You don't even have one death to your credit. I can't hire you. If you're going to stay on Haven, you're gonna have to keep doing the job you registered for. My apologies. I wouldn't want to do it."

When Amanda Sam took me out to dinner and then was Amanda for me in bed, I knew she was going to tell me it was time to work. "I warned you. I warned you. I warned you. And I'll take good care of you and make sure you meet only the best of people. Some of my peers have taken new people under their wing and taken half. I'll only take twenty percent, plus your share of rent and food." The next morning she bought me a big breakfast, and she said how she'd loved every second in bed with me but it was time to learn how to do a few things a little differently. I asked feebly about women, and she laughed. "Young men, they can get for free." Things were flush now, and she had found several people on Haven who would enjoy paying to break me in. And that's how it all started.

I've heard other stories, and I know now how lucky I was.

No one beat me or mistreated me. Amanda Sam always met me at the Wake at the end of an evening to find out how things went, to coach me on how to handle the rude and stingy ones and how to handle the ones who wanted to fall in love with me. And maybe if I were tuned that way, I might have enjoyed myself. Instead I felt like I was living someone else's life. When I wasn't working and when I wasn't with Amanda Sam, I was walking. Long walks with long elaborate dreams. Noriko would appear in the Wake. She'd say she's seen enough battles, and she now wants to take me with her, some place far away. I knew now I would never go home. What would I say? How many lies would I tell just to be comfortable?

She says, You always avoided the truth when it made other people uncomfortable.

I listen for something severe in her voice, but I don't hear it. I say, I'm telling everything the best my memory will allow.

I know. That's what I love about this visit. You know, she says, the subject changing with her tone of voice, I always wondered why you wouldn't change. I did want to try out a life as a man, and I always thought you didn't love me enough to be a woman.

You understand now? I ask. After all those men, after their insistence on their needs . . . the only time they cared about my arousal was when they wanted to boost their own self-confidence . . . after all that, I could never sleep with a man again. You probably would have been a great man, but I couldn't bear to sleep with another one, no matter how nice.

I said I understood. But now I wonder this. Did you stay with me because you loved me or because you wanted a secure life?

There's a giant difference between why I first sought your attentions and why I'm with you now.

It's an awkward moment, given the way our bodies are touching, given the years of abstinence in our last life together, so I return to the story.

When the newborns came, it was a rush. I now dreaded

the sight I had once longed for. Many of the newborns had not seen enough battle to afford a guesthouse, so Amanda Sam and I traded off with the apartment. There would be an occasional woman soldier who hired my services, but mostly I listened to men lament their lives after they'd relieved themselves of their burdens. I kept an eye out for Noriko, but now my plan was to spot her first so I could avoid her.

I started to hang out more with the nurse and the therapist, just to know people who had nothing to do with the Wake and Amanda Sam, though Haven is a small enough place that I'm sure they knew what I did. I'm sure when I got up from lunch, they probably said, He's not so bad. Everyone's got to make a living somehow.

Some nights, I decided just to do nothing, and I stayed in the Wake and drank. Sometimes Amanda Sam would rest her hand on my shoulder and I'd turn to her and she'd tell me it was time to go home. She'd make love to me, comfort me, and I'd pretend to be comforted. "I'll always take care of you," she said. "I'm so glad we found each other." And the next morning she'd take her twenty-percent cut. So I sat in the Wake and foresaw years and years of this, and sometimes in the Wake, but never on my walks, which were just for dreams, I would tally up how long it'd take to build up savings, how long it would take to get off Haven, and how much I'd need to start a new life when her hand fell on my shoulder. I turned and Noriko was looking at me.

"I've been told you've been asking about me," she said.

Oh, no, she says. She doesn't recognize you. She died before she had another neuromap, and she doesn't know you.

I hear the sadness in her voice. For decades and decades I couldn't mention Noriko to her; now, after all these years apart, she sympathizes. How different life would have been if so much separation wasn't necessary to erase whatever had made us bitter.

I stood up to face her. I thought for a second she looked older, as if the job had worn away her friendliness, but then I recalled this look, the way she'd gotten when she'd given out instructions to her companions. There was no recognition on her face, no joy at seeing me, just this military face accustomed to giving orders.

She said, "I thought you'd be gone by now. I made sure the cost of everything was covered."

"I couldn't go."

She stood and waited for me to say more.

"I didn't know what happened to you. I didn't know what happened to me."

She looked around, took my hand, and led me to a table. She sat across from me and ordered herself a beer. She held the glass in both her hands, and I wanted her to hold my hand again. She said nothing for the longest time. I surveyed the entire place, the bar, the booths, to make sure Amanda Sam was nowhere to be seen.

Noriko said, "Here's what happened. We posted as comrades-in-arms. We were set to attack an orbital. They told us that ninety percent of our unit would die. You began to shake in your sleep. You talked about how when you died, once they'd grown you a new body, once you'd been re-assigned, that we'd be apart. But the truth was you were scared to die. When it came time to suit up, you were trembling so much that the captain ordered you to your quarters. He didn't want you to put us at risk. I told you to pack up your gear and move out while I was away.

"The enemy was unprepared. We took the orbital with few casualties. When we got back, you'd hanged yourself."

I felt myself shaking my head. I wasn't the me that would do that.

"I blamed myself for what happened," she said. "Back on Haven, I was so involved in taking care of my own needs that I didn't recognize the warning signs. The one thing I forgot about youth, real youth, the first youth, is how passionate you are about life itself. How it sometimes has to be all or nothing."

I didn't know what to say. I said something about there being no discharge papers.

"You forgot or ignored what you were told. In the military, your life is only to be lost for the cause. The military won't pay for a new life if you kill yourself. They promoted me after that skirmish. I got a pay raise. I had enough money to cover your rebirth. I arranged for some loans to cover the cost of a berth back to your homeworld. I thought I'd made up for everything. I though I'd taken care of you."

We sat there for a while and what more could we say? I wanted to know what warning signs she'd seen. I didn't want to know. And what other subject was there? We'd only been together for three or four days.

Noriko didn't ask about where I was living or what my plans were. She told me she'd recently been assigned to Haven in a supervisory capacity. There would be four units of newborns to organize, plus two units of newbies coming in. The big push was beginning.

She was talking about everything they had to do and how she had to get back to her duties when Amanda Sam walked in and said hello. Noriko looked up at her. There wasn't a trace of recognition on Noriko's face. "I'm sure I'll see you," Noriko said to me and left without saying a word to Amanda Sam.

"I see that soldier girl is back," Amanda Sam said.

"She didn't recognize you."

Amanda Sam looked at me for a moment. I think she was tempted to explain why I was wrong, but she'd taught me the con. I'd already used it a few times, but because I was living such separate lives in my head, I hadn't figured the whole thing out, how everything had stretched back to day one of my new life. The con: you sit down with a newborn, and you talk about the last time you'd been together, the one that must have taken place after the neuromap was recorded.

I walked and walked that night. I told myself I wasn't a coward, I wasn't the kind of person who'd kill himself. Look at what I was living through now. I hadn't been tempted to kill myself in the past months with everything that had happened. And I reminded myself that Noriko had said we'd left Haven as comrades-in-arms. I thought of ways I could see her again, of things I could say to win her back.

But, of course, Haven was a military way station, even though it was run by civilians. Of course, people knew I'd been asking about her, and the local military intelligence guy, whoever he was, must have told her. They'd know how I was making a living, and so Noriko would know.

I didn't see Noriko again. I avoided the hospital, and I avoided other taverns. I only conducted business out of the Wake, and she never returned. I stopped taking my walks. I'm sure she was on Haven until everyone involved with the big push had left. And by the time the newborns and the fresh recruits were gone, I had enough money to start a new life, to be reborn and not remember one bit of this. Instead, I worked for another year and had enough to fly to planets that people liked to talk about, to have some money to live for a little bit and try one unsuccessful business venture or another.

Amanda Sam cried when I told her I was leaving. "I made this possible for you," she said. "I want you to remember that." And my last night there, I let her make love to me the way she liked, and I was so moved by the way she felt that I had my first orgasm while I held her in my arms. This caused her to kiss me passionately. "Please don't leave. Please stay. You think I took advantage of you, but I really do love you." Right then I thought she was begging her twenty-percent cut to stay. Now I think she either loved me or, at least, my company. I think of all the booths I sat in, waiting alone to attract some eager company. I think of those same booths at the end of a long evening when she sat beside me and took my hand in hers.

And the ship I boarded later stopped at some planet or other, and you boarded, and that's how I spent the rest of my lives.

She turns over in the bed and kisses me. I caress her face, and the way time has lined her skin feels wrong against my fingertips. My body betrays me. I say, Talk to me, and I hear her voice and she pulls me into her embrace and it's her I make love to.

The next morning she makes me my favorite breakfast and she packs my bag. I tell her I was more than willing to stay indefinitely. I have no special plans and I like being with her.

She says, These last few days, well last night, especially, were perfect. When I first met you, you told me about Noriko, and I wanted to be with someone who could love so passionately. And I was jealous of her ever since because I couldn't inspire the same kind of love. Last night, you told me about Noriko, and I remembered everything about you I loved when our lives together weren't so difficult. Last night is the memory I want to have of you when I die.

I argue, but if I argue too fiercely, I'll destroy everything these few days have come to mean. I leave her house in the woods, take train after train, come to a port and board a ship for elsewhere. In the decades we were apart—me in a fresh new body, she finding out what happens when the body finally ages—I always thought about her. During those years, I knew that one day, when I had the money for the voyage, I would track her down and see her at least one last time.

I leave her now, but I can't imagine another life.

The Consciousness Problem

MARY ROBINETTE KOWAL

Mary Robinette Kowal (www.maryrobinettekowal.com) is a writer and puppeteer who lives in Portland, Oregon, with her husband Rob. She is currently serving her second term as Secretary of Science Fiction and Fantasy Writers of America. She is the 2008 winner of the John W. Campbell Award for Best New Writer. In an interview she says, "I'm a storyteller. I love world-creation in all its forms . . . When talking about puppetry, I've often paraphrased Orson Scott Card—puppetry is the theater of the possible. That's why I like speculative fiction; I like playing in the world of 'what if.'" Her website described her puppetry career thus: "She has performed for LazyTown (CBS), the Center for Puppetry Arts, Jim Henson Pictures, and founded Other Hand Productions. Her design work has garnered two UNIMA-USA Citations of Excellence, the highest award an American puppeteer can achieve." Tor is publishing her debut novel, Shades of Milk and Honey, *in 2010.*

"The Consciousness Problem" was published in Asimov's. *It is about brain damage from bad and illegal science done in the third world in the not too distant future. And it is a romance, of an original SF kind. The author says, "I had a nightmare involving a clone of my husband committing suicide, and though it has a very limited relationship to the story now, it made me wonder why a clone would do that."*

The afternoon sun angled across the scarred wood counter despite the bamboo shade Elise had lowered. She grimaced and picked up the steel chef's knife, trying to keep the reflection in the blade angled away so it wouldn't trigger a hallucination.

In one of the *Better Homes and Gardens* her mother had sent her from the States, Elise had seen an advertisement for carbon fiber knives. They were a beautiful matte black, without reflections. She had been trying to remember to ask Myung about ordering a set for the last week, but he was never home while she was thinking about it.

There was a time before the car accident, when she was still smart.

Shaking her head to rid herself of that thought, Elise put a carrot on the sil-plat cutting board. She was still smart, today was just a bad day was all. It would be better when Myung came home.

"You should make a note." Elise grimaced and looked to see if anyone had heard her talking to herself.

But of course, no one was home. In the tiny space of inattention, the knife nicked one of her knuckles. The sudden pain brought her attention back to the cutting board. Stupid. Stupid.

Setting the knife down, she reached for the faucet before stopping herself. "No, no Elise." She switched the filtration system over to potable water before she rinsed her finger under the faucet. The uncertainty about the drinking water

408

was a relatively minor tradeoff for the benefits of South Korea's lack of regulations. They'd been here for close to three years, working on the TruClone project but she still forgot sometimes.

She went into the tiled bathroom for some NuSkin, hoping it would mask the nick so Myung wouldn't worry. A shadow in the corner of the mirror moved. Who had let a cat inside? Elise turned to shoo it out, but there was nothing there.

She stepped into the hall. Dust motes danced in the afternoon light, twirling and spinning in the beam that snuck past the buildings in Seoul's to gild the simple white walls. There was something she was going to write a note about. What was it?

"Elise?" Myung came around the corner, still loosening his tie. His dark hair had fallen over his forehead, just brushing his brow. A bead of sweat trickled down to his jawline. He tilted his head, studying her. "Honey, what are you doing?"

She shivered as if all the missing time swept over her in a rush. Past the skyscrapers that surrounded their building, the scraps of sky had turned to a periwinkle twilight. "I was just . . ." What had she been doing? "Taking a potty break." She smiled and rose on her toes to kiss him, breathing in the salty tang of his skin.

In the six months since she'd stopped going into the office at TruClone, he had put on a little weight. He'd always had a sweet tooth and tended to graze on dark chocolate when she wasn't around, but Elise was learning to find the tiny pot belly cute. She wrapped her arms around him and let him pull her close. In his embrace, all the pieces fit together the way they should; he defined the universe.

"How was work?"

Myung kissed her on the forehead. "The board declared the human trial 100 percent effective."

Adrenaline pushed her breath faster and made the backs of her knees sweat. "Are you . . . ?"

"Elise. Do you think they'd let me out of the lab if I weren't the original?"

"No." She shook her head. "No, of course not."

She should have been there, should have heard the success declared. The technology to print complete physical copies of people had been around for years, but they'd started TruClone to solve the consciousness problem. Elise had built the engine that transferred minds to bodies, so she should have gone into the office today, of all days.

She had forgotten. Again.

"I want to hear all about it." She tugged his hand, pretending with a smile to be excited for him. "Come into the kitchen while I finish dinner."

Outside, the first sounds of the market at the end of their block began. Calls for fresh fish and greens blended on the breeze and crept in through the open window of their bedroom, tickling her with sound. Curled around Myung, with one leg thrown over his thigh, Elise traced his body with her hand. The mole at the base of his ribs bumped under her finger, defining the territory. She continued the exploration and he stirred as her fingers found the thin line of hair leading down from his navel.

"Morning." Sleep made his voice grumble in his chest, almost purring.

Elise nuzzled his neck, gently nipping his tender skin between her teeth.

His alarm went off, with the sound of a stream and chirping birds. Myung groaned and rolled away from her, slapping the control to silence the birds.

She clung to him. Not that it would do any good. Myung loved being in the office.

He kissed her on the forehead. "Come on, get up with me. I'll make you waffles."

"Ooh. Waffles." Elise let go of him, smacking his rump gently. "Go on man, cook. Woman hungry."

He laughed and pulled her out of bed with him. She followed him to the kitchen and perched on one of the wicker stools by the counter as he cooked. It almost felt like a weekend back when they were courting at MIT. But the mood broke when Myung laid a pill next to her plate. Her stomach tightened at the sight of the drug. She didn't want the distancing the medication brought on. "I feel fine today."

Myung poured more batter on the waffle iron and cleared his throat. "Maybe you'd like to come in to work?"

The room closed in around her. Elise lowered her eyes to escape the encroaching walls. "I can't." She hadn't gone in since she'd come home from the hospital. Every day she thought that tomorrow the effects of the concussion would have faded. That the next day she would be back to normal. And some days she was. Almost.

Myung put his hand on hers. "Then take your medication."

She had walked away from the car accident, but it had scrambled her brain like eggs in a blender. Head-trauma induced psychosis. On good days, she knew it was happening.

Elise picked up the pill, hating it. "You're going to be late."

He looked over his shoulder at the clock and shrugged. "I thought I'd take today off."

"You? Take a day off?"

"Why not? My clone." He paused, relishing the word. "My *clone* has offered to do my reports today."

"Is that—isn't that a little premature?" As she said it, she realized that she didn't know how much time had passed since the board had declared success. It felt like yesterday but it had been longer. Hadn't it?

"He's bored, which is not surprising since I would be, too."

If she went to the office, maybe she could see the clone. See the thing they had labored toward. Cloned rats and dogs and monkeys weren't the same as a man. Not just any man, but a clone of her husband. She swallowed against a sudden queasiness. "Who's overseeing him?"

"Kathleen. Sort of. I'll have to look over his report later but we've agreed to let him function as if he were me, to see how he does."

Which made sense. The ultimate goal was to make full clones of high-level people who needed to be in more than one place at once. "Am I a clone, Myung?"

"No, honey." He squeezed her hand, grounding her again. "You're not."

The thing that nagged at her was that she could not tell whether she didn't believe him because he was lying or because the accident had left her with delusions to accompany the hallucinations.

Elise wiped the kitchen table, gliding the sponge across the teak in perfect parallel lines. The phone rang. Startled, she jumped and lost the pattern on the table. Putting her hand over her mouth to slow her breathing, Elise glanced at the clock to see how much time she had lost to cleaning. It was only 2:30. That wasn't as bad as it could have been.

The phone rang again.

She picked it up, trying to remember who had called her last. "Hello?"

"Hi honey. I need to ask you to do something for me." Myung sounded tense and a little breathless, as if the phone frightened him as much as it had her.

"What?" She slid a pad of paper across the counter so she could take notes. Clearly, today was not a good day and she didn't want to make that obvious to Myung.

"Would you come to the lab?"

"I . . ." A reflection in the window caught her eye, flashing like an SOS. "Today isn't a good day."

"The clone misses you."

His words stretched out as if they could fill the ten miles between the lab and the house and then everything snapped. "Misses me? It's never met me."

"*He* has all of my memories and personality. From his point of view, he hasn't seen you in months." There was a tension in his voice, his words a little rushed and tight. "Please. It's affecting his ability to concentrate. It's depressing him."

"No." A reflection twitched in the corner of her eye becoming a spider until she looked at it. "I can't."

Myung hummed under his breath, which he always did when he was conflicted about something. She hadn't pointed it out to him because it was an easy way to tell when he didn't want to do something. He exhaled in a rush. "All right. How's everything at home?"

"Fine." She doodled on the pad. There had been something that she'd thought about telling him. "Oh. There are some carbon matte knives I want to get."

"Really? What's wrong with the ones we have?"

Elise hesitated. "These look nice. All black."

"Ah." She could almost hear his mind click the pieces together. "No reflections. I didn't realize that was still bothering you. I'll order them."

"Thank you."

"Sure I can't get you to reconsider?" He laughed a little. "I miss having you around the office as much as he does."

"Not now."

Elise hung up. Back to the office? Her stomach heaved and she barely made it to the sink before vomiting. Gasping, she clung to the stainless steel as the anxiety flung itself out of her. The back of her throat and her nose burned. If she went in, people would know, *know* that she was wrong inside.

In the dark of the bedroom, Elise counted Myung's heartbeats as she lay with her head on his chest. "I'm sorry."

He stroked her hair. "Why?"

She lifted her head, skin sticky from sweat. "That I won't come to the office."

"It's all right. I understand."

At night, the idea seemed less frightening. She could tell herself as many times as she could count that the office was not dangerous, that nothing bad had ever happened to her there, but her body did not believe. "What's he like?"

"Who?" He lifted his head to look at her.

"Your clone."

Myung chuckled. "Just like me. Charming, handsome, devilishly intelligent."

"A troublemaker?"

"Only a little." He kissed her hand. "You'd like him."

"If I didn't, we'd have problems." Elise rolled onto her back, looking for answers on the ceiling. "You want to use me as a trial don't you?"

"What? No. Don't be silly."

"Please, Myung. My brain isn't that scrambled." She poked him in the soft part of his belly.

"Hey!"

"It's the logical next step, if these clones are going to do what we told our investors they would. You need to see if a loved one can tell the difference. You need to dress identically with your clone and let me talk to both of you."

Myung hummed under his breath.

"You could bring him here." Elise kissed his shoulder.

He stopped humming. "Not yet. Too many variables. It has to be at the lab first."

"I'll think about it." Her pulse raced, just saying the words. But the queasiness was manageable.

The knives arrived in the afternoon. Elise pulled them out of their shrink wrap and set them on the counter, forming three matte black voids on the wood. No reflections marred their surfaces. She ran a finger along one edge of the paring knife. Like a thread, a line of crimson opened on her finger. It didn't even hurt.

Elise held the cut close to her face, trying to see what would crawl out of her skin. The blood trickled slowly down her finger, exploring the contours. Without the reflections, her brain needed some other way to talk to her. She could help it if she opened the gap more.

"No. Myung wouldn't like that." Elise clenched her fist so the blood was hidden. "Put NuSkin on it, Elise."

Yes. That was the right thing. As she put the liquid skin in place, it occurred to her that if she printed herself a new body it would come with nothing inside. "But we solved the consciousness problem. It would come with me inside. With me."

She weighed the chef's knife in her hand and dropped it. The kitchen counter had all the vegetables from the refrigerator set out in neat rows. She had chopped a bell pepper without any memory of returning to the kitchen. Elise cursed. Hands splayed on the counter, she lowered her head in frustration.

The front door opened. "Honey, I'm home!"

Elise picked up the knife, then set it down and scooped the closest vegetables into her arms. Before Myung entered the kitchen, she managed to get them into the vegetable drawer in the fridge.

She let the door close and turned, smiling brightly. "Let me get your martini, dear."

Laughing, Myung caught her around the waist and kissed her. "How was your day?"

Elise shrugged. "Mixed. The usual. Yours?"

"Also mixed. My clone is . . . well, let's say I'm learning how stubborn I can be."

She winced. "I could have told you that."

"Not." He kissed her nose. "Helpful."

She stuck her tongue out. Moments like this beckoned her to fall into them with their allure of normalcy. "Thank you for the knives."

"Sorry?"

Elise pointed at the carbon black knives laid out on the counter. "The ones you ordered for me came today."

"I—" Myung crossed to the counter and picked up the paring knife. "Elise, I didn't order these."

The floor of the room fell away from her. Elise grabbed the handle of the refrigerator to steady herself. "But you said you would. We talked about it."

"When?" Myung's nostrils had flared.

"It's not a delusion." She swallowed and her throat stayed knotted. "You called me. You asked me to come to the office."

"Fuck." He slammed his fist on the counter. "Elise, I'm sorry. It's the clone."

Relief swept her so quickly that her knees gave way. She dropped to the floor, one hand still clinging to the refrigerator. The door cracked open letting out a cool breeze that chilled the tears running down her face. Thank God. She had not imagined the phone call. She hadn't ordered the knives herself and forgotten. "The clone did it."

Myung crouched by her, wiping the tears from her face. "I'm sorry. He was working on a report and we let him use my office."

"You're letting him contact the outside?"

"No. I changed the passwords—"

Elise started laughing. "And he guessed?"

Myung's skin deepened in a blush and he shut his eyes. "Should have seen that coming."

"Yes, dear." Elise wiped her eyes. "Oh God. I thought it was another sign of crazy."

At that, Myung opened his eyes, pain creasing his brow. "I'm so sorry."

"Don't be." Elise stood, using her husband's shoulder to push herself off the floor. "He bought the knives I asked for."

"With my money."

"Well . . . he's doing your work."

"Point." Myung got to his feet. "And I would have gotten them for you if you'd mentioned it."

"I thought I did." Giggles overtook her for a moment and they both stood in the kitchen laughing. When she caught her breath, Elise said, "Tomorrow, I'll come to the office with you."

The delight that blossomed on Myung's face almost made Elise withdraw the offer. Not that she resented making Myung happy, but she would disappoint him tomorrow. In the context of the lab, her slips of mind would be more apparent.

Elise shifted on the hard metal chair in the observation room. To her left, a mirrored window hid the staff watching her. She angled her head so the reflections were not so apparent. No time for hallucinations today. The rest of the walls were pale blue Sheetrock, meant to be soothing, but clinically cold. The ballast of one of the fluorescent lights buzzed just at the edge of her hearing. They would have to get that fixed.

She put her hands on the linoleum table in front of her and then in her lap again as the door opened.

Myung came in, dressed in a white T-shirt and jeans. He wore athletic socks but no shoes. Glancing at his feet, his dark hair masked his eyes for a moment, like a K-pop star. "We didn't have matching shoes, so opted for none."

Elise grinned, beckoning him closer. "Are they good for a sock-hop?"

He laughed, voice bouncing in a three-note pattern. "That is not on the set of questions."

"You." She pointed at him accusingly. "Aren't supposed to know what they are."

"I don't." Myung held his hands out in mock surrender. "But I'm guessing that it's not."

"Fine. We'll stick to the standards." Elise waved her hand to command him to sit across from her. Her heart beat like she was at a speed dating service. She looked at the list of questions she planned to ask each man. "When we got married, what did you whisper after you kissed me?"

Myung turned red and glanced at the mirror. He wet his lips, leaning forward across the table. "I think I said, 'How soon can we get out of here?'" His eyes were alive as if he wanted to take her right there on the table.

A flush of warmth spread out from Elise's navel to her breasts. At the wedding, his hands had been warm through her dress and she had been intently aware of how long his eyelashes were.

He looked out from under them now with his pupils a little dilated as if he also found the room too warm. "Next?"

"What is our most intimate moment?" Watching him, time focused itself in a way it had not done since the accident. Each tick of her internal clock was crisp and in sequence.

Myung's eyes hooded for a moment as he thought. "Yellowstone. We might have had the whole park to ourselves but there was also this profound sense that someone would catch us in the act. And that you would . . ." He hummed under his breath for a moment, sweeping his hand through his hair. "Let's just say, I knew that you trusted me."

Elise looked at the paper again. She had thought he would say that it was their first time after his vasectomy. At the time he had reveled in the freedom.

"Last question. Pick a number."

"That's it?"

"Yep."

Myung fingered the end of his nose, and Elise could not doubt that she was talking to her husband. He nodded.

"Very nice. Confirmed memory, subjective memory, and random."

She tapped a finger on the paper. "No opinion please. Number?"

"Thirty-six."

"Why thirty-six?"

He picked at the cuticle on his thumb. "Remember the time we went to see that puppet play, 'Between Two Worlds'?" He waited until she nodded. "The guy who thought that he could win his predestined bride through Kaballah had this line, 'Thirty-six, in that number lies the essence.' It stuck with me for some reason."

Myung came in, dressed in a white T-shirt and jeans. Elise's breath hung in her throat at the palpable déjà vu. She had seen printed clones dozens of times as parts donors but she had never seen one animated. Had she not been a part of the process to give a clone consciousness, she would have thought that her husband had just walked into the room. Like the other one, this Myung wore white athletic socks but no shoes. Glancing at his feet, his dark hair masked his eyes for a moment, like a K-pop star. "We didn't have matching shoes, so opted for none."

Elise pressed her hand over her mouth, trying to remember what she had said to the first one. No wonder they had wanted her to script her questions.

"Are you okay?" Myung—she could not think of him as anything else—took a step closer.

"It's uncanny is all." Wrong. She should not have said that out loud. It might skew his responses. "Shall we get started?" Elise beckoned him to sit across from her. She looked at the sheet of questions, trying to center herself. The calm certainty she felt before had stripped away, leaving her flustered. "When we got married, what did you whisper after you kissed me?"

Myung turned red and glanced at the mirror. He wet his lips, leaning forward across the table. "I think I said, 'How soon can we get out of here?' "

Sweat coated her skin.

He looked out from under his long eyelashes. "Next?"

"What is our most intimate moment?" Watching him, Elise looked for some clue, some hint that he was not her husband. But perhaps he was, and the Myung she had met first was the clone.

Myung's eyes hooded for a moment as he thought. "Yellowstone. We might've had the whole park to ourselves but there was also this profound sense that someone would catch us in the act. And that you would . . ." He hummed under his breath before sweeping his hand through his hair. "Let's just say, I knew you trusted me."

Elise looked at the paper again. Her hands were shaking and she could barely find air to breathe. Every nuance was the same.

"Last question. Pick a number."

"That's it?"

"Yes." Dear God, yes. She had helped create one of these two men, but she wanted nothing more than to get out of the room. Even though she knew he might be her husband, the uncanniness of having the same conversation twice threatened to shred her mind.

Myung fingered the end of his nose. "Very nice. Confirmed memory, subjective memory, and random."

A shiver ran down her spine. "What number?"

"Seventeen."

Elise had to stop herself from gasping with relief. Had they chosen the same number she might have screamed. "Why seventeen?"

"That's the day we were married." He shrugged.

Something, a darkness flickered in the corner of the room. It would be so much easier to drop into crazy than to keep thinking. "May I see you both at the same time?"

Myung stood. "Sure. I'll ask him to come in."

Forcing her mind into order, Elise folded her list of questions in half. Then half again, creasing the edges with her nail to crisp perfect lines.

The door opened and the other Myung came in. Elise had met identical twins before, but no twin had the commonality of experience that these two men had. One was her husband, the other was a copy and she could not tell them apart. They had even printed the extra weight that Myung carried so both had identical little potbellies.

The clone carried microchip transponders in his body, and a tattoo on his shoulder, but neither of those were visible. As they talked, Elise slowly noticed a single difference between the two.

The man to her right watched every move she made. His eyes were hungry for her in a way that—"You're the clone, aren't you?"

She had interrupted the one on her left. The two men shared a look before nodding, almost in unison. The clone said, "How did you know?"

"The way you look at me . . ." Elise faltered. He looked at her like he was trying to memorize her.

The clone grimaced and blushed. "Sorry. It's just that, I haven't seen you in months. I miss you."

Myung, the original Myung picked at his cuticle. "I told you she could tell the difference."

"But you were wrong about the reason." The clone smirked. "She could tell because you don't love her as much as you used to."

"That is a lie." Myung tensed visibly, his fist squeezing without his seeming awareness.

"Is it?" The clone shook his head. "Everything else is the same, why would my emotional memories be any different? The only difference between us is that absence makes the heart grow fonder."

"Stop." Elise stood abruptly, her chair squeaking against the floor. She pressed her hand against her forehead.

Both of them looked abashed. In stereo they said, "I'm sorry."

"It doesn't matter." Her thoughts were fragmenting. The reflection in the window moved, a child trying to get her attention. Elise shook her head. "You brought me down to see if I could tell the difference. Now you know that I can."

Her Myung said, "But not when we were separate."

"No." Elise fingered the paper on the table. "Which of you came in first?"

"I did," the clone said.

They sat in silence, Elise tried to fold the paper into another square. "I think I'm ready to go home."

"Of course." Her Myung stood, chair scraping across the floor.

The clone leaned forward on his. "Won't you stay for lunch?" His voice cracked as he asked, as if the request were more urgent than just a meal.

Elise raised her eyes from the paper to his face. The way his brows curled in the middle. The way his eyes widened to show a rim of white under the dark iris. The way his soft lips hung a little open. All of the minute elements that made the whole of her husband pulled, begging her to stay.

And the other Myung, the original, stood next to him, legs spread wide with a slight tension in his arms as if ready to protect her.

No. Not to protect her, but to protect his right to have her.

"Yes." She put her hand on the clone's, startled by the familiarity of the contact. "Yes, of course I'll stay."

The smell of sautéing onions wafted in from the kitchen. Myung had offered to cook breakfast before going to work, his usual ploy when he felt like he needed to make up for something. Clearly, he had no idea that breakfast was like a confession that the clone was right; Myung did not love her as much as he used to.

That wasn't quite true. Myung loved her the same as before—what had changed was that now there was a version of him that missed her all the time. Elise stretched under the covers and the cotton caressed her body like a lover. "I am the forbidden fruit."

Myung's cell phone rang on the bedside table where he'd left it. Rolling over, she picked it up. Caller ID showed the office. Elise got out of bed, not bothering with a bathrobe, and carried it toward the kitchen.

Myung met her partway down the hall. He took it, mouthing his thanks even as he answered.

Elise lifted the hair away from her neck, knowing that it would raise her breasts and make her torso look longer, daring him to choose work over her. His eyes followed the movement. Lips parting, he reached for her. Stopped.

His face shut down. Myung put one hand on the wall and squeezed his eyes closed. Dropping her arms, Elise shivered at the sudden tension in his frame.

"No. No, I heard you." He leaned against the wall and slid down to sit on the floor. "Did he leave a note or . . ." His eyes were still closed but he covered them with his hand.

Elise crouched next to him. Her heart sped up, even though there was nothing she could do.

"No. I haven't checked email yet." Myung nodded as if the person on the other end of the line could see him. "I'll do that. Thanks for handling this. Tell Larry not to do anything until I get in."

He hung up. Cautious, Elise touched his thigh. "Myung?"

Her husband slammed his head against the wall. Elise jumped at the horrible thud. Cursing, Myung threw his phone down the hall and it ricocheted off the floor. Tears glittering on his cheeks, he hurtled to his feet. "He killed himself. Sent us all a video. By email."

Myung was halfway to the office before Elise could pull herself together enough to stand.

On the monitor, the image of Myung leans close to the screen.

"This is the clone of Dr. Myung Han. I am about to kill myself by lethal injection. You will find my body in the morgue.

"Before I do, I want to make it perfectly clear why I am taking this step. With the animals we tested, the next step in this process is dissection. We must do this to be certain that the cloning has no unexpected side effects and to fully understand the mechanism by which the consciousness transfer works. My original knows this. I know this. He will not do it *because* the experiment has been a 100 percent success. We are identical, more so than any set of twins. He sees terminating the experiment as murder.

"Make no mistake, he is correct.

"Which is why I am terminating the experiment myself. I

am not depressed. I am not irrational. I am a scientist. The experiment needs to continue."

He stands and walks out of the room.

Elise stood behind Myung's chair, scarcely breathing. He reached to restart the video.

"Don't." She stopped him with a hand on his shoulder. It was bad enough seeing it once, but to dwell on it courted madness.

Under her hand, he trembled. "I didn't want this."

"I know."

He slammed his fist against the table. "If it had been me, I wouldn't have done it."

"But—" Elise stopped herself, not wanting to blame him.

"What?"

She saw again the clone begging her to stay for lunch. "He's trapped in the lab all the time. Were you ever going to let him out?"

Myung slumped forward, cradling his head in his hands. After a moment, his shoulders shook with sobs. Elise knelt by the side of the chair and pulled him into her arms. The rough stubble on his cheek scraped her bare skin. She pressed closer to the solidity of him, as if she could pull him inside to safety. An ache tore at her center as she rocked him gently and murmured nothings in his ear.

She had known the clone for a matter of hours, or for as long as she had known Myung depending on how you counted it. The two men had only a few months of differing experience. The bulk of the man who had died belonged to her husband. But the differences mattered. Even something as simple as a number. "Thirty-six," she whispered. In that number lies the essence.

As Myung went to the elevator, Elise stood in the door to watch him. She could not quite shake the feeling that he wouldn't come home. That something about the place would compel him to repeat his clone's actions. When the doors slid shut, she went inside the apartment.

In the kitchen, Elise pulled out the matte black knives that the clone had sent her and laid them out on the counter. He had known her. He had loved her. She picked up the paring knife, twisting it in her hands. It wasn't right to mourn him when her husband was alive.

"Elise?" Myung stood in the doorway.

"Forget som—" Adrenaline threaded its way through all her joints, pulling them tight. He wore a plain white T-shirt and jeans; his face was smooth and freshly shorn. Myung had not had time to shave. This man was leaner than her husband. "I thought . . . How many clones are there?"

He picked at the cuticle on his thumb. "Myung made just one."

"You didn't answer my question." Elise gripped the paring knife harder.

"I'm a clone of the one you met. Unrecorded. I started the process as soon as the building was empty last night." He swept his hand through his hair and it fell over his eyes. "We have about ten minutes of different memories, so for practical purposes, I'm the same man."

"Except he's dead."

"No. Ten minutes of memory and that physical body are all that is dead. "Myung—she could not think of him any other way—crossed his arms over his chest. "It was the only way to escape the lab. I had a transponder and a tattoo that I couldn't get rid of. So I printed this body from an older copy. Imprinted it with my consciousness and then . . . that's where our memories deviate. As soon as we were sure it was a clean print, he went to the morgue and I left."

She should call the office. But she knew what they would do to him. Insert a transponder and lock him up. "Why are you here?"

His eyes widened as if he were startled that she would ask. "Elise—the place where the original and I differ, the thing he cannot understand is what it is like to live in the lab, knowing that I'd never be with you. He doesn't know what it's like to lose you and, believe me, knowing that, I hold you more precious than I ever did before. *I* love you."

The raw need in his eyes almost overwhelmed her. The room tilted and Elise pressed her hand against the counter to steady herself. "I can't go with you."

"I wasn't going to ask you to."

"But you were going to ask me for something."

He nodded and inhaled slowly. "Would you clone yourself? So I'm not alone."

Elise set the knife on the counter, in a careful row with the others. She walked across the room to stand in front of Myung. The vein in his neck throbbed faster, pulsing with life. "Is it any different? Being a clone?"

"There's a certain freedom from knowing that I'm not unique. But otherwise, no. I feel like I am Myung Han."

Putting one hand on his chest, the heat of his body coursed up her arm. "I need to know something."

He raised his eyebrows in question.

"After the accident . . ." She did not want to know but she had to ask. "Am I a clone?"

"Elise, there's only one of you."

"That's not what I asked. The original won't tell me, but you—you have to. Am I a clone?"

"No. You are the original and only Elise." He brushed the hair away from her face. "Everything else is head trauma. You'll get better."

She had braced herself for him to say that she was a clone. That she had died in the crash and the reason she couldn't think straight was because the process had been too new, that she was a failed experiment.

Elise leaned forward to kiss him. His lips melted against hers, breath straining as if he were running a race. She let her bathrobe fall open and pressed against him. Myung slipped his trembling hands inside the robe, caressing her with the fervor of their first date.

Parting from him burned, but Elise stepped back, leaving him swaying in front of her. She closed the robe. "When I'm well, if I can. I will."

Myung closed his eyes, forehead screwing up like a child about to cry. "Thank you." He wiped his hand across his face and straightened.

"They'll notice that another body was printed and come after you."

"Not right away." He picked at his cuticle. "I took my original's passport from the office. Knowing me, it'll take him awhile to realize it's missing."

She felt herself splitting in two. The part of her that would stay here and see her husband tonight, and the part of her that already missed him. At some point, the two halves would separate. "Where are you going?"

He tucked a loose hair behind her ear. "Yellowstone."

Elise caught his hand and kissed it. "I will see you there."

Tempest 43

STEPHEN BAXTER

Stephen Baxter (www.stephen-baxter.com) is a prolific hard science fiction writer who lives in Morpeth, England. He is the author of a number of multibook series, and novels, sometimes in collaboration with Arthur C. Clarke. He has published more than twenty SF novels to date, starting with Raft *(1989). He has remained on the cutting edge of British hard SF. He is also among SF's most reliably good short-fiction writers, though he considers himself more a novelist than a short story writer. His novel* Ark, *the second book in the Flood series, came out in 2009. Most years he gives us several fine stories to choose from for this volume, and this year is no exception, with at least four candidates.*

"Tempest 43" was published in We Think, Therefore We Are, *edited by Peter Crowther. It is the second story in this volume from that book about future artificial intelligences. It is a post-singularity story set centuries hence, in which an archaic space station run by AIs always prevents hurricanes. But a storm has been allowed to happen.*

From the air, Freddie caught the first glimpse of the rocket that was to carry her into space.

The plane descended toward a strip of flat coastal savannah. The land glimmered with standing water, despite crumbling concrete levees that lined the coast, a defense against the risen sea. This was Kourou, Guiana, the old European launch center, on the eastern coast of South America. It was only a few hundred kilometers north of the mouth of the Amazon. Inland, the hills were entirely covered by swaying soya plants.

Freddie couldn't believe she was here. She'd only rarely traveled far from Winchester, the English city where she'd been born, and Southampton where she worked. She'd certainly never flown before, hardly anybody traveled far let alone flew, and she had a deep phobic sense of the liters of noxious gases spewing from the plane's exhaust.

But now the plane banked, and there was her spaceship, a white delta-wing standing on its tail, and she gasped.

Antony Allen, the UN bureaucrat who had recruited her for this unlikely assignment, misread her mood. Fifty-something, sleek, corporate, with a blunt Chicago accent, he smiled reassuringly. "Don't be afraid."

The plane came down on a short smart-concrete runway. Allen hurried Freddie onto a little electric bus that drove her straight to a docking port at the base of the shuttle, without her touching the South American ground, or even smelling the air.

428

And before she knew it she was lying on her back in an immense foam-filled couch, held in place by thick padded bars. The ship smelled of electricity and, oddly, of new carpets. A screen before her showed a view down the shuttle's elegant flank, to the scarred ground.

Allen strapped in beside her. "Do you prefer a countdown? It's optional. We're actually the only humans aboard. Whether you find that reassuring or not depends on your faith in technology, I suppose."

"I can't believe I'm doing this. It's so—archaic! I feel I'm locked into an AxysCorp instrumentality."

He didn't seem to appreciate the sharpness of her tone. Perhaps he'd prefer to be able to patronize her. "This shuttle's got nothing to do with AxysCorp, which was broken up long ago."

"I know that."

"And you're a historian of the Heroic Solution. That's why you're here, as I couldn't find anybody better qualified to help resolve this problem on Tempest 43. So look on it as field work. Brace yourself."

With barely a murmur the shuttle leaped into the air. No amount of padding could save Freddie from the punch of acceleration.

The ground plummeted away.

Tempest 43 was a weather control station, one of a network of fifty such facilities thrown into space in the 2070s, nearly a century ago, by the now maligned AxysCorp geoengineering conglomerate. An island in the sky over the Atlantic, Tempest 43 was locked into a twenty-four-hour orbit, to which Freddie would now have to ascend.

But before proceeding up to geosynchronous, the shuttle went through one low-orbit checkout. For Freddie, snug in her theme-park couch, it was ninety magical minutes, as the cabin walls turned virtual-transparent, and the Earth spread out below her, bright as a tropical sky.

The ship sailed over the Atlantic toward western Europe. She wished she knew enough geography to recognize how much of the coastline had been bitten into by the risen sea. At the Spanish coast Freddie saw vapor feathers gleaming white, artificial cloud created by spray turbines to deflect a little more sunlight from an overheated Earth. Southern Spain, long abandoned to desert, was chrome-plated with solar-cell farms, and studded with vast silvered bubbles, lodes of frozen-out carbon dioxide. The Mediterranean was green-blue, thick with plankton stimulated to grow and draw down carbon from the air. On the far side of the Gibraltar Strait, the Sahara bloomed green, covered in straight-edged plantations fed by desalinated ocean water. And as she headed into evening she saw the great old cities of southern Europe, the conurbations' brown stain pierced by green as they fragmented back into the villages from which they had formed.

Asia was plunged in night, the land darker than she had expected, with little waste light seeping out of the great metropolitan centers of southern Russia and China and India. The Pacific was vast and darkened too, and it was a relief to reach morning and to pass over North America. She was disappointed that they traveled too far south to have a chance of glimpsing the camels and elephants and lions of Pleistocene Park, the continent's reconstructed megafauna.

And as they reached the east coast they sailed almost directly over the Florida archipelago. Freddie was clearly able to see the wound cut by the hurricane. She called for a magnification. There was Cape Canaveral, venerable launch gantries scattered like matchsticks, the immense Vehicle Assembly Building broken open like a plundered bird's egg. The hurricane was the reason for her journey—and, incidentally, the ruin of Canaveral was the reason she had had to launch from Guiana. Hurricanes weren't supposed to happen, not in 2162. Stations like Tempest 43 had put a stop to all that a century ago. Something had gone wrong.

Antony Allen spent most of the orbit throwing up into paper bags.

At last the shuttle leapt up into deeper space, silent and smooth, and Earth folded over on itself.

"Tempest 43, Tempest 43, this is UN Space Agency Shuttle C57-D. You ought to be picking up our handshaking request."

A smooth, boyish voice filled the cabin. "C57-D, your systems have interfaced with ours. Physical docking will follow shortly."

"I'm Dr. Antony Allen. I work on the UN's Climatic Technology Legacy Oversight Panel. With me is Professor Frederica Gonzales of the University of Southampton, England, Europe. Our visit was arranged through—"

"You are recognized, Dr. Allen."

"Who am I speaking to? Are you the station's AI?"

"A subsystem. Engineering. Please call me Cal."

Allen and Freddie exchanged glances.

Allen growled, "I never spoke to an AI with a personal name."

Freddie said, a bit nervous, "You have to expect such things in a place like this. The creation of sentient beings to run plumbing systems was one of the greatest crimes perpetrated during the Heroic Solution, especially by AxysCorp. This modern shuttle, for instance, won't have a consciousness any more advanced than an ant's."

That was the party line. Actually Freddie was obscurely thrilled to be in the presence of such exotic old illegality. Thrilled, and apprehensive.

Allen called, "So are you the subsystem responsible for the hurricane deflection technology?"

"No, sir. That's in the hands of another software suite."

"And what's that called?"

"He is Aeolus."

Allen barked laughter.

Now a fresh voice came on the line, a brusque male voice with the crack of age. "That you, Allen?"

Freddie was startled. This voice sounded authentically human. She'd just assumed the station was unmanned.

"Glad to hear you're well, Mr. Fortune."

"Well as can be expected. I knew your grandfather, you know."

"Yes, sir, I know that."

"He was in the UN too. As pious and pompous as they come. And now you're a bureaucrat. Runs in the genes, eh, Allen?"

"If you say so, Mr. Fortune."

"Call me Fortune . . ."

Fortune's voice was robust British, Freddie thought. North of England, maybe. She said to Allen, "A human presence, on this station?"

"Not something the UN shouts about."

"But save for resupply and refurbishment missions, the Tempest stations have had no human visitors for a century. So this Fortune has been alone up here all that time?" And how, she wondered, was Fortune still alive at all?

Allen shrugged. "For Wilson Fortune, it wasn't a voluntary assignment."

"Then what? A sentence? And your grandfather was responsible?"

"He was involved in the summary judgement, yes. He wasn't *responsible*."

Freddie thought she understood the secrecy. Nobody liked to look too closely at the vast old machines that ran the world. Leave the blame with AxysCorp, safely in the past. Leave relics like this Wilson Fortune to rot. "No wonder you need a historian," she said.

Fortune called now, "Well, I'm looking forward to a little company. You'll be made welcome here, by me and Bella."

Now it was Allen's turn to be shocked. "By the dieback, who is Bella?"

"Call her an adopted daughter. You'll see. Get yourself docked. And don't mess up my paintwork with your attitude rockets."

The link went dead.

Shuttle and station interfaced surprisingly smoothly, considering they were technological products separated by a century. There was no mucking about with airlocks, no floating around in zero gravity. Their cabin was propelled smoothly out of the shuttle and into the body of the station, and then it was transported out to a module on an extended strut, where rotation provided artificial gravity.

The cabin door opened, to reveal Wilson Fortune and his "adopted daughter," Bella.

Allen stood up. "We've got a lot to talk about, Fortune."

"That we do. Christ, though, Allen, you're the spit of your grandfather. He was plug-ugly too." His archaic blasphemy faintly shocked Freddie.

Fortune was tall, perhaps as much as two full meters, and stick thin. He wore a functional coverall; made of some self-repairing orange cloth, it might have been as old as he was. And his hair was sky blue, his teeth metallic, his skin smooth and young-looking, though within the soft young flesh he had the rheumy eyes of an old man. Freddie could immediately see the nature of his crime. He was augmented, probably gen-enged too. No wonder he had lived so long; no wonder he had been sentenced to exile up here.

The girl looked no more than twenty. Ten years younger than Freddie, then. Pretty, wide-eyed, her dark hair shoulder-length, she wore a cut-down coverall that had been accessorized with patches and brooches that looked as if they had been improvised from bits of circuitry.

She stared at Allen. And when she saw Freddie, she laughed.

"You'll have to forgive my daughter," Fortune said. His voice was gravelly and, like his eyes, older than his face. "We don't get too many visitors."

"I've never seen a woman before," Bella said bluntly. "Not in the flesh. I like the way you do your hair. Cal, fix it for me, would you?"

"Of course, Bella."

That shoulder-length hair broke up into a cloud of cubical particles, obscuring her face. When the cloud cleared, her hair was cropped short, a copy of Freddie's.

"I knew it," Allen said. He aimed a slap at Bella's shoulder. His fingers passed through her flesh, scattering bits of light. Bella squealed and flinched back. "She's a virtual," Allen said.

Fortune snapped back, "She's as sentient as you are, you asshole. Fully conscious. And consistency violations like that *hurt*. You really are like your grandfather, aren't you?"

"She's illegal, Fortune."

"Well, that makes two of us."

Two suitcases rolled out of the shuttle cabin, luggage for Freddie and Allen.

Allen said, "We're here to work, Fortune, not to rake up the dead past."

"Be my guest." Fortune turned and stalked away, down a metal-plated corridor. Bella walked after him, looking hurt and confused. Her feet convincingly touched the floor.

Freddie and Allen followed less certainly, into the metal heart of the station.

To Freddie, the station had the feel of all the AxysCorp geoengineering facilities she'd visited before. Big, bold, functional, every surface flat, every line dead straight. The corporation's logo was even stamped into the metal walls, and there was a constant whine of air conditioning, a breeze tasting of rust. You could never escape the feeling that you were in the bowels of a vast machine. But the station showed its age, with storage-unit handles polished smooth with use, touch panels rubbed and scratched, and the fabric of chairs and couches worn through and patched with duct tape.

Fortune led them to cabins, tiny metal-walled boxes that looked as if they'd never been used. A century old, bare and clean, they had an air of staleness.

"I don't think I'll sleep well here," Freddie said.

"Don't fret about it," Allen said. "I'm planning to be off this hulk as soon as possible."

They left their luggage here, and Fortune led them on to the bridge, the station's control center. It was just a cubical box with blank gray walls, centered on a stubby plinth like a small stage.

Fortune watched Freddie's reaction. "This was the fashion a century ago. Glass-walled design, every instrument virtual, all voice controlled."

"Humans are tool-wielding creatures," Freddie said. "We think with our hands as well as our brains. We prefer to have switches and levers to pull, wheels to turn."

"How wise you new generations are," Fortune said sourly.

Bella, with her copycat hairdo, was still fascinated by

Freddie. "I wish you'd tell me more about Earth," she said. "I've never been there."

"Oh, it's a brave new world down there, child," Fortune said.

"In what sense," Freddie asked, "is Bella your child?"

Allen waved that away. "Bella is an irrelevance. So are you, Fortune," he said sternly. "We're here to find out why Tempest 43 failed to deflect the Florida hurricane. I suggest we get on with it."

Fortune nodded. "Very well. Cal? Bring up a station schematic, would you?"

A virtual model of Tempest 43 coalesced over the central plinth. Freddie had been briefed to some extent, and she recognized the station's main features. The habitable compartments were modules held on long arms away from a fat central axis. A forest of solar panels, manipulator arms, and docking ports coated the main axis, and at its base big antenna-like structures clustered. The representation was exquisitely detailed and, caught in the light of an off-stage sun, quite beautiful.

Fortune said, "This is a real time image, returned from drone subsats. Look, you can see the wear and tear." The habitable compartments were covered with white insulating blankets that were pocked with meteor scars, and the solar panels looked patchy, as if repeatedly repaired. An immense AxysCorp logo on the main central body, unrefurbished for a century, was faded by sunlight. "Do you understand what you're seeing? The purpose of Tempest 43 is to break up or at least deflect Atlantic hurricanes. Maybe you know that during the twenty-first century global warming pulse, a whole plague of hurricanes battered the eastern states of the old USA, as well as Caribbean and South American countries, all year round. Excess heat energy pumped into the oceans, you see."

"And Tempest 43 is here to fix that," Allen said.

"Hurricanes are fueled by ocean heat." Fortune pointed to the antenna farm at the base of the station's main axis. "So we meddle. We beam microwave energy into sea water. We can't draw out the heat that's pumping up the hurricane, but with carefully placed injections we can mess with its distribution. Give it multiple foci, for instance. We manage to disperse most hurricanes even before they've formed."

"Where do you get your power from? Not from these spindly solar cell arrays."

"We have a massive fission reactor up here." He pointed at the top of the central axis. "One reason the habitable compartments are so far away from the axis. Enough plutonium to last centuries. I know what you're thinking. This is a dirty solution. They were dirty times. You people are so pious. You kick AxysCorp now, and all the rest of the Heroic Solution. But you accept the shelter of the machinery, don't you?"

"Actually," Freddie said, trying to be more analytical, "this station is a typical AxysCorp solution to the problems of that age. It's a chunk of gigantic engineering, and it's run by absurdly oversophisticated AIs. But it's robust. It worked."

"It did work, until now," Allen said darkly.

"You needn't try to pin the Florida hurricane on me," Fortune said. "The AI runs the show. I'm only a fail-safe. I'm not even in the nominal design. The station should have been unmanned save for non-permanent service crews."

"You keep saying 'AI,'" Freddie said. "Singular. But we spoke to one during our approach, and heard of another."

"Cal and Aeolus," Fortune said. "It's a little complicated. The Tempest 43 AI is an advanced design. Experimental, even for AxysCorp . . ."

The station's artificial mind was lodged in vast processor banks somewhere in the central axis. Its body was the station itself; it felt the pain of malfunctions, the joy of a pulsing fission-reactor heart, the exhilaration of showering its healing microwaves over the Atlantic.

And, alone, it was never alone.

"It's a single AI. But it has *two* poles of consciousness," Fortune said. "Not just one, like yours and mine. Like two personalities in one head, sharing one body."

Allen said, "You're telling me that AxysCorp deliberately designed a schizophrenic AI."

"Not schizoid," Fortune said, strained. "What a withered imagination you have, Allen. Just like grandpop. It's just that when building this station, AxysCorp took the opportunity to study novel kinds of cognitive architecture. After all there are some who say our minds are bicameral too, spread unevenly over the two halves of our brains."

"What bullshit," Allen murmured.

Fortune said, "The two poles were labeled A and C. Nothing if not functional, the AxysCorp designers. I gave them names. Aeolus and Cal. Call it whimsy."

A and C, Freddie thought. It was an odd labeling, with a gap. What happened to B?

Allen said, "I understand why 'Aeolus' for your functional software suite, your weather controller. Aeolus was a Greek god of the winds. But why Cal?"

"An in-joke," Fortune said. "Does nobody read science fiction these days?"

Allen said, "Science what-now?"

Historian Freddie knew what he meant. "Old-fashioned fictions of the future. Forgotten now. We live in an age of aftermath, Fortune. Everything important that shapes our lives happened in the past, not the future. It's not a time for expansive fiction."

"Yeah, well, there's this old classic I always loved, with a pesky AI. Would have fitted better if the 'C' had been an 'H.' Cal's a dull thing, though. Just a stationkeeper."

"So where's Aeolus?" Allen lifted his head. "Are you there?"

"Yes, Dr. Allen. I am Aeolus."

It was another synthesized male voice, but lighter in tone than Cal's—lacking character, Freddie thought.

Allen said, "Let me get this straight. Cal is the station's subsystems. Housekeeping, power, all of that. Aeolus is the executive function suite. You fix the hurricanes."

"Actually, sir, there's some overlap," Cal put in. "The bipolar design is complex. But, yes, essentially that's true."

"So what are you doing, Aeolus?"

"I am enthusiastically fulfilling all program objectives."

"But you let one through, didn't you? People died because of you. And a historic monument was wrecked, at Canaveral."

"Yes, that's true."

"I'm from Oversight. I'm here to find out what happened here and to decide what to do about it. So what do you have to say?" Allen waited, but Aeolus offered no further explanation. "What a mess this is," Allen said to Freddie.

"Actually, this is again typical of AxysCorp," Freddie said. "Given immense budgets, huge technical facilities, virtually unlimited power, and negligible scrutiny, AxysCorp technicians often took the opportunity to experiment. Of course a willingness to meddle was necessary for them to be able to proceed with Heroic-Solution geoengineering projects in the first place."

"They used the climate disaster as the cover for crimes," Allen said. "The purposeless crippling of sentiences, for example. We have to acknowledge their achievements. But it's as if the world has been saved by Nazi doctors."

"Humans are flawed creatures," Fortune said. "Most of them are bumbling mediocrities. Like your grandfather, Allen, whose solution to the world's ills was to exile me up here. To tackle monstrous problems, you need monsters."

"Well, the hell with it." Allen was growing impatient. "I need to study your bipolar AI. I've some gear in my luggage. Freddie, this will be technical. Why don't you take a walk around the station?"

Bella said eagerly, "Oh, let's. I'll show you."

"And you," Allen said to Fortune, "show me back to my cabin. Please."

With bad grace, Fortune stomped off.

Bella gave Freddie a tour of the habitable module and its facilities: cabins, mostly unused, galleys, washrooms, a virtual recreation room. Everything was drab, utilitarian, and old.

Bella told Freddie a little about herself. "My protocols are quite strict." She tried to push her hand into the wall. Sparks scattered from her palm, and Bella screwed up her face in pain. "I can't go flying around in vacuum either. I have to eat and drink. I even have to use the bathroom! It's all virtual, of course. But Fortune says he designed my life to be as authentically human as possible."

Freddie said carefully, "But why did he create you at all?"

"I give him company," Bella said.

Freddie, an academic who was careful with words, noted that she hadn't explicitly confirmed that Fortune had "created" her, as the AxysCorp engineers had created Cal and Aeolus, any more than Fortune had admitted it himself.

They soon tired of the steely corridors, and Bella led the way to an observation blister. This was a bubble of toughened transparent plastic stuck to the bottom of the module's hull. Sitting on a couch, they looked down on the Earth, a bowl of light larger than the full Moon. Freddie was thrilled to see the white gleam of Antarctic ice. But the fragmented remnant cap on that green-fringed continent was the only ice visible on the whole planet; there was none left on the tropical mountains, Greenland was bare, and at the north pole was only an ocean topped by a lacy swirl of cloud.

Bella's thin, pretty face was convincingly painted by Earthlight. "Of course, we're suspended permanently over the middle of the Atlantic. But you can see day and night come and go. And if I ever want to see the far side, I can always call for a virtual view."

She had no real conversation, under the surface. She was an empty vessel, Freddie thought. Beautifully made but unused, purposeless. But then the only company she had ever had was the reclusive Fortune—and perhaps the station's artificial minds, Cal and Aeolus. "I'm no expert. But I can see that this environment doesn't offer enough stimulation to you as a sentience. You've a right to more than this."

Bella seemed moved to defend herself, or perhaps Fortune. "Oh, there are things to see," she said. "It's a marvel when Earth goes dark with night, and you can see the stars. And you can see AxysCorp facilities, studded all over the sky. Sometimes you can even make out the big Chinese space shields. The Heroics, Fortune's generation, saved the world. You can see it in the sky."

Freddie suspected these views were just watered-down versions of Fortune's opinions, the only human mind Bella had ever been exposed to. "But people on Earth," she said, "don't always feel that way. AxysCorp did fulfil the Heroic-Solution strategy, to stabilize the climate and to remove the old heavy, dirty industries from Earth. Billions of lives were saved, and a global technological civilization survived and is now even growing economically. That was a great achievement.

"But the Heroics chose to do things a certain way. The whole Earth is full of their gargantuan, aging machines. Memorials erected to themselves by a generation who wanted to be remembered. *Look at me. Look at what I did, how powerful I was.* Maybe their egos had to be that big to take on the task of fixing a broken planet. But to live at the feet of their monuments is oppressive."

Bella looked lost. "People ought to be more grateful."

"You need to come to Earth. It's not like it is for you, stuck here inside the machinery. Most people just live their lives. They don't obsess about the Heroics and AxysCorp and the rest. Only historians like me do that. Because it really is all just history."

A panel in the window filled up with Allen's blunt features. "Professor Gonzales. Could you rejoin us on the bridge, please? I've made my judgment."

Freddie hurried after Bella, through the maze of corridors back to the bridge.

The room was stripped of virtual displays. Allen sat comfortably on the plinth, the nearest thing to a piece of furniture. Fortune paced about, chewing a silver-colored fingernail.

Allen said, "We'll need a proper debrief. But technically speaking, the situation here is simple, as far as I can see." He showed Freddie the probe he'd been using, a kind of silvery network. "This is a cognitive probe. A simple one, but sufficient. I ran a trace on the AI pole, Aeolus. I can find no bug in the software despite the distorted sentience set-up AxysCorp left behind here. Nor, incidentally, according to station self-test diagnostics, is there any flaw in the physical equipment, the microwave generators, the antenna arrays, the station's positioning systems, all the rest. Aeolus should not have let that hurricane reach Florida. Yet it, *he*, did so."

There was a sound of doors slamming far off. Freddie felt faintly alarmed.

"My recommendation is clear. There's a clear dysfunction between the AI's input, that is its core programming and objectives, and its output. The recommended procedure is clearly defined in such cases. The AI pole Aeolus must be—"

"No. Don't say it," said Fortune, suddenly alarmed.

Allen stared at him. "What now, Fortune?"

"There's no blame to be attached to Aeolus. None at all."

"What are you saying?"

Fortune's mouth worked; his metal teeth gleamed. "That I did it. That Aeolus sent a hurricane into Florida because I asked him to. So there's no need for termination. All right?"

Allen was amazed. "If this is true, we've a whole box of other issues to deal with, Fortune. But even so, the AI acted in a way that clearly compromised its primary purpose— indeed, contradicted it. There's no question about it. Aeolus will be shut down—"

Cal spoke up. "I'm afraid I can't allow that to happen, Dr. Allen."

The station shuddered.

Allen got to his feet. "What in the dieback was that?"

Fortune growled, "I *told* you. Now see what you've done!"

Freddie said to Bella, "Show us your external monitors."

Bella hurried to a wall workstation and began calling up graphical displays. "Our comms link to Earth is down. And—oh."

UNSA Shuttle C57-D had been detached from its dock. It was falling away from the station, turning over and over, shining in undiluted sunlight.

"We're stranded," Allen said, disbelieving.

Fortune clenched his fists and shouted at the ceiling. "Cal, you monster, what have you done? I saved Bella from you once. Couldn't you let her go?"

There was no reply.

* * *

They stayed on the bridge. It made no real sense, but Freddie sensed they all felt safer here, deep in the guts of the station. Bella sat quietly on the plinth, subdued. Fortune paced around the bridge, muttering.

Freddie and Allen went through the station's systems. They quickly established that the station's housekeeping was functioning. Air conditioning, water recycling still worked, and the lamps still glowed over the hydroponic banks.

"So we're not going to starve," Allen said edgily.

"But the AI's higher functions are locked out," Freddie said. "There's no sign Aeolus is monitoring the Atlantic weather systems, let alone doing anything about them. And meanwhile, comms is down. How long before anybody notices we're stuck here?"

"People don't want to know what goes on with these hideous old systems," Allen said. "Even in my department, which is nominally responsible for them. Unless our families kick up a fuss or another hurricane brews up, I don't think anybody is going to miss us for a long time."

Fortune snorted. "Bureaucracies. The blight of mankind."

Allen growled, "You've got some explaining to do, Fortune. Like why you ordered up a hurricane."

"I didn't think it would kill anybody," Fortune said weakly. "I did mean to smash up Cape Canaveral, though. I wanted to get your attention."

Freddie asked, "Couldn't you have found some other way?"

Allen said dryly, "Such as waggle the solar panels?"

Fortune grinned. "Aeolus is compliant. When you have a god at your command, it is terribly tempting to use him."

"So you created a storm," Allen said, "in order to bring somebody up here. Why, Fortune? What do you want?"

"Two things. One. I want my exile to end. A century is enough, for Christ's sake, especially when I *committed no crime*. I'd like some respect too." He said to Freddie, "Look at me. Do you think I did this to myself? My parents spliced my genes before I was conceived and engineered my body before I was out of the womb. I haven't committed any crime. I *am* a walking crime scene. But it's me your grandfather punished, Allen. Where's the justice in that?" There was a century of bitterness in his voice.

"And, second, Bella. My sentence, such as my quasilegal judicial banishment is, clearly wasn't intended to punish *her*. She needs to be downloaded into an environment that affords stimulation appropriate for a sentience of her cognitive capacity. Not stuck up here with an old fart like me. As in fact, your own namby-pamby sentience laws mandate."

"All right," Freddie said. "But what *is* Bella? You didn't create her, did you?"

"No." Fortune smiled at Bella. "But I saved her."

Freddie nodded. "A, B, C."

Allen snapped, "What are you talking about?"

Freddie said, "There weren't just two poles of consciousness in the station AI, were there, Fortune? AxysCorp went even further. They created a mind with *three* poles. A—Aeolus. B—Bella. C—Cal."

"Oh, good grief."

"B was actually the user interface," Fortune said. "Charming, for an AxysCorp creation. Very customer-focused."

Freddie said, "Somehow Fortune downloaded her out of the system core and into this virtual persona."

"I had time to figure out how and nothing else to do," Fortune said sternly. "I'm extremely capable. In fact, I'm wasted up here. And I had motivation."

"What motivation?"

"To save her from Cal . . ."

Inside AxysCorp's creation, three centers of consciousness had been locked into a single mind, a single body. And they didn't get on. They were too different. Aeolus and Bella embodied executive capabilities. Cal, an artifact of basic engineering functions, was more essential. Stronger. Brutal. They fought for dominance. And it lasted subjective megayears, given the superfast speeds of Heroic-age processors.

"Cal crushed Bella. Tortured her. You could call it a kind of rape, almost. He did it because he was bored himself, bored and trapped."

"You're anthropomorphizing," Allen said.

"No, he isn't," Freddie said. "You need to read up on sentience issues, Doctor."

"I had to get her out of there," Fortune said. "This isn't the right place for her, in this shack of a station. But better than in there, in the processor."

Allen asked, "So why did Cal chuck away our shuttle?"

Fortune said, "Because you said you would kill Aeolus."

"You said they fight all the time."

"Do you have a brother, Allen? Maybe you fought with him as a boy. But would you let anybody harm him—*kill* him? Cal defends his brother—and, indeed, his sister if he's called on."

Allen clapped, slow, ironic. "So, Fortune, even stuck up here in this drifting wreck, you found a way to be a hero. To *save* somebody."

Fortune's face was dark. "I *am* a damn hero. We were told we were special—the peak of the Heroic-Solution age, they said. We were the Singularity generation. A merger of mankind with technology. We would live forever, achieve everything. Become infinite, literally.

"And, you know, for a while, we grew stronger. We were transported. Rapt. There aren't the words. But we got lost in our data palaces, while the rest of the world flooded and burned and starved. And we forgot we needed feeding too. That was the great fallacy, that we could become detached from the Earth, from the rest of mankind.

"In the end, they broke into our cybernetic citadels and put us to work. And they made us illegal retrospectively and imprisoned us in places like this. Now we're already forgotten. Irrelevant, compared to the real story of our time. AxysCorp and their ugly machines."

"That's life," Allen said brutally.

"This is Aeolus." The thin voice spoke out of the air.

Fortune snapped, "Aeolus? Are you all right?"

"I don't have much time. Cal and I are in conflict. I am currently dominant."

"Aeolus—"

"I restored communications. I contacted your Oversight

Panel, Dr. Allen. I received an assurance that a second shuttle will shortly be launched. The shuttle will have grappling technology, so Cal won't be able to keep it out. But Cal is strong. I can contain him but not subdue him. Mr. Fortune."

"Yes, Aeolus?"

"I fear it will be impossible to fulfil further objectives."

Fortune looked heartbroken. "Oh, Aeolus. What have I done?"

"As you know, I have always fulfilled all program objectives."

"That you have, Aeolus. With the greatest enthusiasm."

"I regret—"

Silence.

Allen blew out his cheeks. "Well, that's a relief."

Bella was wide-eyed. "Am I really going to Earth? Is a shuttle really coming? I'm going to go look out for it." She ran out of the bridge.

The three of them followed Bella to the observation blister, more sedately.

"Saved by a god in the machinery," Freddie said. "How ironic."

"What an end," Fortune whispered. "Two halves of the same mind locked in conflict for a subjective eternity." He seemed old now, despite his youthful face. "So it's over. What will become of Bella?"

Allen said, "Oh, they'll find her a foster home. There are far stranger minds than hers in the world, in the trail of tears left behind by AxysCorp and their like. We try to care for them all. The station's screwed, however. In the short term I imagine we'll reposition another Tempest to plug the gap. Then we'll rebuild. And we'll let this heap of junk fall out of the sky."

"But not before we've come back to save Aeolus and Cal," Freddie said.

"You're kidding," Allen said.

"No. As Fortune points out, it's actually mandatory under the sentience laws, just as it is for Bella."

"I'd like to see Aeolus spared that hell," Fortune said. "As for Cal, though, that deformed savage can rot."

"But Cal is the more interesting character, don't you think?"

"He locked us up and threw away our shuttle," Allen snapped.

"But there's an independent mind in there," Freddie said. "An original one. Aeolus just did what you told him, Fortune. Cal, born in a prison, knowing nothing of the real world, rebelled instinctively. With a mind as independent and strong and subtle as that, who knows what he'd be capable of, if set free?"

Fortune nodded. "And what of me? Will your indulgence set me free?"

"Oh, we'll take you home too," Allen said, sneering. "You'll stand trial for the hurricane. But there are places for creatures like you. Museums of the Singularity. Zoos," he added cruelly. "After all, there's plenty of room, now the chimps and tigers are all extinct."

Bella came running up, her face bright. "I saw the shuttle launch. You can see its contrail over the ocean. Oh, Freddie, come and see!"

Freddie and Bella hurried on to the blister and gazed down at the shining Earth, searching for the spaceship climbing up to save them.

Bespoke

GENEVIEVE VALENTINE

Genevieve Valentine (www.genevievevalentine.com) *lives in New York City. She began writing for publication in 2007. Her first story was published in Strange Horizons. She is a prolific writer, and over thirty of her short stories have appeared or are forthcoming in magazines such as* Clarkesworld *and* Fantasy, *and in the anthologies The* Living Dead II, Teeth, *and* Running *with the Pack. She is what Jeff VanderMeer terms an "emerging" writer. Her first novel,* Mechanique: A Tale of the Circus Tresaulti, *about a mechanical circus in a post-apocalyptic world, is forthcoming from Prime Books in 2011. She says in the third person: "As "Bespoke" would suggest, she has a particular interest in historical costume and fashion. It's an enthusiasm rivaled only by her insatiable appetite for bad movies, which she chronicles in her columns for Tor.com and* Fantasy Magazine, *and on her blog. She enjoys working within and across all genres of speculative fiction (and finding period films in which anyone wears anything remotely accurate)."*

"Bespoke" was published in Strange Horizons. It is told from the point of view of a clothier of wealthy time travelers, and is an amusing take on costuming and fashion—and time travel. We especially like the ambience.

Disease Control had sprayed while Petra was asleep, and her boots kicked up little puffs of pigment as she crunched across the butterfly wings to the shop.

Chronomode (Fine Bespoke Clothing of the Past, the sign read underneath) was the most exclusive Vagabonder boutique in the northern hemisphere. The floors were real date-verified oak, the velvet curtains shipped from Paris in a Chinese junk during the six weeks in '58 when one of the Vagabonder boys slept with a Wright brother and planes hadn't been invented.

Simone was already behind the counter arranging buttons by era of origin. Petra hadn't figured out until her fourth year working there that Simone didn't live upstairs, and Petra still wasn't convinced.

As Petra crossed the floor, an oak beam creaked.

Simone looked up and sighed. "Petra, wipe your feet on the mat. That's what it's for."

Petra glanced over her shoulder; behind her was a line of her footprints, mottled purple and blue and gold.

The first client of the day was the heiress to the O'Rourke fortune. Chronomode had a history with the family; the first one was the boy, James, who'd slept with Orville Wright and ruined Simone's drape delivery par avion. The O'Rourkes had generously paid for shipment by junk, and one of the plugs they sent back with James was able to fix things so that the historic flight was only two weeks late. Some stamps became very collectible, and the O'Rourkes became loyal clients of Simone's.

They gave a Vagabonding to each of their children as twenty-first-birthday presents. Of course, you had to be twenty-five before you were allowed to Bore back in time, but somehow exceptions were always made for O'Rourkes, who had to fit a lot of living into notoriously short life spans.

Simone escorted Fantasy O'Rourke personally to the center of the shop, a low dais with a three-frame mirror. The curtains in the windows were already closed by request; the O'Rourkes liked to maintain an alluring air of secrecy they could pass off as discretion.

"Ms. O'Rourke, it's a pleasure to have you with us," said Simone. Her hands, clasped behind her back, just skimmed the hem of her black jacket.

Never cut a jacket too long, Simone told Petra her first day. It's the first sign of an amateur.

"Of course," said Ms. O'Rourke. "I haven't decided on a destination, you know. I thought maybe Victorian England."

From behind the counter, Petra rolled her eyes. Everyone wanted Victorian England.

Simone said, "Excellent choice, Ms. O'Rourke."

"On the other hand, I saw a historian the other day in the listings who specializes in eighteenth century Japan. He was delicious." She smiled. "A little temporary surgery, a trip to Kyoto's geisha district. What would I look like then?"

"A vision," said Simone through closed teeth.

Petra had apprenticed at a tailor downtown, and stayed there for three years afterward. She couldn't manage better, and had no hopes.

Simone came in two days after a calf-length black pencil skirt had gone out (some pleats under the knee needed mending).

Her gloves were black wool embroidered with black silk thread. Petra couldn't see anything but the gloves around the vast and smoky sewing machine that filled the tiny closet where she worked, but she knew at once it was the woman who belonged to the trim black skirt.

"You should be working in my shop," said Simone. "I offer superior conditions."

Petra looked over the top of the rattling machine. "You think?"

"You can leave the attitude here," said Simone, and went to the front of the shop to wait.

Simone showed Petra her back office (nothing but space and light and chrome), the image library, the labeled bolts of cloth—1300, 1570, China, Flanders, Rome.

"What's the shop name?" Petra asked finally.

"Chronomode," Simone said, and waited for Petra's exclamation of awe. When none came, she frowned. "I have a job for you," she continued, and walked to the table, tapping the wood with one finger. "See what's left to do. I want it by morning, so there's time to fix any mistakes."

The lithograph was a late 19th century evening gown, nothing but pleats, and Petra pulled the fabrics from the library with shaking hands.

Simone came in the next day, tore out the hem of the petticoat, and sewed it again by hand before she handed it over to the client.

Later Petra ventured, "So you're unhappy with the quality of my work."

Simone looked up from a Byzantine dalmatic she was sewing with a bone needle. "Happiness is not the issue," she said, as though Petra was a simpleton. "Perfection is."

That was the year the mice disappeared.

Martin Spatz, the actor, had gone Vagabonding in 8,000 BC and killed a wild dog that was about to attack him. (It was a blatant violation of the rules—you had to be prepared to die in the past, that was the first thing you signed on the contract. He went to jail over it. They trimmed two years off because he used a stick, and not the pistol he'd brought with him.)

No one could find a direct connection between the dog and the mice, but people speculated. People were still speculating, even though the mice were long dead.

Everything went, sooner or later; the small animals tended to last longer than the large ones, but eventually all that was left were some particularly hardy plants, and the butterflies. By the next year the butterflies were swarming enough to block out the summer sun, and Disease Control began to intervene.

The slow, steady disappearance of plants and animals was the only lasting problem from all the Vagabonding. Plugs were more loyal to their mission than the people who employed them, and if someone had to die in the line of work they were usually happy to do it. If they died, glory; if they lived, money.

Petra measured a plug once (German Renaissance, which seemed a pointless place to visit, but Petra didn't make the rules). He didn't say a word for the first hour. Then he said, "The cuffs go two inches past the wrist, not one and a half."

The client came back the next year with a yen for Colonial America. He brought two different plugs with him.

Petra asked, "What happened to the others?"

"They did their jobs," the client said, turned to Simone. "Now, Miss Carew, I was thinking I'd like to be a British commander. What do you think of that?"

"I would recommend civilian life," Simone said. "You'll find the Bore committee a little strict as regards impersonating the military."

When Petra was very young she'd taken her mother's sewing machine apart and put it back together. After that it didn't squeak, and Petra and her long thin fingers were sent to the tailor's place downtown for apprenticeship.

"At least you don't have any bad habits to undo," Simone had said the first week, dropping The Dressmaker's Encyclopaedia 1890 on Petra's work table. "Though it would behoove you to be a little ashamed of your ignorance. Why—" Simone looked away and blew air through her teeth. "Why do this if you don't respect it?"

"Don't ask me—I liked engines," Petra said, opening the book with a thump.

Ms. O'Rourke decided at last on an era (18th-century Kyoto, so the historian must have been really good looking after all), and Simone insisted on several planning sessions before the staff was even brought in for dressing.

"It makes the ordering process smoother," she said.

"Oh, it's nothing, I'm easy to please," said Ms. O'Rourke. Simone looked at Petra. Petra feigned interest in buttons.

Petra was assigned to the counter, and while Simone kept Ms. O'Rourke in the main room with the curtains discreetly drawn, Petra spent a week rewinding ribbons on their spools and looking at the portfolios of Italian armor-makers. Simone was considering buying a set to be able to gauge the best wadding for the vests beneath.

Petra looked at the joints, imagined the pivots as the arm moved back and forth. She wondered if the French hadn't had a better sense of how the body moved; some of the Italian stuff just looked like an excuse for filigree.

When the gentleman came up to the counter he had to clear his throat before she noticed him.

She put on a smile. "Good morning, sir. How can we help you?"

He turned and presented his back to her—three arrows stuck out from the left shoulder blade, four from the right.

"Looked sideways during the Crusades," he said proudly. "Not recommended, but I sort of like them. It's a souvenir. I'd like to keep them. Doctors said it was fine, nothing important was pierced."

Petra blinked. "I see. What can we do for you?"

"Well, I'd really like to have some shirts altered," he said, and when he laughed the tips of the arrows quivered like wings.

"You'd never catch me vagabonding back in time," Petra said that night.

Simone seemed surprised by the attempt at conversation (after five years she was still surprised). "It's lucky you'll never have the money, then."

Petra clipped a thread off the buttonhole she was finishing.

"I don't understand it," Simone said more quietly, as though she were alone.

Petra didn't know what she meant.

Simone turned the page on her costume book, paused to look at one of the hair ornaments.

"We'll need to find the ivory one," Simone said. "It's the most beautiful."

"Will Ms. O'Rourke notice?"

"I give my clients the best," Simone said, which wasn't really an answer.

"I've finished the alterations," Petra said finally, and held up one of the shirts, sliced open at the shoulder blades to give the arrows room, with buttons down the sides for ease of dressing.

Petra was surprised the first time she saw a Bore team in the shop—the Vagabond, the Historian, the translator, two plugs, and a "Consultant" whose job was ostensibly to provide a life story for the client, but who spent three hours insisting that Roman women could have worn corsets if the Empire had sailed far enough.

The Historian was either too stupid or too smart to argue, and Petra's protest had been cut short by Simone stepping forward to suggest they discuss jewelry for the Historian and plausible wardrobe for the plugs.

"Why, they're noble too, of course," the client had said, adjusting his high collar. "What else could they be?"

Plugs were always working-class, even Petra knew that—in case you had to stay behind and fix things for a noble who'd mangled the past, you didn't want to run the risk of a rival faction calling for your head, which they tended strongly to do.

Petra tallied the cost of the wardrobe for a Roman household: a million in material and labor, another half a million in jewelry. With salaries for the entourage and the fees for machine management and operation, his vacation would cost him ten million.

Ten million to go back in time in lovely clothes, and not be allowed to change a thing. Petra took dutiful notes and marked in the margin, A WASTE.

She looked up from the paper when Simone said, "No."

The client had frowned, not used to the word. "But I'm absolutely sure it was possible—"

"It may be possible, depending on your source," Simone said, with a look at the Historian, "but it is not right."

"Well, no offense, Miss Carew, but I'm paying you to dress me, not to give me your opinion on what's right."

"Apologies, sir," said Simone, smiling. "You won't be paying me at all. Petra, please show the gentlemen out."

They made the papers; Mr. Bei couldn't keep from talking about his experience in the Crusades.

"I was going to plan another trip right away," he was quoted as saying, "but I don't know how to top this! I think I'll be staying here. The Institute has already asked me to come and speak about the importance of knowing your escape plan in an emergency, and believe me, I know it."

Under his photo was the tiny caption: Clothes by Chronomode.

"Mr. Bei doesn't mention his plugs," Petra said, feeling a little sick. "Guess he wasn't the only one that got riddled with arrows."

"It's what the job requires. If you have the aptitude, it's excellent work."

"It can't be worth it."

"Nothing is worth what we give it," said Simone. She dropped her copy of the paper on Petra's desk. "You need to practice your running stitch at home. The curve on that back seam looks like a six-year-old made it."

Tibi cornered Petra at the Threaders' Guild meeting. Tibi worked at Mansion, which outfitted Vagabonders with a lot more pomp and circumstance than Simone did.

Tibi had a dead butterfly pinned to her dress, and when she hugged Petra it left a dusting of pale green on Petra's shoulder.

"Petra! Lord, I was JUST thinking about you! I passed Chronomode the other day and thought, Poor Petra, it's SUCH a prison in there. Holding up?" Tibi turned to a tall young tailor beside her. "Michael, darling, Petra works for Carew over at Chronomode."

The tailor raised his eyebrows. "There's a nightmare. How long have you hung in there, a week?"

Five years and counting. "Sure," Petra said.

"No, for AGES," Tibi corrected. "I don't know how she makes it, I really don't, it's just so HORRIBLE." Tibi wrapped one arm around the tailor and cast a pitying glance at Petra. "I was there for a week, I made the Guild send me somewhere else a week later, it was just inhuman. What is it LIKE, working there for SO long without anyone getting you out of there?"

"Oh, who knows," said Petra. "What's it like getting investigated for sending people back to medieval France with machine-sewn clothes?"

Tibi frowned. "The company settled that."

Petra smiled at Tibi, then at the tailor. "I'm Petra."

"Michael," he said, and frowned at her hand when they shook.

"Those are just calluses from the needles," Petra said. "Don't mind them."

"Ms. O'Rourke's kimono is ready for you to look at," Petra said, bringing the mannequin to Simone's desk.

"No need," said Simone, her eyes on her computer screen, "you don't have enough imagination to invent mistakes."

Petra hoped that was praise, but suspected otherwise.

A moment later Simone slammed a hand on her desk. "Dammit, look at this. The hair ornament I need is a reproduction. Because naturally a reproduction is indistinguishable from an original. The people of 1743 Kyoto will never notice. Are they hiring antiques dealers out of primary school these days?"

Simone pushed away from the desk in disgust and left through the door to the shop, heels clicking.

Petra smoothed the front of the kimono. It was heavy grey silk, painted with cherry blossoms and chrysanthemums. Near the hem, Petra had added butterflies.

* * *

The light in the shop was still on; Petra saw it just as she was leaving.

Careless, she thought as she crossed the workshop. Simone would have killed me.

She had one hand on the door when the sound of a footstep stopped her. Were they being robbed? She thought about the Danish Bronze Age brooches hidden behind the counter in their velvet wrappers.

Petra grabbed a fabric weight in her fist and opened the door a crack.

Simone stood before the fitting mirror, holding a length of bright yellow silk against her shoulders. It washed her out (she'd never let a client with her complexion touch the stuff), but her reflection was smiling.

She hung it from her collarbones like a Roman; draped it across her shoulder like the pallav of a sari; bustled it around her waist. The bright gold slid through her fingers as if she was dancing with it.

Simone gathered the fabric against her in two hands, closed her eyes at the feel of it against her face.

Petra closed the door and went out the back way, eyes fixed on the wings at her feet.

When she came around the front of the shop the light was still on in the window, and Simone stood like a doll wrapped in a wide yellow ribbon, imagining a past she'd never see.

Petra turned for home.

Disease Control hadn't made the rounds yet, and the darkness was a swarm of wings, purple and blue and gold.

Attitude Adjustment

ERIC JAMES STONE

*Eric James Stone (www.ericjamesstone.com) lives in Eagle
Mountain, Utah. He has a degree in political science and a
law degree, and currently works as a website developer. He
began publishing in the genre in 2004, when he was a winner of the Writers of the Future Contest. He has since sold
seven stories to* Analog, *six to* InterGalactic Medicine
Show, *and several more to various other publications. In
2009 he became an assistant editor for* InterGalactic Medicine Show.

*"Attitude Adjustment" was originally written for a con-
test held by the Codex Writers Group (www.codexwriters.
com), of which he is an original member, and was published in* Analog, *which survives by persisting in publishing
the same thing it always has. This story is good old-fashioned
problem-solving space SF in the Astounding tradition, done
well. It has a touch of the Heinleinesque in its characterization and resolution.*

Danica Jarvis switched off the *Moonskimmer*'s main engine, and her stomach lurched in the familiar way that marked the change to zero gravity. She fired the attitude thrusters, turning the mushroom-shaped ship until it floated head-down over the Moon, so the long stem of the engine wouldn't get in the way. The clear diamondglass of the *Moonskimmer*'s hull allowed an unobstructed view of the lunar landscape.

From her pilot's chair in the center, she looked around at the eight tourists strapped to their seats along the circumference of the cabin. "This is the fun part of the trip. Unbuckle your seatbelts and float while you enjoy the view."

"Fun?" A teenage boy—Bryson Sullivan, according to the manifest—snorted. "Can we go back to the Hilton now?" He sported a bright purple datavisor and a shaved head.

Danica mustered her best be-nice-to-the-people-who-pay-my-salary grin and said, "Don't worry, Eddie and I will have you back to Luna City before the basketball game tonight. Right, Eddie?" Lunar-gravity basketball was a major tourist draw.

"Yes," said Eddie, the *Moonskimmer*'s A.I. "Our total flight time is less than two and a half hours. You'll get to see the far side of the Moon, something fewer than a thousand humans have seen with their own eyes. You should enjoy it." Eddie's voice was enthusiastic.

The boy rolled his eyes, then opaqued his visor.

Danica decided to ignore the useless brat and turned her

attention to the rest of the passengers. She pointed to one of the craters below and began her routine tour-guide patter.

"Okay, folks, if you'd please return to your seats and buckle up," said Danica. "I'm going to turn the ship so you can see the Earth rise over the lunar horizon."

It took a couple of minutes for everyone to get settled. For most of the tourists, this was their first zero-gee experience, and it showed.

"Wait, I want to try zero-gee," said Bryson. He began unbuckling his seatbelt.

Danica couldn't believe it. The kid had stayed in his seat the whole time, probably playing videogames on his visor. "I'm sorry," she said, "but we—"

Fwoomp!

The *Moonskimmer* jerked sideways, then lunged forward at its maximum acceleration of 0.75 gee.

Bryson yelped as he hit the floor.

"Eddie, what was that?" asked Danica.

Eddie didn't reply.

Above the engine's hum came the hiss of air escaping the cabin.

Fix the air leak first. That was Sergeant Conroy's first rule of disaster preparedness, drilled into Danica's mind during space pilot training. She quickly unbuckled her seatbelt and stood in order to go get the leak kit off the cabin wall.

But before she took a step, her conscious mind overrode her instinctive reaction.

The *Moonskimmer* was accelerating toward the Moon. Every moment of delay in shutting down the engine meant more altitude lost. She looked at her control panel and found nothing but blank screens. Not just Eddie—all the computers were down.

Manual engine shutdown required her to go down to the ship's lower level through the hatch in the main cabin's floor.

And sprawled on top of the hatch was the teenager.

She was beside him in two steps. "Out of my way," she said, grabbing his arm and pulling him off the hatch.

"Get off me!" He yanked his arm away.

She unlocked the hatch and pulled its recessed handle. It resisted her, and air rushed by her hand to flow down into the lower level. The leak was below.

Pointing to the leak kit's shiny red case, she said, "Someone grab that and drop it down to me." She took a deep breath, then exhaled as much as she could while yanking the hatch open.

Air swirled around her as she slid down the eight-foot ladder. There was still atmo on the lower level, although the pressure difference made her ears pop.

The main engine cutoff switch was right next to the ladder. She twisted it clockwise a half turn, and the engine died. Even though she was now weightless, the airflow from above kept her feet pressed against the deck.

Her lungs demanded air, and she decided it wouldn't hurt to take a breath from the thin atmo. She'd expelled her breath before coming down in case it was hard vacuum.

"Heads up!" said a man's voice from above.

One of the older passengers, Mr. Lyle, gripped the edge of the hatch opening with one hand and held the leak kit in the other.

She waved for him to toss it down. He did, and she caught it with her right hand while anchoring herself to the ladder with her left. She removed the sealant grenade from the kit, pulled the pin, and tossed it into the middle of the room.

The grenade exploded into a cloud of light-blue fibers.

Air currents caused by the leak made the fibers swarm like insects toward the hole in the hull. Some were swept out into space, but some stuck to the edges of the hole and caught others as they passed. In less than a minute the leak was sealed as the fibers congealed over it.

With the *Moonskimmer* airtight again, Danica manually released air from the reserve tanks to bring the pressure up to normal. Then she carefully checked the lower level to assess the damage.

"I think my arm's broke," Bryson said as Danica floated up through the hatch. "My mom is *very* gonna sue you. You'll be lucky to pilot a garbage truck in the future."

At least he was back strapped into his seat.

Danica ignored his comment and returned to her chair in the center of the cabin. "Well, folks," she said, "looks like we got hit by a meteor. Our computers are down, and I had to shut off the main engine manually. But the leak is sealed, and we've still got plenty of air, so I think the danger is past." With the computer destroyed, Danica had been unable to calculate their trajectory to know whether she had stopped the main engine in time. She hoped she had.

"That was very heroic, what you did, young lady," said Mr. Lyle.

She shrugged and smiled at him. "Just doing my job. And thanks for the assist."

"What do we do now?" asked Ms. Paloma, another of the vacationing retirees.

"We wait," said Danica. "Traffic control will realize we're overdue and start searching for us. They'll send a tug to pick us up eventually." She looked at Bryson and said, "I guess you're going to miss that basketball game."

"Why can't we just call and ask them to come get us?" asked Bryson's younger sister, Maddy.

"Coms are out, too," said Danica. "That meteor really did a—"

"It wasn't a meteor," Bryson said.

Danica blinked. "Well, I guess you're right. Technically, it's a meteoroid."

"It wasn't a *meteoroid*." He stared defiantly at her from behind his purple visor.

"Just shut up, Bryson," said Maddy. "Why do you always act like you know everything?"

"You shut up, dumwitch," he replied.

"It doesn't really matter what hit us," said Danica. "What matters is we're—"

"Nothing hit us," said Bryson.

Danica let out a slow breath. "Maybe I just imagined the hole in the hull and the air leaking out of the ship."

Bryson shook his head. "Yeah, okay, I'm just a kid. I don't know zot. But my A.I.—" he tapped his datavisor "—says the engine activated slightly *before* the sideways jolt."

Danica raised her eyebrows. An A.I. small enough to fit in a visor would be so expensive that this kid had to come from one of the trillionaire families. His last name clicked in her mind—Sullivan, as in Sullivan Space Technologies. "Then what did it?"

"Sabotage," said Bryson. "Someone did this to us."

Maddy gasped.

Shaking her head, Danica said, "Why would anyone sabotage the *Moonskimmer*?"

"I know," said Maddy. "Our mom's chief negotiator for L.M.C. The union's made threats."

"Now wait a minute," said Mr. Lyle. "My son's a union steward. They would never—"

Several people began talking at once.

"Stop!" Danica said. "Who did this and why is a matter for the authorities back in Luna City. We survived. That's all that matters right now."

After a few seconds of silence, Bryson said, "We have forty-seven minutes left to live."

As the others responded with shocked exclamations, Danica asked calmly, "Our trajectory?"

Bryson nodded. "My A.I.'s done a nice little animation. In just under half an orbit, we're going to make a tiny new crater on the moon."

Obviously she had shut down the engine too late. But . . . She unbuckled herself and moved to the hatch leading to the lower level.

"Come with me, Bryson," she said as she opened the hatch.

Instead of unbuckling, he folded his arms tight. "You gonna lock me up? I'm only telling the truth!"

"I know," Danica said. "Congratulations! You and your A.I. have just been promoted to navigator. Now get down here and see if you can link up with what's left of the computer."

"Already tried through the wireless. The software's skunked," said Bryson. "No way for my A.I. to make sense of it. And rewriting from zot's gonna take a lot more than forty-five minutes."

Danica tightened her lips for a moment. "Look, it's just our attitude that's the problem."

Bryson snorted. "If we just think positive, everything'll turn out brightwise?"

"No, the *Moonskimmer*'s attitude," said Danica. "The main engine will push us forward if I switch it back on, but we can't turn without the A.C.S.—Attitude Control System."

"There's no manual override?" asked Bryson.

"There was." Danica pointed down to the lower level. "Unfortunately, whatever fried the computer also fried the A.C.S. board. The only way we're controlling those rockets is by computer. Have your A.I. focus on that."

Mr. Lyle's voice came from behind her. "I think I can get your radio working again."

Danica's heart seemed to jump inside her. "Keep working on the A.C.S.," she said to Bryson. She launched herself back to her seat at the center of the cabin.

"What've you got?" she asked Mr. Lyle, who had started taking apart her control panel.

"Well, it seemed strange to me that a computer problem would take out the com, too." Mr. Lyle tugged at some multicolored wires.

Danica shrugged. "It's all digital."

"Yes, but radio doesn't have to be digital. I can remember the days when even TV was still analog. Terrible picture, but at least the shows were better back—"

"Honey," said Mrs. Lyle, "fix the radio?"

"Oh, right," he said. He pulled out a circuit board and frowned at it. "Anyhow, I figure even if the digital part doesn't work, the radio part might. And if we can send an S.O.S., someone might pick it up and come to rescue us."

Danica doubted anyone would be listening for non-digital radio signals, but there was no harm in letting Mr. Lyle try. "Do what you can."

She turned to the other passengers, still strapped in their seats. "Anyone have any experience repairing computer control systems?"

After a few seconds of silence, Maddy said, "We're going to die, aren't we?"

"Not if your brother and his A.I. can get the attitude rockets to work," said Danica. "We just need to get into a safe orbit, and someone will eventually pick us up."

Bryson shook his head. "Can't."

"What do you mean, 'Can't'? Keep trying," said Danica.

"No point. Got into the A.C.S. enough to read the fuel pressure: zero. Explosion must've taken out a fuel line." Bryson shook his head.

"So we can't do anything but float until we crash?" asked Mrs. Park, a retired high school teacher who had chatted merrily with Danica earlier in the trip.

"What about the main drive fuel?" Danica asked.

"Nothing wrong with the main drive, far as I know." Bryson shook his head. "They wanted it to work until it smashed us into the moon."

"So we can accelerate, but we can't turn," Danica said. "We've got to find a way to . . . spacesuit!" She floated over to the cabinet where her spacesuit was stored. "I'll attach a line to the nose and use the suit thrusters to swing us around."

She opened the cabinet and grabbed her suit. The composite fabric, stronger than woven steel, tore like cotton candy. She stared at the wispy handful. Nanobots. That was the only possible explanation: someone had infected the suit with composite-eating nanobots.

With little doubt as to what she would find, she checked the fuel gauge on the thrust-pack. Empty.

She shoved the suit back into the cabinet. She swung over to the cabinet holding the "Breach-Balls," inflatable life-support bubbles with breathable air for two passengers for up to twelve hours. Nanobots had ruined all four of them. No one would be doing any E.V.A.

She turned to face her passengers. All but Mr. Lyle, still working at the radio, stared back at her.

"Anyone have any ideas?" she said.

There was a long pause.

Mr. Godfrey, a wizened bald gentleman who had hardly said two words during the whole trip, broke the silence. "I read a science fiction story once where people were marooned in orbit, and they made a hole in their water tank so that it acted like a rocket."

"Good thinking," said Danica. "Our drinking water tank isn't big enough, though. The only liquid we have enough of is fuel, and we need that for the main engine." She wrinkled her brow. "Plus, the only access to the fuel tank is from outside, and we haven't got a spacesuit. But we need to think of all possibilities."

"Young man," said Mrs. Park, looking at Bryson, "you said we had less than half an orbit before crashing. Is it more than a quarter?"

"Um, yeah," he said.

Mrs. Park smiled. "Then we have nothing to worry about." She made a fist with her right hand. "This is the moon." She pointed at the center of her fist with her left index finger. "Our ship started off pointed at the moon. But without the attitude rockets to keep us facing the moon as our orbit takes us around, our inertia will keep us pointing the same direction." Without changing her left hand's orientation, she moved it a quarter of a revolution around her fist. Her index finger now pointed 90 degrees away from her fist. "When we're no longer pointing at the moon, fire the main engine. All we need to do is wait."

Several passengers sighed in relief.

"There's only one small problem," said Danica. "We weren't using attitude rockets to stay pointed at the moon. We use gravity gradient stabilization—tidal forces. Basically, the long axis of the ship stays pointed at the moon because of the slight difference in the gravitational force on the near end as opposed to the far end."

"Oh," said Mrs. Park.

"What if we made another hole near the nose?" said Mrs. Lyle. "Use some of our air to push us before plugging the hole?"

Danica frowned. "Maybe, if we had something that could make a hole through ten centimeters of diamondglass . . ."

"No," said Bryson. "My A.I. says it wouldn't be enough even if we emptied all the atmo."

"Action and reaction. We need to find something to use as propellant, or else we can't turn the ship," said Mrs. Park.

"Wait," said Mr. Godfrey. "That's not true. I read a story once where an astronaut turned his ship one direction by spinning a wheel in the other direction at the ship's center of gravity."

"Yes!" Mrs. Park's voice was excited. "Conservation of angular momentum. It could work." She looked at Danica. "Where's the center of mass on this ship?"

"It would be in the fuel tank, just above the main engine." Something about the idea seemed to click in Danica's mind, but then she shook her head. "There's no way to access it from here, and even if there were—it's full of liquid hydrogen."

"What if we all got on one side of the ship, made it unbalanced, and then you turned the main engine on?" said Maddy. "Wouldn't that make it curve around?"

"A bit," said Danica.

Bryson puffed in exasperation. "Not enough to keep us from smashing into the moon, picoceph."

"Well, forgive me for not having an A.I. to tell me how to be smart," said Maddy.

"Quiet!" said Danica. "Arguing doesn't help."

"*Nothing's* gonna help," said Bryson. "My A.I.'s smarter than all of us put together, and it's run all the scenarios. In thirty-six minutes we're going to crash. Get used to it."

Danica felt she should protest against hopelessness, but had no idea what to say.

"Ah, 'The Cold Equations.' " Mr. Godfrey made a sound that seemed half chuckle, half sigh. "Did your A.I. calculate how many of us would need to jump out the airlock in order to change the ship's attitude?"

Bryson's eyes widened behind his visor.

"You can't be serious," said Danica.

Mr. Godfrey smiled crookedly. "Deadly so. I volunteer myself as reaction mass, but I doubt I weigh enough on my own."

"Not enough," said Bryson. "Even if *all* of us jumped, it's not enough."

"I've got it!" yelled Mr. Lyle. "It works! I think."

"What?" said Danica.

"The radio. I think I'm sending out an S.O.S." Mr. Lyle tapped two wires together in rhythm. "Dot-dot-dot dash dash dash dot-dot-dot."

"So now we just sit back and wait for them to rescue us?" said Bryson's sister.

"There's a possibility that an ore freighter is in a nearby orbit," said Danica. She figured it was only a five percent chance, but that was five percentage points more than they'd had before.

"Except the freighters are all grounded 'cause the miners are on strike," said Bryson.

"Don't blame this on the miners, boy," said Mr. Lyle. "The working conditions—"

"Stop it," said Danica.

"—are completely unsafe," continued Mr. Lyle. "L.M.C. makes obscene profits while paying sub-standard wa—"

Bryson opaqued his visor.

"Enough!" Danica pointed at Mr. Lyle. "It doesn't matter now."

Mr. Lyle shut up.

"You can either keep sending the S.O.S. on the slim chance someone'll hear it." Danica took a deep breath. "Or you can spend some time with your wife before the end."

He stopped clicking the wires together and looked over at his wife.

"Or," Mrs. Lyle said, "you could do both. Keep trying—I'll come to you." She unbuckled her seatbelt and pushed herself away from her seat, toward her husband in the middle of the cabin.

But her inexperience in zero-gee showed as her right hand caught for a moment on her loose seatbelt. She started spinning as she drifted through the air, and her instinctive move of clutching her arms to her chest only made her pirouette faster.

"Oh dear," said Mrs. Lyle.

Bryson let out a slight chuckle, proving that he could still see through the opaqued visor.

Danica launched herself to rescue the poor woman. For a moment she pictured Mrs. Lyle as a ship, floating helpless in space, just like the *Moonskimmer*. Except Mrs. Lyle was spinning on her long axis . . .

"I've got it!" Danica shouted as she grabbed Mrs. Lyle by the arm. Their momentum carried them across the cabin, and Danica was able to catch a handhold and steady them both.

"We're going to survive," Danica said firmly. "We just need to get the ship spinning on its long axis."

"How?" said Bryson.

Danica pointed at Mr. Godfrey. "Kind of like that story he mentioned. We use my chair in the center of the cabin. And we rotate ourselves around it like we're on one of those playground merry-go-rounds where you spin yourself around by hand power. We'll need everyone's mass for this—some of you will just have to hang on to the people in the middle doing the turning."

"Glad my idea helps," said Mr. Godfrey, "but what good is it to rotate on the long axis? We'll still be pointed at the moon."

Danica turned to Mrs. Park. "Gyroscopic inertia."

Mrs. Park's eyes lit up. "Oh, of course. You all remember my example before? It was wrong because the tidal force kept pulling the long axis toward the moon. But if we're spinning on our long axis, gyroscopic inertia will resist that pull, just like a spinning gyroscope resists the pull of gravity trying to make it topple over."

"Mr. Lyle," said Danica, "can you handle catching people there?"

"I can." He anchored himself with one arm through the seatbelt strap, and Danica gave his wife a gentle push toward him.

"I don't believe it," said Bryson.

Danica paused in making her way toward the next passenger. "Why not? I think it'll work."

"That's just it," he said. He cleared his visor and looked at her with wide eyes. "My A.I. agrees with you."

* * *

Twenty-eight minutes later, and only 160 meters from the lunar surface, Danica activated the main engine. The *Moonskimmer* accelerated toward the clear space ahead, and the Moon gradually fell away beneath them. It was another eight hours before a tug from Luna City caught them.

Just before stepping into the airlock, Bryson turned back to Danica. "I'm not going to let my mom sue you."

Danica smiled wryly. "Thanks, I guess."

Bryson shrugged. "You know, my grandfather runs Sullivan Space Technologies."

"I suspected as much," said Danica.

"He'll track down whoever was behind the sabotage, even if the police don't."

She nodded.

"Gramps just built a luxury cruise ship to go out to Saturn," Bryson said. "He really wants me to go on the maiden voyage with him."

Puzzled as to why he was telling her this, Danica said, "Well, I hope our little adventure hasn't put you off tourism forever."

"Nah." He shook his head. "I'm going to tell him I'll go—if he hires you as the pilot."

He stepped into the airlock, leaving Danica speechless.

Edison's Frankenstein

CHRIS ROBERSON

Chris Roberson (www.chrisroberson.net) lives in Austin, Texas, and, with his wife and business partner, Allison Baker, runs the small press MonkeyBrain Books. He is an up-and-coming writer of fantasy and science fiction, with nine novels to his credit so far. His short stories have appeared in Asimov's, Interzone, Postscripts, *and* Subterranean, *and in original anthologies such as* Live Without a Net, FutureShocks, *and* Forbidden Planets. *He has so frequently been praised as a writer to watch that he remarks, "With all of these recommendations that people should watch me, I get the feeling I can't be trusted." His work has been nominated for awards for writing and he himself for his publishing and editing.*

"Edison's Frankenstein" was published in Postscripts *20/21, the ambitious magazine published and edited by Peter Crowther in England. It is an alternate history Thomas Edison story, in the venerable tradition of the Edisonade, with an unusual central character for this characteristically American form, an Algerian. And so this Year's Best ends as it began, with a non-traditional transformation of the matter of SF.*

It was late afternoon when Archibald Chabane finally found the boy, perched high on the steel trestle of the elevated railway. From that vantage, he could look out across the intersection of 62nd St. and Hope Avenue, over the high fence into the backstage area of Bill Cody's concession, now christened *Buffalo Bill's Wild West and Congress of Rough Riders of the World.*

"Mezian," Chabane called, but over the muffled roar of the crowd in Cody's 8,000 seat arena and the rumble of the Illinois Central Railroad engine coming up the track, he couldn't make himself heard.

"Mezian!" Chabane repeated, cupping his hands around his mouth like a speaking-trumpet. He glanced to the south, trying to see how close the train had come. When Chabane had been a boy, watching the 4-6-0 camelback engines lumbering along the Algiers-Constantine line, he'd always been able to see the black smoke billowing up from their coal-fed furnaces from miles away. These new prometheic engines, though, produced nothing but steam, and virtually all of it used for locomotion, so the trains could be heard long before they could be seen.

Chabane leaned a hand against the nearest steel girder, and could feel the vibrations of the train's approach.

He shouted the boy's name once more, at the top of his lungs.

Mezian looked down, blinking, and his lips tugged up in a guilty grin. "Oh, I didn't see you there, *amin.*"

Chabane had only to cross his arms over his chest and scowl, and the boy began clambering down the trestle like a monkey from a tree.

To the Americans, like Bill Cody—who'd already warned Sol Bloom to keep "his damned Algerians" away from the Wild West Show's Indians—Archibald Chabane was Bloom's assistant, translator, and bodyguard.

To Sol Bloom, "Archie" was just a Kabyle who'd gotten off the boat from Paris with the rest of the troupe, and threatened to throw Bloom into the waters of New York Harbor if he wasn't more polite to the performers. Bloom had offered him a cigar and hired Chabane to be his liaison with the Algerian troupe on the spot.

To the Algerians, though, Chabane was something more. At first only their guide in a foreign land, he had become their elected *amin*, as much the head of their "Algerian Village" concession as if he were sitting in the *djemaa* of a Kabyle village back home.

"Careful," Chabane warned, as Mezian swung from a steel girder. "I promised your mother I'd bring you back in one piece."

The boy just grinned, and dropped a full five feet to the pavement, something colorful fluttering to the ground after him like a lost bird.

"Mother won't give me a dime to get into the show," Mezian said by way of explanation, pointing at the banners which fluttered over Cody's concession, proclaiming *THE PILOT OF THE PRAIRIE*.

"Mr. Bloom has sworn it's my hide if any of our troupe is caught drinking with Cody's performers again," Chabane said, arms still crossed over his chest. Many of the Algerians in the troupe were not the most observant of Muslims, and even now in the final days of Ramadan they could be found passing a flask back and forth once the day's audience had cleared out. "If Cody catches one of us peeking at his show without paying, I'll never hear the end of it."

Mezian scuffed his feet against the pavement, his gaze lowered. "Sorry, *amin*."

"You dropped something." Chabane reached down and

picked up the garishly-colored pamphlet that had fallen from the boy's pocket. It was a story-paper, what the Americans called a "dime novel." The title in oversized letters was *Scientific Romance Weekly*, featuring "Dane Faraday, Man of Justice, in The Electrical World of Tomorrow." Handing it back to the boy, Chabane quirked a smile. "She won't give you ten cents for the Wild West Show, but she lets you spend money on cheap fictions?"

The boy shrugged, slipping the folded pamphlet into his back pocket. "They're meant to help me practice my English." He paused, drawing himself up straight, and then in stilted tones added in English, *"Hands up, the miscreant, you are the surrounded."* Switching back to French, he gave Chabane a quizzical look. "What is a *'miscreant'*?"

"It means unbeliever," the man explained, "or infidel. A villain, in other words." He put a hand on the boy's shoulder and gently propelled him forward. "Come along, your mother is waiting."

As they headed up 62nd to Island Avenue, they could hear the muffled applause from the crowd inside Cody's arena. Open only a little more than a week, and already the Wild West Show was drawing bigger crowds than all the concessions on the Midway Plaisance combined. In another two weeks the Columbian Exhibition proper would finally open to the public, and it remained to be seen whether there'd be crowds left over for any of the outside attractions.

"So your story-papers," Chabane said, as they turned left and headed north up Island Avenue. "Are they any good?"

Mezian shrugged. "They are alright, I suppose. Not as good as the French ones I could get back home, or in Paris."

Chabane nodded. "When I was a boy, I devoured every installment of Jules Verne's *Extraordinary Voyages* I could lay hands on."

The boy pulled a face. *"Verne?"* He shook his head. "Much too dry. No, give me Paul d'Ivoi's *Eccentric Voyages,* any day."

They passed 60th Street, then turned left onto the Midway Plaisance. The looming form of Ferris's still unfinished wheel dominated the horizon, even seven blocks away.

Steel-bodied automata spidered up and down it on their crab-like legs, welding girders into place, stringing high tension wires. The builders promised that it would be ready to start spinning within another week, two at the most, just in time for opening day. Chabane was less than optimistic about their predictions, but knew that if not for the automata, it would not even be *that* far along, and would never have been ready in time.

Chabane couldn't help but think about the boy he'd once been, reading Verne in second-hand story-papers. Not yet Archibald Chabane of London, just Adherbal Aït Chabaâne of Dellys, reading about men who traveled beneath the waves, or across the skies, or to the moon in glorious machines. It had seemed a distant, ungraspable vision that he could scarcely hope to see. Then came the famine, and the oppression of the Kabyle at the hands of their French colonial masters, and finally the failure of Muhammed al-Muqrani's revolt. Chabane had been too young to fight, but his father and his uncles had not, and with the revolt put down his family name had been outlawed in Algeria, never again to be spoken in the *djemaa*. The young Adherbal, seeing no future in his native land, had gone instead to live among the *Romni*, as the Kabyles, remembering the Romans of ancient times, still thought of all foreigners across the middle sea. He ran away to the north, away from the superstitions of his grandmothers and the traditions he had been taught. He had gone looking for the future, to reinvent himself in a rational world. In England he'd made a new life for himself, the bodyguard to a wealthy man, and had tried to forget the past.

In the end, though, he learned the past was something we carry with us, and can never escape. And even though the future had arrived, it had not been quite as he'd expected.

Chabane and the boy continued up the Midway, past the various concessions just shutting down for the day. Like the Wild West Show, they'd been able to open early, while work on the Columbian Exhibition was still being completed. Some of the concessions, like the Algerian Village, had been open as early as the previous summer. And like the Algerian troupe's "exhibit," the other concessions were all, in one way or another, caricatures of the countries they purported to represent, pantomimes of pasts that never existed. There were Irishmen in green felt, Germans in lederhosen, Lapps in fur, Turks in fezzes. But as clownish as the others often seemed, it struck Chabane that the worst indignities were always reserved for those from the African continent. Like the natives of Dahomey, only recently conquered by the French, being presented as "cannibal savages" for the amusement of American audiences. A once proud people, reduced to the level of sideshow performers.

As they neared the towering wheel, beyond which lay the Algerian concession, Chabane heard his name called. It was one of the performers from the Street in Cairo concession, which was proving the most popular of the Midway's attractions.

"Another of our monkeys has been stolen, Chabane," the Egyptian continued in Arabic. "You Kabyles haven't been breaking your Ramadan fast with monkey stew, have you?"

"Keep your ruffians away from our women, Zewail," Chabane answered, good naturedly, "and I'll keep my people away from your monkeys."

As they passed under the lengthening shadow of Ferris's wheel, the Algerian Village concession coming into view, Mezian drew up short, looking behind him, a look of alarm on his face. "I've lost my story-paper." He patted his pocket, craning his head around and twisting to look down over his back, as though the dime novel might be clinging to his shirt-back.

Chabane turned in a slow circle, scanning the ground at their feet, looking back the way they'd come. "You must have dropped it."

Mezian looked up, his eyes wide. "My mother will *kill* me."

Chabane gave a sympathetic smile, but before he could answer he heard the sound of footsteps fast approaching. He spun around, expecting trouble, instinctually dropping into a defensive posture, but relaxed when he saw it was only Papa Ganon, the Algerian troupe's glass-eater.

"*Amin!*" Ganon shouted. "Come quickly!"

Chabane tensed once more when he saw the blood darkening the front of Papa Ganon's *burnous*.

"What is it?" Chabane said, rushing forward. "Are you hurt?"

Ganon responded with a confused look, then followed Chabane's gaze to his blood-stained front. He shook his head. "It isn't mine, *amin*. There's a stranger, badly bleeding and confused, found hiding behind the theater."

Chabane drew his mouth into a line, and nodded. "Run along and find your mother, Mezian." Then he started with long strides towards the Algerian theater, Papa Ganon following close behind.

The Algerian Village was almost identical to that which the troupe had originally set up in the Paris Exhibition four years before. It had been there that a young Sol Bloom had seen them, in the shadow of Eiffel's tower, and hired them to come perform in the United States. But when the time had come to leave Paris, the troupe had been uncertain about venturing into the unknown wilds of America.

At the time, Archibald Chabane had not heard his native tongue since leaving Dellys, years before, but traveling to Paris on business he had chanced upon the troupe on the *Quai d'Orsay*. After a friendly meal and reminiscences about their erstwhile home, Papa Ganon had spoken for the others in begging the assistance of the worldly, mannered Chabane. Ganon had called up Kabyle tradition, which held that a Kabyle journeying abroad was obliged to come to the aid of any Kabyle in need, even at the risk of his own fortune and life.

Chabane had thought he had put such traditions behind him. But looking into the hopeful faces of the Algerian troupe, he couldn't help but remember the sacrifices his family had made during the famine of 1867. Tradition demands that every stranger who enters a Kabyle village be treated like an honored guest, given food, lodging, whatever he requires. But even with more than ten thousand strangers from all over Algeria pouring into Dellys, not a single person died of starvation, nor had the *djemaas* been forced to ask aid from the government. Among the European settlers in the larger cities, police measures were needed to prevent theft and disorder resulting from the influx of strangers; in Dellys nothing of the kind was needed. The Kabyles took care of their own affairs.

There on the *Quai d'Orsay*, to his own astonishment, he found himself agreeing to act as the troupe's guide in America. He had tried to escape his past, but his past had eventually outrun him.

In the shuttered Algerian Theater, Chabane and Papa Ganon found the unconscious stranger being tended by two of the troupe's female performers. Though they went veiled when in the public eye, in *chador* or *hijab*, in private they favored western dress.

"I tell you, it is Salla," one of the women said, dabbing blood from the stranger's face with a wet cloth. Piled on the ground were shards of glass they'd pulled from his wounds. "Look, he has Salla's eyes."

The other woman, Dihya, shook her head. "Taninna, you've gone mad. Salla is dead and buried. Besides, eyes or no, this man looks nothing like him."

Chabane crouched beside Taninna, looking closely at the man. There were cuts all over his face, arms, and hands, and underneath the wool blanket the women had thrown over him, the stranger was completely naked.

The ministrations of the two women had already staunched the flow of blood from the stranger's arms, and Chabane reached out to touch one of the scars, which looked older than the others, already healed, running like a ring around the stranger's upper arm. But when Chabane's fingers brushed the scar, he got a slight shock, like a spark of static electricity, and pulled his hand back quickly.

"What shall we do with him, *amin*?" Dihya asked, wiping her forehead with the back of her hand.

Chabane was thoughtful. "I'll go speak with the tin soldiers, see what they have to say."

Just opposite the Algerian Village, across the Midway Plaisance between the Old Vienna concession and the French

Cider Press, was a Fire and Guard Station, manned by members of the Columbian Guard, the private police force of the Columbian Exhibition. The Guard was headed by Colonel Edmund Rice, a former infantry officer who had gained some small measure of fame during the Battle of Bull Run, where the Union army's new-minted prometheic tanks had put an end to the short-lived southern insurrection. Under Rice's command, the Columbian Guard was meant to be a model peacekeeping force, committed to the safety and security of all who strode upon the Exhibition grounds. In their uniforms of light blue sackcloth, white gloves, and yellow-lined black capes, though, they looked more like spear-carriers in a Gilbert & Sullivan production than officers of law. And their talents at peacekeeping, often, left something to be desired, more interested in presenting a dashing profile than in seeing justice done. It wasn't for nothing that the concessioneers had taken to calling them "tin soldiers."

As Chabane approached the Station, framing how best to broach the subject of the unconscious man who lay bleeding in the Algerian Theater, a trio of Columbian Guards rushed through the narrow door, the one in the lead shouldering Chabane aside.

"Out of the way, darkie," the Guard sneered in English, patting the buttoned holster at his side. "We don't have time to hear about any damned stolen monkeys."

Chabane held up his hands, palms forward, and stepped back out of the way, presenting as inoffensive a profile as possible. "My apologies," he answered, in his best drawing room English. If he'd wanted, he could have swept the legs out from under all three Guards, and taken their firearms from them as they fell. At the moment, though, he was more interested in what had stirred the normally laconic Guards to such a frenzy.

The three guards were hustling up the Midway, around the wheel and towards the Columbian Exhibition itself. A few of the other Midway concessioneers were still in the street, and Chabane could hear them muttering suspiciously to one another, like wives gossiping over a garden fence. Some had overheard the Guards within their hut, and had heard the summons to action.

There had been a *murder* in the park.

As he trailed behind the Columbian Guards at a discreet distance, keeping them just in sight as they hurried up the Midway, Chabane tallied up the number of deaths in the park since the previous summer, when the Algerian troupe had arrived from New York. Like the Algerian sword-swallower Salla, who had been working in a construction position in the park while waiting for the Midway to open, the deaths had all been accidents, all of them workers killed at their duties because of poor safety conditions. Salla had fallen from the airship mast and drowned in the waters of Lake Michigan, others had broken their skulls when masonry had fallen on them from improperly lashed cranes, or been crushed under piles of girders that slipped from the pincers of poorly programmed automata.

And it wasn't just the dead men buried in paupers' graves south of the park that had been affected. Even now, in the city itself, striking workers agitated for better working conditions, or for assurances that they would not lose their jobs to automation. The motto of the Columbian Exhibition was "Not Matter, But Mind; Not Things, But Men," but Chabane could not help but wonder whether such noble sentiments were any salve to men who had been replaced at their posts by "things" in recent months and years. He knew it came as no comfort to those men who had died in automata-related accidents.

But accidents were one thing. A murder was a different matter entirely. And as much as the Exhibition's Board of Directors might turn a blind eye to the loss of a few workmen, news of a murder would be bad business indeed for the fair.

It seemed a likely explanation that the bleeding and bewildered man now lying in the Algerian Theater was another victim, one who had escaped the killer's grasp. But it seemed to Chabane just as likely that the Board of Directors would be eager for a scapegoat on which to hang the crime, and a confused stranger, unable to defend himself, would suit their needs perfectly. He wasn't about to hand the stranger over to them, until he knew he wouldn't be signing the man's death warrant to do so.

Chabane followed the Guards through the 60th Street entrance and into the Columbian Exhibition itself. With only two weeks to go before the grand opening, it was clear there was still a significant amount of work to be done. The grounds were covered with litter and debris, with deep ruts cut across the greens. Lumber was piled haphazardly at the intersections of pathways, and empty crates and the discarded remains of worker's lunches were strewn everywhere.

The Guards continued east, past the Children's Building and the north end of the Horticultural Exhibition, before turning right and heading south along the western shores of the Lagoon. Chabane trailed behind, and when he rounded the corner of the Horticultural building, he could see the gentle rise of the Wooded Island in the middle of the Lagoon. Since he'd last come this way, they'd finished work on the fanciful reconstruction of the "Antediluvian" temple at the southern tip of the island. Supposedly based on archeological findings in Antarctica, it looked more like something out of Mezian's story-papers. Also new since he'd last seen the Lagoon were the miniature submersibles bobbling along on the water's surface, waiting for patrons to rent them for brief excursions to the bottom of the Lagoon once the Exhibition opened.

Chabane couldn't help wondering what Captain Nemo would have made of *that*.

For that matter, what might Verne himself have made of the airship now drifting at anchor atop the mast just visible on the far side of the Lagoon, past the Manufactures building, on the pier out over Lake Michigan? It was a prometheic airship, its envelope buoyed by the red vapor produced by the reaction of prometheum and charcoal.

Prometheum was such a simple substance. It looked like water and flowed like mercury. Add it to water, and it would set the water to boil. Add it to charcoal, and it turned the charcoal into still more prometheum. Put it in a vacuum and shake it, and it glowed bright white.

Now that the sun had slipped below the buildings to the west, the park's lamplighters had set to work, cranking the clockwork mechanisms at the base of each lamppost that set the cut-glass globes at the top of the posts to vibrating, agitating the prometheum within. Chabane had a pendant on his lapel, a little crystal flask, stopped with silver. If he were to shake it now, the clear, viscous liquid within would glow soft white, and not dim until almost sunrise.

Chabane watched as the Guards continued past the Transportation building, then turned left into the so-called Court of Honor, with the golden dome of the Administration building at its center. Chabane hurried his pace, so as not to lose sight of which building they entered.

As he rounded the corner of the Automata Exhibition, Chabane watched as the three Guards hurried through the massive doors of the Machinery Exhibition across the way. He followed behind at a somewhat more leisurely pace.

To Chabane's left, opposite the massive Machinery hall, were the twin Automata and Prometheum buildings. Between them stood the fifteen-foot tall statue of Cadwalader Ringgold, in one hand a sextant, in the other a model of the crab-like Antediluvian automaton he'd brought back from the South Pole.

Of course, Ringgold hadn't been the first to return with one of the automata, the first proof of the existence of the "Antediluvians." That honor had fallen to James Clark Ross, who had brought back the broken husk of a mechanism with articulated limbs from the island that now bears his name in 1843, the year after Ringgold and the rest of the Wilkes Expedition had returned from the south seas. This had set off a race to the Pole, to find other examples of this strange, unknown technology. The Ringgold Expedition had won the golden ring when they returned with another, more intact automaton from deep within an icy mountain crevasse, in whose tiny engine there still rested a few precious drops of prometheum. A few drops were enough to change history, though, since added to charcoal they quickly produced more. And in short order, the automaton itself had been reverse-engineered.

The debate still raged about just who the Antediluvians had been. Had they been some forgotten race of man? Or visitors from another world or plane of existence? Some wild-eyed savants even suggested that the Antediluvians were actually the originals of the Atlantis myth, their existence remembered only in legend. All that was known for certain was that they had left behind a scant few examples of a technology that far outstripped that of modern man in the 1850s.

It had not taken modern man long to catch up, Chabane mused, as he passed through the entrance into the Machinery Exhibition.

The interior of the building was massive, looking like three railroad train-houses side-by-side. And though many of the stalls and booths were already installed, there was still considerable work to be done before the park opened, and the massive steam-powered cranes mounted overhead still hurried from one end of the building to the other and back again, time and again, moving the heavy machinery into place.

At the far left of the building, the west end of the hall, were installations from other countries—Canada, Great Britain, Austria, Germany, France—with the rest being American products. Behind the far wall, on the southern face of the building, was the boiler-house, where tanks of lake water were impregnated with small amounts of prometheum, which set them to boil almost immediately, transforming hundreds of gallons into steam in a matter of moments.

Nearly all of the exhibits drew their power from the steam-powered line shafts spinning at between 250 and 300 revolutions a minute, running from one end of the hall to the other at fourteen feet above the ground. Pulleys were strung from the drive shafts down to the exhibit stalls, strung tight as guitar strings, powering more kinds of machines than Chabane had known existed: water pumps, bottling mechanisms, refrigerating apparatus, trip-hammers, sawmill blades, printing presses, stone-saws, refinery mechanisms, and others whose uses he could scarcely guess. All powered by pro-metheic steam and, according to the banners and type-written signs hung on each installation, all of them profitable, the marvels of the age.

In the south-east corner of the building, though, where Chabane could see the Columbian Guards congregating, could be found less marvelous, less profitable exhibits. And it was around the smallest of these that the Guards were now milling.

There wasn't much to the exhibit, just a shack, a banner proclaiming *The Latter-Day Lazarus*, a podium, a few ped-estals, and a table designed to lever up on one end. The only machinery in evidence appeared to be some sort of motor, attached by a pulley to the drive shaft overhead. But the mo-tor wasn't attached to anything but a pair of long, thick ca-bles, one of which snaked towards the shack, the other towards the levered table. It took Chabane a moment to rec-ognize it as the same sort of device he'd seen displayed in London, years before. It was a machine for generating elec-tricity.

Outside of Mezian's dime-novel, Chabane had heard pre-cious little about electricity in years. It had been something of a novelty a few years back, and marketed as a new brand of patent medicine before the danger of electrocution had driven it from catalog pages all together, but aside from its use in telegraphy it was now all but abandoned. What was the product or device promoted by this "Lazarus" exhibit, and why the unnecessary risk of electricity?

The Columbian Guards he'd trailed had joined with the others already on hand, inspecting the area. Most of them were already inside the shack, which appeared to be the scene of the crime. Intent on their work, none seemed to pay any notice to Chabane. It wasn't surprising. Like many of the Americans he'd encountered since the last summer, the Guards seemed to look upon men and women with dark complexions as nothing more than menials—janitors, gar-deners, busboys, maids—and so Chabane had found it pos-sible to slip in and out of groups of them all but unnoticed, effectively invisible.

With his eyes down and an unthreatening expression on his face, Chabane slipped into the shack. He had expected to see a body, perhaps some blood or signs of violence. What he found, instead, was like something from a Grand Guignol.

On the dusty floor, covered by a sheet, was a still human form, presumably the body of the dead man. Overhead, wire cages hung empty from the tarpapered ceiling, the floor of each caked in excrement.

The center of the shack was dominated by a bed-sized bench, with casters on the legs, and straps at either end and in the middle. Affixed to the top of the bench was a boxy metal frame, from one corner of which a thick cable snaked down and under the shack's thin wooden wall. The ground around the bench was strewn with jagged bits of glass that crunched underfoot.

Beside the bench was a low table, on which were piled strange implements, saws, pliers, and clamps, along with what appeared to be various automata components. And what Chabane at first took to be strips of meat were scattered on the table and the surrounding ground, and pools of dark liquid congealing scab-like.

An abattoir stench hung thick in the air, and as Chabane stepped over to the nearest of the three barrels at the rear of the shack, he found the source of the smell. In the barrel was heaped viscera, blood, flesh, and bones. Chabane started, covering his mouth and gagging, then recognized the tiny child-like limbs as those of a monkey. Beside the limbs he saw the remains of a monkey skull, cut in half like a grapefruit, the brain scooped out. He remembered the animals missing from the Street in Cairo concession, and suppressed a shudder.

"What in God's name is *this*?" came a blustering voice from the shack's open door.

Chabane turned to see the chief of the Columbian Guard, Colonel Edmund Rice, shouldering into the shack, behind him another man with thinning hair and a prominent mustache.

"There's been a murder," one of the Guards explained, unnecessarily.

Rice shot the man a bewildered look, then shook his head, muttering something about the quality of officers he had at his disposal, comparing them unflatteringly to the 14th Massachusetts Infantry Regiment.

Chabane had accompanied Sol Bloom to a few meetings with Colonel Rice, but doubted the man had ever noticed he was there. Certainly, Rice hardly seemed to notice him *now*.

"Well, Robinson?" Rice turned to the mustached man behind him, whom Chabane now recognized as L.W. Robinson, chief of the Columbian Exhibition's Machinery department. The colonel reached down and flicked the blanket off the body on the floor. "Do you know this man?"

Robinson peered down at the burnt and bludgeoned man on the floor, and with a queasy expression quickly nodded. "Yes, I know him." He straightened up and looked away. "That's Tom Edison."

Rice narrowed his eyes in concentration, and looked from Robinson to the dead man. "I know the name, but can't place it."

Robinson nodded again. "Was a bit famous for a time. He invented the phonograph, you may recall?" The colonel shook his head. "In any event, I only spoke with him briefly when he secured his spot in the hall, but it appeared that he'd sunk his fortunes into electricity years ago, and simply couldn't see a way out."

"Electricity?" the colonel repeated, disbelievingly. "Whyever for?"

Robinson shrugged. "Who can say? I tried to explain to him that there simply wasn't any call for such things, not with prometheic steam engines and lights and automation and such, that he might as well try selling butter-churns. But Edison was not to be deterred. He had that wild-eyed look you see in religious zealots, you know the type? He was *determined* to find a way to make his . . . now what did he call them? Oh yes, his *dynamos* profitable."

"That's a 'dynamo' out front, I take it?" Rice asked.

The Machinery chief nodded. "Sad, isn't it? Still, Edison wasn't the only one. I've heard of a number of inventors and investors who'd hung all their hopes on electricity, in the years before prometheum really took hold. Most ended up going off into industries or trades, sooner or later. I even heard of one, a Serbian I believe, who became a writer of cheap fictions." He looked back to the dead man on the ground, grimacing at the gruesome sight. "Clearly, though, Edison hadn't been able to adapt. And it got him in the end. Unless I'm mistaken, he shows every sign of being electrocuted."

One of the Guards stepped forward, and Chabane recognized him as the one from the Midway who was so quick with the racial epithets. "What do these dyna . . . dynami . . . dyna . . ." He shook his head. "What do these things have to do with this 'Latter-Day Lazarus' business? Was your man here intending to raise the dead with this electric thing?"

"If he was," another Guard called from the rear of the shack, "I think he was doing it one piece at a time." The Guard held aloft a severed arm, far too large to have come off any monkey.

"Jesus *wept*!" Rice spat, rearing back.

The Guards began muttering to one another, and Chabane distinctly heard several mentions of "grave-robbing" and "workmen's bodies."

"What?" Chabane said, stepping forward, for the first time making his presence known. "What did you say about the workmen's graves?"

The others turned to him, most of them seeming to notice him for the first time.

"You're that Jew's Arab, aren't you?" the colonel said, narrowing his gaze.

Chabane drew himself up straighter, and in perfect Queen's English replied, "I am Kabyle, sir, and not of Arab descent, but I am presently in the employ of Mr. Bloom, if that is what you mean." His hands at his sides tightened into fists, but he managed to maintain a calm exterior. "What was the mention of grave-robbing and the remains of the workmen?"

Rice glanced to Robinson, who looked as confused as Chabane, and then back. "It's not public knowledge, and if the papers get word of it I'll know where from. But some of the graves to the south have been disturbed, and the bodies laid to rest there have gone missing."

"Would that include the Algerian who drowned in the lake?" Chabane asked.

Rice shrugged. "Only the Christian graves are marked, as I understand it."

Chabane ignored Rice, and looked back to the barrels, from which the Guards were still pulling cadaver parts. There were severed hands and feet, a leg, two arms, bits of skulls, even a complete torso. He bared his teeth in a snarl, and turned to look down on the dead man on the floor. "My grandmothers always said that no one is to be lamented who dies during Ramadan, during which the gates of hell are closed and those of heaven always open. It doesn't seem quite right that a man such as this should get into the gates of heaven uncontested, even if he *was* murdered."

"Now hold on," Rice objected, holding up his hands. "No one said anything about murder."

"They didn't?" Robinson asked, eyebrows raised.

Rice turned to the chief of Machinery, fixing him with a hard glare. "You yourself said this was an electrocution, right? An *accidental* electrocution?"

Robinson's hands fluttered like caged birds. "I suppose it *could* have been," he allowed. "But what about . . ."—he waved at the broken glass, the scattered tools, the splattered blood and viscera—". . . all of this?"

"*This*," Rice said evenly, "could well be simple vandalism. And vandalism is an entirely different order of magnitude to murder. Murder will get plastered over every paper in the country, and run the risk of turning paying customers away, if they think the killer is at large. One more accidental death and a spot of vandalism, *that* we can handle."

"You're joking, of course," Chabane objected. "Have you no interest in seeing justice done?"

Rice glared at him. "There must be *some* jobs down south the automata won't do, boy. Why don't you get down there with the rest of the darkies and make yourself useful?"

Chabane bristled. There *were* still a few slaves in the southern United States, not yet supplanted by cheap automata. That this man could so casually dismiss their continued suffering in an off-hand slight brought Chabane's blood to boil. For an instant, he almost forgot the welfare of the troupe to whom he'd pledged himself, and the stranger who had stumbled beneath the shelter of Chabane's protection. If he'd been on his own, not responsible for anyone but himself, Chabane would have wished for nothing more than a flyssa saber in one hand and a Webley pistol in the other, and he would show these pale-skinned buffoons his worth. But he *wasn't* on his own, and he was responsible for many more souls than just his own.

Marshalling his last reserves of restraint, Chabane strode to the door, and left the shack of horrors behind.

As he made his way back to the Midway, the stars had come out in the darkened skies overhead, and the prometheic lamps were now bathing the park in the soft white glow that had given the exhibition its unofficial name, the White City. But as clean as the white-clad buildings looked in the pure prometheic light, Chabane knew that they were only plaster and boards, hiding the rot and void beneath.

Of course Rice and the rest of his tin-soldiers were more concerned with paychecks than with justice, happy to paint a murder as an accident if it suited the Board of Directors, whitewashing away any chance of bad publicity. Still, Chabane wasn't sure that justice hadn't been done, anyway. He remembered another Kabyle superstition his grandmothers had taught him, that there are never any demons abroad during Ramadan, because God compels them to remain in hell throughout the sacred month. Having seen the gruesome work of the dead man, Chabane doubted any demon ever did worse.

Passing the Terminal Station, he exited the park grounds through the 64th Street entrance, heading north up Island Avenue. Just before reaching the Midway, something bright caught his eye, a splash of color on the pavement reflecting back the prometheic light from above. It was Mezian's dime-novel. Picking it up, Chabane flipped through the pages as he continued on towards the Algerian concession.

The prose was lurid, the action improbable, but there was something about the image of this future of electricity and equality presented by the author, that resonated with Chabane. This Nikola Tesla was no Jules Verne, but still Chabane was reminded of the sense of boundless potential he used to feel when reading the *Extraordinary Voyages* story-papers.

Before turning onto the Midway, Chabane saw a handbill posted to a lamppost, advertising the impending Opening Day celebrations for the Columbian Exhibition. In addition to the last living relative of Christopher Columbus, the duke of Veragua, the most honored guest at the ceremony would be the octogenarian Abraham Lincoln, former president of the United States, who would be on hand to cut the ribbon on the Exhibition.

The imagery of "Dane Faraday, Man of Justice" still rolling in his thoughts, Chabane tried to imagine a world in which James Clark Ross had never returned from the south seas with a broken automaton, in which Ringgold had never discovered prometheum, in which the modern age knew nothing of the forgotten Antediluvian civilization. Perhaps in such a world, there would now be an Electricity exhibit instead of a Prometheum one, with Tom Edison's dynamos at center stage. And perhaps instead of an Automata building, one devoted to some other industry, metal-working perhaps, or mining. But then, in the world in which the United States army lacked prometheic tanks, perhaps they wouldn't have been able to subdue the southern insurrection, and the Union might have split in two over the question of slavery. Perhaps there might not be a Columbian Exhibition at all.

What Chabane couldn't decide was whether such a world would be better, or worse, than the one he knew.

By the time Chabane returned to the Algerian concession, the sun had long since set, and the fourth prayer of the day, Maghrib, had been completed. Now the troupe was breaking their Ramadan fast. Even the non-observant among them, like Chabane, usually had the good graces not to eat and drink in front of the others while the sun was shining in the holy month. Fast or not, though, Chabane knew that a fair number of the performers, once their meals were done, would slip off and drink spirits, perhaps swapping Algerian wines for the "firewater" favored by Cody's Indians. Perhaps tonight, instead of trying to stop them, Chabane just might join them.

The stranger sat among the Algerians, in his lap a plate of food, untouched. He had been cleaned up, his wounds bandaged, and dressed in a suit of borrowed clothes. He was awake, but unspeaking, and it was unclear what, if any, tongue he comprehended. He simply sat, watching the others silently, his expression mingling confusion and interest.

"Keep your distance, *amin*," Papa Ganon said, as Chabane crouched down beside the man. "My hand brushed his bare skin while we were dressing him, and I got the shock of my life. He's like a walking thundercloud, this one."

Chabane nodded, and kept his hands at his sides. In the soft white glow of the prometheic lights overhead, Chabane examined the stranger closely. His coloration, what little of it could be seen beneath the bandages, cuts, and scars, was somehow . . . off. His skin was a darker shade than his light hair would suggest, the little hairs on the backs of his hands darker than his feathery eyebrows. And his features seemed mismatched, his nose too long and narrow, his mouth a wide slash in his face, his overlarge ears too low on his head.

"What will we do with him?" Dihya asked, coming to stand beside Ganon. Taninna came with her, staring hard at the stranger's disfigured face, as though trying to find something hidden there.

Chabane thought about tradition, about the past and the future. He remembered the superstitions he'd been taught as a child, and the story-papers' fantastic futures into which he'd fled.

In many ways, the future promised by Jules Verne had arrived, but not in the way the young Adherbal Aït Chabaâne had imagined. But the future that young Mezian now dreamt of, the future promised in Nikola Tesla's colorful stories? That would never arrive. That wasn't tomorrow, but was *yesterday's* tomorrow. The world of Dane Faraday would never arrive, with its heavier-than-air craft, and wireless communications connecting distant nations, and incandescent lights dangling from wires, and massive dynamos. A world of phosphorescent gas tubes on lampposts, and power-lines crisscrossing the countryside, and antennas atop every house picking symphonies out of the air. Of men and women of all races and nationalities, each measured by their conduct and their character, not by their language or the color of their skins.

Chabane thought about the frisson he'd felt on flipping through Tesla's story, the familiar thrill of boundless potential. But he realized now it wasn't a hope for a new world to come, but a kind of nostalgia for a future that could never be. He thought about the dead man in the blood-covered shack in the Machinery building, so committed to a particular view of yesterday's tomorrow that he had been willing to commit horrible acts to get back to it, whatever the cost.

"Amin?" Dihya repeated, seeing Chabane lost in thought. "What will we do with the stranger?"

Chabane took a deep breath, and sighed. He had tried to escape tradition before, and now knew he never would. "We do what our grandmothers would have us do. No stranger who comes into the village for aid can ever be turned away."

Maybe it wasn't all of the tomorrows that mattered, Chabane realized. Maybe what was truly important was preserving the past, and working for a better *today*. Perhaps *that* was the only real way to choose what kind of future we will inhabit.

But Taninna was right, Chabane knew, looking back to the silent man sitting in the cool glow of the prometheic light. The stranger *did* have Salla's eyes.

Story Copyrights

"Infinities" by Vandana Singh, copyright © 2008 by Vandana Singh.

"This Peaceable Land; or, The Unbearable Vision of Harriet Beecher Stowe" by Robert Charles Wilson, copyright © 2009 by Robert Charles Wilson.

"The Unstrung Zither" by Yoon Ha Lee, copyright © 2009 by Yoon Ha Lee.

"Black Swan" by Bruce Sterling, copyright © 2009 by Bruce Sterling.

"Exegesis" by Nancy Kress, copyright © 2009 by Nancy Kress.

"Erosion" by Ian Creasey, copyright © 2009 by Ian Creasey.

"Collision" by Gwyneth Jones, copyright © 2009 by Gwyneth Jones. First published in *When It Changed*, ed. by Geoff Ryman, Comma Press, Manchester, UK.

"Donovan Sent Us" by Gene Wolfe, copyright © 2009 by Gene Wolfe; first appeared in *Other Earths*; reprinted by permission of the author and the author's agents, the Virginia Kidd Agency, Inc.

"The Calculus Plague" by Marissa K. Lingen, copyright © 2009 by Marissa K. Lingen.

"The Island" by Peter Watts, copyright © 2009 by Peter Watts.

"One of Our Bastards Is Missing" by Paul Cornell, copyright © 2009 by Paul Cornell.

"Lady of the White-Spired City" by Sarah L. Edwards, copyright © 2009 by Sarah L. Edwards.

"The Highway Code" by Brian Stableford, copyright © 2009 by Brian Stableford.

"On the Destruction of Copenhagen by the War-Machines